THE BRINGER OF LIGHT

The Second Dreambringer Book

KATHRINE EATON

Foreword

The '~~Tribe of Morpheus~~' *'Bringer of Light'* is a sequel to my first novel 'The Soul's Domain.' If you have read 'The Soul's Domain' you may want to skip the Dreambringer Lore and A Dreambringer Legend sections, or maybe read them as a refresher. If you have not, <u>you should probably read 'The Soul's Domain' before continuing with this book</u>.

You can read this book as a standalone story if you choose but it would mean missing out on the dramatic back story behind it. Plus, there will be major spoilers if you later decide to go back and read the first book.

If you do wish to continue without reading the first book you will need some background information first which is what this forward is about.

Whichever choice you make I hope you enjoy the world of the Dreambringers.

DREAMBRINGER LORE

Do you ever wonder why you dream? What dreams are, and what they mean?

Well, it is simple really, DREAMS ARE THE SOUL'S DOMAIN.

Every human has a soul, and a soul never sleeps. So, whilst our minds and bodies rest our souls take control and drawing from our resting minds all that has happened and all that we wish or fear will happen, it gives us ways to heal and learn and solve our troubles. It brings us insight and gives us wish fulfilment. It is not always clear to our waking minds what we have learnt from our dreams. Some barely remember what they dreamt at all, and some dismiss what is remembered, but believe me the knowledge is there and it always helps.

And now we come to a special few, those who dream deep and awake understanding, at least in part, what they have learnt. They find answers in their dreams and as they help them in life, they also express what they learn through art because these special few always have artistic leanings. So out of all the great painters, musicians, writers, or those who have a talent in any other artistic field there are a special few, and out of these few special people the elite will be chosen for a special task.

Primitive man dreamt but not as we do as their souls and the dreams they brought were as basic as their primitive minds.

As the human race evolved, they were watched. The watchers were of this earth but of a species far more evolved. They were 'spirit forms' their spirituality and intellect were superior, but their physicality and numbers restricted. The weak dreams of the humans fed them, but poorly.

Over time however they discovered that a select few humans dreamt a little deeper. The souls of these special humans were stronger, and they possessed skills that their fellow humans did not. These humans were the first to discover art, though primitive and restricted they stood out and the spirit forms were attracted to them as they dreamt and after a while, they decided

1

that an alliance needed to be made. And so, when they felt the time was right, they made themselves known to a select few of the more gifted humans through their dreams and gradually an amazing partnership grew.

The sprit forms fed the humans with their spirituality, heightening their dreams and therefore their waking lives. And through the spiritual energy produced from.their art the humans fed them in return forming a partnership that benefited all. Over time the partnership flourished, and they discovered together that they could enrich the life of all humans through their dreams.

The newly formed partners met with danger and resistance however from some who did not understand and so another set of humans with their own unique talents were tasked with their protection and over the years the spirit forms and their special humans went underground and became a secret that only their protectors knew of.

They spread in small groups across the world in order to better remain hidden and although the spirit forms did not increase in numbers their protectors did. And so, with the help of their human partners they worked in secret to enlighten the human world through their dreams, enriching the souls and minds of the human race.

As with any group of sentient beings these protectors evolved over the centuries forming their own hierarchy and setting their own rules and procedures taking on many forms until now, in the modern world, they have become a Global Organisation. This organisation is known as The Somnium Foundation.

The Somnium Foundation was set up and is run by an incredibly old, extraordinarily rich, and powerful family named Vecchini. This family have been prominent amongst those who protected the spirit forms and their human partners for centuries.

To most of the world the Foundation is an organisation that funds a network of art communes across the globe. Most people are unaware it exists at all as it does not advertise its work, and those who do know of it have no idea of its real purpose.

Outside of family members The Foundation employs a global network of lawyers, accountants, and stockbrokers who help raise funds to run the communes via investments in real estate, antiquities trading, small businesses, and the stock exchange. Only its members are privy to its secrets and even then, there are levels of knowledge amongst its employees. The Foundation has a strong Ethos with a solid hierarchy where everything and everyone has a name, a distinct identity, and a defined purpose.

The name given to the spirit forms that are the heart of this amazing organisation is THE ETERNAL DREAMERS (Eternals or ED's for short). They do not have a solid form, and some believe them to be the embodiment of pure soul. They are immortal and with the help of their human 'partners' they enrich our dreams. Their human partners are needed to strengthen them by acting as a 'conduit' to bridge the gap between them and the human race. And so, in order to do their work, they must join with a special human being and these special people are known as DREAMBRINGERS.

These Dreambringers are people who have a particularly strong talent for dreaming. They are prolific dreamers who need little help from the Eternal Dreamers. They dream much more than others and their dreams are filled with vivid and diverse images. This is because when they dream, they tune into the dreams of others around them as well as their own.

These select few humans are also born with an artistic talent of some kind. Their dreaming talent is what connects them to the Eternals and their artistic talent is what 'feeds' them. The energy created as they work on their 'art' enables the Eternals to enter and enrich the dreams of those who sleep during the day and at night the Dreambringers connect with them and together they join with our souls to bring us inspiration and insight, helping us to learn and grow.

A Dreambringer set consists of one of each of the six 'kinds' of Dreambringer. They are The Dreamcatcher, The Dream Mate (female), The Dream Mate (male), The Gatekeeper of Dreams, The Seer of Dreams and The Soul Healer of Dreams, plus six Eternal Dreamers. Within the set each Dreambringer forms a strong bond with one particular Eternal Dreamer and together they help to bring the kind of dream specified by their Dreambringer role. Outside of this paring they are all linked by an artistic energy that feeds the whole group.

The sets of Dreambringers are not joined with their Eternal Dreamers for life. The years they spend at their task varies, there is no set time they are expected to serve, no average time, each group is different.

There is one other kind of Dreambringer. They are called DREAMWISHERS, and they have similar talents as the others, the differences being that they are not part of any particular set and are not joined to one specific Eternal Dreamer; they are able to link, on a lesser level, to any Eternal Dreamer.

They are transient members of the organisation who travel around the different houses in pairs on a rota giving the group an extra boost every now and then. They are also used on rare occasions to fill in for those that are long term sick or who need to be away from a house for more than a day at a time.

Once a set of Dreambringers feel they have given all they can of themselves to the Eternals it is then their task to bring together a replacement group. This is almost always a joint decision made by all.

Once the decision has been made and agreed the Dreambringers, with the help of their Eternals, must contact their replacements through dreams. Prospective candidates are found quite easily as they stand out in the dream world. All current Dreambringers need do is send out feelers that will be picked up by their natural replacements in their dreams. Once the connection has been made the Current Dreambringer can begin to instruct the New Dreambringer in their new task via their dreams.

Once the New Dreambringers have been told what they need to know they are then told to reach out to each other through their dreams. Once the group has connected with each other they are given a meeting place where they will come together and where they will be initiated into the Somnium Foundation and told of their task.

This initiation is undertaken by a member of the Foundation known as a Dreamteller. These Dreamtellers are ex-Dreambringers who have taken on the new role after retiring from their Dreambringer role. The new recruits will then be brought to the home of their particular group.

These homes are all large, impressive houses purchased over the years by the Foundation and set up as art communes. They live together in these houses for the duration of their time as Dreambringers. The Eternal Dreamers reside in a nearby dwelling that only the Dreambringers have access to as they are protected by an incredibly unique security system. Once at their assigned house they will receive further instruction and be introduced to and joined with their Eternals ready to begin their task.

And now for their protectors.

All employees of the Foundation are carefully vetted through their dreams by a few special family members via the Eternal Dreamers. These special family members are known as MARSHALS.

The Vecchini Marshals have existed almost as long as the Dreambringers and Eternal Dreamers themselves. Future Marshals are spotted at an early age by the current Marshals through dreams. They are first tested, and if they pass, they are then initiated into the family secret.

The Marshals have a dream talent too. Like the Dreambringers they are prolific dreamers and possess an artistic talent, however, their connection to the Eternal Dreamers is different as is their purpose. Whereas the Dreambringers have a strong connection to one particular Eternal the Marshals have a more general connection to all Eternals. The Marshal's connection is in the dream world only; they cannot come into direct contact with the Eternals only the Dreambringers can do that. The Eternals communicate with them through their dreams on a basic, instinctual level. They guide them by sending dream messages via emotions rather than instruction. This communication between Eternals and Marshals is needed in order for the Marshals to carry out their own task.

3

The Marshals task is as follows.

They must vet prospective new employees of the Foundation for trustworthiness. They do this with the help of the Eternals through dreams. When a set of Dreambringers decide that their task is over they must contact their appointed Marshal who will then come to the house in order to ensure that the changeover goes smoothly. With the help of the Foundation, they must make the necessary arrangements for the new Dreambringers to move in and the current Dreambringers to be moved out and all the many arrangements that entails. If there are any problems, it is the Marshals job to sort them out either alone or with the help of other Foundation members depending on what the problem is. In-between change overs it is the Marshal's job to monitor the houses in their 'area' to make sure things are being run well which includes regular visits.

There is one other important member of each house and that is THE WARDEN.

A Warden is appointed to each house after each set of new Dreambringers has been initiated. Their job is to look after the house and its inhabitants. They deal with any minor, practical problems at the houses, however, if any major problems arise, or if any big decisions need to be made then the Warden must contact the Marshal who deals with them, usually in person.

It is the job of The Marshal to choose the new Warden from amongst the most trusted of Foundation employees. They choose from those employees who have a higher dream/artistic talent than normal (but not high enough to make them a Dreambringer). They are let in on the secret of the Dreambringers without being told of the added existence of The Eternals and cannot access the nearby house where they live. Although they are aware that they have not been told everything and that the Dreambringers travel to a nearby place where they cannot go, they trust their employers and accept this with no questions asked.

When a Dreambringers task has ended some choose to go back to normal life and others choose to stay within the Somnium Foundation in a different role. These roles range from menial jobs to skilled jobs that they had been trained for before their Dreambringer work (e.g., Doctors or Lawyers), to very specialised and important roles. Whatever role they take on they will remain part of something very special for the rest of their lives.

THE DREAM REALM & THE DREAMBRINGERS ROLE WITHIN IT

A Dreambringers night's sleep is split up as follows; for the first half hour or so hour their bodies are relaxing and then when fully rested their soul takes control. At this point the connection between their souls and the Eternals takes hold pulling them into what is called by those in the know the Dream Realm.

Along with their Eternal Dreamers the Dreambringers souls interact with those of the normal dreaming souls, learning what they need from their dreams and helping them to achieve it, becoming what the dreamers need them to be.

After five or six hours of this work their souls are pulled back into their still sleeping bodies. Then for the next couple of hours they can enjoy their own dreams enriched by the Eternals before waking fully.

The Dream Realm is not a physical place, it is the Souls Domain. Its everchanging landscape created by the souls who inhabit it in their dreams. In the dream realm normal dreamers do not have a physical form their souls are simply represented by vague, white, misty human shapes. The Dreambringers however have more of a physical presence. Their souls appear within the ever-shifting dream landscape as ethereal forms of their physical selves. They are a ghostly and insubstantial yet perfected version of themselves. Their forms appear frail yet are smoothed of all their imperfections and their attributes are enhanced. They are their dream selves.

Whilst the Dream Realm is not a physical place it does have its own unique type of geography. It does not have physical territories and boundaries as such, but dreaming souls tend to inhabit the same area of the Dream Realm as others who live/sleep in the same physical area of the world as them.

Dreambringers are able to 'travel' to any area in the Dream Realm and help the dreaming souls there but if all the Dreambringers were to roam wherever they liked it could be chaotic and some areas/dreamers may get missed. This is why it was decided many years ago that rather than travel erratically through the Dream Realm the Eternal Dreamers and their Dreambringers should split off into smaller groups and disperse to different areas of the world and for each group to keep to the area inhabited by the local dreaming souls in order to properly cover as much of the worlds dreamers as possible.

These groups would later become the art communes of today and so for many years Dreambringers have helped those souls who live/sleep in the physical area surrounding their commune and this has meant that these days a Dreambringers talent tends to become stronger within the area of the Dream Realm where local dreaming souls are as they are physically as well as spiritually near them. This also makes distance travel withing the Dream Realm not only unnecessary but less effective.

There is one slight exception, and that is when Dreambringers are 'calling' their replacements. It is a different thing to Dreambringing itself but the 'call out' can reach further than a Dreambringers area of the Dream Realm. The call goes out to the nearest suitable candidate and its unlikely all the candidates for one group will come from the same area. The candidates are likely to be in the same country as the Dreambringer they are to replace but distance can vary and although they have been known to come from another country it is rare.

Dreaming souls are unaware there is such a place as the Dream Realm when they are awake and whilst there, they cannot travel within it, but then they have no need to. Their 'local' Dreambringers interact with them giving them dreams in which they can then interact with their fellow dreamers either known, unknown, nearby, or far away.

Simply put the Dream Realm is the place where dreams are made and is I repeat The Soul's Domain.

A DREAMBRINGER LEGEND

Several hundred years ago there lived a man; he was a Dreambringer, a Soul Healer of Dreams to be exact. He was a very skilled Dreambringer and revelled in his task. Over the years however he grew very arrogant and self-important. This was not an unusual occurrence back in the days before the Foundation had stricter rules and fail safes in place, but what was unusual was the extreme actions that the man's arrogance led him too.

He discovered that the others in his group were thinking of bringing their time as Dreambringers to an end as they had been in place for many years. He did not agree with them. The thought of being separated from his Eternal Dreamer and possibly never doing Dreambringer work again was too much for him. He also felt his Dreambringer talent was too impressive to come to an end. And so, he decided on an extreme solution. He decided that he could make his link to his ED not only stronger but permanent by properly merging with it to become one entity. Although he knew that this was something that had never been thought of before let alone attempted, he was convinced he could do it. Deep down he knew that his Eternal did not agree with him but in his desperation and arrogance he decided to go ahead anyway.

His Dreambringer skill enabled him to project his spirit from his body and for it to merge with the spirit form of the Eternal, but he did not have the necessary skill to fully extract his soul from the earthly bond of his body and send it with his spirit. This and the fact that the Eternal Dreamer was not totally complicit meant that the spirit form instinctively resisted the merge.

5

There was a spiritual struggle as the Dreambringer was unable to complete the full merging but refused to let go the connection he had made. As the struggle continued his body without its essence began to die. When the Eternal finally began to eject the Dreambringer he began to return to his dying body but at the last minute he managed to increase his hold and instead of strengthening his attempt at merging he managed to pull the essence of the spirit form back into his body trapping it there with him, and a new hybrid being was formed.

In appearance this new 'being' took on the basic form of a man, but the spirit form within it shone through those parts of its body which had begun to die. This meant that from its eyes there shone a white light and a white glow emanated under the skin of its torso where the dying organs had been. The skin of its fingers and toes also glowed white and if it opened its mouth a white light shone from within.

Its brain was also transformed making it not quite human and giving it powers it was soon to discover. The more immediate discoveries made were that it could not see well, only in shapes and shadows and it could not speak. Its movement was also impaired, partly due to poor sight but mainly because its limbs had become leaden and hard to control.

When the other Dreambringers discovered this new creature, they were understandably appalled and frightened. Word was immediately sent out to their protectors for help. In the time before that help arrived the new being discovered it could communicate through telepathy. Although disconcerting at first the other Dreambringers were glad of the connection as It could tell them what had happened and how It was feeling but in turn as It probed their minds It discovered how horrified they were by what It had become, and how wary they now were of It. This knowledge made It nervous and a little angry.

Others arrived to help but were at a loss what to do as this was an unprecedented event. More help was sent for. And whilst they waited and discussed what to do It began to come to terms with what It had become and what It could and could not do and It discovered that It could 'control' those around It. To start with it was just trivial things like putting thoughts in their heads about what they should be doing but this only confused them.

After a while It was able to control their thoughts and movements, first in little ways and then it learnt to take control of one of them totally for short periods of time. When they discovered what It was doing there was widespread panic. The new being's powers could not affect the Eternals, but they could not protect the humans from It and their own powers were suffering because of it. Therefore, when the new batch of helpers finally arrived, they were met with chaos and fear.

This new group were made up of a number of very powerful ex-Dreambringers. It was discovered that due to their stronger Dreambringer talent and there having been forewarned they were, with a little effort, able to resist the creatures mind control. Now armed with this new knowledge these protectors were able to make plans. The creature's mental power was restricted by distance and so It was taken by the three who could resist Its control the most to a remote property and as physically restraining the creature was easy a locked room was sufficient to contain It for the time being.

Back at the house where the creature had been born things would never be the same. Those Dreambringers who had been most affected by what they had been made to do under Its control were retired and replaced as soon as could be managed, with one notable exception. There was no new Soulhealer of Dreams. There could never be a replacement as the set were now missing the required Eternal Dreamer. Therefore, at this particular house there would from then on only ever be five Eternal Dreamers and five Dreambringers. The short fall would be made up to some extent by regular visits from Dreamwishers, but this house would forever remain different from all the others.

It was suggested by some that the creature should be killed but although it was likely they could destroy Its body they had no idea how this would affect the creature and it was thought possible that it may become stronger if freed from the body that was restricting It physically. And so, it was decided that It would need to remain imprisoned until a better solution was found.

The temporary prison nearby was made more permanent and a dwelling was quickly built beside it in which the creatures' captors were to live. They were given a new role and title within the organisation. They were THE CUSTODIANS and through the years many retired Dreambringers would take on this inherited role. It had been established that the creature could not influence dreams, It's talent for mind control only worked on those who were awake and in close proximity. Therefore, their task was to ensure that the creature remained locked away to prevent It from encountering anyone susceptible to Its influence and to keep It secret and safe from outsiders.

At first the Custodians tried to communicate with the creature, to find out what it wanted and why it was so hostile but after Its initial contact with Its fellow Dreambringers the creature became increasingly unresponsive. Gradually over the years less and less time and effort were put into understanding the creature and the Custodians job became one of simply monitoring and confinement. They made sure It stayed safely locked away and monitored It to make sure Its mind control talent did not evolve into something even more dangerous.

Also, less and less effort was put into finding a better solution until it was no longer something that was even discussed. The confinement of the creature simply became the norm as no other solution has even been found.

At some point someone gave the creature a new name. From then onwards it was known as THE SOUL STEALER.

Kathrine Eaton March 2021

Chapter 1
The Origination

All those with the dreaming talent felt it, that moment of creation.

Those nearest to its source experienced it as a second long waking dream that soothed and uplifted their souls.

Those further away felt it as a moment's relief from any troubles, fleeting but healing. This healing, though brief would later be passed on in dreams.

The person nearest, the first one to see the new Being, was not afraid and as she looked into his eyes, she felt a deep pain from her past ease.

A new force within the Dreambringer world had been created and most felt it was a good thing, this merging that was to become known as the Origination.

Something special had been formed, an alliance that would work, but to what end?

Chapter 2
Eight Months After the Origination

Eddie Oakley and Sofia Vecchini stood before the new structure awed by its unexpected beauty. They'd been expecting a basic log cabin, but this was far beyond what they'd envisioned. Rather than looking like it had been built upon the woodland ground it appeared to have grown from it like all the trees that surrounded it. Each log had been artfully carved and flowed into the next as if the trees had willingly joined together rather than being felled and attached by human hands. The arched, beautifully framed windows looked like naturally formed apertures in the wood and the tree carved into the door looked formed by nature not tools.

'I can't believe how beautiful it is' breathed Sofia.

'It's amazing. I mean I saw all the materials arrive but never imagined it would look like this. I thought those guys were builders but they're really artists' said Eddie.

'I agree. Do you think he designed it himself or left it to the architects?'

'I have no idea but either way he's a lucky man, if man is the right word.'

'What do you mean?'

'I mean is he still a man or is he something else?'

'I'd say he was something more, rather than something else.' Sofia's tone was quite harsh, and Eddie felt bad about what his words had implied.

'I'm sorry, I didn't mean to imply he was a monster or anything.'

'It's okay,' Sofia reassured him, 'I know you didn't I'm just a bit on edge, we don't really know what to expect of him do we and it's a little unnerving.'

'I totally get that and it's gonna be weird for everyone but a good weird, I'm sure.'

'Yes, you're right it'll be fine, let's go inside.'

Taking the lead, she strode towards the cabin. She was wearing jeans, trainers and a white t shirt, her usual 'uniform' of pencil skirt and high heels being unpractical for a walk in the woods. Her long black hair was pulled back in its usual ponytail, her pale skin and delicately pretty, if slightly severe features were free of make-up.

There were three steps leading to a balustraded veranda at the front of the cabin and even these were expertly carved. There were no artificially straight lines, just natural curves and angles. When they got to the door Sofia couldn't resist running her hands over the tree design carved into it. She was surprised to find it felt warm which only adding to its strange charm. The beautifully carved wood just leant itself to being touched.

There was no lock on the door, a requirement insisted on by the cabins soon to be inhabitant, but the door was large and heavy, so it took a little effort for Sofia to push it open. Eddie entered the cabin behind her and leaving the door ajar they walked to the middle of the structure before stopping to take it all in.

The single storey cabin consisted mainly of one large, open plan room with a beautifully polished wooden floor. To the right of the door there were several comfy chairs arranged around a wood burning stove. In the left front area, there was a double bed with an expertly carved base and headboard. There was a small bedside table on the left of it, and next to that a double door wardrobe, both expertly handmade.

Next to this bedroom area was the only enclosed part of the cabin, a bathroom with a large, beautifully tiled walk-in shower. The walls of the bathroom were cleverly covered in wood panels, so they blended perfectly with the other walls. The back right area held a small kitchen where the modern appliances were cleverly integrated into the wooden theme by handmade cabinets and superbly crafted surfaces.

To the left of the kitchen area there was immaculate shelving and a large cupboard with ornately carved doors ready to hold the occupants' belongings.

In the centre of the large space there was a startlingly original table. It had been carved from the base of a very large tree, the supporting leg shaped like the base and neck of a wine glass. The tabletop was the slightly uneven circle of the tree, its top sanded and varnished, the trees rings clearly and beautifully visible. Around the table there were six hand carved chairs, each one unique yet still clearly part of the set.

'Its fantastic' stated Sofia as she circled the table taking the whole place in.

'It's even better inside' said Eddie 'I thought it'd be like an American log cabin and that if I just had a buffalo hide coat and a fur hat I'd look right at home, but this is something else.'

'It sure is' agreed Sofia supressing a laugh at the thought of Eddie in a fur hat. She got what he meant though, with his big build, long strawberry blonde hair, darker red handlebar moustache and beard he did look a bit like an old west fur trapper. Then again, with all his tattoos and rock band t-shirts maybe a modern-day redneck was more accurate.

'On a more serious note, how long until he gets here?' asked Eddie.

Sofia glanced at her watch 'About two hours' she said feeling her stomach lurch at the thought of his arrival.

'We'd better head back then just in case he's early.'

'Good idea.'

After a short walk back through the woods Eddie and Sofia emerged from the trees onto the sloping lawn that led up to The Gateway House. Approached from the back it wasn't quite as impressive as the front, but the red brick building still had that beautiful Georgian style with large, symmetrically placed sash windows. As they reached the French doors at the back of the house Sofia realised that there were now three remarkable buildings on the surrounding land, all holding their own secrets.

Clea Monroe greeted them as they entered the large kitchen.

'Hello lovey's' she said with the usual accompanying friendly smile. She had an apron on over one of the brightly coloured dresses she had made herself, fluffy slippers on her feet and a tea towel in her hand. 'How's the cabin?' she enquired 'everything ready for him?'

'Yes, and it's actually quite amazing' Sofia told her as she and Eddie sat at the kitchen table 'it's like a craftsman's showroom, full of beautifully carved wood, not the simple home we were expecting.'

'Sounds intriguing, I can't wait to see it. He'll be here soon, and I have to admit to being rather excited about it. I've just finished making an apple pie and it won't take long to prepare the cold meat and salad once he's here, I just hope there's enough to go around and that he's okay with the food, I mean does he eat normally?' her question was aimed at Sofia but before she could answer a gruff, male voice said, 'Stop fussing woman' and they all turned to see Geth Hudson entering the kitchen. Walking over to Clea he gave her a quick kiss on the cheek to take the sting out of his words and she playfully flicked him with the tea towel.

'Don't be a grump' she told him 'This is an important day and I just want everything to be perfect.'

Geth made a sound somewhere between a grunt and a growl as he joined Sofia and Eddie at the kitchen table.

'Is there any tea going?' he asked.

Clea tutted but went to put the kettle on saying 'I'm only doing this because I expect Sofia and Eddie could do with some tea.'

'We could' agreed Eddie smiling at the dynamic between his two unlikely friends. There was curvy Clea in her bright colours with the sunny disposition to match, all mumsy with traces of flour in her long, wavy red hair. Then there was Geth, the sullen tattooist in his black clothes

10

and dark, scowling look to match. He wasn't always grumpy but the contrast of his dark demeanour against Clea's brightness was vast. Eddie wondered then what the male equivalent of resting bitch face was because whatever it was Geth had it. The scar next to his left eye didn't help. Despite their differences though the pair got on really well as did everyone who lived at the Gateway, that was the beauty of the process that had brought them all together.

On the face of it The Gateway was an art commune funded by a worldwide organisation called The Somnium Foundation, but really these special people were much more than just artists.

Just then Max Millig entered the kitchen. The sculptor was his usual dishevelled self with clay smeared on his jeans and the t shirt that Clea had made him before they'd even met. There were even small pieces of clay in his long, light brown hair and patchy beard and a smeared fingerprint on one lens of his glasses.

'Want some tea lovey?' asked Clea 'you look like you've been working hard.'

'Tea would be great, thanks.'

Max was the quiet one of the group, a thinker not a talker. Clea mothered him, well she mothered everyone even though she wasn't old enough to actually be the mother of most of them. But Max was her favourite 'child', he was the first one of the group she had met, and they had formed a strong bond very quickly.

He joined the others at the table whilst Clea bustled around them.

'How's the new piece going?' Sofia asked Max.

'Okay I guess.'

Max was working on a small figure piece of a woman he had discovered in a painting on the wall in the art room/lounge. She was an interesting study, but he found he wasn't really feeling it. Sensing that Max was a little uncomfortable talking about his work Sofia changed the subject.

'Where are the other three?' she enquired of no one in particular.

'They were in the art room about twenty minutes ago' Geth told her.

'I think they're still there, or they were when I left them just now' added Max.

'Okay, I'm going to go and ask them to join us as I think we need a little conflab about the imminent arrival,' said Sofia.

Sofia only found two of the three other Gateway residents in the art room/lounge, the lovebirds Mary and Aaron.

It was a large room with two distinct areas. Looking in from the doorway the right side of the room was the lounge area consisting of two large, comfy, black leathers sofas and two matching armchairs set around a large TV system, and nearest the door was an upright piano and bench.

The whole left side of the room, nearest the windows, was taken up by the slightly more incongruous set up of an art area with work benches and stools in the middle, and a stainless-steel sink and cupboards full of art supplies against the back wall. The walls were painted a delicate dove grey, but you could not see much of it under all the works of art displayed on the walls around the lounge area and those parts of wall on the art room side not covered by cupboards. In between two of the tall cupboards against the back wall there was a door that led to the guest room where Sofia stayed on her visits.

Mary and Aaron were referred to as the lovebirds because they were a loved up young couple. The first of the group to meet in person they had fallen in love fast and hard. Their love was part of their special talent and important to their roles within the group.

Mary was curled up in the corner of one of the black leather sofas, a laptop on a special tray perched on her knees. Small and slim she almost looked like a child dwarfed by the large sofa her long, auburn hair tucked behind her ears as she hunched over the laptop screen. Sofia wasn't sure if she was working on her novel or some poetry but whatever it was, she looked like she was struggling as she was staring at the screen with a look of frustration on her pretty face her hands just hovering over the keyboard.

Aaron stood before an easel in the art area staring intently at the beginnings of a self-portrait in oils, his tall frame hunched, broad shoulders tense. In one hand he held a paintbrush the other clutched at his dark hair in consternation.

Having already painted the portrait of everyone else in the house including Sofia who was only an occasional resident, and Mary several times, it was a new direction for him. A vague, part image of his handsome young face peered at him from the canvas, but he clearly wasn't happy with it. Judging from their demeanour and how Max had been about his work Sofia wondered if the pending visitor was causing a lack of concentration amongst the artists.

'I think maybe you two could do with a break' she said making both of them jump as neither of them had realised she was in the room.

'Fucks sake Sofia!' exclaimed a startled Aaron.

'I think that proves her point' added Mary, and then to Sofia 'we definitely need a break.'

'Everyone else is in the kitchen, we're having a little chat about our impending guest. Clea's making tea so come and join us.'

'Gladly' agreed Aaron 'and sorry for the swearing.'

'No problem?'

She was just about to ask them where the seventh member of the household was when she heard footsteps behind her and turned to see him entering the room.

'Hay Sofia, what's up?' asked Mason Winchester.

The tall Black man wore a warm, easy smile and was holding a half-built guitar in his hand. He was a handsome man with a lean, muscular build, short, neat dreadlocks and a tidy beard. He was a talented Luthier, the guitar in his hand obviously a work in progress.

'We're having a sort of meeting in the kitchen; will you join us?' Sofia asked him.

'Of course,' he answered.

Mason was a weird mixture of the latest member of the Gateway 'team' and yet a member of the old one and was just settling into his new role within the Gateway community.

Once everyone was sat at the table with a mug of tea before them Sofia began the conversation.

'In less than an hour your new, sort of, tenant will be here, Eddie and I have seen the cabin and its fantastic so I'm sure he'll be happy. Now you all know about the Origination and what that involved but understandably we're all a little unsure how we will react to who he is now and how he will be towards us.

As you know he's spent the last eight months being 'assessed' by various high-ranking members of the Foundation. Now although it's still not been established 'what' exactly he has become, the Foundation are sure he is no danger to anyone. It is believed that he may possess some new, unique talent, but it has not yet been determined what that talent is. He is coming here as he feels that it is the place he needs to be in order to explore his new talent and the Foundation agrees with him. I have been told that he will explain things to us in more detail himself, but right now I just want to gauge how everyone is feeling about it all.'

Aaron was the first to speak, 'I'm looking forward to meeting him and I'm not worried at all, what he's achieved is awesome and although no one really knows exactly what he is I know he's something good.'

'I'm with Aaron' was Mary's not unexpected opinion 'though I'm a little more nervous about it than he is, I'm not exactly sure why.'

'Well, I'm a little nervous too' added Max 'but I believe it's just a healthy fear of the unknown, I know he won't hurt us or anything, but I really don't know what to expect of him now and in the future.'

Clea spoke next whilst laying her hand on top of Max's and giving it a little squeeze.

'I'm not nervous at all, I'm only expecting good things from him, I haven't had a strong sense of what's to come but I can sense that it will be good.'

'Don't you ever have a negative thought in that shiny mind of yours?' asked Geth and although his words were a little harsh his affable tone softened them.

'Do you ever have anything but negative thoughts in that dark mind of yours?' was Clea's playful retort.

This was the closest the group ever got to arguing which was a feat in itself since they were all so different. And it was mostly Clea and Geth who sparred like this.

'You have some negative thoughts about him then?' Eddie asked Geth.

'I wouldn't say negative, I'm just not as unconcerned as Clea is. We don't really know what this new thing is exactly.'

'Thing!' exclaimed Sofia 'He's a person not a thing.'

'I'm sorry, we don't know exactly what this 'person' is and so I think we need to be a bit cautious at least.'

'You may be right Geth' agreed Eddie 'but I don't think the foundation would have let him come here so freely if they thought he was a danger.'

'I guess not, they built him a bloody cabin after all, but there's still the possibility that they're wrong you know, they're not infallible.'

'I get your point, but I agree with Eddie' said Mason 'I really don't think he poses any danger to us.'

'Maybe not, but that doesn't change the fact that no one knows what it, sorry he, could be capable of.'

'But that's why he's coming here Geth' said Sofia 'to try to work out exactly what he's capable of and I hope you are all willing to help him with it, to all work together to find out.'

'I'm willing to do anything I can' Clea assured her, then to the others 'we all are right?'

'Sure' said Aaron and the others nodded their agreement, except Geth.

'Geth?' Clea enquired.

'Well yeah, I'll help of course I'm just urging caution okay.'

'That's sensible Geth' said Sofia 'of course we need to be careful but let's keep things friendly, okay?'

Geth nodded his agreement.

'Good, that's settled we'll leave it at that shall we. He'll be here soon and some of our questions will be answered, we'll discover the rest in time, I'm sure.'

And that was the end of the conflab, it was now time to get ready to greet the subject of their debate.

The big, heavy gates began to slowly open in order to let the car pass through giving its passenger time to admire with new eyes the unusual design woven in the black iron. The metal formed strange leaf and vine like structures that looked organic yet were unrecognisable as any known flora. The pattern was familiar and somehow comforting.

Once through the gate the car travelled sedately along the winding, tree lined driveway until finally arriving at the semi-circle of gravel in front of the red brick house. The house's occupants stood waiting on the gravel; a scene reminiscent of the house's Georgian heritage when a group of servants would stand waiting to greet the master of the house on his return from a long trip abroad. The times and situation were very different yet at the same time there were similarities.

He wasn't their master, more of a mentor he hoped and though he had never lived here exactly a part of him called somewhere nearby home and that part was returning after a very long absence.

Sofia stood slightly in front of the waiting group ready to be the first to greet the new member of the household. *'How should I greet him?'* she wondered; he'd been Samuel Raven the last time she saw him, but he was 'more' than that now, so she decided not to use his name. The car door was opening now and then he was finally there before her.

He was a striking figure of a man at six foot five, his slim legs and hips clad in black jeans, his broad chest and shoulders accentuated by a plain white t shirt. He was wearing sunglasses which hid his eyes, but his Native American heritage was still very evident in his strong features, long, flowing black hair and naturally bronzed skin.

It was a little disconcerting not being able to see his eyes, but the beauty of the man still took Sofia's breath away.

Before the Origination she'd started to have feelings for Samuel, feelings she had never had for anyone before, and she had not known what to do about them. She had managed to mostly dampen these feelings over the last eight months telling herself that the Samuel she had known was gone and there was no chance of any relationship with him even if she still wanted it. Seeing him again now she was frustrated to find that the attraction was still there, but she was determined to harden herself against any deeper feelings.

'Welcome, it's so good to see you again' she said in greeting her voice a little shaky.

'It's good to see you too' he replied.

He looked and sounded the same as he had when they had first met but he wasn't the same and Sofia could feel that now. He had a different aura about him, it wasn't visible, but she could definitely feel it. There was a sense of power radiating from him, but it wasn't a frightening power it was strangely soothing, and Sofia felt her fears about their meeting melting away. She still had questions and did not really know how to act around him, but her worries were gone. She wanted to touch him and knew that shaking his hand would not be a strange thing to do but somehow, she just could not bring herself to do it.

The others were greeting him now and everyone was smiling, but she noted that none of them had proffered any physical greeting either, not even Clea.

Sofia led them into the house, their honoured guest behind her followed by the rest in a ragged group. Eddie was last in after helping the Foundation chauffer to unload the car of their guests' belongings and offering the man refreshment. He declined saying he had somewhere to be and drove off leaving Eddie to carry the bags into the house. Or to be more exact the one bag plus various cases containing musical instruments.

Inside Sofia ushered them into the art room/lounge where she offered the new arrival a seat in one of the comfy armchairs and everyone else found a place to sit. Eddie followed after having stowed the luggage in the large hallway and found himself a seat. No one had said anything for a few minutes, so Clea decided to break the slightly awkward silence.

'Are you hungry?' she asked the man that had been Samuel Raven 'only we have a nice lunch prepared when you're ready.'

'That would be lovely' he answered, 'but not just yet, I have a few things to say first.'

'Yes, of course, sorry' said Clea feeling a little silly.

'There's no need to apologise, I realise you're all a little unsure what to do or say right now and that you have questions so I'm going to address some of the issues you may have. Firstly, I think we need to establish what you should call me. As you all know I am no longer just the man known as Samuel Raven, and that part of who I am now was once known as The Soul Stealer and later Talionis. None of those names seem fitting anymore so I have given myself a new name, and that name is Morpheus.'

'Like the guy in The Matrix' blurted Aaron, then immediately regretted it feeling embarrassed.

'Morpheus is the Greek god of dreams' stated Geth surprising them all. Seeing their shocked looks he added 'what, you all think I'm a complete philistine or something?'

'No of course not' Sofia reassured him, 'but let's not get side tracked, let Morpheus finish what he has to say.' The name felt alien on her lips, but it was obvious why he had chosen it and at least they knew what to call him now.

'So now you know what to call me' continued Morpheus seemingly unphased by the interruption, 'I'll explain a few basic things you are no doubt wondering about, then you can ask me questions if I haven't covered what you want to know.

To start with I can confirm that I am still human in most physical senses. I eat, sleep and shit just like you do. My difference lies within the less physical sense of the soul, but we will get to that later.

The one physical aspect in which I do differ explains these' he said tapping the expensive looking sunglasses he wore with a long finger. 'My eyes were the only part of me that was physically changed by the Origination and so I wear these sunglasses when I first meet certain people until I have explained because although the change is subtle it is strange, so I don't like to spring it on anyone. I'm going to take them off now and set my gaze upon each of you in turn so that you can witness this difference.'

After taking the sunglasses off Morpheus sat staring into the distance above their heads for a few seconds before slowly turning his gaze first to Sofia. After a few seconds she gave a little gasp of awe but continued to stare into his eyes as if mesmerised. He held her gaze for about a minute before breaking it by closing his eyes briefly, then he continued on to the next member of his captivated audience.

At first each of them could see nothing unusual, they just saw the deep brown eyes of the man who used to be Samuel. Then as he held their gaze, they glimpsed deep within the blackness of his pupils a white light which pulsed with the regularity of a heartbeat. They each then discovered that the longer you stared at the light the stronger it became, and after a while the pupils became a swirling, milky white rather than the usual dense black. Having been prewarned none of them, despite a few exclamations, were alarmed by what they saw, what they felt was curiosity and a touch of wonder.

'What you are seeing' explained Morpheus after breaking eye contact with the last of them 'is a physical manifestation of the Eternal Within me. I have found that It likes to demonstrate Its presence whenever anyone with a dream talent looks into my eyes, and this brings me to the other explanation I need to give you: what exactly happened at the Origination.'

It was obvious that he had everyone undivided attention, so he continued.

'You all felt it happen, you are aware of the events which led to it, and you know the general facts, but I will now explain a little more about what actually took place.

As you know in order to neutralise any further danger from the damaged soul known as Talionis Samuel, with your help, first healed It through dreams. Samuel then came to the realisation that the flawed human body that encased Talionis would hold It back from any further development and he began to form an idea of how to release the entity from the flawed human flesh it was trapped in. It was a perilous venture into very much unknown territory, but he thought it worth the risk.

Samuel bravely put his idea into practice. He knew that the Eternal could never be released and restored to its natural state as there was no way that the human soul could or would be parted from It, but what he could do was provide the joint entity with a stronger, more suitable host. This could only be achieved by mutual consent, and so working together using spiritual force he managed to pull the willing Eternal Dreamer and human soul out of the damaged body they were trapped in and take them into himself.

And so, we became Morpheus, the unification of two human souls and an Eternal Dreamer.' Pausing there he waited for someone to ask the obvious question, and that person was Clea.

'So how exactly does that work?'

'As you can see, excluding my eyes, physically I am Samuel and his is the dominant soul within me except for when I enter the Dream Realm when the Eternal Within has equal dominance with that soul.'

'And what about the other soul, the damaged one that caused all the trouble?' asked Mason the pain that soul had caused him and his friends clear in his expression.

'That soul dwells in this body experiencing through it the things it was denied for years. It now vicariously enjoys the benefits of a healthy body, the joy of making music once again and the ability to dream. It is no longer the essence of the arrogant Dreambringer whose attempt to merge with his Eternal went so terribly wrong. Nor is It the tortured soul that was twisted into the being known as Talionis by rejection, a lack of dreams and many years of incarceration. It is just a remnant of those things now and what remains has been purified and rendered powerless. Our two souls are linked, It feels and experiences what I do, It is an important part of me, but It is a passenger only and will never be a dominant force again.'

'But does it deserve to enjoy those benefits after what it did?' Asked Eddie.

'Maybe not, at least in the eyes of those it hurt most, but there is no changing the situation, I could not be free of it even if I wanted to be. I can assure you that It is content with Its new role whether It deserves to be or not. This Passenger Soul is part of me and as I intend to do good with whatever new talents I may now possess maybe this soul's part in that will make up for the harm it has done in the past.'

'Well let's hope so' muttered Mason.

Morpheus could see that most of the group were placated by his words on this subject although Mason and Eddie were understandably still a little upset, but he had done all he could to reassure them. The group were still understandably full of questions though and it was Sofia who asked the next one.

'Physically you are still Samuel, and you say that his soul is dominant so why do you feel the need for a new name, why are you not just an improved Samuel Raven?'

'It's hard to explain. I am still Samuel in every way, I have his thoughts, his memories, his body but I'm not 'just' him anymore, I don't feel the same, I feel like someone new, plus people are unsure what or who I am now, so I thought it made sense to give myself a new name to go with my altered identity. I have two souls and an Eternal within me, we are joined forever so I felt we needed a collective name, it seemed only fair.'

'That makes sense,' said Sofia.

'Are you happy as you are now?' this from Clea.

He was taken aback a little by a question that no one had thought to ask him before and replied, 'What a thoughtful thing to ask, thank you Clea, and yes I am happy, very happy.'

'That's good lovey.'

There was a slight pause as everyone took in the information they had been given so far before Max asked the next question.

'What happens when you're in the Dream Realm? How do you affect it in your new state?'

'Good question, and this is the part that hasn't quite been figured out yet. All I know at the moment is that when I enter the Dream Realm my interaction with the dreaming souls there feels different. I can connect with them and bring them specific types of dreams as you Dreambringers do, but I also have a more general influence. I have discovered that I give off a healing aura in person and this translates more strongly in the Dream Realm. As I roam within the Dream Realm any dreaming soul that passes near me benefits from this healing influence without any effort on my part.'

'Samuel was a Soul Healer of Dreams as was the Passenger Soul' interjected Sofia 'so it makes sense that as Morpheus you have a strong healing presence. I know I felt the benefit of your healing aura both when the Origination happened and when we met you earlier, so is that not your new talent, a strong healing ability?'

'Yes, my healing talent is strong but as important as that is it seems insufficient; I feel that I am capable of more, I just can't work out what that more is.'

'I see.'

'After working with members of the foundation for the last few months I felt that something else was needed and decided that communing with the Eternals here at the Gateway might help. The Eternal Within was once a member of the group here and reuniting with them could help me realise my full potential. That's why I asked for the cabin to be built so I could be near them at all times, and I intend to commune with them in person too.'

'And the Foundation agreed obviously.'

'After a little persuading yes.'

In fact, the leaders within the Foundation had taken a lot of persuading. He had spent months at a secluded Foundation safe house being questioned and tested. He did not blame them for being afraid and therefore cautious to start with, but he believed it had been established quickly that the result of the Origination, namely him, was all for the good. Yet they still insisted on keeping him away from others and using various talented ex Dreambringers to test him.

Even after a strong endorsement from Dorothea Attwood, the woman who had been sent with Samuel to deal with Talionis at the beginning of it all, the slight mistrust persisted, as did the tests.

Nothing much was learnt in all those months he spent confined and when, after a couple of months, he had suggested a visit to the Eternals at the Gateway might help he had simply been told it would be considered. This consideration had taken months and as the months passed, he had become more and more frustrated.

It would have been easy for him to just break out of the place they were holding him (because holding was a strong word, he was not exactly a prisoner) and make his own way to the Gateway, but he had decided it would not be wise. A move like that on his part would reawaken their fears of him being a danger and cause a major upset he was sure. The thing he needed from them most was trust and leaving like that would have the opposite effect.

So, he had bided his time, submitted to all their tests and had occasionally reminded them of his idea until, finally, without any other options on the table they had agreed to it. They'd even agreed to the cabin being built for him. It had been a bold request but an important one in his opinion.

He knew that he mainly had Cedric Neale, the head of the British division of the Foundation, to thank for it. Although as cautious as the rest Cedric had the most faith in Morpheus and as leader had the last say. And now here he was.

'So that's why you're here, to commune with the Eternals?' asked Eddie now bringing Morpheus back to the present.

'Yes', he told him.

'And that is possible, that you'll be able to access their chamber?'

'I believe so yes.'

'When do you intend to do that?' this from Geth.

'Later today.'

'You're eager' stated Aaron.

'I am' Morpheus agreed with a warm smile.

'Well, I hope it works out then,' said Mary.

'Thank you,'

At this point Sofia suggested that they leave it there for now and go have some lunch. Although everyone was still full of questions and opinions, they all agreed that a break was a good idea. There would be plenty of time to discuss things further, Morpheus wasn't going anywhere. So, they all headed to the kitchen for something to eat.

Chapter 3
Morpheus is Home

'It's even better than I imagined' exclaimed Morpheus as he turned a small circle in the middle of the beautifully crafted log cabin that was his new home.

'It is pretty special' agreed Eddie standing beside him.

It had been, reluctantly, decided that Eddie was the only one who would accompany Morpheus to the cabin at this stage. The others were desperate to see the amazing cabin, but they would have to wait a little longer. The two of them had brought some of Morpheus' belongings between them along with some basic food and drink but the rest of his musical instruments were still back at the house. The plan was for the others to have staggered visiting times the next day so they could see the cabin, and each bring one of his instruments with them.

'I feel at home already' Morpheus said as he headed back towards the door where they had dumped his bags.

'Do you want me to help, I can put the groceries away for you?' Eddie suggested.

'No thanks I can manage' he replied as he lifted a bag.

'Okay, I'll leave you to it then' said Eddie reluctantly taking his leave.

Twenty minutes later Morpheus had finished unpacking and was stood in the open doorway looking out into the woods at the bright, early evening sunshine filtering through the trees. It was time for Morpheus to take a walk through those sun dappled trees, but it would not be an aimless stroll, he had a very special destination in mind. Not too far off through the woods was another unusual dwelling and this was the home of the Gateway Eternal Dreamers.

It had been nice getting acquainted with the Gateway artists but what he was really excited about was communing with the Eternals, even being this near them was thrilling. His body was almost vibrating with the joy that both souls and the Eternal Within were feeling at the prospect of this meeting.

The Eternal Within had been apart from It's fellow Eternals for many years as had the Passenger Soul and their torment at the separation had been one of the reasons that their former selves had been twisted into the being known as Talionis. Now after the healing help given by Samuel and the miracle of the Origination, they were able and ready to commune with the Eternals once again. As for the soul that had been Samuel, he was excited about what the meeting could accomplish.

Closing the heavy wooden door behind him Morpheus headed off into the woods. As Samuel he had been to the Eternals dwelling, the place that Gateway artists jokingly called The Factory, therefore he needed no directions. He knew that the building would not be cloaked from him either, the Eternals knew he was coming, he could sense their welcoming vibes.

He reached the place where the mental barrier created by the Eternals shielded their dwelling from strangers. Those who were unwelcome would see only a grassy clearing surrounded by trees, but those in the know could perceive the unusual dwelling within that clearing. It was a strange, circular, single storey castle like structure of ancient grey stone with arched windows and a porched doorway.

As he neared the building Morpheus saw a shimmer in the air where the protective mental barrier was and passing through it, he headed for the entrance to the building.

He stood before the big oak door for a while examining the symbols carved into it. The same leaf and vine design he'd seen in the iron gate leading to the Gateway house was carved into the wood entwined around six carved circles set in a clock face pattern. Each circle encased a carved symbol that represented a kind of Dreambringer. There was the bare branched tree of the Dream Mate Male, the full moon of the Dream Mate Female, the portcullis gate of the Gatekeeper of Dreams, the feather and web of the Dreamcatcher and the swirl pupiled eye of the Seer of Dreams.

The sixth circle held no symbol and as Morpheus reached out to touch the smooth, uncarved wood the thought came to him that maybe there would be a symbol there one day soon.

In a smaller, separated circle in the upper right corner of the door there was also the crescent moon and star symbol representing the Dreamwisher. The whole thing was a beautiful work of art even more impressive than the work on his cabin if only for the fact that it had been made so long ago.

Reaching for the ornate iron handle Morpheus let himself into the building.

Inside the huge, high ceilinged, mostly open plan space was a strange mix of ancient and modern. The bare stone walls and large, grey slate slab floor were ancient but well preserved and the stone arches of the windows had been in more modern times expertly framed and glazed. The furniture throughout was a mixture of antique and modern, all well made.

For several feet into the enormous room there was just bare, slate floor with a small cloakroom area and storage cupboards against the walls on either side of the door. The specially made cupboards contained fold out beds and bedding for if the Dreambringers wished to spend the night here amongst other things. Further in the space resembled a bigger version of the front lounge area of the Gateway in that it was littered with work benches, easels and other art equipment and machinery, with the left-hand wall taken up by a large stainless-steel sink and storage cupboards.

In the back left hand corner, there was a seating area with a couple of large, comfy sofas around an ornate, antique rug. Next to that there was a small kitchen area with tea making facilities, a small sink with a storage cupboard underneath, a small fridge and a table holding a microwave oven. At the back on the right-hand side were the only closed off parts which consisted of a small bathroom and a well-equipped recording studio.

The large, arched windows along with several skylights in the high ceiling provided the room with plenty of natural light making the space any artists dream. It also helped that although the building was very old it was fitted with modern lighting, heating and electrical systems. It was a marvel, but what lay beneath this amazing room was what really made the building unique and special.

Morpheus could feel the joy emanating from the Eternal Within as It returned to the place where It had once happily dwelt. The Passenger Soul had known this place too though long ago and It too felt joy at being back. Samuel had visited this place once but had not ventured into the real heart of the building, but now the three of them would venture there together.

Turning to his left Morpheus walked slowly forwards weaving a strange pattern as he endeavoured to step on each separate slate floor slab, his eyes alert for a symbol. He wasn't sure that the symbol he was seeking was still there and if it was that he would be able to activate it, but he was sure that he would be granted access somehow. Maybe any of the other symbols would work for him?

He just about made out the first symbol, it was etched faintly into one of the slate slabs, a human eye with a swirling pupil, but it did not light up as his foot touched it, so he moved on. Next, he found the moon symbol but again it did not light up, so he continued his search.

Three steps later he gave a start as light flashed under his foot for a second and taking a step back, he looked closer at the slab. He had thought that particular slab to be symbol free so maybe the etching was fainter than the others he thought straining to make out any etched lines on the slabs surface. Or maybe it had been scrubbed smooth like the circle in the door, but it didn't matter it was here. Placing both feet on the slab he watched as the symbol lit up beneath them.

The symbol depicted a basic human shape with rays of light emanating from its core, the symbol representing The Soul Healer of Dreams. He waited, and although it took a little longer than he had expected he finally felt a slight vibration through his feet and heard a brief grating sound. Then several of the large slate floor slabs a few feet in front of him dropped down a few inches before sliding back underneath where he stood. And now instead of a solid slate floor before him there was a set of stone steps leading downwards into darkness.

In his haste Morpheus was a few steps down before he realised his mistake. The staircase had begun to spiral to the right, and he realised that it would become very dark. 'Damn it' he muttered retracing his steps.

Heading for the cupboards on the left-hand side of the door thinking them his best bet he hurriedly opening a few doors until he found what he was looking for, an LED lantern. Turning it on he walked quickly back to the head of the staircase and began to descend the stone steps.

After spiralling to the right in an eighty degree turn the staircase straightened out and continued down another twenty feet before finally terminating in a small stone chamber with a wooden door set in the roughhewn stone wall facing him. The door was a smaller, unadorned version of the one above.

Next to the door on the right was an iron lever set in a vertical slot carved into the stone wall and just as he was wondering about its use, he heard the hatch about close with a clang. He then, rightly, conjectured that the lever was what would open the hatch again when he wanted to leave. Now grabbing the iron handle of the door Morpheus pushed through into darkness.

The light from his lantern did not penetrate far into the darkness beyond the door but unperturbed he walked further inside then turned to close the door behind him. He then used the lantern to examine the stone wall either side of the door looking for some sort of light switch not knowing exactly what to expect. He found nothing and was moving slightly to his right in order to widen his search when small spots of light began to appear spreading out in an arc from where he stood. So, it was automatic then he thought to himself as his surroundings became illuminated by warm, subdued lighting.

The room, or rather chamber, was about half the size of the room above and was also circular, the wall, floor and ceiling all roughhewn in stone. Morpheus marvelled at the skill involved in carving a perfect circle into solid rock and wondered who could have achieved such a feat of engineering. Peppered around the wall from floor to high ceiling were numerous stone shelves and recesses of various sizes. These shelves and recesses contained works of art of all kinds – paintings, sculptures, books and any number of other weird and wonderful artistic creations. The warm lighting was coming from small LED lights scattered amongst these treasures.

Taking a few more steps into the amazing chamber Morpheus put the lantern on the floor at his feet and stood taking in more of its marvels.

In the centre of the room there was a circular depression carved into the stone floor. It was three feet in circumference the depth gradually deepening from the outside in until about a foot deep in the middle, however, the spiral pattern carved into the stone gave the optical illusion that the circle was in fact deeper.

Arranged around this central circle were six rectangles, five of which were large blocks made of stone each two foot high, seven foot long and three foot wide at one end narrowing to two and a half foot at the other. On top of each block of stone was a fitted wooden frame encasing padded purple velvet cushioning. The sixth however was simply a rectangle of equal length and width carved into the stone floor.

The six rectangles radiated from the central circular depression in a pattern reminiscent of a clock face with their narrowest end nearest the centre circle. The five stone rectangles each had a pattern etched into the side at their wider end, but the rectangle carved into the floor was blank.

On the floor at the wider end, or 'head' of each stone rectangle there was a slightly raised stone circle about a foot in diameter. Like its adjacent stone rectangle, the sixth circle was a plain flat circle carved into the floor. Each of the other five stone circles had a pattern etched into the middle of it. The symbols etched in the stone rectangles were the Dreambringers symbols, and the patterns etched on the stone circles represented the inhabitants of the amazing chamber, The Eternal Dreamers. They were the symbols depicted in the Iron Gate and on the carved oak door, the flower/leaf like symbols at the ends of the 'vines', each one subtly different.

Morpheus took in these astonishing sights in a matter of seconds and felt a brief pang of anguish at the sight of the flat, unadorned sixth rectangle and circle as like the blank circle on the door they were a sad sign of the eradication of The Soul Healer of Dreams from this group. But his focus was on the real treasures of the astounding chamber, its inhabitants, the Eternal Dreamers.

There were five of them each hovering above the raised stone circle at the wider end of one of the raised stone rectangles. Roughly seven feet tall they have a vaguely human shape with an elongated head and limbs, but they are not made of flesh. They are not solid, yet not transparent, their unnameable substance seemingly made of smoke and light, their white, ghostly shape constantly shifting as little specks of white light move within the swirls of white mist. There was no definition to them, no facial features just an aura of soft, smoky white light in constant but gentle motion, ever changing and mesmerising to behold. As they gently move and subtly change shape there is a hint of what could be flowing hair or a delicate hand, but it is all fleeting.

The sight of these beautiful spirit forms triggered a strong reaction within Morpheus as the three parts of his being each rejoiced in their own way. The soul that was Samuel was in awe of the Eternal's beauty and felt thrilled and honoured to be in their presence for the first time. The Passenger Soul experienced these emotions vicariously, but the depth of the experience is such that It also experienced a remembered joy of Its own. But the biggest reaction was from the Eternal Within as It jubilantly expressed without words 'I am home'.

As a physical manifestation of these emotions a tear escaped Morpheus' left eye and rolled down his beautifully defined cheek bone.

The three entities that made up Morpheus now set about communing with the five Eternal Dreamers in a frenzy of elation and reunion.

At the Gateway house the residents and Sofia were all scattered around the art room/lounge working on their respective arts. When Morpheus began his communion with the Eternals the new Dreambringers felt it, as did Sofia, Mason and Eddie in their own ways.

Her role as a Marshal with The Somnium Foundation meant that Sofia had full knowledge of the Foundations secrets and she had her own kind of link with the Eternals within the art communes in her care. Her link was only through her dreams, she never came into contact with them on a physical level, but the link was there.

For Eddie it was his newly acquired Dreamwisher talent that linking him with the Eternals. His own introduction to and first commune with the Eternals was still fresh in his mind having only taken place a few months before. As a Dreamwisher he did not have a strong connection to one specific Eternal, his was a weaker and more general link, but he now held a new and important role within the group.

Before the tragic events at the Gateway which had culminated in the Origination Eddie had been the Warden there and although aware of the special talent that the artists he looked after possessed he had, as was normal, been unaware of the Eternals themselves.

The unusual events had led to him being upgraded in terms of the knowledge he had been given and this in turn had led to him being offered the chance to train to become a Dreamwisher. The thinking behind this being that after the recent troubles a permanent, inhouse Dreamwisher would be prudent especially given the groups long term lack of a Soul Healer of Dreams. It was a shame that no one had thought to do this earlier but a lone, inhouse Dreamwisher was a slight twist on a long-established role, so it wasn't something that anyone had considering before.

Dreamwishers were usually transient, travelling in pairs to stay for short periods with Dreambringer groups that were temporarily weakened by short absences or illness. Their role was mainly to help 'feed' the Eternals through their artistic energy.

Within the Dream Realm they held less power than the Dreambringers, their presence giving more general comfort rather than the more directed, individual help of the Dreambringers. Dreamwishers were always recruited from existing foundation staff who over time had shown trustworthiness and a strong dreaming talent. Although made aware of the Eternal Dreamers the Dreamwishers never actually came into physical contact with them, only making their temporary connection with them through art energy and dreams.

In Eddie's case it was decided that he would be allowed to make physical contact with the Eternals as this would give him a stronger connection to them therefore allowing him to maximise his input. He did visit them physically less often than the Dreambringers however and could only do so if in the company of one or more of them. Eddie was well aware of the privilege he had been given and was very grateful for it his life having been enriched by his link to the Eternals.

Now the group were part of another Dreambringer first and although it was thought a good thing it was still a lot to deal with on top of everything else they had gone through.

As well as his new role as Dreamwisher Eddie still performed some of the duties he had done as Warden. There had been talk of recruiting someone to take over the role of Warden, but Eddie had insisted it wasn't necessary and then when another decision had been made a new/old addition had meant he now had someone to share his Warden duties with; and that someone was his friend Mason.

The first few weeks after the Origination had been hard for Mason Winchester, he'd lost three of the things he loved most; his job, his home and the companionship of his friends. Maybe job was the wrong word to describe his work as a Dreambringer, words like vocation or calling were more accurate, but whatever you called it he had still lost it.

His time as a Dreambringer had been brought to a premature end after the very traumatic few weeks when he had been part of the event that had caused great upheaval within the Dreambringer community. He had come out of it well, his successful handling of a very unusual situation gaining him the admiration of even the highest members of the Somnium Foundation, but his retirement had come before he was ready for it and that was hard to deal with.

Mason had not been the only one to have been pushed into early retirement, three of his friends had suffered the same fate, but things were different for them. Claude Grey and Gina and Blake Summers had suffered physical and mental harm at the hands, or rather mind, of the creature self-named Talionis and this meant that they had no longer felt capable of fulfilling their Dreambringer task which had made it easier for them to let go. As for Mahesh Choudhary, the other member of the Dreambringer group, he had paid an even higher price, his death having been the beginning of their troubles.

His good friend Eddie Oakley had actually benefited vocation wise from the changes that had needed to be made, but he had still suffered the same ordeal and being apart from his friends was hard for him too. Mason was still able to visit his friends regularly, but it was not the same as living together at the Gateway and he missed the strong link with his Eternal too. The premature breaking of that connection had been devastating in itself.

After the ordeal was over and the fallout dealt with Mason had taken a break to think over his options. There was no way he would even consider leaving The Foundation, but none of the options they offered him felt right.

The Foundation members felt that the role of Dreamteller would be a good move, but Mason knew that although the best part of a Dreamteller's job was initiating and training a new group of Dreambringers, he was also aware that it was quite a rare occurrence and with other Dreamtellers to choose from who knew when he would get a chance at this prize job. This had bothered him because other than the rare Dreambringer induction the Dreamtellers job appeared to consist of office training for new members of the Foundation, most of whom would not even get to know about the foundations real purpose. So, he had turned down that offer and eventually come up with a role for himself, which he had pitched to the head of the British division of the Foundation, Cedric Neale.

Mason wanted to become a second inhouse Dreamwisher at The Gateway, after all Dreamwishers always came in pairs and each pair had to be compatible, therefore, as Eddie was his best friend, they would be a great match.

'If one Dreamwisher is an asset to The Gateway, then surely two would be even better' he had told Cedric Neale as part of his pitch.

'Is it not a step down though?' Cedric had asked.

'No more than taking on the role of Dreamteller would be' Mason had countered.

'But a Dreambringer becoming a Dreamwisher is unheard of, would it even work?' Cedric had retorted.

'Until recently a Warden becoming a Dreamwisher had not been heard of but that's worked out, and that's the least of the unheard-of things that have happened recently' Mason had countered.

After that initial conversation a lot of discussions had taken place until, finally, it had been agreed that Mason would join Eddie as a Dreamwisher at The Gateway and that the friends would share the Warden duties.

The Foundation had insisted that he go through the Dreamwisher training first even though he was basically overqualified, his Dreambringer talents being superior to those of other Dreamwishers. He had agreed though as he would have done anything to get back to his 'home'.

He had of course passed the Dreamwisher training with flying colours and had in fact found it quite interesting, not least because the trainer had turned out to be Dorothea Atwood. Her job as Custodian having become defunct after the Origination she had taken on a role as Dreamteller and as part of the group that had gone through the Talionis ordeal along with Mason the Foundation had decided to give her the job of conducting his Dreamwisher training.

Mason and Dorothea had inevitable talked about the event from their different perspectives and she had told him how she had felt privileged as the closest one to the Origination, to be the first to witness its result and that being that close to the creation had had a profound impact on her. Where some had felt soothed and uplifted, and others had felt momentary relief from their troubles, Dorothea had experienced a deeper healing; in that moment a deep pain from her past had been eased changing her in a small but significant way. She had not elaborated on what that deep pain had been, and Mason did not pry, it was enough to know it had happened.

The next problem had been finding room in the house for him. Mason had suggested that the two guest rooms that were usually used by the visiting Dreamwishers, and occasional other guests, could be converted into one bigger suite for him.

This had then started a debate on whether The Gateway would still need visits from normal Dreamwishers, and if so, where would they stay? After all the new in-house Dreamwisher idea had been seen as a long-needed solution to the lack of a sixth Dreambringer at The Gateway so if they were to be a substitution for the missing sixth Dreambringer there might still be need for Dreamwisher visits if there was long term sickness or absence. Plus, there was always the possibility of other visitors.

Again, it was Mason who came up with a solution. The attic rooms could be renovated. They were currently only used for storage, but half of the space could quite easily be converted into two guest bedrooms with small en suites, and there would still be ample storage room in the other half. Plus, there was the double guest room which Sofia used on her visits.

It took a while, but eventually The Foundation agreed that Mason's ideas were acceptable and so plans were put in place for the necessary renovations and a few weeks later Mason returned home.

It was a little weird at first being in the same house but a new room, and also having new housemates and a new role within that group. But he was home, back with his friend Eddie and near to his Eternal, and that was what mattered most. Although he could never have a singular link to the Eternal he thought of as his own he could still communicate with It and that was enough.

Mason and Eddie missed their friends, the previous group of Dreambringers, but had taken to this new group quickly and Eddie particularly felt the need to look after them as he had done their predecessors.

'I take it you all feel that?' Mason asked the group. He was experiencing the initial communion between Morpheus and the Eternals as a jolt of inner energy that then levelled off into the calming feeling of being part of something good. It felt like there was an invisible tether joining him to everyone in the room and that also stretched out into the woods and joined them all to the inhabitants of that amazing stone chamber.

There was no perception of the exact messages being passing between the newly joined entities, just a projected sense of the elation that the reunion was creating.

Eddie gave him an answering nod, but Aaron was the first to answer verbally.

'I'm sure as hell feeling something' he said with an expression on his face that was a strange mixture of a frown and a smile 'and although I'm not exactly sure what it is it feels good.'

'I'm taking it as a good sign' Sofia told them with a subtle smile.

'It feels wonderful' exclaimed Clea her face beaming with joy.

'Like pure happiness' added Mary.

'Get a grip you big drama queens' grumbled Geth.

'Do you not feel it?' asked Clea.

'Of course I do, and I agree it's a good thing, but there's no need to act like it's the second coming or something.'

'Why do you always have to be so negative?' asked Aaron.

'Because you're all so airy fairy at times and it gets on my nerves.'

'Let's not argue' interjected Max 'what's happening is a good thing, we're agreed on that, so why don't we just allow each other to experience it in our own way without criticism.'

'Okay, fine' Geth agreed looking a little abashed.

'I know this sort of thing makes you a little uncomfortable Geth but please tell me you are feeling just a little bit of happiness right now' said Clea.

'Don't push it' he told her, but he was smiling now. These days his grumpiness was always short lived, and he realised his reaction had been a reflex rather than a true indication of what he was feeling, and despite their initial irritation his friends all knew that too.

The group lapsed into silence then as they all let themselves relax and enjoy the communal feeling of happiness and belonging whilst they continued with their artwork.

A short while later Clea startled the group with a sudden outburst as a thought occurred to her.

'Ooohh loveys' she exclaimed 'you know what we should do.'

'What?' said several of the artists at once all a little shocked by her sudden outcry.

'We should show Morpheus the artwork that The Origination inspired.'

'Do you think he'd really be interested?' enquired Geth.

'Of course he would' insisted Clea 'don't you want him to see your tattoo design, he might want you to tattoo it on him.'

'I think that's highly unlikely' Geth stated. He'd drawn the design with Samuel in mind and although it was a great design, he hadn't been sure the man would want it etched on him forever. He had even less confident in the idea of Morpheus wanting to be tattooed with it.

'There's no harm in asking' insisted Clea 'I'm going to show him the t shirt I made.'

'You do what you like.'

'I will.'

Ignoring Geth now Clea turned to Aaron saying, 'You should show him your painting of him, it's amazing.'

'I'm up for it' agreed Aaron 'it's a pretty good portrait if I say so myself though I have no idea what Morpheus will make of it.'

'I think he'll be impressed' said Clea.

'Maybe.'

'But you will show it to him.'

'Yeah, why not.'

Having got her yes from Aaron Clea moved on to Mary.

'I'm sure he'd love to read your poem Mary.'

'I'd feel a little weird giving it to him to read' said Mary looking and sounding nervous 'but poems should be read right so okay I'm in.'

'Good girl. What about you Max?'

'Errrmmm, okay I guess' was Max's unenthusiastic answer, but it was enough for Clea.

'That's great, so that just leaves grumpy to persuade.'

All eyes turned to Geth who looked angry, but after a few seconds under the encouraging gazes of his fellow artists he began to waver and then gave in.

'For fucks sake, I'll show him the design if it'll make you happy but I'm pretty sure he won't want the tattoo.'

'Excellent' said Clea ignoring the negative part of Geth's statement 'we just need to find a time to do it. When do you think will be best Sofia?'

'I'm not sure' said Sofia a bit taken aback by her sudden inclusion in the conversation 'he'll probably stay with the Eternals until late, probably even overnight so why don't we wait until tomorrow morning and make a decision once we establish what Morpheus' plans are for the day.'

'Okay' agreed Clea.

They all went back to their artwork then all wondering in their own way what Morpheus would make of the artwork the Origination had inspired.

Morpheus did indeed spend the night on one of the pull-out camp beds at The Factory and it had left him feeling energised, hopeful and sure that he was where he needed to be in order to find his true purpose.

After returning to his cabin for a shower and change of clothes he decided to go to the Gateway house for breakfast. It wasn't that he felt the need for the company of the Gateway residents, in fact he would prefer to be alone in the cabin, but he thought they would want to know how things had gone with the Eternals. He was sure they would have sensed things had gone well but had a feeling they would want to talk to him about it and he might as well get it over with.

As he had expected they were all in the kitchen having a noisy breakfast. Their loudness almost made him turn back but he made himself enter the kitchen.

The noise ceased briefly after the artists became aware of his presence and then came the greetings and the offers of food. They were a very welcoming group and despite his initial reluctance he decided their company was not so bad after all.

When asked how things had gone with the Eternals Morpheus was happy to tell them his feelings about how well it had gone stating that although he was no nearer to finding out his true purpose after just one visit, he was hopeful that further communing with the Eternals would give him answers.

The group all made positive comments on the matter and then conversation turned to what everyone's plans for the day were. Once everyone else had stated their plans all eyes turned to Morpheus.

'I hadn't really made any definite plans' he told them 'Except maybe taking a long walk through the woods whilst I processed my nights dreaming. There may be an inkling of an idea there if I think on it.'

'That sounds like a nice idea lovey' said Clea 'but before you do that, we have some things we'd like to show you.'

Even though they knew what she was talking about the other artists were a little shocked she had come out with it like that without discussing their approach, but that was Clea, always straight to the point. And so, they waited for Morpheus' reaction.

'What sort of things?' he asked.

'Artwork.' she told him 'We want to show you the work we did under the influence of the Origination.'

'The influence?'

'Yes. As you and Talionis were doing your merging thing we all had these spurts of inspiration, and the resulting work was some of our best so as it was inspired by you, we thought you might like to see it.'

'You know what, I think I would like that' said Morpheus finding the woman's directness refreshing.

'Come on then lovey, you go on through to the lounge with Sofia and Eddie and we'll fetch our art.'

Once they were all congregated in the lounge, being the instigator, it was decided that Clea would present her work first. She'd been keeping the t shirt she'd made hanging in her wardrobe and now presented it to Morpheus on its hanger.

The garment Clea proudly held out to him was a basic t shirt in a soft, bright, white cotton but as with all Clea's work it was the embroidery that made it stand out. The simple, but stunning design was sewn onto the left chest area of the t shirt in three colours.

Depicted in a shimmering silver thread there was a basic human outline in a pose reminiscent of the famous Vitruvian Man. Within this figure there was a circle sewn in spirals of yellowy gold thread except for the centre of the circle, which was a smaller, less perfect circle made up of random, conflicting stitches in a silvery grey thread.

There was a moments silence as Morpheus took in the design and reached out a hand to feel the softness of the material. And everyone waited for his reaction.

'It's us' he finally said sounding impressed.

'That's right', said Clea 'the figure depicts Samuel, the larger circle the Eternal Within and the smaller circle the Passenger Soul. Obviously, I didn't fully understand this when I first drew the design but that's how I perceive it now.'

'Yes, it's exactly right, the design, the colours, everything' Morpheus told her 'it's beautiful.'

'I'm glad you like it, but would you wear it?'

'It's for me?'

'Of course it is lovey.'

'Then I would be proud to wear it.'

Clea was almost glowing with pleasure and pride as Morpheus took the t shirt from her.

'Right, I'm going next then, get it over with' said Geth into the following silence 'my tattoo design is kinda similar, but I didn't copy Clea, it wasn't like that.'

'I understand' Morpheus told him.

Geth handed his design over to its inspiration and waited for a reaction.

There was silence as Morpheus studied the artwork. Geth, like Clea, had drawn a basic human figure with arms outstretched and containing a circle within. In this case however it was depicted in black, grey and an absence of colour depicting white. The figure was outlined in black blurring into a grey aura around it. Inside the figure was white except for the rough circle

26

at its centre which was a swirling design in shades of grey with an irregular black circle at its core.

'So, what do you think?' asked an impatient Geth.

'I think it's great. Like Clea's your design portrays us perfectly.'

'Would you have it tattooed on you though?' this was what Geth really wanted to know.

'I've never really thought about having a tattoo before, but now I'd say I'm pretty tempted to have this on me, I'm not sure if that would be a bit strange though. I mean this design is basically a depiction of me and it's a bit arrogant to have yourself tattooed on your own skin isn't it.'

'People do it and its no worse than wearing a t shirt with yourself on' Geth told him 'some have their own name tattooed and, in some cases, its literally a portrait of themselves, at least this isn't obviously you to an outsider, and to us it wouldn't be weird or big-headed right guys?'

Geth looked around for confirmation and received nods and yeses from the others.

'You could class it as your Dreambringer symbol, and we've all had our symbols tattooed on us so it would be the same as that' Aaron pointed out.

'He's right' added Sofia 'this could be your new Dreambringer symbol. Whatever your new Dreambringer talent turns out to be this symbol can represent you.'

'I get it, you're right it would make a great Dreambringer symbol' agreed Morpheus 'so I'll make a deal with you Geth. When I discover what my new Dreambringer talent is then you can tattoo this design on me.'

'Okay, it's a deal' agreed Geth 'but what about Clea's t-shirt, are you going to wear that now or when you find out your new talent?'

'I see your point, and okay, I'll wait to wear the t-shirt until my talent is discovered too.'

Clea and Geth both felt a little disappointed by this decision, but they understood the reason for it and what else could they do but accept it.

'It's my turn now' announced Aaron. He then stood up and went over to one of the storage cupboards to retrieve his painting. Carrying it facing himself he walked over to Morpheus and then when he was directly in front of him, he turned it around for the man to see.

Aaron's take on the three entity's that made up Morpheus was a little different to that of Clea and Geth in that it was from before the Origination. In the two previous works of art the three entities were depicted as they were now, joined, whereas in Aaron's portrait they were depicted before the joining.

Off centre in the painting was a full length, standing portrait of Samuel as seen in the Dream Realm. His ethereal yet perfected form was clothed in a long, flowing, white robe, his arms stretched out in front of him with the palms of his hands upturned. His long, black hair was artfully painted to show motion like it was being moved by a breeze or had a life of its own. The face was a perfect likeness showing Samuels chiselled beauty at its exceptional best. The expression on his face along with the figures pose spoke of calmness and entreaty. Aaron had somehow managed to depict that strange mix of etherealness and strength perfectly.

Behind Samuel's left shoulder there was another figure, this one depicting Talionis as It has appeared in the Dream Realm. This figure had a dark, indistinct human form within which there were small swirls of lightness and at its core, a brighter mass made of whirlpools of silvery smoke and small flashes of white light.

The background was a beautiful wash of blue, starting with dark blue at the bottom and blending upwards into lighter hues into sky blue at the top. The whole image was very striking and stunningly beautiful.

'It's magnificent' exclaimed Morpheus 'the likeness is spot on and Talionis is done so well, it's almost like a photo, you're a very talented man Aaron.'

'I am pretty proud of it' admitted Aaron.

'And so you should be. What's it doing hidden away in a cupboard, it should be on display, it's much better than any of the other paintings on the walls in here.' Morpheus told him.

'That's what I told him' said Mary proudly.

'We should get it up on the wall ASAP' added Clea.

'So, we're not going to wait until Morpheus has discovered his new Dreambringer talent then?' asked Geth with a touch or sarcasm.

'This is different' Morpheus told him 'This is before we were joined, it tells the story of how we came together, it represents the past whereas I feel yours's and Clea's work represents the future, do you see?'

'Yeah, okay I get it' Geth agreed 'I don't really have any objection to Aaron's painting going on the wall, it's a great work of art, I was just being my usual arsy self, sorry.'

'No need to apologise' Morpheus told him 'And don't forget once you tattoo your design on me it will be on display too. In the meantime, you could always frame your artwork and put it up somewhere.'

'No need for that, I'll wait, its fine.'

'Okay, good.'

Then, after a short pause.

'Right, who's next?'

'Me I guess' said Max sounding a little unenthusiastic. He wished he had gone first now because the other three had been so impressive he was worried his work would look poor in comparison.

'Don't look so worried lovey' Clea told him showing her usual talent for reading someone's emotions 'Your work is amazing too.'

'Come on, I'll help you get it out' offered Eddie 'we'll put it on that work bench behind Morpheus so he doesn't see it until it's properly displayed.'

Whilst Max and Eddie went to another of the storage cupboards to get the sculpture Morpheus dutifully looked away until the work was ready to view. Once the sculpture was in place Max had something to say before letting Morpheus view it.

'My work represents a phase somewhere between Aaron's, Geth and Clea's. You can look now.

Morpheus stood up, turned around and walked to the table on which the sculpture was displayed.

The sculpture was two foot high and like Aaron's painting was a full-length depiction of Samuel as he appears in the Dream Realm. Even in clay Max had managed to portray the flowing robe and even the flowing hair very well if to a lesser extent. The face was instantly recognisable as Samuel's the clay being a good medium for his chiselled features. Max's depiction of the Eternal Within and the Passenger Soul were closer to Geth and Clea's but with a slight twist. Instead of a 2D circle within the human form the figure held a sphere in front of him, one hand on top, the other underneath. Most of the surface of the sphere was sculpted into a smooth, swirling pattern with the exception being a band around the widest part of the sphere. This band was sculpted into a pattern of pits and bumps.

After studying the sculpture Morpheus put Max out of his misery 'That is really impressive' he said, and Max let out a breath he hadn't realised he was holding.

'It really looks like me and the sphere is beautifully done, so clever, and like Aaron's painting I think it deserves to be on display'

'Thank you,' said a blushing Max.

'Yes, we need to find some sort of stand for it and put it somewhere prominent,' said Sofia.

'I always thought the hallway needed a little something' added Clea 'you know, a statement piece next to the staircase that you see as you enter the front door.'

'That's a great idea' agreed Sofia.

'I'll get something sorted then' offered Eddie.

There was a little more chat about displaying the sculpture and the painting until Morpheus realised something.

'Hold up, before we get to the displaying there's one more person to go.'

All eyes turned to Mary and the smile she had been wearing was instantly replaced by a look of dread.

'I can't' she said.

'Can't what lovey?' asked Clea

'I can't let him read my poem now, it will be such an anti-climax.'

'Of course it won't' insisted Aaron putting a reassuring arm around Mary 'your poems are great.'

'I'm proud of my poem but compared to all your brilliant artwork it just doesn't stand up' Mary elaborated.

'Poetry might be a very different medium but it's just as valid' Max told her.

'Max is right' Morpheus assured her 'I don't know a lot about poetry in itself but through my love of music I have always had a high regard for the talent of writing lyrics. Words are what makes some music mean so much. I really want to read your poem Mary.'

'Okay, fine, but I want to know what you really think of it not just a load of guff to make me feel better.'

'I promise to give you my honest opinion.'

Mary nodded her agreement but her slowness in finding the poem in her notebook showed her reluctance was still evident.

When she finally handed her notebook to Morpheus, he thanked her and said, 'I'm going to read it to myself first and then read it aloud okay.'

Mary nodded and Morpheus began to read. Mary found she could not look at him whist he read and so turned her head into Aaron's comforting shoulder.

When Morpheus was finished reading, he cleared his throat as an indication he was ready to read the poem out loud and with Mary still hiding her face he read the following:

The Path to The Origination

A twisted creature in need of redemption,
Transformed anew through perseverance and bravery,
By one man's belief and the aid of others,
Setting us on a path to something new.
A warped soul was returned to music and dreaming,
Though not without loss, it was a great achievement,
With confidence, strength and compassion,
An ancient mistake was finally reversed.
That last leap of faith took courage and conviction,
Taking a hazardous path never ventured before,
And we all felt that cumulative, wonderous moment,
When something true and good was bravely created.

There were a few moments silence after Morpheus spoke the last word before he gave his opinion.

'You have a great way with words' he told Mary 'And although the others show who we are beautifully in a visual way, your words go much deeper, they tell our story and so are powerfully evocative in a way the others can't be. I'm just as flattered and honoured by these words as the other's beautiful images. Never underestimate the power of words Mary.'

'I don't' Mary told him 'I just underestimate my own sometimes.'

'Well, you shouldn't'

'Thanks, and I'm glad you like my poem.'

'We should get the poem written up all fancy, frame it and put it on the wall' suggested Clea.

'Fantastic' exclaimed Eddie 'it's about time we had new art on these walls.

There was a bit of general chatter now that the artwork show was over, and then after a few minutes Morpheus interrupted them all to remind them of his plan to take a walk to process his evening with the Eternals.

'I've really enjoyed seeing all your artwork' he told them 'But I need to get back to the business of working out my true purpose now.'

'Of course lovey, we understand,' Clea assured him, 'maybe we'll see you for dinner later then.'

'Yes, that would be nice' he agreed.

'Good.'

Morpheus headed off leaving them all discussing where to put Aaron's painting and where to get a stand for Max's sculpture. He really had enjoyed seeing their artwork, it had given him very positive vibes.

Chapter 4
Darkness on the edge of Light

It was three weeks since Morpheus had first communed with the Gateway Eternals and in those few weeks, he had spent a lot more time in the physical presence of the Eternals than was normal. The time a Dreambringer spent actually inside the Eternal Dreamers chamber with them was totally up to the individual. Some Dreambringers have a set routine for when they do this, some just do it when they feel the need to because a visit to the chamber gives both the Dreambringer and their Eternal Dreamer a boost of energy.

The amount of time spent in this way does not make one Dreambringer any better than another it is purely a matter of choice.

In the case of the new Dreambringers at The Gateway none of them had settled into any sort of routine in that respect yet and since Morpheus has arrived none of them had visited their Eternal in person. Morpheus had felt a little bad for 'hogging' the Eternals, but it was hopefully only temporary, and the group would be able to get into some sort of routine soon. For now though his work took precedence.

Although he was sure he was where he needed to be he had for most of those three weeks felt frustrated at his lack of progress. Although he was now a very dominant visual presence within the Dream Realm his role within it appeared a very superficial one and this bothered him.

In the Dream Realm Dreambringers appear as an insubstantial yet perfected version of themselves, their ghostly forms smoothed of earthly imperfections, their physical attributes enhanced. They move through the landscape in these beautified forms noticeably different to the vague, white human shapes of the dreaming souls.

As a Dreambringer Samuel's Dream Realm appearance had been impressive and now with a new element to it Morpheus' Dream Realm presence was even more remarkable to behold. He was a giant, his long hair seeming to have a life of its own as it billowed around him, his face chiselled perfection and the new element being, as in the flesh, his eyes, which became shining white orbs emitting smoky beams of white light.

It soon became apparent that this light soothed any dreaming souls that he turned his gaze upon and although it was a development it seemed an insignificant one. He'd known almost from the beginning that he had a healing presence and this was just a stronger manifestation of it brought on by his time with the Eternals.

The only other related discovery had been that instead of searching out those souls in need as Dreambringers did, souls found him. They hovered around him in groups taking turns to bathe in the healing rays from his eyes. All he need do was look at them to do them good and the ease of it bothered him. There was no real interaction between himself and the dreaming souls, and no effort needed on his part. He felt that there must be something more he needed to be doing but he had not figured that out yet.

Then a few nights ago he had noticed something unusual. On the periphery of a group of dreaming souls he saw a darker mass and when he realised what it was, he was shocked and then thrilled. What did this mean? Was his true talent finally starting to make itself clear?

Whatever it meant he did not have time to explore it that night because he began to feel the pull as he was drawn back to his physical body, his nights work being over.

The next night Morpheus was glad to note the dark presence was there again. Unlike the ghostly white human forms of the dreaming souls this presence did not seek the healing rays of his eyes, in fact it seemed to purposely avoid them. Over the course of the night however it was the only constant presence within Morpheus' changing band of followers. He did not try to communicate with the presence, he only noted the traces of emotion he could sense from it deciding that he needed to observe it some more first because although he knew what it was, he did not yet know why it was there.

For a further two nights Morpheus observed his unusual follower noting no discernible change in its behaviour. It still appeared to purposefully avoid his healing gaze but remained near to his dream self for most of his time in the Dream Realm.

This dark follower was what was known as a Dark Soul. These Dark Souls belonged to severely damaged humans who either through their own dark personality, or because of severe trauma, could not or would not dream.

The would nots were those people who had such a disturbed personality and consequently warped soul that they would not allow themselves the luxury of dreaming, it was not in their nature, and they could not be helped. In the distant past this type of person had been a danger to the Dreambringers and their Eternals, but the work of the Somnium Foundation had eradicated that threat. This type of person was still a threat in the waking world in various ways, but it was not the job of the Foundation to deal with them.

The could nots were those people who had been severely traumatised in life and had lost the ability to dream because of it. This latter group could be helped, in fact Morpheus, or rather Samuel, had met a Dreambringer called Xiu Bo who specialised in helping this type of Dark Soul. The knowledge he had learnt from Xiu Bo had helped Samuel devise a way to help the creature formerly known as Talionis; help which had eventually resulted in the Origination.

The help Xiu Bo was able to give these Dark Souls was minimal but still important and so now Morpheus wondered if the talent the Origination had given him was an elevated version of the skill that Xiu Bo had taught him. He decided that the idea needed a little more thought before he tried putting it into practice.

There had of course been the usual three-way internal discussion of the subject between the entities that made up Morpheus, but he felt more input was needed. A conversation with Xiu Bo would be helpful, but first there was someone else he thought he should discuss his ideas with, he needed to sound his idea out, get another opinion. So, sure that the Dark Soul would still be there the next night Morpheus decided an attempt to commune with it could wait.

A strange sound reached Sofia's ears as she approached the cabin through the morning sun dappled trees. At first, she felt apprehensive as it was a slightly eerie and unfamiliar sound, but then she realised that it sounded musical, and that the eeriness was actually sort of beautiful. She knew that Samuel's and therefore Morpheus' artistic talent was musical and that he could play many instruments, but she couldn't quite place what instrument this was, bagpipes maybe? No, it was more complex than that

The door of the cabin was wide open and when she reached the threshold, she stopped not wanting to interrupt the strangely hypnotic music. She could see Morpheus, he stood next to the table in the middle of the cabin, his back to her. He was obviously totally involved in the music, his tall frame rocking slightly as he played, his right arm was moving in a circular motion, his left arm out of view as was the instrument he was playing.

'I could watch and listen to him for hours' Sofia thought, but just then he turned as if sensing her presence and a few seconds later the music stopped.

'I'm so sorry' she told him 'I didn't mean to interrupt you.'

'It's not a problem, please come in' he said putting the strange instrument he had been playing down on the table 'after all I did invite you here. Please take a seat' he added indicating a chair around the table 'and I'll put the kettle on, would you like tea or coffee?'

'Coffee please' answered Sofia as she sat down.

For a few minutes she sat watching Morpheus noting that he moved gracefully for such a large man and what a pleasure it was to observe him even in the mundane act of making coffee. Then her eyes were drawn back to the instrument on the table. It was squat and pear shaped looking a little bit like a violin but with a lot more going on. There was a thin, raised box running through the middle of its body under one side of which there was a strange sort of keyboard. There were two strings going across a raised wooden 'bridge' and into the box and two more either side of the raised box. One end of the instrument went into a 'head' with turning pegs like on a guitar or violin, and at the other end there was some sort of hand crank.

'Have you seen one of those before?' asked Morpheus as her returned to the table with the coffees.

'No, what is it?'

'It's a Hurdy Gurdy.'

'A what now?' said Sofia with a laugh.

'I know, it sounds silly but it's quite a complex machine.'

'I can see that, and it makes quite a complex sound from what I heard. I couldn't see it properly when you were playing before so would you mind showing me how you play it now?'

'Sure' agreed Morpheus, lifting the instrument from the table and proceeding to play raising his voice to explain what he was doing over the strange music.

'As I turn the crank wheel it rubs against the strings much like a bow on a violin! Then I can make melodies by using the keyboard here which presses small wedges against one or more of the strings to change the pitch! The drone strings are what make that constant pitch that sounds similar to bagpipes and accompanies the melody!'

'I'm impressed!' Sofia told him loudly 'It looks very complicated; how long did it take to learn how to play?!'

Morpheus decides to stop playing and explain.

'A few months to perfect it but the basics came pretty much instantly.'

'What? You must be really talented then.'

'Not exactly, my musical talent helped but my ability to play it was inherited rather than learnt.'

'How do you mean?'

'The Passenger Soul played the Hurdy Gurdy back when he was simply human so when we merged I inherited that talent somehow.'

'That's amazing.'

'It's one of the perks of The Origination' said Morpheus and the smile on his face made Sofia's stomach do a little flip. He didn't smile often, and this rare smile was far too brief in Sofia's opinion as he was quickly back to his usual serious self.

'As nice as this little musical interlude has been I'd really like to get back to why I asked you here.'

'Of course, I'm sorry, why did you want to see me?'

'I have some news.'

'What is it? Good news I hope.'

'Potentially very good' was Morpheus' teasingly short answer.

'Please elaborate' requested Sofia eager to find out more.

'I think I may be on to something; I have an idea about what my new role within the Dream Realm may be, but it needs more thought and I need a sounding board.'

'You want me to be your sounding board?' asked Sofia feeling unduly thrilled at the idea.

'Initially yes, there is someone else I feel I need to speak to, but I thought you would be a good starting point if that's okay with you.'

'Of course it is' said Sofia a little deflated by the starting point comment but still pleased to be the first to hear Morpheus' theory, 'give it to me' she told him then blushing a little and internally cringing at her choice of words she quickly added 'your idea I mean, tell me your idea.'

Seemingly unaware of Sofia's embarrassment Morpheus began to talk. He told her about his experiences in the Dream Realm and about the recent development involving the Dark Soul. Then he spoke about Samuel's time with Xiu Bo and how what he had learnt had led to the

Origination and how it now linked in with his new theory about his evolved Dreambringer talent. Sofia knew some of this of course, she had been a part of the lead up to the Origination after all, but she listened intently taking it all in hoping that she would have some intelligent input to give him.

'So, what do you think?' asked Morpheus when he had finished all he had to say.

'To be honest I feel I need a little time to process it all properly, but my initial feelings are that you are on to something, but I'm not sure what that is.'

'Me neither so you should ask me some questions because that's the stimulation we need to solidify ideas.'

'Okay, so how do you know that the Dark Soul that follows you is definitely the same one every night?'

'In the Dream Realm you can't visually recognise individual dreamers, it's a person's soul that inhabits it not their body, so they have no recognisable features. You get a sense of the person the soul belongs to though, that's how Dreambringers connect with them by means of the emotions that emanate from them. I recognise this same Dark Soul in a similar way. Although its emotions are much harder to read the Dark Soul still emanates something of itself, something original to it and therefore recognisable. It's a sensory rather than visual recognition, sort of like knowing a person by their scent.'

'I get it, but what exactly are you sensing from this Dark Soul?'

'I've only got a general sense of it so far; I haven't probed it yet as I didn't want to frighten if off. I've just been letting it follow me whilst I work out how best to approach it. I have sensed traces of two emotions from it though and they are sadness and curiosity.'

'Curiosity about you?'

'Yes.'

'And the sadness?'

'I won't understand that until I probe it further.'

'Of course, and when do you plan to do that?'

'When I've worked out a strategy which I'll do after I've finished speaking to you and have spoken to Xiu Bo,'

'Okay, so what makes you think that the appearance of this Dark Soul has something to do with the new talent you believe the Origination has given you?'

'It's just a feeling, an unexplainable one, and it may turn out to be nothing. The idea that the Origination has given me some sort of special talent may be a false one, it may turn out that the Origination was just a singular event that created a new kind of being, me, and that's the full extent of it.'

'But you don't really believe that?'

'No, I feel there has to be more to it.'

'And you think the appearance of this Dark Soul may be the key to it all?'

'I do. What do you think?'

'Like you I think that there has to be more to the Origination than just the merging of three beings. I also think that whether it leads to you discovering a possible special talent or not this Dark Soul is definitely worth investigation.'

'I don't want to jump into this too quickly though, I don't want to ruin it.'

'That's understandable and I agree it needs a bit more thought.'

'I really want to speak to Xiu Bo.'

'I can help you set that up, you'll have to come to the house though, this cabin gets decent mobile reception, but I think a call to China needs a more stable telephone line.'

'Definitely. Bo lives in a village in Qinghai province, and they don't have the best telecommunications there although the Foundation make sure that his Commune have the best available. China is seven hours ahead of us so as its early evening there, we'd better get a move on and hope that Bo is available to talk.'

'Let's go back to the house and get the ball rolling then. We can get Xiu Bo's telephone number through the Foundation.'

'Do you think they'll need to know why we want the number?'

'Not if we ask the right person, why?'

'It's not that I want to keep them in the dark I just want to speak to Bo before I explain it fully to The Foundation.'

'I get that. It'll be fine, I know just the person to call so let's get going.'

Eddie and Geth were the only ones at the Gateway house, the others having left for the Factory after breakfast. Both men were in the kitchen drinking coffee and talking about tattoos when Sofia and Morpheus entered.

'Hey guys there's more coffee if you want some' said Eddie in greeting.

Geth just gives them a cursory nod as a hello.

'Maybe in a little while' Sofia told Eddie 'We need to go and make a few important phone calls from the office first.'

'Okay, just give me a shout if you need anything' Eddie told them as they headed out of the room, and he received a parting thanks from Sofia.

'Wow, that Morpheus guy is even less into casual chat than you' Eddie commented to Geth.

'Good for him.'

'What do you think the important phone call is about?'

'Don't know, don't care.'

'You're not even a little curious as to what our new friend is up to.'

'Nope.'

'You're so weird.'

Geth just shrugged and took a gulp of his coffee.

Morpheus followed Sofia out of the kitchen into the large hallway where Max's sculpture of him now stood on a small, round, pedestal table at the base of the staircase, and then into the room to their left.

This room was known as the Office and was a slightly smaller version of the art room/lounge opposite with identical nine pane sash windows looking out onto the circular driveway in front of the house and the woodland beyond.

The area in front of the windows held two large, comfortable, cream coloured leather armchairs with a small, wooden table between them. Towards the back of the room in the centre stood a large, antique wooden desk, behind which was a black leather swivel chair, and against the left-hand side of it there was a second swivel chair. On the desk there were two telephones, two computer screens and the control box for the gate intercom. Along the wall to the right of the desk were three five-foot-tall metal filing cabinets and along the wall to the left was a large wooden cupboard next to which there was a door which led to Mason's new room.

The walls of the office were painted the same delicate dove grey as the art room/lounge; however, again like the other room, little of the paint was visible as the walls around the furniture were liberally covered in a collection of impressive drawings, photographs and paintings of all ages and styles. The furniture free back wall held the larger works as well as a set of shelves containing small sculptures and ceramics. The floor was original, polished wooden floorboards.

Sofia headed for the desk and sitting in the swivel chair she picked up one of the telephones whilst Morpheus sat in the chair at the side of the desk. As she'd told Morpheus she knew exactly who to contact at the Foundation for the information they needed. She dialled a memorised head office number and listened to the familiar telephone answering manner of the foundations General Secretary.

'Hello, Barbara its Sofia.'

'Hello Sofia, what can I do for you?'

'I need the telephone number for the commune in Qinghai province China.'

'I can get that for you just give me a minute.'

Whilst she waited Sofia retrieved a pad and pen from a desk draw in readiness so that when, within the stated minute, Barbara was back on the line reeling off the telephone number she was ready to write it down. And that was it, done, no questions just helpful efficiency. Sofia thanked her and put the phone down.

'There you go' she said handing Morpheus the piece of paper she had written the number on and standing up so they could swap chairs.

'Thanks, now let's just hope Bo is available to talk.'

Settling himself behind the desk Morpheus dialled the number and after it was answered it was soon established that not only was Xiu Bo available to talk, but he was also very happy to do so. He obviously knew about the Origination and having been a friend of Samuel's was eager to speak to the new entity that his friend had become.

Realising that the first part of this telephone conversation was going to be a question-and-answer session that she did not really need to hear Sofia decided to go and get them some coffee to help lubricate what would be a long discussion. She informed Morpheus of her intention using hand signals and gestures and headed for the kitchen which she found was still occupied by Eddie and Geth.

'Is everything okay?' Eddie asked as she entered the room.

'Yes, everything's fine' she replied heading over to the counter that held a half full coffee pot and some clean mugs.

'Only you said something about important phone calls and in this place that often means problems' said Eddie.

'I promise you there's no problem' Sofia replied as she poured coffee into two mugs. She then went to the fridge for some milk as she mulled over what to tell them. There was no need for secrecy, it was just a matter of how much to say at this point. After finishing the coffee making, she turned to the two men and gave them the short explanation she had decided on.

'Morpheus has a theory about his possible new Dreambringer talent, and he wanted to talk it through with a Dreambringer he knows as he has special expertise that could be helpful. I don't want to go into details right now, but I assure you that once this call has been made and Morpheus has had time to process it all you will be told what's going on. We don't intend to keep anything from you, or anyone else, Morpheus just needs to clarity things in his own mind before he shares his theory with everyone.'

'That's fair enough' said Eddie 'I just wanted to be sure there were no problems.'

'There's definitely no problem, hopefully quite the opposite.'

'Okay, good.'

'If any of the others come back before we've finished, can you tell them what I just told you and make sure no one disturbs us.'

'Will do.'

'Thanks.'

Geth hadn't contributed to the conversation and in fact looked totally disinterested and Eddie seemed happy with her explanation, so Sofia picked up the two mugs of coffee and headed back to the office. She entered the room just as Morpheus was finishing telling Xiu Bo about his recent experiences in the Dream Realm and what he thought they might mean. Putting one mug of coffee on the desk next to Morpheus she sat in the spare chair and listened sipping from the other.

When Morpheus had finished what he had to say he explained to Xiu Bo who Sofia was and that he was going to put him on speaker so that she could hear him too. After a brief greeting, they got straight down to business and as Bo began to discuss his thoughts Sofia was pleased to discover that his English, although strangely phrased at times was very good.

'During my work with Dark Souls, none have followed me around Dream Realm, so my thought is this is a new and interesting development. Maybe it is curious like other normal souls, you are new entity in Dream Realm now.'

'Yes, but if that's the case why is it just the one, what about the other Dark Souls?' countered Morpheus.

'You are definite it is same one every night?' queried Bo.

'As definite as I can be yes.'

'Maybe there is something special about Dark Soul.'

'Rather than there being something special about me?'

'Possible, or is something special about both. Maybe Dark Soul is only first to brave approaching, or maybe will be only one.'

'Do you think it can have benefited at all from being near me like the normal dreamers?'

'Is very hard to say.'

'You're right, it's all speculation right now, but you do agree that this is an important event?'

'Most definite, only have not discovered how is important yet.'

'And how do we do that?'

'That strange question, you know how do that, Samuel help me and help Talionis. You must try to communicate with Dark Soul.'

'I know it was an obvious question, but this feels really important, and I just want to sound everything out. With Talionis Samuel worked it through mainly alone and took some risks, but this time I feel the need for outside input from an expert however basic it may be to start with. Just bear with me okay, I just want to get it right.'

'I understand but believe after Samuel work with Talionis you are more expert than me.'

'Talionis was different, this is a normal, fully human Dark Soul we are dealing with and that's your area of expertise.'

'Are you sure is normal Dark Soul not like Talionis?'

'I don't believe there is another like Talionis, and this one looks the same as all the other Dark Soul's whereas Talionis stood out. But maybe it is different or special in some other way.'

'Yes, this possible but we not know without interaction with Dark Soul.'

'But what form should this interaction take, I need to know more about it without scaring it away.'

'It takes delicacy I think, gentle probing.'

'That's how Samuel approached Talionis at first.'

'Yes, you go gentle, be patient, this is best approach. It hard but need to be slow, you know this, you not need my help.'

'You have helped though, just hearing your voice has helped me remember everything you taught Samuel and to crystalise my plan of action.'

'It make me happy to help.'

'I'm very grateful for it, and I may need to talk to you again.'

'I be ready to help.'

'Great, thanks.'

They said their goodbyes and ended the call. Morpheus was happy that he had got what he needed from the conversation and now it was time for him and Sofia to discuss a few things.

After a good ten-minute talk, they had made their plans. Their first task was to inform the Foundation, so Sofia put a call in to Cedric Neale her immediate boss. She called him regularly with updates, but this was the first time she would actually have something worth telling him.

He took her call almost immediately obviously aware that it would be to do with Morpheus' progress. They had the phone on speaker again so they could have a three-way conversation and between them Sofia and Morpheus brought Cedric up to date.

When they had finished the head man's first comment was 'I would rather you had contacted me before Xiu Bo, but I understand your reasoning for speaking to him first. Please do not make a habit of this however because from now on I insist you keep me fully updated and make no important decisions without consulting me first.'

'We will do sir' agreed Sofia.

'Good. As to the situation itself I must say it sounds both intriguing and promising, it appears that The Gateway will again be at the heart of a new chapter in the history of The Somnium Foundation.'

There was a little more chat but nothing important was said and once the call had ended both Sofia and Morpheus felt the need for some alone time to relax and process all that had been said. Morpheus headed out to his cabin for his few hours alone time but before she could retire to her guest room for her own Sofia had to make arrangements for a meeting with the Gateway artists for later in the day.

Entering the art room/lounge Sofia's eyes were immediately drawn to Aaron's painting of Morpheus which now held pride of place on the wall to her right. Eddie had moved a few pieces of work around to make space for it as well as Mary's now framed poem which had been placed underneath the painting. It was a striking addition to the room's art display.

The room was currently occupied by Geth and Eddie as Geth was giving Eddie yet more ink. Despite him not having much use for it The Foundation had willingly supplied Geth with a comfortable stool for himself and a tattoo chair/table for his 'client'. He had brought his own tattoo machines with him, and Eddie made sure he had stock of ink, but whereas the others could practice their art anytime they liked Geth could only practice his when he had a willing subject to ink.

He did have the option of getting in touch with old contacts in the tattoo world and getting himself small guest spots at nearby tattoo studios, but with time away from the Gateway being restricted he had not bothered looking into it yet. He wasn't too bothered about it as he'd welcomed the break after nearly twenty years tattooing and had been enjoying doing some Japanese dragon and koi paintings rather than flash art. He could still draw flash art but if he wanted to actually tattoo someone for now it had to be someone at the Gateway.

He had inked his fellow Dreambringers on the day they had all met giving them a permanent reminder of their own Dreambringer symbols. Later on, he had tattooed Mason with a slightly different interpretation of the Dreamcatcher symbol to the one he had given Max. At the time it had been a poignant parting gift to the reluctantly retiring Dreambringer.

Now, thanks to Eddie, he was keeping his hand in occasionally with this being his fourth tattoo. The first had been done soon after the Origination once all the drama had died down. At Eddie's request Geth had added a koi carp to his already extensive ink. It wasn't something that Eddie had considered before, but after looking through Geth's flash art and some photos of his past work Eddie had taken a liking to the Japanese style koi designs. Geth had then custom designed one for him and tattooed it onto the calf of his left leg.

The next had been done after Eddie returned from his Dreamwisher training and began his new duties when Geth had etched the moon and star symbol of the Dreamwisher into the inside of his left wrist forever. This was shortly followed by a Crow in honour of Eddie's favourite TV show 'Game of Thrones'. This one had been expertly tattooed onto his right, upper arm.

And now for his new tattoo Eddie had decided on a dagger and skull design which was more in keeping with his older tattoos. The problem was that now some of Eddie's older tattoos looked poor in comparison to Geth's work, so they'd come up with a plan of action for after this fourth new tattoo.

Firstly, Geth would re-colour a couple of Eddie's oldest tatt's as they were quite badly faded. Next, there were a few, small pieces of work that Eddie did not like much anymore so Geth was going to work on new designs that he could tattoo to cover them.

Lastly, both Eddie's arms would now be pretty much covered so Geth would design work to link them all up covering all the remaining bare skin to make what was called a sleeve on each arm. Both men were very happy with this arrangement, with Geth getting to practice his art and Eddie getting some real quality tattoos.

The only other Gateway resident to have had a second tattoo so far was Aaron. He had chosen a Celtic Dara Knot design as its meaning was linked to strength and the oak tree which Aaron felt fitted with his Dreambringer symbol. He had it tattooed on the inside of his right forearm in mirror of the Dream Mate symbol on his left forearm.

Mary and Clea had both expressed a wish to have another tattoo but only when they decided on something they really wanted and that had not happened yet. Max was less keen but not completely opposed to the possibility of having another and Mason was currently debating whether or not to have the Dreamwisher symbol tattooed on him. Sofia was the only one who said she would not have one, but that was fine, tattoos were not for everyone.

'I'm sorry to interrupt' said Sofia now as she entered the room 'but I need to tell you something.'

The sound of the tattoo gun ceased, and the two men gave Sofia their attention.

'Are the others still at the Factory?' she asked.

'As far as we know' replied Eddie.

'Right, we need to have a meeting later today, so if they're not back in say three hours can one of you contact them and ask them to come back to the house.'

'We can do that though I expect they'll all be back before dinner time anyway. I take it this it to do with Morpheus and his new theory,' said Eddie.

'Yes, exactly. Morpheus and I need some down time, so he's gone back to the cabin and I'm going to spend some time in my room, but later we'll share everything with the group.'

'Okay, so how about we plan to get everyone together for about five o'clock then?' Eddie suggested.

'Sounds good.'

And so, with the plan made Sofia headed for her room leaving the two men to chat whilst Geth continued to tattoo.

'I wonder what Morpheus has come up with?' mused Eddie as the sound of the tattoo gun started up again.

'It'll just be more mumbo jumbo no doubt.'

'Come on man it's not mumbo jumbo and you know it; this is important stuff.'

'I know' Geth said with a sigh 'but you know this stuff makes me uncomfortable.'

'Still, even after months as a Dreambringer?'

'Yes, I still can't quite get my head around this strange turn my life has taken. I'm just about getting used to my new role but when more stuff like this comes up it just makes me uneasy again.'

'But at least this time it's all good.'

'How do you know that?'

'I just feel it. Morpheus is unique and I think his new Dreambringer talent, whatever it is, is going to be immense and exciting.'

'Maybe, but personally I can do without excitement after all that's happened recently.'

'Ever the grump' Eddie's tone was playful and Geth just grunted in return signalling the end of the conversation.

At five fifteen everyone was gathered in the lounge area eager to hear what Morpheus had to say. After several hours alone Morpheus was ready to talk through his thoughts.

'I believe that my new role within the Dream Realm may be to do with helping the Dark Souls that haunt the outskirts of the Dream Realm' he began.

'Like Talionis?' asked a worried looking Aaron.

'No, Talionis was a one off, I'm talking about the usual Dark Souls.'

Seeing the slight frowns and questioning looks of his audience Morpheus at this point decided to give them a little revision on what exactly the Dark Souls were, or rather who they represented. So, he gave them a quick refresher and then went on to tell them about the work he had done with Xiu Bo in the past and about what he, Bo and Sofia had discussed.

Once he had finished it was Clea who spoke first.

'So, you've helped these Dark Souls a little in the past and now in your elevated Dreambringer state you believe that you can help them further?'

It was more a summing up of what he had said than a question, but he answered her anyway.'

'Yes, that is basically it and with Bo and Sofia's help I have worked through the plan of action in my head as I've outlined to you.'

'The gently, gently approach right?' said Mary.

'Yes, but after thinking it through I still have other questions. I believe that I can help them, that I can heal them, but the question is to what extent can any healing I give improve their dream life? And is that help all I have to offer from my new Dreambringer talent?'

'Well, if all you can do is help even a little, I'd say it was enough lovey' Clea told him 'But I'm guessing that with all that you went through with Talionis and the Origination you feel that this new talent needs to be bigger somehow.'

'Yes, I do, does that sound big headed?'

'Yep' is Geth's blunt reply eliciting several scowls and tuts from his friends.

'No, it doesn't' countered Sofia 'it means you expect a lot of yourself rather than think a lot of yourself, its different.'

'Exactly' agreed Clea.

'Either way it doesn't answer my questions' said Morpheus flatly.

'I don't think any of us can answer those questions right now' Sofia stated.

'You just need to give it a go and see what happens' was Aaron's suggestion.

There were a few more comments along the same lines with Geth's typically blunt comment being the last.

'Why don't you just stop talking and start doing, you said you had a plan right, well just get on with it.'

And that was pretty much the end of the conversation.

Chapter 5
The Darkness of Sleep

Constantine Howard was lying on his bed staring at the ceiling. It was 1.30am but even after the trials of the day sleep seemed far away. Every day of his life was a nightmare but today had been particularly bad though he could not explain why that was which was maybe why he could not switch his mind off to sleep.

He had woken up that morning feeling a little more positive than usual and he still had not worked out why, he had nothing to feel positive about after all and that little touch of positivity had soon been knocked out of him so what had been the point of it?

The new hell in his life had started about two months ago when his father had declared that at eighteen it was time that he got a proper job.

Since leaving school at sixteen with no qualifications Constantine had worked various menial jobs for very little pay. Then recently his father had somehow got him a job working on a building site with some old mates of his now that he was 'unfit' for the work himself. More like unfit for life the bastard.

His father Donald was a waste of space, violent alcoholic who'd not done a day's work for over a year. They had gotten by on benefits and what little Constantine earnt, but that was not good enough anymore apparently.

Donald was a big man, the all brawn and no brains type, with fists like hams and a foul mouth. The muscle was turning to flab now, and he had grown an impressive beer gut, but his fists could still do damage and he was even more prone to shouting his mouth off. Why his old mates had agreed to take his boy on the boy himself did not understand because he was not cut out for building work being nothing like his father either mentally or physically.

Constantine was only five foot five with a slight build, shoulder length reddish brown hair, big brown eyes and a weak chin. He'd hated the job even before starting it and once he did, he was not sure what he hated most about it, the gruelling physical work or the constant tormenting about his girlishness. He got enough abuse at home so he really didn't need it at work too.

He would like to say that his friends and work colleagues called him Con, but he did not have any friends and the guys on the building site had taken to calling him Missy. His father just called him Sonny, but not in an affectionate way, it was more a sneering insult. As for using his actual name his father would not dream of uttering the 'ridiculous' name that his mother had given him.

The abuse from his fellow workers was only verbal and nowhere near as bad as the tongue lashings he got from his father, but it was still more abuse. Then there were the aches and bruises the physicality of the work caused, which added to those he received from his father's fists at home.

The only break he got was when he was asleep and even then, it was an empty reprieve. Whilst he may have got about six hours of sleep most nights, he never seemed to feel any real benefit from it. Yes, his physical aches and pains were eased a little when he first got up, but he never felt the emotional recuperation that others apparently got from a good night's sleep.

He never dreamt either which was weird surely, or maybe he did dream but just didn't remember them. Either way he awoke each day from the darkness of sleep to the greyness of his life. At least he didn't have any nightmares either, but then his life was the nightmare wasn't it.

To him sleep was just a six-hour break from abuse and that was all.

Finally overtaken by tiredness Con drifted off to sleep and in time drifted to his place on the dark outskirts of the Dream Realm. He began to wander through the dimness but this night his wandering was not aimless, he was instinctively seeking something.

It was a new pattern for Con's dream self, one that had begun a few nights ago and remained unremembered by his waking mind. He was looking for the giant figure with the flowing hair and light beam eyes, though he didn't really understand why, he just knew that he needed to be near this being again.

After what felt like endless searching, he finally saw the figure of the giant in the distance and felt compelled to brave leaving the dark safety of the outer edges in order to be near it once again. He was gripped with fear but knew that fear would abate once he was near the figure he sought.

As before there was a cluster of smaller, bright but indistinct figures surrounding the giant and he took his usual place on the outskirts of the group. He basked in the feeling that came off the giant in waves whilst at the same time avoiding the bright beams emanating from its eyes. The feeling was hard to describe, it was unfamiliar, yet he yearned for it. As for why he avoided the beams of its gaze he didn't really know, it's not that he sensed danger it was just another step outside his comfort zone, a step too far. For now, he was happy to savour that tingling, calming, wonderful feeling for as long as he could.

After a while Con sensed that something was different this time, it began to make him a little nervous and he became torn between a need to remain within the giant's ambience and an instinct to flee. Although he had continued to easily avoid the giants gaze, he now began to sense that the giant was very aware that he was there.

He was hovering behind the giant and on the verge of fleeing when something happened to stop him. Words suddenly erupted into his mind, words that were not his own thoughts and those words were *'Do not be afraid.'* The giant was speaking to him, putting words directly into his mind and he was not sure how he felt about that. There was a strange struggle going on within him. The alieness of it all made him want to run from the giant, but that wonderful, calming feeling was keeping him in place. As for the voice in his head it was strangely frightening and reassuring at the same time.

But in the end the instinctive fear and mistrust born from a life of abuse won out and Con withdrew from the giants influence fleeing to the dim outskirts where he felt he belonged.

When Con woke up, he felt strange. Remembering nothing of his Dream Realm experience he was left with conflicting emotions that had no apparent origin. He felt that touch of positivity again along with a hint of unease. *'If I had a dream, I don't remember it'* he thought, *'but maybe I did have one and that's the cause of these strange feelings. But what sort of dream leaves you feeling both positive and uneasy?'*

Whatever the reasons he had no time to ponder them, it was time to get up and go to work, to live through another day of hell, the only sort of day he knew.

Morpheus also awoke with conflicting emotions. He had known that helping this Dark Soul would be a slow process but the part of him that had been Samuel felt frustration at the smallness of that progression. Yes, he had communicated with the Dark Soul and knew it had heard him, but its reaction had been to flee without any interaction. The Eternal Within on the other hand, having a more patient nature, felt hopeful that it was a good enough start. The little trickle of emotion coming from the Passenger Soul was impatience, its mirror of the emotions felt by the soul that was Samuel.

Whatever he was feeling there was nothing Morpheus could do about anything until his next visit to the Dream Realm. All he could do now was report his small progress to Sofia who would then pass it on to the Foundation.

After a shower and some coffee Morpheus decided he would take a walk up to the Gateway house rather than speaking to Sofia on the phone as it was a nice day and a walk through the woods would be pleasant. At least that is the reason he gave himself but deep down on some level he was aware that was not the real reason.

When he had first thought of returning to The Gateway, he had known that room could have been made for him at the house but living with six people had not appealed to him. There had been a lot of fuss around him after the Origination and he'd had to spend way too much time talking with and being around others. Those months with the Foundation had created a need within him for some alone time which is where the idea of the cabin had come from. In the cabin he would be near the Eternals and the residents of the Gateway yet have his own space in which to be alone. Not that a being that was the integration of two souls and an Eternal Dreamer could ever be truly alone.

The last few weeks had been just what Morpheus needed and although he still felt the aloneness of the cabin was what he wanted unconsciously he was beginning to enjoy his interactions with the residents of the big house and particularly to its temporary resident. He was burying these growing feelings however as he knew they would complicate things. So, for now he chose to believe the woodland walk was his motivation for the visit to the house.

As Morpheus came through the open French doors and into the back hallway of the house he was met by the sound of animated chatter and laughter. The house's seven residents and their house guest were in the kitchen having breakfast. He paused out of sight by the open kitchen door part of him recoiling at the noise and wanting to retreat, but as he hesitated, he began to feel the warmth emanating from the room. Not in the heat sense, what he felt was the warmth generated by the friendly banter and mirth created by a group of people who clearly cared for each other.

He stood listening for a minute before stepping into the room giving the open door a knock as he did so in order to get their attention.

There were a few seconds silence as the chatter stopped and seven heads turned in his direction. But once they saw who it was, he was greeted enthusiastically and ushered into the extra chair that Eddie had brought down from storage for their new guest.

'Tea or Coffee mate?' asked Eddie.

'How about some scrambled eggs and toast?' suggested Clea.

'Coffee please, and sure eggs would be great' he replied a little taken aback by all the fuss.

Sofia sat across the table from him and glancing at her he could tell that she was eager to find out how he had got on, but there was so much else going on it did not seem the right time. And was he actually enjoying all this noisiness and attention? It would appear so.

The coffee and eggs appeared in what seemed like seconds, and he drank and ate whist taking in the group around him.

Aaron and Mary were hunched over a mobile phone watching something that was making them both laugh. Clea and Max were at the sink, she was washing, he was drying, and they were having an aminated discussion about something they had watched on TV the night before. And Eddie was telling Geth, Mason and Sofia an outlandish story from his time as a Hell's Angel. It was all so normal, and Morpheus marvelled at the way this group of extraordinary people could still maintain this level of normality in their lives.

He realised that he could not remember a time when life had been this normal for him. Obviously, life for Talionis and the Eternal had not been normal for a very long time, but Samuel had led a similar life to these people it just seemed so long ago now. Morpheus wondered if he would ever lead anything like a normal life again, and did he even want to?

As soon as he finished eating his plate was whisked away by Clea to be washed and having finished his story Eddie offered Morpheus a coffee refill which he accepted. Things then began to quieten down a bit and the group all congregated at the table as if a bell had been rung or something. The little pockets of chatter stopped, and everyone's attention was suddenly on Morpheus.

Surprisingly it was Geth who started things off with a blunt 'So what happened then?'

So, they had been wondering then thought Morpheus, though you would not have guessed it from their casual behaviour. Looking at their expectant faces now though it was obvious they were ready to get down to business.

'Not a lot' was Morpheus' disappointing answer.

'Did the same Dark Soul appear again?' asked Sofia desperate for more information.

'Yes, it did, and I left it alone to follow me most of the night hoping to gain its trust.'

'But you did try to communicate with it in the end, didn't you?' enquired Aaron.

'Yes'

'And?' urged Clea.

'I told it not to be afraid. I know it heard me and understood me but I'm afraid after a moment's hesitation it fled.'

'That's it, you said don't be afraid and it ran away, for fucks sack that's poor' exclaimed Geth.

'Whoa, Geth, that's a bit strong,' said a shocked looking Max.

'We always knew this was going to be a slow process remember Geth' added Sofia 'so please show a little more understanding.'

Geth just scowled in reply.

'I'm frustrated too' admitted Morpheus taking Geth's anger in his stride 'I had hoped to do a little better but as much as I wanted a more positive outcome it was only my first try. It took me a while to get through to Talionis so why should this be any different.'

It was weird but Geth's outburst had actually made Morpheus realise that he had been expecting too much of his first try and had put it all into perspective. It had taken patience and time to get through to Talionis and that was what was needed now as frustrating as that may be.

'Could we be of any help?' asked Mary tentatively 'you know like we did with Talionis.'

'Maybe somewhere along the line, but not right now. I think too many of us would scare the Dark Soul even more.'

'Oh yeah, sorry' apologised Mary blushing and looking down at her hands causing Aaron to instinctively put a supportive arm around her shoulders.

'Don't be sorry, and never be afraid to offer help or put forward suggestions' Morpheus reassured her the sound of his voice instantly making Mary feel better 'that's how you can help me by talking things through, saying what you think, it all helps.'

'Even negativity?' enquired Max, whilst giving Geth a pointed look.

'Yes. I want to know what you're all thinking and feeling, and I want to hear any suggestions however small or silly they might seem. I may need your help in the same way I did with Talionis further down the line or I may need it in different ways, all we can do is work through it together.'

'What happens now?' asked Mason.

'Well, Sofia will pass on my small progress to the Foundation and then I'll try again tonight.'

'With the same approach?' queried Eddie.

'Pretty much yes. I need to gain the Dark Souls trust and that will take patience.'

'Maybe you should try communicating with it earlier on in the night' suggested Mason.

'But then it would just be frightened away sooner' countered Eddie.

'Yes, but it would possibly come back again later in the night, and he could give it another go' Mason elaborated 'or maybe Eddie's right and it's just a silly idea.'

'No, it's not a bad idea' said Morpheus 'I could give it just enough time to relax around me before trying to communicate with it then if it does flee again there is enough time to see if it will approach again later in the night and I could give it another try.'

'But what if it doesn't come near you again the first time let alone giving it a second try in one night?' this the inevitable negative comment from Geth causing a few dirty looks and a loud tut from Clea.

'It's okay' said Morpheus seeing the groups' reaction 'we have to discuss the negatives too and it's a valid question. And to answer it I can assure you that it will be drawn to me again because the one thing I have established is that certain souls are drawn to me in the Dream Realm and it's a pull they can't resist. I just have to work at gaining its trust and that could take a while.'

'If it runs away again, could you not go after it' suggested Aaron 'I don't mean chase after it shouting 'wait up' or anything, I just mean you could maybe follow it.'

'Maybe, but I'm not sure what that would achieve.'

'You could maybe just observe it, you know see what it normally does in the Dream Realm.'

'I think my strong presence in the Dream Realm would make that a little difficult, it will definitely know I was watching it and I think that could ruin any trust it may have in me.'

'Yeah true, never mind it was just a suggestion.'

'Actually, I think the idea does have a little merit if mixed with Mason's idea and one of my own' interjected Sofia

'Okay, go on' urged Morpheus.

'First can I just confirm that last night for the most part you pretended to ignore the Dark Soul, right?'

'Yes.'

'Whilst spying on it could be counterproductive and pursuing it if it flees would be bad there is another approach that might work in certain scenarios. Rather than ignoring it make it aware that you know it's there from the beginning. By that I don't mean try communicating with it straight away, I mean gently but constantly move in its direction just subtly making it clear that you have an interest in it without being forceful about it. If it starts to move away, then slowly follow. Then after a while, once it gets used to that you can try communicating with it. If it flees early on, then as Mason says you may get another go later on if it returns.'

'I see your point; show an interest in it without the direct confrontation of attempting mental communication. I'm always aware of where it is around me even though it actively avoids my direct gaze and I believe I can make it clear I know it's there without being too intimidating.'

'Exactly, and once it's used to your interest you can try to communicate, but you'll have to gauge when and if that happens. This approach may scare it off too but it's another option.'

'And options are what I need. That's great, thanks all of you, this little talk has really helped.'

With the main conversation now over there was a slight pause before Clea took things in a different direction.

'So, what's everyone's plan for the day?'

'Me, Mary and Geth are going to the Factory this morning,' said Aaron.

'Mason and I are going out to get some art and food supplies, then after lunch we're going to the Factory' added Eddie.

'I'm going for a quick bike ride in a minute' Max told them 'then I'll work on the big sculpture piece I've just started as it's too bulky to carry out to the Factory.'

Max had been into extreme mountain biking before he became a Dreambringer and having brought his bike with him he occasionally liked to ride it through the rough terrain of the surrounding woods. It wasn't quite as extreme as he was used to, but he enjoyed it and he always made up the time he'd spent riding later in the day by extending his artwork hours.

His bike was kept out in the triple garage along with the VW Camper van he'd arrived in. The garage also housed his new state of the art kiln as supplied by the Foundation along with Eddie's van.

'I think I'll stay here with Max' stated Clea 'my stock cupboards in a bit of a mess and I need to sort it before the boys come back with more supplies. Then I can make a start on something new.'

Sofia spoke next 'Morpheus and I need to update the Foundation then I have some Marshal duties to deal with by email and phone. One of my communes is trialling daytime shifts and I need to check in with them, see how things are going.'

'Daytime shifts, that's a thing?' asked Aaron.

'Yeah, it's not common practice but some Dreambringer groups do it regularly and others give it a try every now and then which is what this group are doing.'

'I guess those who sleep during the day, shift workers etc, need help too,' said Mary.

'The daytime Dream Realm is a lot less populated and there are always Dreambringers in the Dream Realm somewhere in the world plus the Eternals are obviously always there, but yes a little extra help during the day is always welcome' explained Sofia.

'The Eternals bring the dreams during the day with the help of the energy we produce from working on our art' stated Mary 'but I've been wondering are the sort of dreams they bring different to those we bring?'

'Yes, although they can be vivid, they are often stranger, more fleeting and less useful to the dreamer without the influence of their Dreambringer, especially when the dreamer is just taking a short nap.'

'Maybe we should try daytime Dreambringing sometime' Aaron suggested.

'Haven't we got enough drama to deal with at the moment' said Geth brusquely.

'I didn't mean we should do it right now, it's just an interesting idea that all' was Aaron's defensive reply.

'So will your Marshal duties take all day?' Max interjected with a question for Sofia in an effort to defuse the situation.

'They shouldn't do so I might have time to join you and Clea later.'

'Okay, good.'

'What about you Morpheus?' Clea asked 'after updating the Foundation I mean?'

'I haven't really thought about it.'

'Well, we all know you're a talented musician and can play all those instruments you brought with you, but can you play piano?'

'Yes, it's not one of my specialities but I can play pretty well, why?'

'Well, we have that great piano in the art room that none of us can play, it seems such a waste so I thought maybe you could give the ivories a tinkle for us.'

'I'm a bit rusty but as long as you don't mind the odd bum note I could play for a bit later on I guess.'

'That's fantastic lovey.'

Morpheus was a little surprised by his own answer but suddenly the idea of playing for an audience was appealing to him and it would be good to brush up his keyboard skills. As for Clea she had been trying to get Morpheus to interact with the group more and was therefore pleased she had finally persuaded him to spend some real time with some of them.

'I want to visit the Eternals this afternoon though, so it won't be for long' Morpheus added.

'That's fine, it'll just be nice to work to live music for a change. Eddie and Aaron have both given the piano a try, but they weren't very good' Clea told him with a laugh.

'Hey! I did okay' exclaimed Aaron his tone offended but he was smiling.

'You played chopsticks, badly' said Eddie making Mary and Clea giggle.

'Well, you weren't much better, and you've had more practice' Aaron retorted good naturedly.

'I'm just sorry I won't be here to hear someone play it properly' said Mary with a cheeky grin.

'Maybe Morpheus will play for us another time when we're all here' suggested Clea.

'We'll see how it goes today' Morpheus told her.

'Good enough.'

And so, after a brief chat to clarify all their plans they split into their small groups and got on with their day.

After making their update to the Foundation Morpheus and Sofia decided to take a walk before he made his piano debut. It had been Sofia's suggestion and she'd been surprised when he'd agreed. On Morpheus' part he had simply thought it a good idea to get some fresh air, but it meant more to Sofia.

They didn't really talk about much of import, it was just casual and relaxed, but Sofia enjoyed it immensely. Morpheus had a nice time too, he enjoyed Sofia's company, but he didn't want to analyse that fact too much, there were more important things to spend his mind power on.

After their walk Sofia went back to the office to do some work and Morpheus went to the lounge/art room where he found a clay splattered Max, who after his short but exhilarating bike ride, was now working feverishly on a large lump of clay set on one of the benches.

He stood watching for a minute or two as Max worked to mould the clay into what looked like a crude human form. It was obvious that this was a new piece and needed a lot of work and Morpheus was slightly mesmerised by the frenzied way that Max worked at the clay. It must be exhausting he thought.

A sudden clattering noise diverted his attention away from the sculptor. He had not spotted Clea on his initial glance around the room but now she rose from behind a work bench which had until then hidden her from his view. She had her back to him and was muttering what he thought were swear words under her breath. He now realised that she had been crouching or kneeling in front of an unusual set of drawers, presumably the one she had told them all she needed to sort out before new supplies arrived.

It was in fact the piece of furniture she used for her sewing and embroidery patterns and equipment and had been brought from her home by the Foundation.

'Are you okay, do you need some help?' Morpheus asked walking towards her.

Clea gave a little start and turned towards him.

'Oh, hello lovey' she said looking and sounding a little flustered 'it's okay, I'm fine I just pulled out a box and the bottom fell out so now I've made even more mess.'

'I'm sorry if I startled you but I can give you a hand if you like.'

'Thank you but it'd be awkward the two of us scrambling around in here, it's something I need to do myself.'

'Okay, if you're sure.'

'Yes, but you could play me a nice soothing tune on the piano whilst I sort the mess out.'

'I'd be glad to.'

He glanced over at Max then intending to apologise for interrupting him as well as Clea but saw that he was still intent on his work.

'Don't worry about Max' Clea told him 'He's in the zone right now, I doubt he even knows you're here.'

And it appeared she was right; the man was totally absorbed in his art and Morpheus couldn't help but be impressed and a little envious.

'It's gonna be a good piece' Clea continued 'it always is when he gets like this. Now that his work is ever bad it's just that he's been a little lacklustre lately so it's nice to see him so inspired.'

'Will it bother him if I start playing?'

'No, he'll hardly register it he's so engrossed.'

'Maybe I should leave it then'

'No chance, I'm looking forward to it and I'm sure Sofia will enjoy it too, it'll be nice background music for her from here. I take it she is working across the hall?'

'Yeah.'

'So come on then play us a tune.'

Moving towards the piano Morpheus felt a strange mixture of disappointment and relief at having such a limited audience and now he had to decide what to play.

'Any requests?' he enquired.

'Anything but chopsticks' was Clea's cheeky answer making him smile and relieving the tension he hadn't realised he was feeling.

Sitting down at the piano he decided that as she wanted soothing it should be a nice classical piece and choosing 'Clair de Lune' by Debussy he began to play. It had been a while but despite his self-deprecating comment earlier there were no bum notes and he began to really enjoy himself. At the end of the piece, he paused to think what to play next and was started by the sound of applause. Turning he saw that not only was Clea clapping him Max was too and so playing to his audience he stood up and took a bow.

'That was beautiful' said Clea when she'd stopped clapping.

'Very good' added Max.

'Thanks.'

'Can we have more please?' asked Clea.

'Sure, do you want more classical or something more modern?'

'Can you sing?'

'I'm not the best but I can hold a tune.'

'Then we'll have something more modern with singing please.'

'Okay.'

And so, he played the first song that came to mind, an old favourite of Samuel's, 'Imagine' by John Lennon.

When he had finished there was more applause and he turned to see that Clea was now perched on a work bench and Max was leaning against another.

'Were you working whilst I played that or just listening?'

'Just listening' said Clea swinging her legs like a child.

'Yep, just listening' echoed Max.

'Haven't you both got work to do?' Morpheus asked in a mock stern voice.

'Yes, but we got distracted' Clea told him.

'Maybe I should stop then.'

'No!' they both said in unison.

'Okay, I'll play some more but you have to work whilst I do.'

His small audience agreed to this and so switching between classic and some more modern works Morpheus played whilst they worked.

After about half an hour Sofia sidled into the room carrying her laptop. She had made all her calls now just had some emails to do, and after hearing the music faintly from across the hall had decided she wanted to hear it properly. Plus, there was the added draw of being able to watch Morpheus as he played. It might mean getting a little distracted, but she had all day to send a few emails so if each one took an hour it would not matter.

Morpheus noticed her arrival and felt flattered by it. This idea of Clea's was turning out to be very enjoyable, and when Eddie and Mason joined them shortly after Sofia, he realised just how much he enjoyed playing to an audience.

Clea packed the large hoard of supplies that Eddie and Mason had purchased for her into her newly tidied drawers' whilst the two men set about putting away the rest of the art supply purchases. Max worked on his sculpture and Sofia dealt with her emails, and although his audience did not sit in rapt attention but moved around the room doing their own thing and even having the occasional quiet little conversation, he knew that they were enjoying it and that pleased him greatly.

When Mary, Geth and Aaron turned up they said it was for lunch but really they had been hoping to catch Morpheus' playing and everyone knew it. Morpheus played for nearly an hour more before declaring that the concert was over, and it was time for lunch. Whilst sad that the music was over everyone agreed they were hungry, and it was definitely time for some lunch.

Lunch was a joyous affair with everyone on a high, the sort of high you only get from pure artistic energy.

Morpheus was surprised to find that he was really warming to this group and was even beginning to feel like one of them. Would it be a mistake to get too involved though? He did not know where the search for his new Dreambringer talent would take him but there was always the chance that it would take him away from here. Away from his wonderful cabin and from these people who he was beginning to get attached to. So maybe it would be best to stick to his original plan to keep himself at a mental and physical distance from them.

On the other hand, becoming part of this group and therefore feeding off their combined artistic energy could be beneficial to his search. There was so much to think about and as much as he had enjoyed his morning with the group, he now felt his mood shifting. He now felt the urge to be alone again, to spend a little time by himself in his cabin before his intended commune with the Eternals.

As soon as he could politely do so Morpheus excused himself from the boisterous group and set off for his peaceful cabin. The group were sorry to see him go, particularly Sofia who had enjoyed hearing and watching him play immensely but she understood his need for solitude.

Soon after Morpheus' departure the group dispersed with Aaron, Mary, Geth, Mason and Eddie heading for the Factory and Max and Clea heading back to the art room. Having finished her Marshal work whilst Morpheus played Sofia decided to join Clea and Max. It would be nice to relax and work on her own art for a while. Her head was full or images of Morpheus as he played the piano, the speed of his large yet somehow delicate hands across the piano keys, the way his long mane of black hair rippled as his body moved to the music he was creating. Her medium was charcoal, and she thought it ideal for the subject and couldn't wait to translate the images in her head onto paper.

Eddie and Mason had thoughtfully added charcoal and her favourite Strathmore charcoal paper to their shopping list and so now she retrieved some from an art room cupboard and headed for one of the sofas in the lounge area where she made herself comfortable and within seconds, she was emersed in transferring the images in her mind onto paper with sweeping strokes of charcoal.

Clea had also made herself comfy in one of the armchairs and was looking very happy. She had a new sketch pad in front of her and was about to start work on a very exciting new piece of work.

Eddie and Mason had brought her a bolt of beautiful white silk material and embroidery silks in many beautiful colours for an adventurous project she had in mind. But before she got to those, she had to sketch out her ideas.

Her intension was to create a set of embroidered panels depicting the story of Talionis, the bringing together of herself and her fellow Dreambringers and culminating in The Origination. It was the sort of thing that was more usually portrayed in a tapestry but that wasn't her thing. When the panels were finished, she would frame them somehow and then they could possibly be displayed somewhere in a similar way to religious panel art.

The designs would include the Dreambringer symbols, her own unique depictions of all those involved and tell the story of what had happened to them. The last panel would depict Morpheus in all his Dreambringer glory.

She had never actually depicted humans in her embroidery, the occasional animal, but not people. The figures would be stylised of course and although a little daunting she was confident in her talent especially because of the new flow of artistic energy she was experiencing.

She was not sure how the others would react, especially Morpheus himself, but for now, until she began work on the actual embroidery itself, she would keep her plans to herself, just in case things did not work out.

With the piano concerto over Max was back in the zone working on his new sculpture. It was the first of a planned set of seven figures. He had been formulating the idea and preparing materials for a while and now he was finally getting to the good part. Working on a set gave him the extra advantage of being able to work on one at the house and another at the Factory meaning he did not have to constantly haul his work between the two.

After he had finished the Morpheus sculpture, he had hit a bit of a lull but more recently his zeal had returned.

Again, the subjects of his work would be his fellow Dreambringers, but these would be full figure rather than busts and he would be depicting them as they appeared in the Dream Realm. He was also attempting to do one of himself. Each figure would be about a foot high and dressed in flowing robes. They would be quite a challenge, but he felt he was up to it, in fact he had never felt so confident in his work, and he was enjoying the feeling. He was starting with Clea, and her figure was coming along nicely. He was going to take the clay needed for his sculpture of Aaron to the Factory on his next visit and begin that one there.

Max was understandably proud of his sculpture of Morpheus which was now displayed in the hallway, and he hoped these would be just as good.

As Morpheus approached the castle like domain of the Eternal Dreamers, he found himself in an optimistic mood. His time at the piano had done him the world of good and after a little time alone to rest and think his head was in a good place. He was feeling a lot more optimistic about things and now a session with the Eternals could only improve his mood further.

As always, he paused at the entrance to the extraordinary building to admire the artistry of the carved wooden door and ran his hand over the smooth circle where the Soul Healer of Dreams symbol should be before pushing open the heavy door and stepping inside.

The five artists currently working in the 'Factory' looked up as Morpheus entered and greetings were exchanged. There was no need for any other conversation though, they all knew he was here to see the Eternals and they had their work to get on with. So as Morpheus activated the hidden stairway and disappeared below the floor the artists continued to work.

Eddie had always been good at comic style art but in the past his lifetime goal of writing and illustrating his own graphic novel had always eluded him. The art talent had always been there, and he had produced many simple comics but in the past, he had struggled with creating a unique lead character strong enough for a graphic novel, plus he had thought that the actual story writing part was beyond him. However, during a sudden surge of inspiration they had all experienced during the Talionis drama he had finally come up with a solid lead character and the basis of a plot.

He still wasn't quite ready to tackle the story writing part yet but was making good progress on defining the images of the character's he had invented so far. He had spent months rough drawing them over and over in different poses just to get them solidified in his mind and was now making a start on the actual artwork for the graphic novel and was finding it exhilarating.

With all that had happened over the last few months Mason had not started on a new instrument until very recently. Up until then he had just been finishing off a few works in progress, but none had felt really inspiring. Now though he was working on a new guitar that he was becoming more and more happy with. He had finally started to work with some quality materials that he had been saving for something special for a while now.

A lot of his work was on commission, but he had thought he would use this special material to make himself a great instrument, now however he had decided that this piece would be a gift to Morpheus. Whatever else the man was he was a very talented musician and therefore worthy of what Mason hoped would be his best work yet. He just hoped Morpheus would be pleased with the offering.

Mary had been making tea for them all when Morpheus came in, but she was now back at her laptop working. Her novel had been coming on very slowly until recently when she'd had a series of breakthroughs regarding plot and the approach to her writing. She had found inventing the characters easy, but her initial plot idea had been very vague which had stifled the actual writing somewhat.

She had spent a lot of time writing notes and had only typed a couple of chapters onto her laptop. And with no clear way to go with her story rather than forging on with new chapters she had spent her time going back over what she had already written again and again making small improvements.

Then about two weeks ago a big plot idea had suddenly popped into her mind, and she had spent a day filling her notebook with plot outlines and doing small pieces of research online. She still had a few small things to work out and the big thing of thinking how the novel would end, but it gave her something to work on finally.

After getting it all clear in her mind she had made a few small alterations to what she had written so far to align them with her new plot ideas and had then managed to type up another two chapters all in one day.

The next day however, rather than carry on with a new chapter she had slipped into old habits by going back over the last two chapters in order to make sure they were perfect. That day she had only managed to write a couple of new paragraphs. She had gone on like this for a few days, and although happy with what she had written, she began to feel frustrated at her lack of forward momentum. Then she'd had the second breakthrough.

She realised that the chapters she had written could never be truly completed until she had the whole plot worked out as even the few chapters she had initially written had needed minor changes made to them when the plot idea had come to her. Therefore, the breakthrough came in the form of a new way of working on her novel. Yes, she wanted her writing to be a good as possible before anyone read it, but she realised that the constant re-writing was really stifling her flow therefore, her approach to her writing needed to change.

This new approach involved getting it into her head that this was just the first draft of the novel, and it did not have to be perfect at this point. She would no longer spend time going over the previous day's work. Instead, each day she would write as much as she could even if some of it was below par just so that she could get the whole story down. This way her work would flow better and there would be time to go through the whole thing and make improvements once the first draft was finished. Also, if she was struggling with a particularly hard part and was unhappy with the way it was written she would not worry about it but move on and come back to it later. There remained the little worry of not having an ending yet, but she thought that would come to her as she worked. For now, it was all about flow and forward momentum.

Whilst Mary had been progressing with her new approach to writing, Aaron had also made his own kind of breakthrough. He had recently decided to attempt a self-portrait for the first time and had been finding it tough going. How on earth did you approach depicting yourself like this? With other people he painted them as he saw them based on a mixture of their superficial appearance as he perceived it by eye and on the sense he got of their personality through studying the look in their eyes and their demeanour.

For posed portraits most people chose to smile but Aaron always saw beyond that smile whether natural or fake. If that smile felt genuine, he focused on it but if not, he liked to concentrate on some other emotion that they betrayed through their eyes or in the way they held themselves. It was easier if he knew the person, but he was good at capturing the essence of a person even when they were a stranger as the portraits he had done of his fellow Dreambringers before he had even met them showed.

Some people did not like his finished work because of this, especially if it highlighted an unpleasant trait in that sitter's personality, but Aaron did not care. He always refused to rework a portrait at the sitter's request and if that meant he did not get paid he didn't care. This was probably one of the reasons he had never made a living out of his work, but his artistic integrity had always been more important to him than money.

He had discovered that a self-portrait was different though. No one ever saw themselves as others saw them and it was hard to depict the truth in yourself that others would recognise. A self-portrait could easily go to one or other extreme in that there would be a tendency to either highlight your good points or your bad and it was hard to find the truth in the middle. Of course, even in extremes any version of you in paint would still be the truth in part but it was more likely to be on a superficial level and that was not what Aaron was aiming for.

Aaron had tried painting himself with the use of a mirror but had found that he could not maintain the same expression in the mirror when moving his focus between mirror and canvas. So, then he had used a photo that Mary had taken of him using his mobile phone. It had taken a long time to get a photo that Aaron was happy with but he'd finally chosen one which they had then transferred to a tablet belonging to Clea so he had the bigger image to work from.

The problem this time had been that the more Aaron stared at his photo the more he hated it. He just could not see the truth of himself in the posed photo and studying his own face so hard made him uncomfortable.

Seeing him struggle Mary had suggested that a more natural photo would be better, one where he was unaware of the photo being taken or at least one where he was not actively posing for it. He told her that would not work, not for the type of portrait he did. Yes, that sort of photo would be more candid in one respect, catching the person as they reacted truthfully to what was going on around them, but it would also be less focused. Aaron liked his subjects to have a focused gaze, either directed at him if the subject was sitting for him in person or into the lens of the camera that took the photo he was working from. Also acceptable was if the person was staring through the artist or lens their mind on something unseen and a more natural photo could never hold that sort of intensity.

Mary's next suggestion had turned out to be more helpful although this had not been immediately apparent.

'This self-portrait is a new direction for you right' she had stated 'so maybe your approach should be different. Maybe you should try a new style, give the less focused option a go. It'll be challenging but hopefully worth it. It's worth a go at least surely.'

He'd muttered something about giving it some thought but had not really taken the idea on board. In fact, he had secretly felt a bit sulky about it feeling a distinct reluctance to change his usual approach. Or at least that was what he had thought.

A couple of mornings later he had been having a sleepy early morning chat with Mary as they lay in bed. They had gotten into the habit of discussing their experiences in the Dream Realm as they lay in that half sleeping state before waking properly. As they chatted, their eyes closed, Mary's head resting on his chest, he still had the image of her Dream Realm self in his mind and in those last few seconds of sleepiness he had an idea; *'I should paint myself as I appear in the Dream Realm.'*

This new idea would be challenging but he felt he was up to it. He would be working without a visual reference, but he knew what he looked like, and he knew how he felt as he travelled the Dream Realm helping souls dream and he would translate this onto canvas. There would be an element of invention to this new approach, and it was a new concept for him, but the idea excited him. It was not the new direction that Mary had suggested, but he felt that her idea had been part of the inspiration for this better one. All his fear and reluctance regarding taking a new direction was gone and he had been exhilarated by it.

By painting his Dream Realm self, he would be painting something he had never seen with his own eyes, but the image would be the truest essence of himself that he could ever achieve.

His new self-portrait was only in the very early stages, but he was enjoying every minute of this new style of working.

Like Aaron and Mary Geth had also had a bit of an epiphany recently. His had taken the form of being inspired to draw a load of tattoo designs, some small, some more elaborate. He had never been as prolific as this, and it was a bit weird seeing as he was unlikely to get to tattoo any of them anytime soon. This fact could have been frustrating, but he was surprisingly unbothered by it. It had seemed a shame that the designs would never be used though especially as he felt they were his best work yet.

Then he'd had an idea.

Recently there had been a spate of books published of tattoo designs, and even some of the new fad of adult colouring books had a tattoo theme. He was not keen on the colouring book idea but with the number of ideas for flash art he currently had in his head he felt he could fill a book all on his own.

He had decided to keep churning the designs out for as long as this stint of inspiration lasted and then he would investigate the practicalities of getting them published. He was sure The Foundation would help in that regard and his reputation within the tattoo world would not hurt either. He could possibly even write some text to accompany the designs. He was not exactly sure what context that text would take but he felt that pages of just designs was not enough.

Anyway, that sort of decision could wait, for now he would just enjoy converting the plethora of ideas in his mind onto paper.

No one had properly dissected this new surge in inspiration yet but none of them doubted that it stemmed from the presence of Morpheus. Before his arrival, and for a week or so after, they had all felt a little discombobulated, but things had settled and the longer he had been there the more inspired they had begun to feel.

As the Gateway artists revelled in their newfound inspiration Morpheus basked in the joy of communing with the Eternals. Without a place of his own within the chamber when communing with the Eternals he had taken to randomly choosing one of what the Dreambringers had jokingly taken to calling their 'commune cribs' to lay upon. Today he had chosen the one belonging to the Gatekeeper of Dreams.

He lay there now with the Eternals stood in their usual places each at the foot of their Dreambringers crib. For some reason he felt that he was getting even more from them today, the air inside the Eternals chamber buzzed with even more energy than usual and after just an hour communing with them Morpheus felt like his 'batteries' had been supercharged. It was exhilarating and he did not want it to end.

The artists upstairs felt it too. It was like an electricity in the air that made the hair on their arms stand on end and stimulated their creativity even more. Even those back at the Gateway house felt it and though none of them fully understood what was happened they sensed that it was something good.

After nearly three hours, when the artists at the Factory were reluctantly packing up for the day, they received an unspoken message from Morpheus as did those back at the house.

'I'm spending the night here' were the words that he sent them telepathically.

'That's not unexpected news,' said Mary feeling a bit weird commenting on something that had not been said out loud but that she knew they had all heard.

'Do you think Morpheus has had some sort of breakthrough?' asked Aaron of no one in particular.

'Let's hope so,' said Eddie.

'I feel like something good is going to happen,' stated Mary.

'I think you could be right,' agreed Geth causing them to all look at him.

'What?' he said seeing the surprised expressions on their faces.

'That's unexpectedly positive for you,' Mary explained.

Geth just shrugged feeling a bit embarrassed.

'It must be the Morpheus effect,' suggested Aaron.

'And what exactly is the Morpheus effect?' asked Eddie.

'You know, this thing he has that calms people and stuff,' Aaron said feeling a little frustrated at his own lack of eloquence.

'Well, whatever his talent is exactly it's impressive if it's made Geth more positive,' said Mary sensing Aaron's frustration.

'Hey, I can be positive,' insisted Geth making the others smile.

'Sure you can,' said Eddie 'now let's finish packing up and get back to the house, I'm hungry and Clea said she's gonna cook her famous cottage pie for dinner.'

As the four artists were preparing to leave the Factory Morpheus was making plans to make his overnight stay more comfortable. It wasn't unusual for a Dreambringer to spend the night with the Eternals, Mason has done it when calling the new Dreambringers, but this was usually done on the fold out beds upstairs.

Morpheus wanted to stay in the Eternal's chamber, and thought that The Gatekeeper of Dreams crib on which he currently lay would be comfortable enough, but it felt wrong somehow, he felt that maybe he should lay where the missing Soul Healer of Dreams' crib should have been. However, a rectangle etched into the stone floor was not an appealing bed for the night. Then he had an idea and not wanting to break his commune with the Eternals to go upstairs he decided on an unconventional way to get what he needed.

The group were almost out the door when Mary suddenly stopped in her tracks.

'He needs something,' she said making it sound more like a question than a statement.

'What? Who does?' enquired Aaron.

'Morpheus.'

Then they all understood as the telepathic message reached them too, and so working as a team they set about providing Morpheus with what he had requested. Whilst Eddie and Mason pulled one of the foldaway camp beds out of the cupboard and set about removing its mattress Mary sorted out a pillow and blanket, Aaron readied an LED lamp to light their way and Geth stood on his symbol on the slate floor to open the staircase.

Whilst all of this was going on upstairs Morpheus rose to his feet intending to walk the short distance to the etched stone rectangle without breaking his communal link to the Eternals.

The Soul Healers place was diagonally across from the Gatekeepers place, so the quickest way was to go across the middle and as he began to move he felt a strange pulling sensation. At first, he thought it was proof of his theory that he should be on the Soul Healers etched rectangle, but then he realised he was being pulled to the centre, to the strange spiral circle in the middle of the clock face formation of the Dreambringers cribs.

He stopped beside the circle as a memory was triggered in his mind. When he was just Samuel, he had done a lot of research on Dreambringer history and the use of the strange spiral circles which existed in some form in each of the Eternal Dreamers chambers throughout the world had been something he had come across.

Nobody these days really knew what it was for, it was never used and considered merely decorative by most. But Samuel had found a very old account from a Dreambringer who had learnt from their Eternal that it was used by the Eternal Dreamers to give themselves an energy boost. They never did it when humans were present which is maybe why there was only the one, ancient account of it. There was not much detail in the account either, just that if an Eternal felt weakened in any way, through the extended absence of its Dreambringer for instance, they would somehow use the circle to rejuvenate themselves.

Now, as Morpheus stood at the edge of the spiral circle, he felt the pull grow stronger and realised it was coming from the Eternal Within. It wanted him to step into the circle. He felt it would be quite awkward to stand in because of its bowl shape but he figured as the Eternals did not stand, they hovered, it was not usually a problem. But despite the awkwardness of it he stepped inside the circle by putting one foot in the centre and with the other leg bent the other foot braced against a sloping side.

Once both his feet were within the circle a sudden, shuddering jolt shot through his body followed by a strange sensation of lightness and a feeling of something being released from his body. This could have been alarming but knowing instinctively that he was in no danger Morpheus gave himself up to the sensation eager to learn its source.

The sight that greeted the five Dreambringers as they entered the Eternals Chamber left them all stunned. Although some of what they saw was familiar it was the unusual elements that had them transfixed.

Six figures hovered around and within the circle of cribs and intertwining them were ribbons of a smoky white fog like substance within which sparks of iridescent light glittered. Whilst they were used to the beauty of the diaphanous figures of the five Eternal Dreamers, and had witnessed less impressive versions of the misty, shimmering ribbons that swirling around linking their forms together it was the sixth figure that took their breath away.

The body of Morpheus hovered several inches above the spiral circle at the centre of the chamber floor, his figure suspended in a relaxed, upright pose, beams of white light radiated from his eyes. His floating body was encased in a swirling, white fog which as they watched began to form a vaguely human shape around his solid human form and into which five tendrils of the shimmering ribbons merged.

As the onlookers took in this extraordinary sight their minds began to comprehend, at least in part, what they were witnessing. Somehow Morpheus and the Eternal Dreamers had achieved something remarkable.

Having stepped onto the centre of the Chamber the Eternal Within had been partially released from the body of Samuel so the human was now encased within the Eternal rather than the other way around. Exactly how and why this had been achieved and what the ramifications of it would be did not matter to any of them at this point, they were all too wrapped up in the spectacle of it to analyse it too deeply.

Each of the three entities within Morpheus were rejoicing in their own way. The Human soul that had been Samuel was revelling in the fact that a major leap forward had been achieved. The Eternal Within was delighting in the feeling of being more fully its true self and the Passenger Soul was basking in the healing emotions the other two were emitting. Along with this elation the three of them were also experiencing a glimmer of enlightenment. They knew that this development was a significant one in their quest to discover the true extent of Morpheus' new talent and that was exhilarating. They also understood that this new 'state' was not a permanent one but one that they could achieve anytime they wanted from now on and they realised that they knew when they should use it.

Eddie was the first to get himself together enough to talk though he only managed to say, 'Shit, this is big.'

'What do we do?' questioned Mary in a shaky voice.

'Fuck knows' was Geth's unhelpful input.

'Should we leave?' asked Aaron.

'I really don't know,' said Mason.

But as they stood dithering someone made the decision for them.

'*WAIT!*' was the instruction they were given without words, and so they waited, and watched.

Although reluctant to end the new metamorphosis the three entities within Morpheus knew that they could and should 'come out of it' for the time being. They knew this simply meant that the Eternal Within needed to reign in its newfound strength in order to give back control to the human soul and the physical body encasing them. The Eternal Within had no problem with this, as much as it was rejoicing in its newly returned power it knew instinctively that it was time to relinquish its dominance, it would have its time again later.

As the Dreambringers watched the diaphanous shape encasing Morpheus' body began to dissipate into swirls of mist which then appeared to be absorbed into the physical body. The beams of light from Morpheus' eyes disappeared and then his body slumped to the ground. The five shimmering tendrils linking Morpheus to the other Eternals also dispersed their commune session having ended.

Morpheus remained slumped and motionless on the floor.

'Is he okay?' Mary enquired taking a couple of tentative steps towards him.

Before anyone could say or do anything however Morpheus' body jerked violently, and they watched as he sat up and took in a long, loud gulp of air. A few seconds later he was up on his feet.

'Are you alright mate?' Eddie asked him.

'That was really intense,' added Aaron.

Morpheus looked at the four concerned artists and smiled. 'I feel amazing,' he told them.

Chapter 6
A Little Light

After a strangely silent walk through the woods Morpheus, Eddie, Geth, Mason, Aaron and Mary were heading up the slope towards the back of the house. Sofia, Clea and Max were out on the patio waiting for them. They may not have witnessed what the others had but the three of them knew that something momentous had happened and even had an inkling of what had occurred due to their own connections to the Eternals. They were still eager to hear what their friends had to tell them though.

The initial conversation was very garbled with everyone talking over each other in excitement. There were three variations of 'What Happened?' Mary and Aaron exclaiming 'It was amazing!' in unison and various other excited comments until Morpheus silenced them all.

'Enough!' he shouted, and then once they were quiet 'Let's just get inside and discuss this properly.'

They all filed inside, and each took a seat around the kitchen table. They were silent now, but their excitement was palpable. It was obvious that Morpheus would take charge, so they all waited for him to speak.

'As you know I decided to have a long session with the Eternals this afternoon' he began 'I didn't expect them to have any answers I just wanted their input on top of everyone else's and thought that the build-up of energy that communing with them in person always brings would be beneficial. It turned out better than that as for some reason the session energised me even more than usual and so encouraged by that I decided to extend the session intending to spend all night with the Eternals. Then whist preparing for that something unexpected happened.'

And so, Morpheus explained to the group how whilst waiting for the mattress etc to be brought down for his night's stay he had stood upon the central spiral circle and how that had somehow triggered the event. He then went on to explain how he'd felt when it happened and then speaking for the group who had witnessed it Mason explained it from their point of view.

After Mason finished speaking there was a few moments silence before Clea spoke.

'I'm so glad this breakthrough happened; I just wish I'd been there to witness it.'

'I'm kinda glad I wasn't there' added Max 'I would probably have been freaked out at bit.'

'You would have been fine' Mary told him 'It wasn't like that, freaky I mean, it was shocking for a few seconds but then it was just amazing.'

'What happens now?' was Sofia's question aimed at Morpheus.

'Now I rest for a couple of hours, then I go back to the Eternal's chamber and get back into this new state and enter the Dream Realm from there.'

'Do you think it's possible to enter the Dream Realm that way?' enquired Sofia.

'I'm certain it is, otherwise, what is the point of it? In this new state the Eternal Within is more fully its true self, meaning it is stronger and that can only be beneficial to my time in the Dream Realm.'

'You're right of course' said Sofia 'it's just that it's so beyond the norm that I haven't quite processed it all yet, sorry.'

'No need to apologise, I'm still reeling a little myself.'

'I think we all are' added Clea.

'But what difference do you think it's actually going to make to your dream self?' asked Max.

'I can't know exactly; I just know it will give me strength and that strength may mean I can finally release the new talent I know that I have within me, I really believe that this is the key to it.'

'I say go for it then man,' said Aaron.

After a light meal and a couple of hours rest Morpheus set off from his cabin to the Eternals abode. The Gateway Dreambringers usually avoided walking through the woods at night as it was a different world then with the capacity to cause disorientation and no one wanted to get lost in the woods at night. It didn't bother Morpheus though and even if it had he would have braved it to get where he needed to be.

When he was in the Eternals Chamber at last, he felt at peace. The mattress etc lay in a heap just inside the door where the startled Dreambringers had left them, but he would not be needing it all now. There was no preamble, he was eager to get going and so strode across the room and lay down on the Gatekeeper's crib. He needed to start there whilst he made a connection to the Eternals.

As for the Eternals they were as glad to see him as he was to be amongst them, and the Eternal Within was ecstatic at the prospect of being close to its true self again. As usual the Passenger Soul was basking in its fellow's joy.

The connection was made quickly and easily and for a short while the group of special beings communed, shimmering ribbons of mist linking them together. Then, when Morpheus felt the time was right, he slowly got up, moved towards the spiral circle, then stepped inside.

He welcomed the sudden, shuddering jolt followed by the strange sensation of lightness and the feeling of something being released from his body and gave himself up to the sensations.

Once again, his body was suspended in a relaxed, upright pose as the Eternal Within was partially released through beams of white light radiated from his eyes and a swirling, smoky aura around his human form.

Now it was time to make the new step, to enter the Dream Realm in this state. For this to happen usually the human body had to be asleep so that the soul could have domain over the brain. Was sleep even possible in this form? But even before this question was fully formed it was answered. Morpheus realised that in this state the two souls within him were already dominating the brain and the Eternal had dominance over them both and suddenly he was there in the Dream Realm.

Morpheus' presence in the Dream Realm had always been impressive but now it was even more so. He was still the magnificent giant with the flowing black hair and white light beaming from his eyes, but now there was a new element to his beauty. Whereas before his calming presence had just been felt when near and more so when within the beam of his eyes, now it was visible. His whole form glowed with a white light that emanated outward and had a super charged calming and healing effect on those it touched.

It was early evening so there were fewer dreaming souls, but those there began to flock towards this healing light patiently waiting their turn to be touched by it before moving on to experience heightened dreams with the help of the other Eternals.

Morpheus was revelling in his new power feeling enriched by every soul that passed through his light.

He spent some time with the dreaming souls, then, as the night wore on the Dream Realm became more populated, the Dreambringers began their night and Morpheus turned to the task he believed he had been given this power in order to perform; to help the Dark Souls.

He began then to look for the Dark Soul he had encountered previously on the edges of the crowd of dreaming souls seeking his light.

Then he saw it, as usual on the edge of the crown staying near but shying away from the light whilst the other souls moved toward it. What must he do to coax it into the light? Surely this new strength would prove irresistible eventually. Morpheus thought it possible that he could push the light purposefully towards the Dark Soul and force it within its beam but that felt wrong somehow. He must have patience and keep the light strong until the Dark Soul could resist no longer.

Morpheus did not want to scare the Dark Soul away again, so he tried to concentrate on the other souls whilst keeping a subtle eye on his real target. Over time the reluctant soul began to venture nearer to the light and then it made its bravest move. Coming closer and closer it finally came near enough to move briefly into the light before quickly darting away again. It was testing the water and the fact that it still hovered nearby meant its fleeting time in the light had not frightened it. Of course it hadn't thought Morpheus, but still it hesitated.

Finally, it darted in for another try and this time Morpheus made a slight move himself so that the Dark Soul would remain in the radius of his light for longer if it tried to move away again. And move away it did but after a longer stay this time. It was still only seconds but even seconds in the light could heal.

Over the course of the night the Dark Soul mainly remained on the perimeter of the crowd, but it did make a couple more brief darts into the light. Morpheus decided that for the time being just being in his light would be enough and that he would not try to use his basic Dreambringer talent to search the soul to find out what it needed from dreams yet. He also felt it was definitely too soon to try to communicate with it, that could all come later when the Dark Soul was more confident in him.

When Morpheus felt his time in the Dream Realm coming to an end, he felt pleased with the progress he had made. It wasn't giant steps yet, but he'd had some success and that was all he could expect on a first try. Plus, he was sure even the short time the Dark Soul had spent in the light would have done it some good. Now he just needed to get used to his new power and hone it. There were more breakthroughs to come he was sure of it. Therefore, as he felt himself being pulled from the Dream Realm Morpheus felt happy with his nights work.

Morpheus awoke lying on the floor of the Eternals Chamber. The Eternal Within was back 'within' but the ribbons of mist still linked him to the other Eternals. He got up slowly and staggering slightly moved over to the nearest crib where he collapsed. The Eternals were sending him messages of praise and hope as he drifted off into a revitalising sleep.

Mary and Aaron awoke in each other's arms as usual, but their normal post Dream Realm chat was a lot more animated than normal.

'Wow, how amazing did Morpheus look' Mary effused.

'I know, the guy is incredible, and the souls who I helped dream after they left his light were so energised by it, they were buzzing.'

'Yeah, I think they all had supercharged dreams and I feel great too.'

'Yep, so do I.'

'I wonder what happened with the Dark Soul though?'

'Surely with that mega light it must have benefited.'

'I agree, but we'll have to wait and see what Morpheus says.'

A little later the couple joined the others for breakfast and learnt that Clea, Geth, Max, Eddie and Mason had had a similar conversation. Sofia had been there too, but her experience had been different. She was a Marshal not a Dreambringer so although she, unfortunately, had not been able to witness Morpheus' magnificence she had experienced amazing dreams and had woke feeling invigorated yet relaxed.

'I dreamt of Morpheus and his Hurdy Gurdy' she said wistfully.

'Morpheus and his what?!' exclaimed Aaron making Sofia blush as she realised what she had admitted out loud.

'I, errmm, well it's you know his instrument' she stammered and then when they all started to laugh was mortified to realise she had made it worse.

'Musical instrument! It's a musical instrument!' she exclaimed 'I saw him play it the other day.'

'Still sounds iffy' Eddie told her with a big grin on his face.

But finally, Clea came to her rescue though she had laughed with the others to start with too.

'Don't be so childish' she told them 'A Hurdy Gurdy is a musical instrument, it's perfectly innocent, I'm sure.'

'It still sounds like a sex dream to me' said Geth.

'Clea's right, that's enough now' interjected Mason, then to Sofia 'I'm sorry I laughed.'

'Don't worry' Sofia assured him 'I can see the funny side, but I'd rather we dropped it now.'

'Okay then' said Clea 'changing the subject, slightly, do you think we should go and check on Morpheus?'

'I don't know' answered Sofia 'maybe we should leave it a bit longer, see if he shows up here.'

'But what if he's not okay?'

'Why would he not be?'

'I don't know, but he was really impressive last night, and it could have been hard on him, he could be suffering this morning.'

'It's sweet of you to worry Clea, but I'm sure he's fine.'

'If there was a problem, I'm sure we'd sense it' added Mason.

'I know I'm just an old worrywart, but I can't help it.'

'It just shows you care,' said Mary.

'Let's just give him another hour and then some of you are due to go to The Factory anyway right so you can check on him then' suggested Sofia. In truth she was dying to see Morpheus and find out how he was feeling about his exploits, but she knew he would come to them in his own time. 'You know how he likes his own space' she added.

'You're right' agreed Clea 'we'll just go about our day as normal and see what happens' then with a cheeky grin she added 'but I'm glad it's my turn to go to The Factory' making them all laugh.

The days plan was for Clea and Max to go to the Factory and for Mary, Aaron and Geth to work in the house art room. Eddie and Mason had a few Warden jobs to catch up on then they intended to join the group in the art room. Sofia had her usual Marshal work to deal with by email and phone then she planned to join the others too. They all knew the plan so got on with it.

He sits crossed legged on soft grass. Dappled sunlight plays on his skin and the canopy of a tree rustles and sways slightly in the breeze. He is at peace.

Constantine Howard woke from the darkness of sleep expecting the usual grey start to the day but as his mind came into focus, he realised something felt different. Then he realised what it was.

'I had a dream' he said aloud.

And what was even more amazing he realised that he'd remembered it quite vividly. He could still almost feel the grass beneath him and the sunlight on his skin. It had been a brief dream, or maybe he only remembered a small part of it, but either way it was a small miracle.

It was his day off today, the one day in a six-day working week, so he had time to lay and enjoy the remembrance of the dream.

He usually had a lay in on his day off, not that he really slept, he just lay there enjoying the physical aspect of not going to work. He called it his healing time if only in a physical sense. His father was never up early so he was able to enjoy this simple pleasure. Once he heard his father up and about however, he would have to make sure he was up too in order to avoid a telling off for being lazy despite his father having slept in too.

What he did with the rest of his day mostly depended on what his father did. If his father went out, then Con stayed in and rested some more in front of silly daytime TV. If the old git felt like lazing around the flat himself then Con would go out. He never had anywhere particular to go, no friends to go see, no money to spend, so he would just pick a random destination and take a slow walk there.

Sometimes he'd walk to a nearby park, find an empty bench and sit and watch people. Other times he would just walk into town and wander around the shops, not that he ever bought much. If he felt less aimless, he went to the library. He had enjoyed reading when he was younger but wasn't a big reader these days, but if one of the computers was free, he would sit and google stuff. If not, he would stroll around the non-fiction books and take a look at whatever took his fancy that day, preferably something with lots of pictures in. He never checked any of the books out, he was too worried about what his father would say. Although the library was never as silent as people may think he did always find it quite peaceful.

Emerging from his bedroom Con found his father in an agitated mood.

'Where are my keys?' he barked at Con when he saw him.

Con refrained from saying 'How am I supposed to know' as he knew that would likely earn him a smack around the head or worse, so he said, 'I'll help you look.'

Less than a minute later Con spotted the keys in plain view on the coffee table in front of the sofa. But again, having learnt from experience he did not point them out to his father, instead he wandered away slightly pretending to look elsewhere but suggested 'Did you leave them on the coffee table?' leaving his father to find them himself. He did not receive a thank you for his helpful suggestion, but he had not expected one.

'I'm off out' his father said after picking up his keys and Con let out a sign of relief when the front door closed behind him. He was glad the old git had gone out, he felt like a lazy day in front of the TV.

He got himself some cereal and a cup of tea and after getting as comfortable as he could on the lumpy old sofa, he grabbed the remote, turned on the TV and started channel hopping. He didn't really mind what he watched, it was all just mindless crap anyway and most importantly, a painless way to spend his day. He did at least try to find something good though and today he actually found a gem.

It was one of those retro music shows and this one was a look back at the best of the pop charts in the 1970's. Con was way too young to have memories of the 70's themselves but the song that was on when he flicked over to the show was one that brought back memories for him none the less.

The song was 'Make Your Own Kind of Music' by Mama Cass, it had been a favourite of Con's Mum Lily and he could not help but sing along now. She had told him that as well as sounding great the song held a special meaning and she had not needed to explain what that meaning was, he had listened to it and got it straight away.

His mum had always told him to be who he wanted to be no matter what others thought and she had personified that philosophy. Although she had not been old enough herself to remember it first-hand, she'd had a love for 1960's and 70's music, and when Con was little she had played her old LP's and they had sung along whilst dancing around the room. She'd had a lovely voice and had always told him that he had the voice of an angel. That may have just been a mother's pride, but he had thought they sounded great together anyway and those times had been the best in his life.

Lily had been beautiful both inside and out. She was small and slim with long, strawberry blonde hair, big, blue eyes and a pretty, freckled face. She had only just had her eighteenth Birthday when she had given birth to Con and maybe because of her youth their relationship had been more like sister and little brother and Con had idolised her.

His father was nearly ten years older than Lily and had never shared their love of music and definitely not their fondness for singing. He had not been a drunk back then but had always had a temper. He did not like noise of any kind except that of his own making, so their singing and dancing sessions only happened when he was out at work.

Con had never understood why his parents had got together, they were like light and dark, and he had been too young to have a conversation with Mum about it. But perhaps back then in those days his father hadn't been too bad, yes, he had been a bit grumpy and short tempered, but they'd still shared some good times.

The violence must have always been in him though and all Con could think was that maybe his mum had been a calming influence over him. As far as Con knew his father had never physically abused his mother, and whilst she was still alive, he had not beat Con either, that had all started after her death.

His mum's death had been traumatic and heart-breaking, she had not deserved to go like that, her death had left a massive hole in his life and turned his father into a monster.

Con had been eleven years old when she died, and he had witnessed her death first hand.

The two of them had been walking along a crowded street during a shopping trip. Suddenly there was a horrible screeching sound followed by a series of thumps and people screaming.

Con had turned to look at his mother questioningly, confused about what was going on. His mum had a look of horror on her face and shouting 'Quick, in there' had pushed Con backwards into the doorway of a shop. Before she could follow him into safety however, she had suddenly been swept away. The sight and sound of the car hitting her had been horrific. One second she had been there, the next she was wiped out by a hunk of mental driven by a madman.

Con had been paralysed by shock for a few seconds, the sounds of screaming had continued and then a loud crash. When Con emerged from the doorway seconds later in was to a scene of carnage. To the left of him several mangled bodies lay on the pavement some with people wailing beside them. To his right he saw a large, green car smashed into the wall at the end of the street. Between him and the car there were two more bodies on the ground, the closest one to him had been his mum.

He rushed over to her his screams now joining those of the other victims and witnesses. She lay on her back one of her legs crushed to pulp where the car had driven over her after hitting her and throwing her twenty feet. One arm was twisted underneath her and there was blood coming from various wounds, soaking through her floral print dress and pooling around her. But she was not dead, not yet. Con had fallen to his knees beside her and grabbed her hand.

'Mum please don't leave me' he'd pleaded.

She was trying to say something, but he could not hear her over the sounds of screaming and approaching sirens, so he bent his head closer.

'Sing me a song my angel' his mother requested before coughing a spray of bloody spittle over him. Con was crying now and the last thing he felt like doing was singing but the pleading look in his mum's eyes made it hard to resist her request. So, in a shaky voice wracked with tears Con did his best to give Mum her last wish. And continued to sing after she had taken her last breath only stopping when a policewoman gently pulled him away.

He had watched the light go out in his mum's eyes and he had thought he would never recover from it. His father had taken it badly and instead of comforting Con he had shunned him and started to drink heavily consumed by anger and self-pity.

Con had suffered nightmares to start with so had spent several nights resisting sleep for as long as he could. Then when he finally slept properly from sheer exhaustion, he had a few nice dreams about his mum, but waking up and remembering she was gone had been a torture.

Then his father had turned his anger on Con, taking it out on him verbally to start with, blaming him for his mum's death and saying all sorts of terrible things. Then the physical abuse had started and that was when the dreaming had stopped altogether.

Con had felt numb and hollow, just a shell of a boy going through the motions of a life. A miserable, lonely life where days were a torture, and nights were simply a dark, dreamless haven from pain both physical and mental.

A stray tear slipped down his cheek as he remembered that terrible day. But then another song drew his attention back to the TV show. This one was 'Daydream Believer' by The Monkees, another favourite of Mum's, and one that had always made them smile. He let the music wash over him and then began to sing along.

All too soon though the song was over, and it was also the last song on the show. As the credits rolled Con muttered to himself 'I want more.'

He looked over to his left at the cabinet that held his mum's vinyl record collection and the little record player she had played them on. The cabinet had stayed shut, the records unplayed for nearly eight years now, but maybe now was the time to play them again. It had been too painful before now, but today Con had the urge to listen to some of her favourite music and to sing along.

The sight of the neatly stacked vinyl LPs brought a lump to Con's throat, but he was determined to play something. He flipped through and found the LP with 'Make Your Own Kind of Music' on and placed it on the turntable. Within seconds he was dancing around the room singing along with a smile on his face and tears streaming down his cheeks as he was filled with both joy and pain.

He played song after song and sang his heart out realising that this was the first time he'd sung for years. What he did not realise however was just how good his singing voice was.

When Clea and Max entered The Factory, they found the large upper room empty.

'He must still be downstairs with the Eternals' remarked Clea.

'Unless he's gone back to his cabin' suggested Max.

'Maybe, should we go downstairs and check?'

But before they could make that decision, they heard a familiar sound and knew to make sure they were away from a particular part of the room as a selection of the slate floor began to move to reveal the stone staircase. And then there he was moving fluidly up the stairs towards them, Morpheus.

'Hello lovey' Clea said in greeting 'we were wondering if you were still down there.'

'I heard you arrive and thought I'd better re-surface' he told her with a smile.

'It went well then' stated Max.

'It did, yes' agreed Morpheus still smiling.

'It's so good to see you smile' said Clea.

'It's good to have something to smile about.'

'Do you fancy a cup of tea and a chat?' Clea asked.

'If you make that a strong coffee, I'm up for it' Morpheus told her.

'You have a deal' agreed Clea.

Clea made the drinks and they made themselves comfortable on the sofa's ready for their chat. Morpheus realised that he would need to have this same conversation again with the others back at the house, but he was still on a high, so he did not mind.

Morpheus enjoyed telling them about what happened from his perspective, and hearing it from theirs, he was not so keen on hearing Clea gushing about how amazing he looked in the Dream Realm though, but it was a compliment, so he took it gracefully.

He spent a pleasant enough half hour with the two artists then headed off to see the others.

Morpheus found Geth, Mary and Aaron in the art room, and not wanting to repeat himself twice more he sought out Sofia, Mason and Eddie and asked them to join the group in the art room.

There was the expected praise and excitement but, in the end, it was Sofia who asked the pertinent question.

'What happens now?'

'Now I just keeping trying, I go back every night and hone these new stills and hopefully get that Dark Soul to stay longer in my healing light. Then once I feel it is more trusting I'll try to gauge its needs and later try to communicate with it.'

'Did you notice any other Dark Souls hanging around?' asked Mason.

'No, I didn't, but then I was so concentrated on that one Dark Soul I may not have noticed any others.'

'Did you see any others Mason?' asked Sofia.

'I thought is saw a couple briefly, but they were quite far away from the main event.'

'Really. That's interesting' Morpheus mused, then to the group 'did anyone else see them?'

He got a no from Eddie, Mary and Aaron but a hesitant yes from Geth and all attention turned to him.

'Look, I think I may have seen some vague dark shapes out of the corner of my eye that's all' he explained 'but I can't say for sure they were Dark Souls.'

'I'm not sure of what I saw either' added Mason.

'Okay, fair enough' said Morpheus 'but that's something we need to check on another time. So, whilst I concentrate on that one adventurous Dark Soul maybe the rest of you should look out for any others lurking about.'

'And what do we do if we see any?' enquired Geth.

'I'd say nothing, not on the first night anyway, just report back if you see any, at this point I think all we need do is clarify if there are indeed any others following me.'

'Okay, will do' Geth told him, and the others nodded their agreement.

There followed a few minutes comfortable silence as the group processed this new information, then it was Sofia who reluctantly broke the silence.

'We need to update The Foundation' she told Morpheus.

Morpheus grimaced 'I forgot about that' he said thinking how he'd have to have the same conversation yet again 'But can I have something to eat first?'

'Oh shit' exclaimed Eddie 'sorry mate, I should have asked if you wanted something.'

'Its fine, I can't eat and talk anyway.'

'Tell me what you want, and I'll go make it for you' Eddie offered.

'No need, I'll fix something for myself, its fine.'

'If you're sure?'

'I am.'

'Okay mate.'

'You all get on with your art or whatever' Morpheus suggested 'and Sofia, I'll come and get you when I've finished eating and we can go and update The Foundation.'

'Okay' agreed Sofia, then to Eddie and Mason 'how about you, do you have much more Warden work to do?'

'No, not really' answered Mason.

'Good, so how about we all get together here when we're done, and maybe you can play us some more music Morpheus.'

'Sure' agreed Morpheus making them all smile.

Just over an hour later the art room was full of artists and music. Morpheus once again played the piano and sung whilst the others worked on their art.

Then, a couple of hours later, just as the group were sitting down to lunch, Clea and Max returned and joined the others for something to eat.

'By the way we're not going back to The Factory this afternoon' Clea told them as they ate.

'How come?' asked Geth.

'I know' Mary interjected 'Clea somehow knew how much fun we've been having here and didn't want to miss out.'

'Well, I am the Seer of Dreams' said Clea making them all laugh.

Con had spent a good couple of hours singing and dancing along to his mum's records collection, but his voice had started to get hoarse, and the dancing had worn him out a bit. He now lay on the lumpy, liquor-stained sofa breathing heavily. He had no idea when his father would return home so maybe it was a good idea to stop anyway. If the old git caught him dancing and singing there would be hell to pay.

He made sure to close the cabinet up properly so his father would never know that he'd opened it. He remembered how a little while after his mum's death his father had caught him half-heartedly singing and dancing around the living room. Con had done it in an effort to make himself feel better, but it had not worked, and then he had been caught, called a sissy and had received his first clip around the ear.

That first taste of physical abuse had been nothing compared to what was to come but it had shocked him deeply. This was the first time he had touched his mum's vinyl LP's since then and he was sure his father never played them. It was a shame really, but he decided that he would do this again the first chance he got. It would always be risky, but he felt it was worth it.

Now though he went to make himself some tea and toast for lunch then took it back to the sofa, turned the TV on and started channel hopping again. He did not find any good music shows this time but settled on an old black and white comedy film that seemed watchable and made the most of the rest of his alone time.

His father came home about two hours later. He was of course pissed but he was thankfully in one of his better moods, so he joined his son vegging out in front of the TV but not before taking the TV control off of Con and doing some channel hopping himself. Finally, he decided on a sports channel showing a cricket game.

Con was not a fan of cricket, he did not like sport much at all, just football when he was in the mood. This was another sticking point with his father who loved pretty much all sport so Con did what he always did and pretended to be enjoying the match whilst letting his mind wander.

He remembered his dream then and comforted himself with the vague memory of it and the enjoyment that it, and later the singing and dancing, had brought him. To some they might be small, ordinary things, but to Con this had been the best day he'd had in years.

That night Morpheus headed towards the Eternals dwelling with hopeful expectations. He felt he was really on to something now and could not wait to get back to 'work'.

Chapter 7
A Journey Begins

Over the next seven nights Morpheus gradually worked his magic on the Dark Soul. He took it slowly which was a little frustrating, but he felt it was the way to go.

The Gateway Dreambringers all liked to take a few minutes out from their nightly task to observe the Dark Souls progress for themselves, but they did it singularly, from a distance, and not for too long. They also kept an eye out for other Dark Souls and although they all glimpsed a few that briefly ventured outside their usual dark outskirts when Morpheus drew near none were brave enough to approach him and they quickly slid back into the murky outskirts.

Each night the Dark Soul entered Morpheus' light sooner and stayed for longer, and then on the seventh night Morpheus noticed a slight change in its appearance. He noted that the darkness of its mass seemed to have lightened a little and this discovery gave him the confidence to move things on a little. He decided it was now time to use his basic Dreambringer talent to gently probe the Dark Soul to find out what its dream needs were.

He was delighted to discover that with just a slight bit of effort he was able to find out some useful information and he also made a small but important discovery that gave him a little more insight into who the souls owner was.

Each morning Morpheus updated the others over breakfast, and they would have a short discussion adding their own observations before Morpheus went off to update Cedric Neale. They were all quite relaxed about it realising that as with Talionis progress would be slow, but it was positive, and everyone was feeling optimistic about the eventual outcome without actually fully knowing what that outcome would be.

Contantine Howard was dreaming again. Ever since that morning when he had felt the urge to play his mum's music again, he had woken each day remembering a dream. The first few had been like the initial one, just vague images of him sitting feeling the grass beneath him, the tree's branches above him and the dappled sun on his skin.

He had woken from these dreams feeling a little happier deep inside. His days at work were still nightmarish but he had felt able to cope with them better. The nasty jibes of his co-workers hurt less, and he felt somehow stronger physically too.

On the day after the third dream, whilst working he had noticed the faint sound of music and seeking out the source, he had found a co-worker had brought in a small radio. He had done his best then to find work to do nearby so that he could hear the music. It was not all to his taste and the inane chat of the DJs in between the songs was annoying, but he still got some pleasure from it.

On the evening after the fourth dream, after his father had gone out, he had braved playing some of Mum's LPs again. He had kept the volume low and had worried a little that his father would return unexpectedly and catch him. But he had not been caught and the music had lightened his recent mood further.

The next couple of dreams he remembered after that evening were longer and more detailed. In these dreams he stood up and raising his arms began to sing one of his Mum's favourite songs. And through singing he felt joy and peace.

After the second singing dream he woke and realised that he knew where that tree was. He had remembered that it was in one of those city gardens, one where his Mum used to take him occasionally. They would sit under that one lone tree and have a picnic. His Mum also brought along a small transistor radio and they would sing along to the pop songs they knew, not caring if people stared or commented on the strange mother and son singing duo.

After that revelation he could not decide if a visit to that garden would make him happy or sad.

Then the next night he had the dream of her. He was in the garden again, singing and he suddenly realised that someone was singing along with him. He looked around but could see no one yet that same, sweet voice continued to join him in song, and after a while he came to realise that he knew that voice.

'Mum is that you?' he asked.

Then he woke up.

He woke with tears in his eyes and realised that they were tears both of sadness and joy. He had dreamt of his mum, and though he had not seen her the sound of her voice had brought back beautiful memories. In the past thoughts of his mum had only ever made him feel sad and alone, dwelling on what he had lost rather than cherishing happy memories of her.

It was his day off so he decided he would spend it reliving happy memories of his Mum. If his father went out, he would play her music again, if he did not, he would visit that garden if he could still remember where it was.

When Morpheus arrived at the house that morning, he was very eager to tell the others his news because he finally had something exciting to tell them.

'I've made a breakthrough' he announced as soon as he was through the kitchen door and before half of them even knew he was there. But his words got everyone's attention, and they all stopped what they were doing to listen to him.

They had all started referring to the Dark Soul simply as DS during their morning discussions, so Morpheus began with "I know how to help DS.'

There was a chorus of 'How?' and a lot of eager expressions that almost made Morpheus laugh, but he stifled it and told them his news.

'It's simple and obvious really, I have to give DS what they need. It's what Dreambringers do after all, we analysis each dreamer to find out what they need from their dreams, what problems they need solving, or what they need to calm their fears, and we give it to them through dreams, so why should DS be any different excepting that it might be more difficult to achieve in their case.'

'And what does DS need?' asked Sofia.

'It's mother' stated Morpheus.

'How do you mean?' enquired Mason.

'Well, I'm not a hundred percent sure yet but I know I'm on the right lines. DS stayed in my light for quite a long-time last night, so I took a risk and concentrated my energies on them for part of that time like I do with all the normal souls who seek my light. I was worried my attention would scare them away but thankfully it didn't. I tried not to probe too deeply though, just enough to get an inkling of what they were about. I'm now pretty sure that DS is a young male and that he has suffered some sort of trauma regarding his mother.'

'Oh, the poor boy' said Clea.

'Yes indeed' said Morpheus 'whatever this trauma was exactly I believe it is what caused this boy to become a Dark Soul.'

'You said that what he needs was his mother, so does that mean she is the cause of his trauma through abuse somehow and he needs to make peace with that somehow, or was the trauma that he lost her, that she died maybe?' this from Mary.

'I'm not sure yet, I feel its most likely the latter but that's what I need to find out, the full nature of his trauma, then I can help heal him. I'm sure that he has had some short, weak dreams just from being in my light, but now I need to probe deeper and find out specifically what sort of dreams he really needs.'

'So, you'll do that tonight?' enquired Sofia.

'Definitely.'

'Is there a chance that this might scare him off?' asked Max.

'Yes, or course, but what else can I do. Besides I think he's beyond being scared off, I get the feeling he's going to be eager for more help now.'

'I think so too' agreed Clea, always the optimist.

'Do you think you'll find out all you need to know in one night?' asked Aaron.

'I doubt it, normal dreamers are easy to read but I think Dark Souls will be harder. Talionis was very hard to communicate with to start with but then he was a different creature altogether. I think that DS will be harder work than normal dreamers but less work than Talionis. I told you about my friend Xiu Bo and what he taught me about helping Dark Soul's, well he has managed to help them in his own way by giving them the small, vague dreams as I believe I've done with DS, but Bo took weeks to achieve what I have in days. Therefore, I feel it must be within me to help these Dark Souls more fully and in a lot less time.'

'So, is this your new talent then?' asked Eddie.

'I believe so yes. The Origination supercharged Samuel's Dreambringer talent so that now I can help those who until now have been beyond Dreambringer help.'

'Well except for this Xiu Bo guy' Geth pointed out.

'Yes, but as I said Bo's help is limited, I think I can go beyond that. I'm not playing down Bo's efforts especially because I think that what he taught Samuel contributed to making me what I am now, he is a pioneer and I intend to give him all the credit he is due, but I am going to be the one to carry what he achieved further.'

After that no one had any more questions, so Morpheus and Sofia headed to the office to update Cedric Neale. Then Morpheus put in a call to Xiu Bo to tell him the news and thank him for his part in his success. Sofia and Morpheus then joined the others for a hearty breakfast cooked by Clea and Eddie.

As Morpheus predicted DS was not at all wary that night and joined the throng around him very early on. Morpheus had to help those dreamers that had arrived before DS first and he was a little nervous that DS would move away before he got to him but luckily that was not the case as when it was finally DS's turn he was there waiting.

What Morpheus really wanted to find out was the whole story of DS's trauma but try as he might he only got that his mother's death had been a traumatic one for the boy and that his life since losing her had been a nightmare. However, he also gleaned that DS and his mother had loved to sing together and that was enough to start with. And armed with that knowledge he sent DS a dream.

He is in the garden again. He sings as he sits in the dappled sunlight. He feels at peace. And then another voice joins his, a high, sweet voice, one that he remembers from long ago.

'Is that you Mum?' he asks.

'I'm here my angel' the voice replies. And then she continues to sing.

He cannot see her, but her voice is enough, it fills his heart, and he joins his voice with hers once again. They sound so good together. They sing for hours.

Con awoke, his face awash with tears once again, but he felt happy, and stronger than he had for a very long time. He wished he did not have to go to work, but that was nothing new. The day before he had gone out in search of that garden but had not managed to find it, so he wished he had another day to search again. It would have to wait for his next day off now though.

Work had been the usual hell and his father had been in a foul mood that evening, but things had not got to Con as much as they usually did, he had let his co-workers' taunts and his father's drunken rants wash over him, and he had slipped away to bed as soon as he could.

The next two nights and days had gone much the same for Con, he'd had the same dream and it had once again helped him through his days.

Then his next dream had been a little different. It had started the same as before but then just before he woke, he had sensed that someone was sitting beside him and turning his head he had for an instant seen her, his mum, her long hair moving in the breeze, a big smile on her beautifully freckled face.

'Hello Mum' he said as he awoke.

Then Con did something he'd never really done before; he turned over and went back to sleep in the hopes of returning to the dream and seeing his mother again.

But the dream had not returned, instead he'd had a rude awakening when his father burst in shouting 'What the fucking hell do you think you're doing still in bed you lazy piece of shit!'

He was then roughly dragged from his bed and as he lay startled on the floor his father had shouted 'You'll be late for work you fucking layabout!' then kicked him hard in the stomach.

'Get up and go to work' he had added with another kick, this time to the ribs, before dragging Con to his feet and half carrying him to the bathroom where he instructed him to 'Wash that grubby little girly face first though you snotty little bastard.'

The rest of the day did not get any better. After the beating from his father his stomach and ribs hurt but he still had to go to work. His boss gave him a good telling off for being late and he was given the shittiest jobs they could find for him that day, but at least they did not involve heavy lifting and so he struggled through them the best he could.

When he got home his father seemed to have forgotten about his tardiness that morning but was in a demanding mood and Con had to go back out again to get him some cigarettes and fish and chips for his dinner, which Con had to pay for.

Luckily, after scoffing down his dinner his father went out and Con was able to rest at last. His stomach was still painful as were his ribs, and he knew without looking that he would be bruised. He tried to eat a cheese sandwich but only managed half, and then he had a good cry. He knew that if his father came back and caught him crying he would get another beating, but he could not stop himself.

After a while he was too exhausted to cry anymore and just lay on the sofa staring at the ceiling.

For the last few days, he had felt better than he had for years, but now he was back down in the shit again. He could not take much more of this, he really couldn't, but what could he do about it, how could he get away from this hellish life? Suicide popped into his mind, not for the first time, but he had long ago decided he did not have the guts to jump off a tall building or tie a rope around his neck and choke the life out of himself, and even the thought of a painless death from an overdose scared him.

He had also thought about running away, but when he was younger that had been scary too, there were bad people everywhere and as a child alone he would be easy prey and his life could take an even more sinister turn. Now as an adult that option was more viable, but not much more, he still looked like a kid and his lack of strength made him vulnerable, and what about money, plus where would he go?

He had to do something though, and soon, so struggling up from the sofa he staggered to his bed for an early night thinking he would sleep on it and maybe a plan would come to him.

'Somethings changed in DS's life' Morpheus told the group the next morning.

'How do you know?' asked Sofia.

'His needs have changed.'

'How exactly?' enquired Mason.

'As you know until now his needs have been about his mother so I've been giving her to him in dreams as best I can, but this morning, just before I was pulled from the Dream Realm, I sensed a new element has been added to his needs.'

'What element?' asked Max.

'Escape, he feels a need to escape from someone or something, but what exactly I'm not sure.'

'What sort of life is that poor boy living?' wondered Clea, tears in her eyes.

'I real bad one' suggested Aaron.

'That's obvious' added Geth 'but what can we do about it, or rather what can you do about it?' he queried indicating Morpheus.

'It's difficult to give someone the dreams they need when you don't know exactly what it is they want. I'm not really sure at this point, I need to know more about this new need for escape.'

'What did you do for the Dark Soul last night then?' asked Eddie.

'I carried on with the dreams of his mother but added an extra level of comfort, you know to make him feel safe. I'm going to have to think about how to approach him tonight and any suggestions are welcome. I'd really made a breakthrough, but I have a feeling that this has put things back a bit which is frustrating.'

'Setbacks are a part of life' said Max his old Youth Councillor training kicking in 'but you can help him through it I'm sure, you just need patience, especially if he's young as you believe he is.'

'I know you're right and it's not like I have a time limit on this, I just need to keep at it.'

'And keep positive' added Sofia.

'Yes, keep positive, that's the attitude' agreed Morpheus and the smile he gave her made her heart flutter. Then she blushed hating the girly way she reacted to him sometimes. Luckily, he did not seem to notice the effect he had on her. and she was grateful for that.

'What happens now then?' asked Mary.

'I guess I try to delve deeper into where this need for escape comes from and decide what to do from there' answered Morpheus 'I know that's a bit vague but that's all I have.'

'Can we help at all?' asked Clea.

'Not in terms of communicating with and helping DS directly no, but if you all put the hours in with your artwork and support me like you have so far then that will boost me, I'm sure, and that will help me in my task. I do appreciate you all you know, and although much of this falls on my shoulders I can only do it because I have you backing me up.'

It was the most emotional Morpheus had been and his kind words brought tears to Clea's and Mary's eyes.

'Thanks for that' said Aaron 'it's nice to be appreciated.'

'And we will always have your back' added Mary with a slight catch in her voice.

'Okay, now it's getting too sentimental' Geth cut in 'that's enough, let's just eat our breakfast and get on with our day.'

The others agreed, some reluctantly, but they did as he suggested.

For a couple of minutes after waking that morning Con had felt good, the memory of his dream still lingered, and he felt safe. He had been singing in the garden with his Mum again and this time as well as seeing her for a few seconds she had moved to embrace him, and he had felt her love in those few seconds before he woke.

He was cruelly brought back to the real world however when he made a small movement that sent pain shooting through his bruised ribs. He groaned and felt on the verge of tears but tried to hold them back with memories of his great dream. But then, scared of falling back asleep again, he forced himself to get up.

His ribs protested as he went through his morning routine, and he tried not to think about the pain to come at work. He may have had more than a valid reason to take a sick day but there was no way he would get away with that. If he told them he could not work because he had hurt his ribs, it would get back to his father and even though he would keep him out of it his father would take it as him telling on him and that would not go down well. And giving a fake reason would also get back to his father who would punish him for throwing a sickie. No, taking a sick day was not going to happen, but how would he get through another day of hell?

Luckily at work the first block of apartments in the development they were working on was almost completed and so whilst the others did small finishing jobs it was Con's job to follow behind and clear up after them. This meant his work was not too physically demanding and that he was alone most of the time. Therefore, without anyone to hear him he got through the day by using the coping strategy of singing quietly to himself as he worked. He still suffered from his bruised ribs and stomach, but it was just about bearable.

He also used other mental tricks to take his mind off the pain; he thought about the wonderful dream he'd had that morning and he tried to think of a way out of his terrible life. He had already ruled out suicide so now his mind went back to the possibility of running away, away from his job and away from his father.

Would living on the streets really be any worse? He lived with the ever-present fear of physical harm being done to him at home anyway and at least on the street he would not have to do heavy manual work, he could just find a quiet corner somewhere and sleep whenever he wanted. He was used to not eating much and if he left just after pay day he would have a little money to get by on to start with.

By the time he got home he had decided it was probably his best option but that it needed a little more planning. Yes, a little more thought was needed, but he was fairly sure he was going to run away and try to find a better life even at the risk of ending up with a worse one.

There was a part of him that realised trying to make it alone on the streets might be a form of assisted suicide, but he tried not to think of that. Instead, he tried to think of it as a positive move to finding a better future.

The Dark Soul was one of the first to claim Morpheus' light that night and whilst the other dreaming souls flitted in and out of his light quickly Morpheus was glad to note that the Dark Soul again remained within the light.

Morpheus started as he had the last few nights by gently seeking out the Dark Soul's needs and sensed the usual need for his mother, but this time that need was eclipsed somewhat by the new need for escape.

Until now Morpheus had been very gentle with the Dark Soul only probing deep enough to get a vague idea of what he needed. Now he decided it was time to interact with him more directly. It was a bit of a risk but during the day Morpheus had decided to take that risk and the other Dreambringers had agreed that it was worth a go.

Using the skills he had learnt when dealing with Talionis he sent out a gentle, non-threatening communication.

'My name is Morpheus, do not be afraid, I want to help you.'

He did not receive a response, but he did not sense fear either, and the Dark Soul remained within his light, so he continued.

'Tell me, what is it you need to escape from?' he gently enquired.

There was a pause, and he was just beginning to lose hope in an answer when faint words came to him.

'My life.'

71

Morpheus found this reply alarming. Was the poor soul suicidal he wondered, and then was again shocked by an unsolicited communication from the soul.

'Not suicidal, just need to get away.'

It had read his thoughts without him having to emote it which was a wonderful development.

'Get away from what?' Morpheus enquired.

Then instead of words in answer Morpheus received a sudden influx of mental images; images that were vaguely informative but also quite harrowing.

Morpheus was taken aback; this was something new and he felt a mixture of shock and delight. Shock at the nature of the images and delight at the new development. The question was who was the instigator of this new phenomenon, himself, or the Dark Soul? He would have to dissect that later, now he needed to stay in the moment.

'Thank you' he told the Dark Soul *'I can help you now, but first can you tell me your name?'*

'It's Constantine.'

'Hello Constantine, now I know what you need I will send you the dreams that will help you.'

When Morpheus woke that morning, he felt elated. The Dark Soul was far from being cured but he had made a great start and he was learning more about himself and the nature of the Dark Soul so things could only get better.

The strange thing was he was a little unsure exactly what this new information had achieved in terms of the actual dream he had brought from it. It was usual for Dreambringers to ever actually 'witness' the dreams their input created but they usually had an idea what that dream involved. In this case all that Morpheus knew was that the dream would help the soul in some way, but he did not know any details which was slightly worrying. Morpheus pushed that slight worry away though, another small but significant breakthrough had been made, and even though he did not fully understand it he knew it was a good thing.

When Con awoke it was after the following dream.

He sits as before on grass, his skin touched by tree dappled sun. He sings and after a while her voice joins his and he is happy.

Then suddenly before him he sees something, not a person but a place, a place that does not belong in this garden.

He sees a winding gravel pathway bordered to left and right by trees.

A woodland.

A woman appears upon the driveway and as she draws near, he recognises her.

'Hello Mum' he says.

'Hello my angel' she replies, 'come with me.'

And then she steps into the trees and disappears from sight.

He leaps to his feet crying 'Wait!' and runs towards the place she disappeared.

And there the dream ends.

For a moment after waking Con felt disappointed that the dream had ended but consoled himself by thinking how good the dream had made him feel. Then he realised that beyond the joy of the dream itself and the diluted joy of remembering it he now felt something else, hope. This was shortly followed by the revelation that this dream was telling him that he had somewhere to go. He had no idea where that somewhere was, but he believed he would find out soon and that was enough for now.

He also decided that this dream was reinforcing his idea that running away was his best chance at a better life. It was definitely time for him to start making real plans. The next day was his day off so he would struggle through work today bolstered by his dream and the prospect of escape, and then the next day he would have time to really make some plans.

Morpheus was so eager to tell the others of his success that he arrived at the Gateway kitchen before most of them were even up. There was only Sofia and Mason in the room when he entered. They exchanged good mornings and then Mason said, 'We were just talking about you.'

'All good things I hope,' said Morpheus with a rare cheeky smile.

'Of course,' Sofia told him returning the smile.

'We were just saying that we both woke up with the feeling that things went really well last night,' explained Mason. He was talking to Morpheus, but his eyes were on Sofia who he had noticed had seemed to light up since Morpheus had entered the room. It's not that she had not been in a good mood already and had greeted him with a friendly smile, but the smile she had given Morpheus was different. Something was going on here, but Mason was not sure what exactly.

'Yes, it did, but you'll have to wait until the others are here before I tell you what happened,' Morpheus told them taking Mason's attention off of Sofia briefly until she spoke.

'You big tease' she said.

She's flirting thought Mason and then Sofia saw him looking at her and blushed.

'I errmm… you know I…erm I was just joking,' she stammered making Mason feel bad. He had not meant to embarrass her, but she must have read his expression. Luckily it did not seem like Morpheus had picked up on the flirty vibe because he simply said 'Sorry, I just don't want to have to repeat myself, especially as I'm going to have to tell it again to Cedric later.'

Just then, to Sofia's relief, Clea entered the room, closely followed by Max and the focus was taken off her.

Not long after Eddie and then Geth joined the group, and then last as usual Aaron and Mary arrived. And once the greetings were over and everyone was settled Morpheus could finally tell them his news.

'I now know that the Dark Soul's name is Constantine, and I know some details of the trauma he suffered and what he is suffering now.'

'What a lovely name' interjected Clea.

'Sounds a bit pretentious to me' said Geth causing Clea to scowl at him, but Morpheus continued as if they had not spoken.

'As I'd already surmised the trauma that turned his soul dark was the death of his mother when he was quite young.'

'The poor boy, what happened?' asked Clea.

'I don't know any details, but the basics are his mother died and since then he has suffered physical and mental abuse. I'm not sure who exactly is abusing him but it's bad.'

'So that's what he wants to escape from,' said Sofia 'abuse.'

'Yes, exactly.'

'It's heart-breaking,' said a tearful Mary.

'Don't worry, Morpheus will help him' Aaron reassured her as her put his arm around her 'right?' he added to Morpheus.

'Of course. Now I know more details I can really start to heal him properly. In fact, I already started.'

'How exactly?' enquired Eddie.

'In the usual way, by giving him the dream he needed. It will have only been a brief dream, but it's a start, my task now is to give him more substantial dreams.'

'What sort of dream did you bring him?' enquired Max.

'It was a dream of his mother with and added element of hope I guess.'

'What do you mean you guess?' asked Mason.

'Well, I gave him a touch of hope for his wanted escape but I'm not quite sure what context that would have taken in his dream.'

'How can you not know what dream you brought him?' enquired Geth.

'Because this is all new remember. Dark Souls aren't like normal dreaming souls, there are barriers that they've put up. Constantine may have shown me a snapshot of his life, but he still has barriers that I haven't broken through, he only let me see what he wanted me to see so I could understand him a little. He isn't able to communicate well in mind words, but I discovered he can understand what I am thinking and trying to convey, he just hasn't got the hang on answering me with more than a few basic words. And what he actually dreamt was hidden from me.'

'That's a little worrying don't you think,' said Eddie.

'What's worrying about it' countered Morpheus 'I did what Dreambringers always do, I brought him the dream he needed and just because I'm not a hundred per cent sure what that dream was it doesn't matter, it's not going to be anything bad.'

'Okay, maybe worrying is the wrong word' Eddie conceded 'maybe weird is better.'

'Yes, that's better, it is weird, but this whole thing is weird, its new territory and so there's an element of having to be careful, but I am being and so far I see nothing to be worried about.'

'Sorry mate, I'm just trying to process it all and I spoke before I thought it through.'

'No need to apologise, I'm never going to condemn anyone for saying what they think, so don't hold back, criticism helps as much as praise.'

'Okay, thanks.'

'So what's you plan going forward?' Sofia asked Morpheus.

'So far I've just been able to give him vague dreams that can make him feel a little better, but now I know his situation it's obvious he needs more than that.'

'He needs to escape to somewhere safe, that's what he needs' Max interjected, then feeling bad for interrupting continued 'sorry, you were probably getting to that, I'm just getting a bit emotional. I've counselled abused teenagers in the past and its always heart-breaking and is never simple.'

'Exactly' agreed Morpheus, 'he needs more than the average dreaming soul as Talionis did. He needs a lot of mental healing first before we can really tackle his living conditions.'

'But that's the problem' this from Max again 'I know you can help him a lot through dreams, but what he really needs is to get away from the abuse, he'll never heal properly whilst it's still going on. I understand that that's not in our power though.'

'Morpheus can give him the confidence to leave home though,' said Mary.

'Yes, but that's not easy, where would he go for a start?'

'There are charities and organisations that can help.'

'He might not know that, he may not know where to go for help. Can we give him that information in a dream?'

'It's a bit specific and reality based for a dream,' Morpheus told her.

'I just wish we could find the poor boy in the real world and help him,' said Clea.

'Can we not do that?' enquired Mary of no one in particular.

'It's not really what we do.' Sofia said, 'besides how would we find him?'

'He's got a pretty original name' stated Mason 'and if he's in our area of the Dream Realm then he must be reasonably local and with the Foundations connections it couldn't be too hard.'

'But that sort of thing just isn't done' Sofia told him.

'There have been a lot of things 'done' since Talionis showed up that just weren't done before,' he countered.

'Not something like this though.'

'You both have a point' interjected Morpheus 'but Sofia is right, seeking out Constantine in person just isn't the right thing to do. It's not how we work. For instance, when a Dreambringer calls their replacement I'm sure if they tried, they could find out that person's name and then where they are and go and get them, but it's just not how it's done.'

'Right, I see your point, I was just worried about the kid's physical wellbeing as well as the mental side, he could be in danger.'

'There is that risk, but it doesn't change the fact that we don't work that way. I'm convinced that our way is the best way to go, but if I do sense that he's in real danger we can look at the options okay?'

'Okay, fair enough.'

'Good, that's settled. So now my plan is to work at giving Constantine the dreams he needs to heal enough mentally to take that step to help himself and get away from his abusers. I realise that I don't know enough to know exactly how to guide him, but I know enough to begin with. We can all analyse things again each morning like today and I can make changes to the plan accordingly. Is everyone happy with that?'

To Morpheus' relief they all consented and now it was time for him to update the Foundation and see what their input was.

It turned out that Cedric gave him an easier time than the Dreambringers had. He was pleased with the progress that had been made, was happy with Morpheus's plan for going forward and did not have much input himself. The foundation boss had only advised caution and reiterated his need to be kept fully updated.

What Morpheus and the others did not know was that not everyone was as pleased with his progress as Cedric Neale was. Cedric was a cautious man but not as stuffy and old fashioned as some people thought or expected. He was quite progressive compared to a couple of other high up members within the British division of the Foundation. He had already met with some resistance from certain quarters over his handling of the whole Talionis affair, not to mention the Origination itself. It was part of the reason that Morpheus had been 'held' by the Foundation for so long before being allowed to go to the Gateway.

A couple of other members, though younger than Cedric, were very old fashioned and distrustful of change. The Foundation had been very set in its ways for many years and the business with Talionis had really shaken up those in charge. Most felt that the eventual outcome of the Origination was a good thing and were willing to accept the changes it could bring, but others were not so sure.

One of those was a man named Patrick Chapman. He had worked his way up the Foundation hierarchy and at fifty-eight was the head of the Foundations Law department. He was good at his job but was a bit pompous and vain.

He was always neat and well-groomed, his thin, brown hair clipped short at the back and sides, the top left longer and neatly slicked back. The dark blue pin striped suits he wore were immaculate and expensive but never seemed to fit his short, stocky body right.

Like Cedric he had never been a Dreambringer, his talent, like his boss' and other high up members was more along the lines of the Marshals. They too tended to be descendants of families that had for many years had a hand in protecting and looking after the Dreambringers. In Patrick's family's case they were a legacy of Lawyers within the Foundation.

All those who worked within the Foundation were fundamentally good people, but that does not mean they were perfect. In Patrick's case he had a rather high opinion of himself and had felt for many years that he would make a better leader than Cedric.

This inflated self belief had taken a couple of hits lately however. Firstly, his wife of thirty two years had recently left him for someone else, that someone being a woman.

Although he had obviously felt hurt by this betrayal, what he mostly felt was humiliated. It would have been bad enough if she's left him for another man, but a woman, well that was just too much.

He had of course done his best to keep it all quiet, not many people knew, but even one person knowing was humiliating enough.

The fact that his wife Irene was insisting on a divorce had made it all worse because to him as a lawyer having to go through the courts citing adultery as the reason for divorce was just embarrassing. He had asked his wife if they could use another reason, irreconcilable differences for instance, but she had insisted on telling the truth which was rich coming from an adulterer. He got the feeling that she was enjoying making a fool of him.

The second blow had come after a visit to a doctor. He's been having some health issues and thinking they were just stress reactions to his impending divorce he had gone to the doctors for some advice. But the actual diagnosis he'd received had shocked him. Apparently, he had Multiple Sclerosis. This was not good news for his career or his life in general. At least his illness was easier to keep secret, for now at least, until his symptoms got worse, as they inevitably would. He definitely had a lot on his plate right now.

His long held dream to inherit Cedric Neale's job now seemed out of his reach and this did not sit well with him. With all the stress he was under was it any wonder that the changes that the Origination may bring made him nervous. There were too many bad changes going on in his life, he really didn't need the stress.

He was unhappy with the way Cedric had dealt with things but felt helpless in doing anything about it. If he had his way Morpheus would be locked away as the aberration Patrick believed he was.

In the end he and another dissenter had been outvoted, the others trusted in Morpheus, and he had been allowed to leave and was now involved in this Dark Soul nonsense. To Patrick the Dark Souls were bad news, their name said it all and he believed that Morpheus was courting danger and should be reined in. He was in the minority however so could do nothing about it, not through the usual channels anyway.

Unaware of the depth of one man's distrust in him Morpheus was seeking a way to pass the time until he could return to the Dream Realm and continue his work. He was sure the other Dreambringers could help him with that, so with that in mind he and Sofia returned to the kitchen to have breakfast with the others and make plans for the day.

They were all deciding who was going to Factory that day when Morpheus had an idea.

'There's a recording studio at the Factory isn't there,' it was a rhetorical question, so he continued with an actual query 'have any of you used it at all.'

There was a chorus of no's before Mason spoke.

'No ones used it since Blake' he told them a note of sadness evident in his voice.

Morpheus was aware that Blake was the previous male Dream Mate who had been seriously injured at the hands of his friend, and fellow Dreambringer, Claude whilst he had been 'possessed' by Talionis and that this was still a little raw for Mason and Eddie.

'I take it Blake was a musician, what did he play?' asked Morpheus.

'He was a great guitarist. He wrote, played and sang his own songs.'

'Are there any recordings of him here, I'd be interested to hear some.'

'The collection of CDs he'd made of himself were sent on to him recently along with his and Gina's other belongings, but there might still be something in the studio, I must admit I haven't checked.'

'Would you, or anyone else, mind if I took a look at this studio? Being a musician myself I'm really interested in checking it out.'

'I don't have a problem with that' Mason told him.

'Me either,' said Eddie and no one else had any objections.

'Thank you,' said Morpheus. He had noted a touch of reluctance in both Mason and Eddie, but it was understandable, and he had every intention of being respectful.

'Do you know how it works?' he then asked Mason and Eddie.

'I have a rough idea' said Eddie 'but Mason knows more.'

'Would you mind giving me a little tutorial then Mason?'

'Okay' agreed Mason.

'So that's me and Mason headed for the Factory, who else is coming?'

'We're due for a sharing day' Clea told him 'We have a kind of informal Rota, most days we split into two groups and one group has a whole day there, but on sharing days one group spends the morning there and the other the afternoon.'

'Okay, so I'd like to be in the morning group with Mason, that way I can have a break before going back in the evening. If that's okay with everyone of course.'

It was. There was a little bit of lighthearted debate as it was obvious most of them were intrigued to know what Morpheus would do in the recording studio, but they got there in the end. Clea and Eddie would go with Mason and Morpheus leaving Geth, Mary, Aaron and Max with the afternoon shift. As for Sofia she had never felt more disappointed about not being able to go to the Factory.

On the way to the Factory the 'morning' group detoured to Morpheus' cabin so he could pick up his electric guitar and violin.

'I don't get to use the electric one much' he told the group as they continued through the woods 'I only have a small amplifier and it's not often worth the bother when I have the acoustic. And I think the violin would just be interesting in a studio.'

'You're not bringing your Hurdy Gurdy then?' asked Eddie stifling a laugh and causing Clea to let out a reluctant giggle.

Morpheus obviously did not get the 'in' joke and just assumed they were laughing at the instruments silly name saying 'I know, it's a stupid name for an amazing instrument' making Eddie feel a bit bad about his comment, but no harm was done.

When they got to the Factory Mason gave Morpheus the promised tutorial whilst the others got on with their artwork. Then once Morpheus had the basics down Mason got on with his own work leaving Morpheus to experiment to his heart's content.

Clea soon realised that the soundproof studio meant that they could not hear what Morpheus was up to, but if he made any recordings, she hoped he would share them. She ended up disappointed though because when they were getting ready to leave, he informed her that he had only experimented, and nothing was worth a listen.

A bit later on it was Sofia's turn to be disappointed when she found out that she would not have the pleasure of Morpheus' company that afternoon at the Gateway house as he informed them all that after lunch he was going back to his cabin for some alone time and a rest.

'I need to be as rested and prepared as I can for tonight's session with Constantine' he told them, and they all understood.

When Con went to bed that night he was just looking forward to the rest and hoping to dream of his Mum again. He was totally unaware of all the work that was going into giving him this dream just like all the other dreamers in the world.

As soon as Constantine entered his light that night Morpheus established communication with him.

'Hello Constantine'

'Hello' came the caution reply

'I'm here to help you'

The rest of the communication was done without words, even metal ones, as was usual. Instead, Morpheus used his supercharged Dreambringer skills to extract the information he needed whilst the healing light he radiated continued to sooth and heal.

The other dreaming souls demanding his attention were a slight distraction but helping them only required minimal effort, so he was able to concentrate most of his energy on the Dark Soul.

By the time Morpheus sensed the end of that night's session coming he felt that he had succeeded in his aim to bring Constantine the dreams he needed. His healing light had eroded the Dark Soul's barriers further enabling him to access his needs more fully and as he was pulled back to his own sleep Morpheus was confident he had done a good night's work.

Con woke with a smile on his face. He did not remember the healing light of Morpheus or communicating with the impressive looking being in the Dream Realm, but he did remember his dreams. Yes, dreams plural.

The clearest dream had been almost the same as the one the night before. This time however he had found his Mum on the edges of the woodland, she had taken his hand and they had walked further into the trees together.

He only remembered flashes of his other dreams, or maybe the dreams themselves had just been brief. Either way he remembered walking along a street. The street had seemed familiar, yet strange, but he walked with purpose. '*I know where I'm going*' his dream self had thought.

Another remembered fragment was of him standing in a doorway. Where that doorway was he did not know but as he stood there, he heard a voice say, '*You can do it*' and stepping forward he was suddenly transported to the woodland where his Mum walked ahead of him. He followed her for a few steps and then she turned and beckoned him with a hand gesture '*This way*' she told him.

The last thing he remembered dreaming was a strange conversation with his father. They stood in a slightly off kilter version of their lounge, face to face.

'*I'm leaving*' he told his father.

'*Good riddance*' his father retorted with a sneer '*but before you go, take this.*'

Sensing what was coming Con darted to the side as his father's fist punched the air where he had stood which put him off balance causing him to fall at Con's feet.

'*Before I go, you take this*' Con said before aiming a kick at his father's ribs. But suddenly he was striding down the street again. '*I'm free*' he thought. And that was when he woke up.

Con lay in bed thinking how there was no way that he would have that confrontational conversation with his father in real life. When he left it would be without his father knowing, but somehow the dream made him feel more confident that leaving was the right thing to do even though it was scary.

He remembered then that it was his day off and therefore time for him to do some real planning if he really did mean to leave, he just hoped his father went out at some point that day because he needed him gone for at least part of what he had planned for that day.

Luckily, his father did decide to go out, but he took his time about it making Con feel edgy and frustrated. Once he was out the door though Con took a minute to get himself together before beginning the first part of his plan. This first part involved looking through his meagre belongings and making a mental inventory of what to take with him. He dare not make a physical list just in case his father found it. He was probably being a bit paranoid, but it was better to be safe than sorry.

His complete wardrobe consisted of two pairs of jeans, two pairs of work trousers, five t shirts, a black hoodie, five pairs of boxer shorts, four pairs of socks and a scruffy, green bomber jacket. In one of his drawers he still has some pajamas, but they were old and a little small for him, he slept in his boxers now.

He had two pairs of shoes; a battered pair of trainers and a secondhand pair of work boots he had been forced to buy when he started work on the building site.

He then checked that his old backpack from school was still under his bed to put them in when the time came. It was a bit battered and dusty, but it would do. He would leave the boots and work trousers behind, wear a pair of jeans, t shirt, hoodie, jacket, and trainers to go and the rest could go in the backpack. It was a bit too warm to wear that many layers, but he would not get it all in the backpack.

Apart from his clothes and a cheap watch he had very few possessions. He had a few old comics, but he had read them all several times so decided none of them were worth taking. As for his mobile phone, it was old school and on a pay as you go tariff. He hardly ever used it as he did not use social media; there was no real point when he had no friends and no real interest in it. Plus, there was the issue of the tracking thing. His father might call the police to report him missing, but then again, he might not.

On the one hand his father would be glad to see the back of him he was sure, but then without Con he would have to make all his own meals, do housework, pay the bills and all without Con's wages. Would that be enough for him to make an effort to try to find Con? He doubted it, but he would leave the phone behind just in case.

Toiletries wise he would take deodorant, toothbrush and toothpaste, a bar of soap, a flannel and his comb. He was not sure where he would be able to wash but they were small, and he felt necessary items.

The next part of his mental inventory would include a bit of risk. He needed to go through the draws in his father's bedroom to see if he had any valuables he could pawn for extra money. It was risky because he was not going to take anything yet so he would have to be careful to leave everything as he had found it because his father would notice he had been there if he did not. He was not allowed in his father's room, and he would go mental if he thought Con had been in there. It would mean a beating for sure. But it had to be done even though finding anything worth money was a long shot.

His father's room smelt of stale sweat, beer, and cigarette smoke, it was also dark as the curtains were still drawn. Con dare not touch the curtains so he turned the light on instead.

The room was tidier than he had expected but the bed was unmade. He went straight to the large, old-fashioned chest of draws on the far side of the room and carefully opening the top draw started to cautiously rummage through the contents. The contents consisted of his father's underwear but nothing else.

The middle two draws contained clothes but again no hidden treasure. There was something hidden under the clothes in the bottom draw, but it was only his father's small stash of porn magazines.

Next Con looked under the bed. The only thing there, apart from balls of dust, was an old, dust covered suitcase. It was possible it held something useful but Con thought it more likely it was empty. Either way moving it in order to find out seemed too risky, disturbing all that dust might leave signs of him having been in there.

His last chance of finding something lay in the three draws of the bedside table. Gently opening the top draw, he discovered a mess of small junk. There were cigarette papers, matches, an old watch strap, a stub of pencil, an old pocketknife, half a pack of mints, and a couple of used hankies. What the hankies had been used for Con did not want to know.

The middle drawer held a small, half empty bottle of cheap whisky.

At first Con thought that the bottom drawer was empty but then he realised there was a brown envelope lying flat in one corner. Taking note of its exact position so he could put it back how he had found it he picked it up.

What he found inside made even the possibility of a beating worth it. It may not have any monetary value, but this was definitely treasure. In his trembling hand he held a photo of a woman and a child. The woman was his mother, and the child was Con at what he guessed to be about seven years old.

It was a full length shot of the pair with Con stood in front of his mum, her hands on his shoulders. She was wearing a blue, knee length summer dress, he wore only a pair of shorts. Their bare feet were sunk in soft sand and behind them was sea and a cloudless sky.

'I remember this day' Con said quietly to himself.

He remembered that the photo had been taken by his father on a rare family day out at the seaside. They had been so happy that day and now tears came into his eyes, but were they tears of joy or sadness? Maybe a bit of both.

His reverie was interrupted then by a loud bang. For a heart stopping moment he thought that his father had come home but then he realised it was just a neighbor's door slamming. It brought him back to the real world though and he reluctantly slipped the photo back into the envelope, put it back where he had found it and carefully closed the drawer.

He had always thought his father had thrown out all the family photos but for some reason his father had kept this one. Maybe it showed that he did love them deep down, or at least he had done at one time. You would not know that now though.

He was disappointed not to have found anything worth pawning but he had found something of value in another way. One thing was for sure; that photo was coming with him when he left.

After his search of the bedroom Con returned to the lounge and collapsed onto the sofa. He needed a minute to relax as his heart was hammering after the tension of the search, his emotional reaction to the photo and the scare of the banging door.

When his heartbeat had returned to normal, he set his mind to more planning. Firstly, should he take a couple of Mum's LPs with him? His heart said yes but his head said no. It was not really practical was it? And what use would they be to him without the record player? It had to be a 'no' then didn't it, he told himself, but he also decided that one day he would buy his own copies. It was not quite the same, but it was not like he would never hear those songs again.

His next dilemma was a matter of safety. Should he take one of the kitchen knives with him for protection or would that be asking for trouble? Then he remembered the pocketknife he had seen in one of his father's drawers. Maybe that would be better? It could come in handy in other ways too. Yes, add that to the inventory he thought.

Now the big decision was when to leave and tied in with that was the question of money. As was usual a few days away from payday he had very little left of the previous pay packet and he had no savings, so in order to leave with as much money as possible his departure would have to happen as soon after he received his wages as possible.

On pay day he would usually come home with his wages in cash as his father insisted. His father would take the money off him as soon as he walked in the door and then divide it up as he thought fair. This consisted of him taking a quarter of it for himself (to spend on alcohol and cigarettes mostly), giving Con a paltry fiver for himself, then the rest would go in the rusty old biscuit tin they kept in the kitchen cupboard.

The money in the tin was to use to buy food and pay the bills, and although Con was in charge of both these things, he could not take any money out without explaining to his father what it was for. The rule for his father was different, he often took some without letting Con know which often made it harder for him to pay the bills or buy enough food.

His father never let him get away with keeping any loose change either, however little it always went back in the tin, and somehow the old bastard always knew exactly how much was in that tin at any time so Con could not risk taking any for himself. The penalty for taking money without permission was a severe beating.

He could see no way to avoid losing the amount of money his father took right away but he would definitely take the money in the tin. This meant that in order to leave with the most money possible he would have to leave the night he got paid, or early the next morning. But which one would depend on what his father did, so he went over his father's usual routine in his mind.

After dividing up the money his father usually went straight out to stock up on beer and cigarettes, then after popping back to drop off his home provisions and eat the dinner Con had cooked, he would go out to meet his mates at the pub. He would stumble back blind drunk later that night and then sleep half the next day.

His father's absence during the evening made a nighttime escape a good bet in terms of being undetected but Con did not relish his first steps to freedom being taken in the dark. No, he would use the time his father was out to pack his bag ready to leave as soon as it was light. His father would be in a deep, drunken sleep by then and when he did finally get up, he would assume Con was at work.

Having decided that was the best plan Con could not help but wonder how long it would take his father to notice that he'd gone. And then what would he do when he did realise? Would he call the police? And if so, would it be out of worry or because he had 'stolen' all their money? Would he notice that the pocketknife and photo had gone, and would he care? Con guessed he would never know unless he somehow ended up back there and that did not really bear thinking about.

With most of his plan now in place Con had one more thing to decide; where to go? He knew that there was no actual place he could head for, but he needed some sort of basic plan.

Should he spend a little of his money on a cheap form of public transport so he could get further away quickly, or should he just take the slower option of walking, after all what else would he have to do all day? With either option he would have to decide on a vague direction at least surely. But then again randomly picking a destination at a bus depot or train station might be good, or if he took the walking option, he could just wander in whatever direction he felt was right.

As he was pondering this, he started to get a headache and decided that was enough planning for the day. The inventory was done, the day of departure was decided, and now he had a couple of days to decide on a direction/destination.

Now he would have his usual lunch of tea and toast and play some of Mum's vinyl LPs for the last time. After eating he would have a good sing a long, make the most of it while he could.

Morpheus was in a good mood that morning at breakfast again. He had one bit of new information to pass on and another successful night to report. The only issue was if they asked him exactly what dream he had brought Constantine he would not be able to tell them again. It was a bit weird, but he felt it was insignificant against what he had achieved.

He started off with the new information.

'The physical abuse Constantine is suffering is at the hands of his father' he told then 'but as for the metal abuse that seems a bit vague, but I get the impression it's from various sources.'

'That's terrible' said Clea.

'It is, I agree, but be reassured that I am helping him, I'm sure of it.'

'I don't doubt you' Clea told him 'But it's just so sad and you'll never fully undo the harm that's been done to that poor boy.'

'It's true I can't change his past, or erase it, but I can, and will, help him to try to move on from it.'

Clea had simply nodded at that clearly overcome with her emotions, a mixture of sadness, pity, hope and gratefulness.

'There's a clear change going on with Constantine's Dream Realm self, it's definitely becoming lighter' Morpheus now told them all.

'That's a good sign' said Sofia and some of the others added similar comments.

The rest of the conversation was shorter than the last time and Morpheus was relieved when no one asked the question about the details of the dreams he had given Con this time or suggested they look for him in the real world. The last question was the usual 'What happens now?'

'I carry on as I am and see where it takes me. I'm learning as I go here so you can't expect me to know all the answers at this point.'

'We don't' Sofia told him.

'Okay, good.'

That was the end of the discussion for that day, and it was back to the routine of Morpheus and Sofia going to the office to make their report to the Foundation and the rest of them deciding on who was going to the Factory that day.

The next few nights and days went pretty much the same way for Morpheus and the Gateway residents. The only difference being Mason and Eddie going on a food and supplies run on the second day.

As for the artwork the group were producing it continued to be of even higher quality than normal. Aarons so called 'Morpheus Effect' theory was in full effect with the group not only feeling more relaxed and positive, but their artistic output was on a new level.

The whole group were feeling the benefits, and they were all aware that the Eternal Dreamers were feeling it too. It was not just Morpheus who had been supercharged, he was passing it on to all of them. But more importantly, he was working his magic on the Dark Soul.

Morpheus was noticing a continuing change in the Dark Soul. Communication was easier each night and he felt Constantine was feeling a new confidence, but at odds with that Morpheus had detected something else, indecisiveness. He gleaned that the boy had made a big decision but was still debating something. He did not want to interfere with that decision, he just needed to give him the confidence to make the right choice.

With the question of what dreams his sessions were actually producing always on his mind Morpheus tried to glean what exactly the boy dreamt but without much success. He knew that the boy dreamt of his mother because he had orchestrated that. The singing was also down to Morpheus as he had picked up on Constantine's forgotten love of singing with his mother. But however hard he tried he could not see what context or surroundings the boy's dreaming soul interpreted these things into. He figured this was due to the barriers his dreaming soul was putting up.

All Morpheus could do was continue to heal with his light and send the boy unknowable dreams of this mother infused with positive vibes to give the boy tranquility and confidence. He also added self-worth and belonging to the mix.

As for Con he was surprised by how calm he felt during those few days. His head was full of plans and decisions to be made but he was remarkably unstressed by it all. Yes, when he really thought about actually leaving, he felt a shiver of fear deep inside, but he was mostly excited.

He continued to have several dreams each night, all very similar, but that was reassuring, they were good dreams. After seeing the photo his mother's face was more vivid in his dreams and they continued to sing together beautifully. The woodland in which they walked was becoming familiar to him now, like it was a real place, though he was fairly sure he had never been there. It must have just been the number of times he had dreamt of it.

His other dreams were all related to leaving. They featured walking through doors and striding confidently down unrecognised streets. He had not dreamt of confronting his father again though and he was kind of glad about that.

Work was still a nightmare, and although his father had not laid a hand on him, he was in a foul mood more often than not which meant a lot of swearing and insults aimed at Con. He was also still a little sore from the recent beating, but again, this strange new calmness meant none of it bothered Con as much as it used to. He figured it was due to the fact that he was leaving it all behind soon and as scary as life on the street might be he had a weird feeling that it would all work out okay.

Chapter 8
The Leaving

It was finally pay day and Con received a surprise, a bonus. With the first stage of the development finished in good time the whole team had received a little extra cash for their good work.

As he walked home Con debated keeping the extra cash for himself, then he remembered that one of the friends his father drank with on pay day was Con's boss. He was bound to tell him about the bonus, but would he say how much? Maybe he could just keep some of it and tell his father the bonus was less than it was. But that was still a risk, his boss may tell him how much it was, he told him everything else. No, it was too risky. The good news was that there would still be more in the tin than usual, though he had a horrid feeling his father might take all of the bonus straight away.

By the time he got home Con was resigned to losing all the bonus having told himself a few extra pounds would not make much difference anyway. Keeping some or all of it was definitely out of the question, the risk of a beating was too high, and he had not really lost anything had he, he would still be leaving with the amount of money he had expected. Besides, if he received a bad beating, he would have to delay leaving and he could not risk that. He had to go, and he had to go the next morning.

His father was waiting for him when he got home, and he dutifully handed over his pay packet saying, 'We got a bonus today.'

His father's eyes lit up at the news and he greedily counted the money out. As expected, his father pocketed the whole of the bonus but then, to Con's surprise for his 'cut' he gave his son a ten-pound note instead of the usual five.

Whilst his father headed to the kitchen to put the rest of the money away in the tin, Con stood for a few seconds holding the tenner, feeling stunned. Well, that was unexpected he thought as he pocketed it. An extra fiver wasn't much, but it was better than he had expected. Maybe it was a good omen.

The early part of the evening went as usual. Whilst his father was out buying his stash of alcohol and cigarettes Con made them dinner. It was always a poor effort on pay day as Con did not do the food shop until after work the next day. His father was always too intent on a big night at the pub to be bothered about dinner anyway and usually Con was not bothered either but this time he wished he could've had a bigger meal inside him to fuel the adventure ahead. Plus, some food to take with him.

Then he realised something, he would have all the money in the tin to do with as he pleased soon, so he could buy himself a cheap, but substantial breakfast to eat as he walked to freedom plus some other supplies. This thought made him smile.

His father was out the door headed for the pub even before he had swallowed his last mouthful of dinner. Con finished his own baked beans and contemplated the washing up; should he leave it for his father to do after he had gone? That would be a great 'fuck you' leaving present Con thought with a rare laugh. Then he decided yet again it was another risk not worth taking as there was the slim chance that his father might discover the dirty dishes when he got home, and his punishment would scupper his plans.

Con decided that the thought of his father's reaction when he found the money missing was enough.

It would be a good few hours before his father came staggering home so Con decided to watch some TV. He had thought he would be too jittery to just sit like that, but the strange calmness was still with him. His mind did wander occasionally though, going over his plan.

His decision to leave as soon as it was light meant that he would not get as much sleep as he would have liked but it was still the best plan. There was the issue of a wake-up call though. He usually woke up naturally at the same time each morning but this would be earlier so he could not risk leaving it to chance. His phone did have an alarm setting so he had decided to use that, he had picked the least piercing tone though so there was less chance of waking his father too. His father was a heavy sleeper, especially after a big drinking session and the bathroom was in between their rooms giving extra sound insulation, but you could never be sure, in this instance though the risk was one that had to be taken.

Con usually had a shower before bed so he did not disturb his father in the morning so that did not need to change, but he intended to go to bed earlier than usual to counter the early morning, and although he usually had no trouble falling asleep due to physical exhaustion, he was worried that he would have trouble that night because of all that was on his mind. The main problem on his mind at this point being what if the phone alarm does not work or failed to wake him up. He consoled himself with the thought that even if he woke at his usual time his father would still be fast asleep, it was just that the extra time made him feel more secure.

Finally, it was time to pack. Fetching his old school backpack from under the bed he packed his clothes, minus those he would wear the next day, as neatly as he could. Then he carefully retrieved the pocketknife and photo from his father's room. After a quick look at the photo, he packed the stolen items safely in the backpack then stashed it back under the bed. He just preyed his father did not notice them missing, it was highly unlikely but again it was a risk he needed to take. He would leave adding the toiletries and the money to his pack until the morning though because the least left to chance the better.

Now it was time to go to bed. He checked the alarm setting and battery level on his phone, it looked fine, so he climbed into his bed for what would be the last time.

He lay awake for about twenty minutes before physical and mental exhaustion thankfully pulled him down into sleep.

Morpheus was working his usual magic on the Dark Soul that belonged to Con and he was soon able to detect new emotions from the soul, those being excitement with a hint of fear. There was obviously something going on in Constantine's life, so Morpheus had communicated more specific questions in order to find out what that was.

'Why are you so excited?' he asked without words.

'It's a secret' was the reply.

'You can trust me with your secret' he assured the soul.

There was no answer and he sensed resistance. This would take some work; it was obviously a big secret and the Dark Soul's natural instinct was to protect that secret. For the time being Morpheus returned to a less direct approach intending to 'ask' again later after more time to work on healing the soul.

He needed to gain the boy's trust so that he would drop his remaining barriers. So now Morpheus needed to bring the soul dreams that would gain his trust.

Therefore, as Con's soul bathed in Morpheus' light Con dreamt dreams that Morpheus sensed were needed.

Firstly, he sent dreams similar to those he had sent before, there was comfort in the familiar. But then he stepped it up some and without knowing exactly what Con dreamt Morpheus was confident it would help him extract that secret later.

Con was cradled in his mother's arms.
'You can trust me' she whispered in his ear 'I love you and I will protect you.'
'I love you too Mum' he told her.
'Let's take a walk' his mother suggested.
And suddenly they were walking through the familiar dream landscape of woodland.
'You feel safe here, don't you?' his mother enquired.
'Yes, especially when you're here with me.'
His mother smiled 'And you trust me, don't you?'
'Yes, of course.'
'And you know you can talk to me about anything.'
'Yes, I know.'
'I'm here for you my angel, and always will be' she told him 'We can talk later, but now let's sing.'
And so, they walked hand in hand singing in perfect harmony.

Deciding it was time to try again Morpheus prepared to convey another question. Before he could pose that question however something unexpected happened. The Dark Soul suddenly disappeared from the Dream Realm.

Morpheus was momentarily alarmed until he realised it was a normal phenomenon. Usually when a person wakes in their normal fashion, be it naturally or by some wake up device, their soul's presence in the Dream Realm fades as they return to consciousness, and by then the Dreambringers have usually returned to their own sleep leaving the Eternal Dreamers to continue their work.

But when a person is rudely awoken, especially if earlier than is normal they are gone from the Dream Realm in an instant. Until now the Dark Soul had always faded before Morpheus was pulled from the Dream Realm making him an early riser. This was really early though and if left Morpheus wondering what could have woken the boy so suddenly. He hoped it was not in a traumatic manor, and now he regretted not making his second attempt at communication earlier. There was nothing he could do about it now though; the Dark Soul's secret would remain his own until the next night at least.

Con was not used to waking like that and it took him a few seconds to realise what the noise was. As soon as he realised, he moved quickly to turn the alarm off. He then collapsed back onto the bed his heart racing. He held his breath for a moment whilst he listened for any sounds indicating that the alarm had woken his father, but he heard nothing, so he let his breath out.

He had not enjoyed that rude awakening, especially as he had been having a particularly good dream, but the alarm had obviously been necessary. His heart was still pounding in his chest and now his stomach was churning as he realised the day was finally here.

For a second, he felt like crying and almost pulled the bed cover over his head. In other words, he almost chickened out. But instead, he managed to swing his legs over the side of the bed and sit up. He needed a minute before he could get up properly as he felt a bit sick, but he was definitely going to do it.

Five minutes later he was pulling on his clothes. His stomach was still churning, and his heart continued to beat faster than usual but he carried on regardless, he had to, there was no way he was chickening out now.

Once he was dressed, he pulled his backpack out from under his bed, slowly opened his bedroom door and crept into the lounge. After putting his backpack on the sofa, he held his breath and listened for any sounds coming from his father's room. Detecting only the faint sound of snoring he let out a sigh of relief.

He retrieved his toiletries and comb from the bathroom as quietly as possible, but the sound of snoring filtering through the wall reassured him. Next, he padded through to the kitchen and careful removed the money from the rusty old biscuit tin. He then put some of the cash in his pocket and the rest he stashed in the inside pocket of his backpack.

Lastly, he carried the full backpack over to the alcove next to the front door where the coats and shoes were kept. He put on his trainers and bomber jacket, and he was ready. Or was he?

He froze then the fear taking hold.

Then he remembered the dreams he had had where he stood in a doorway, and he heard the words in his head. Words spoken in a voice he did not recognise.

'You can do it' the voice told him and so he did, he opened the door and stepped outside.

As Morpheus strolled through the trees on the way to the Gateway house, he wondered what the others would make of his news. There was no way of knowing what had happened to pull Constantine from the Dream Realm like that, it could be something quite normal, or something more sinister going by what they knew of his life. He might find out something the next night, but it would mostly remain a mystery. Also, what would they make of the 'secret' that the Dark Soul was keeping?

After telling them his news Morpheus discovered that the group were concerned about the reasons for Constantine's quick exit and puzzled over what his secret could be.

'I really hope nothing bad has happened' commented Clea.

'With the type of life that boy has its likely something bad did happen' stated Geth.

'But he was excited' said Mary 'which must be a good sign.'

'I'm sure he's fine' Aaron said, 'Morpheus has been helping him so his life must be a little better and if he was excited about something then maybe something good is happening in his life.'

'The excitement might be a sign of something good happening but disappearing from the Dream Realm like that might not be' was Eddie's input.

There was more discussion, but no one had any answers, how could they.

'I'll just have to see if I can find anything out tonight' said Morpheus in conclusion.

Having walked for nearly two hours Con decided it was time to find somewhere to have breakfast. It took him another twenty minutes to find a suitable place and by then he was in need of a rest.

The café was small and a bit grubby looking, but he figured it would be cheap. It had only just opened for the day and being almost empty he had his pick of tables so chose a small two-seater in a corner. A young, bored looking waitress ambled over to him. She was very skinny and had her dark, greasy looking hair tied back in one of those high, tight ponytails which gave her elfin face a severe, sly look.

'Wot do ya want?' she asked not even looking at him.

It was the first time Con had ever ordered food for himself other than in fast food take away places and her manor made him a bit nervous, but he managed to stammer out his order of a full English breakfast and a mug of tea.

He had been to cafes before when he was younger with his Mum, and he had never been in a proper restaurant so this solitary, sit down meal was a new experience for him. He expected there would be more new experiences to come and not all of them would be as pleasant as this one, because even with the lacklustre waitress he was kind of enjoying himself.

The only other diners were a couple of middle-aged men in scruffy work clothes. They reminded Con of his work colleagues which depressed him for a few seconds before he remembered they were now his ex-work colleagues.

When the waitress plonked his meal down in front of him, he was shocked by how much food there was. He had cooked a full English for himself and his father on many occasions, but it had never been as big as this. It was a much larger meal than he was used to at that time of day, he usually only had cereal, but he had worked up an appetite with that long walk, still, he was not sure he would get through it all.

He bolted the first few mouthfuls down thinking only about how good the food was, but then as his hunger was sated a little, he slowed down and his mind wandered onto the subject of what to do next. His only plan at the moment was to find a cheap supermarket and get a few provisions which he would make last. This was a good meal to set him up, but after this he would eat sparingly and as cheaply as possible.

He felt he had walked far enough now not to bump into anyone he knew, not that he knew many people, and that made him feel strangely safe. But would he still feel safe when he was spending the night on the streets?

He was starting to feel full now but did not want to waste any of the food, so he started to eat really slowly, even if that meant the food was getting cold. He needed to pace himself to get it all eaten, plus he needed as long as possible to ponder his next move. After the supermarket he really needed to have some idea where he was headed. Should he stick to the populated parts of town, or head out to the suburbs a bit? In the town he would merge into the crowd more, but there were more people to be a danger to him. In the suburbs there would be less danger from other people, but he would stand out and might find trouble that way.

Then there was the question of distance and means of travel. Should he stay walking, which was more tiring but the cheaper option, or get a bus to the next town which would give him more distance but cost him money? How much did a bus ride cost anyway? Con had not been on a bus for years and this made him realise just how small and restricted his life had become. He walked to work and to the shops, then walked about locally on his day off, all within about a two-mile radius and that was it. How sad was that?

Maybe he could ask someone about the bus fares, but who? He glanced at the waitress who was now sat at an empty table staring into space. She did not come across as the friendly, helpful type but maybe if she was bored, she would welcome the chance of a chat.

'Excuse me' he said trying to attract her attention. And when that didn't work 'Hello, can you help me with something?'

For a few seconds he thought she had not heard him again, but then before he could try again, she got up and walked over to him.

'Ave ya finished?' she asked.

'Erm, no, not quite' he answered glancing at the remainder of his breakfast 'I just wondered if you could give me some information.'

'About wot?'

Her tone definitely was not friendly, but he felt he had to explain himself now.

'I'm err, new to the area and was just wondering what the bus fares are around here.'

She looked confused for a moment, but then to Con's surprise she took the seat opposite him.

'That's a bit of a weird question mate' she said, 'but I've had weirder I guess.'

She then proceeded to give him the information he needed telling him he would be best off getting a travelcard if it was more than a one-off ride he was thinking of.

'There's a newsagent just down the road what sells 'em' she told him.

'Okay, thanks' he said taken aback a little by how helpful she had been, and then she surprised his again by saying 'You've run away from home ain't ya?'

'What, no, no I haven't' he stammered, but she gave him a look that said, 'I've got your number' but what she actually said was 'I know the signs mate, I've been where you are.'

Con did not know what to say to that so just sat silent as the waitress continued.

'I can give ya some 'elpful tips if you like' she told him, and he just nodded. Tips would be good.

'Daytime it ain't too bad on the streets but nights can be fuckin' scary. I don't know 'ow much cash ya got, and don't worry ya don't 'ave to tell me, but if ya got enough you should go to that newsagent and get a fiver put on a travel card. 'Ave ya got enough?'

Con nodded.

'Good, cos I'm gonna give ya some directions and the bus numbers to get ya near to a shelter I know 'bout, I'll write it all down for ya' she said starting to scribble on her waitress pad.

'I erm, I was gonna find a cheap supermarket and get some supplies' he told her as she wrote.

'Nah, don't bovver 'bout that right now mate' she told him 'There ain't no supermarket that near 'ere anyways. Just go get a travel card and find the shelter okay.'

'Whereabouts is this shelter?' he asked worried that she would be sending him back towards home. But he need not have worried, it turned out the shelter was in a place he had vaguely heard of and knew was quite a way in the other direction.

'It'll take ya nearly two hours to get there' she told him 'But it's not like ya got anyfing else to do right?' and she smiled for the first time then. It looked kind of awkward on her, like she was not used to smiling, but it still made her look more friendly.

'Ya won't be able to get in 'til the evenin' but ya can hang 'bout nearby 'til they open up. They'll give ya somefing to eat and a bed for the night then chuck ya out in the morning. It can be a one off if ya like, or ya can go back as much as ya like. They'll 'elp ya with stuff too, advice and fings, they 'elped me' she gestured around her at the café 'this job ain't much but I got a room to stay in too so life ain't too bad, better than it was before anyways.'

'Thank you' he managed to say whilst trying to digest all the information and take in the fact that she was being so nice to him, he was not used to it.'

'Was it really bad at 'ome?' she asked him then.

All Con could manage was a nod. He felt close to tears and did not want to cry in front of her.

'Yeah, it was for me too, but I'm safe now, maybe not exactly 'appy, but I'll get there one day.'

Con felt bad for her then, and finally found his words.

'Thank you so much for all this, and I hope one day you are happy.'

'You too mate' she said, 'now how 'bout another cup of tea before ya set off, on me.'

'I can pay.'

'Nah, you save it where you can mate, nevva refuse a freebee, that's another tip.'

There was that underused smile once again and this time Con smiled back at her.

'Thanks.'

'Oh, and on the subject of cash, hide what you've got as best ya can okay. The shelters pretty safe but ya nevva know, and on the streets its best to keep it hid. Don't let no one else on the streets see ya buy nuffing, plead complete poverty right.'

'Okay, I will.'

When she brought his tea, she also gave him a greasy white paper bag.

'Ere's a sarnie to tide ya ova 'til tonight' she said.

'Thanks so much' he said.

'Its nuffin' really' she said with a shrug.

'But it is, I never expected help like this, you're a great person for helping me. I'll try to repay you one day I promise.'

'No need for that mate, but pass it on maybe, ya know, one day when you're betta off and you see someone else in trouble then you try 'n' 'elp 'em out yeah?'

'Okay, I promise to pass it on.'

'Good, now get that tea down ya and then and I'll go through the directions with ya, oh and ya betta use the bog before ya go.'

Forty minutes later Con was sitting on the first of two buses to the shelter when he realised that he had not asked the waitress her name.

The place that Con found himself in after the second bus ride was completely alien to him, but with the waitress' directions he managed to find the shelter reasonably easily. Now what to do? He had hours to kill, and he did not want to wander too far away in case he could not find his way back.

The shelter itself was on a small side street but it was off a long, busy high street so he decided to walk to the far end and see if he could find somewhere to wait. He was pretty tired by then but after sitting on buses for so long he really did need to stretch his legs.

He made metal notes of the shop names and other landmarks as he walked so he would recognise the way back, and when he came to a busy crossroads with traffic lights at the end of the street he stopped.

What way should he go? To his left and right were streets of shops and businesses. The one on his right went straight on for quite a way but the one on the left veered off to the right so he could not see where it went. The street straight ahead looked a bit different as there was a small block of flats on one side and a short row of terrace houses on the other. Beyond the flats he thought there might be more houses but after the nearer houses he could see green railings. Could it be a park? He decided to investigate.

When he reached the railings, he found that it was a park of sorts, but not much of one. It was basically a scruffy field with a crappy kid's playground at one end. There was one rickety looking bench but it was near the playground so he might look a bit dodgy if he sat there. Not that there were any kids there right now, but there might be later. No, he would look right out of place if he sat there doing nothing.

He looked down the road but all he could see was more terrace houses and a big, blocky building that could have been some sort of office or maybe a school, so he decided to turn back.

At the crossroads this time he decided to check out the road that went around a corner to see what was there because the other road was just shops and businesses as far as he could see. He was getting weary now and his backpack felt heavier and heavier, but he walked on in search of somewhere to rest.

Around the corner he saw a petrol garage on one side, and a Tesco Express on the other. The small supermarket could come in handy at a later date, but he was set for today what with the large breakfast, the sandwich the waitress had given him and the meal he would hopefully get at the shelter.

Beyond the garage there were more blocks of flats and on the supermarket side there was another row of terrace houses. Past the houses was a single storey building with a board outside which Con could not quite read so he decided to investigate.

When he got near enough to read the sign his heart lifted, it was a library. On closer inspection he saw that the library was only open until 2.00 that day but that would give him a couple of hours anyway. Besides staying longer than that might cause suspicion.

It was a small library so he would be a bit conspicuous, but he had a plan. He was used to wasting time in libraries without checking any books out.

As Con entered, he noted four people, a scruffy old man sitting reading a paper on one of three chairs arranged around a low table and a middle-aged woman perusing the shelves. The other two where members of staff, one, a tall, bony woman in a tweed skirt, old fashioned blouse and sensible shoes was shelving some books from a wooden trolley, the other, a young woman with limp, blonde hair sat on a high stool behind the counter by the door. She was wearing a cheap but fashionable dress over thick, black tights partnered with a pair of imitation Doc Martens that made her feet look too big for her body. As Con entered, she gave him a weak but friendly smile. He smiled back and asked, 'Can you point me in the direction of the books on art please.'

He followed her directions and found the art books discovering on the way a table ideal for his uses. It was his intention to look like a student doing a bit of research the old-fashioned way.

He had chosen art books because he found them more interesting to look at than books on computer programming or World War history and the like, he just hoped they had some good ones that he had not seen before in his local library. He doubted they would have much of a range in such a small library, but they must have something.

He managed to find a big, heavy tome on art history which was perfect. Taking it over to the desk like table he had spied he put his backpack on one of the four chairs set around it and sat on another one. Then he began to leaf through the book. It felt so good to sit down and rest for a bit. He wished he had some paper and a pen so he could look like he was taking notes, it would look more authentic, but then he had an idea. He began to rummage in his backpack as if he was looking for something just in case anyone was looking. Then feigning exasperation, he got up and walked over to the young woman behind the counter.

'I've forgotten my notebook and pen' he told her 'Do you have a pen and some paper I can use?'

'The pen I can do' she told him producing one from a draw under the counter 'but not sure about some paper' she continued as she hopped off the stool and bent to look under the counter 'we have membership cards but what about paper, let me see' then after a little rummaging 'oh here we go, these might work' and straightening up she proudly produced a small stack of pale blue A5 paper with some printing on. Something about a used book sale.

'They're out of date now' she told him turning the stack over 'so you can write on the back if that's any good.'

'That'll do fine, thanks' he said taking the paper and pen from her.

'You're welcome' she said as she perched herself back on the stool.

For the next hour Con leafed through the book looking at the pictures and occasionally copying down some of the text so he looked like he was making notes. He just hoped no one came near enough to read what he had written.

He looked up occasionally and had a long stretch giving him time to check out the other library users. There were not that many, but he got to do a little bit of people watching without appearing to do so.

After that hour he got up to put the book back on the shelf and picked another one, this one on Modern Art. He would do the same with this book until the library shut, but then what? He would still have several hours to kill, and he could not spend them all walking around.

Con left the library about ten minutes before it was due to close, not wanting the attention involved in being chucked out. He had a very weak plan of what to do next. After sitting in the library for all that time he was up for walking again so he started to stroll back towards the shelter with the intention of walking in the other direction to see what he could find.

He walked slowly past the shops and businesses trying to blend in with the other shoppers and people going about their business.

Halfway down he realised he was really thirsty so he stopped at a small convenience store and brought a cheap brand can of soft drink and continued to stroll along whilst he drank it. Then he realised he needed the toilet. The library had not had a public toilet and he had not seen one on his travels. What was he going to do? It was not like there were any convenient bushes to hide behind and he had not even gone past any alleyways he could nip down. He would just have to hold on until he found somewhere.

He was coming to the bend in the road now, so he hoped he would find somewhere to pass the time and to relieve himself.

And then there it was, the perfect place, a train station.

It was a big station with a large, paved area outside on which were a few public benches and a kiosk selling newspapers and confectionery. He would be able to sit there a while without looking too suspicious. Before doing that though he wanted to check out the interior of the station in the hopes of finding a public toilet.

The station was very busy and noisy. The concourse contained, over to the right, a small takeaway outlet, a newsagent, a coffee bar and a small branch of M&S. There was also a seating area set with electric boards showing train times and destinations set high above them, and along the left-hand side were the ticket machines and a ticket booth. At the far side were the barriers you needed a ticket to pass through, behind which he could just make out the sloped tunnel leading to the platforms. And there, in the far left corner was the hoped for public convenience.

After relieving himself Con decided to sit on one of the outside benches and watch the world go by. He entertained himself by playing a game with himself that he had recently remembered his Mum had liked to play with him.

The game was you chose a stranger passing by and judging by their appearance and demeanour you made up a little back story for them. He remembered that his Mum had been so good at it he had often wondered if she was actually psychic rather than just being good at making up stories. He had mostly been content to listen to his Mum's ideas but had piped up with a few things himself, usually tagged on to something she had started.

For instance, his Mum would say something like 'See that old lady over there in the green coat and red hat? Well, she looks so angry because her neighbour still hasn't fixed his side of the garden fence and his dog keeps getting into her garden and trampling her flowers.' And then he would add something like 'And doing its business on her lawn.' Then the two of them would giggle.

They always kept the stories light like that, and it was a fun game. It was not quite the same playing on his own, but it passed the time.

After a while Con decided on a change of scene and moved to the seating area inside the station, but first he took a stroll around M&S and then the newsagent before going to sit on one of the seats pretending to be looking for his train time on the board just in case someone was watching him. He then continued to sit there as if waiting for his train.

He had been there for about half an hour when he noticed that someone had left a newspaper on one of the seats, so he changed his seat, picked up the paper and put in it his backpack. He figured it would come in handy later to keep him occupied or make him look less conspicuous.

Soon after that Con decided to move back to the outside seating area where it was quieter and eat the sandwich the waitress had given him.

He spent the rest of the afternoon and early evening switching from the two seating areas breaking them up with the occasional wander down the road either side window shopping.

Geth had just finished his usual monthly telephone meeting with the manager of his tattoo studio.

'How did it go?' asked Eddie as Geth came back into the art room/lounge to re-join him and Clea.

'Fine thanks.'

'He still buying your story?'

'Yeah, I think so.'

'You'll have to rethink it again soon you know.'

'I know but it's hard to think of something convincingly long term.'

'You should get Sofia to have a chat with the brains at The Foundation, they're used to this sort of thing so I'm sure they'll have some good ideas.'

'Yeah, good idea, I'll ask her.'

Geth was the only one of the new Dreambringers who had owned their own business and premises in his old life. When he had taken up the call to become a Dreambringer he had left his tattoo business Studio Ink in the capable hands of his employee Chris James.

At first, after meeting up with the other Dreambringer candidates at Artfest he had simply told Chris that he was staying away for a few days to do a large commission piece that he had been offered at the festival. Then, after passing the necessary tests and agreeing to take on his role as a Dreambringer he had given the further excuse of having received other commissions on the back of that and was doing a kind of tattooing tour.

Then when that excuse grew thin, he told Chris that he now needing an extended holiday and time to think about what he wanted to do with his career next. He had left it vague and although out of character Chris had accepted things as they were. It helped that he was obviously enjoying being in charge of the studio whilst his boss was away. He had been given free reign in employing another tattoo artist which they had needed even before Geth left, and in completing their apprentice Rick's training. He also got to stay in Geth's flat above the studio rent free so that was another reason for going along with Geth's vaguely explained absence.

Geth really did need to think of a more long-term reason for his absence now though because he was likely to be living at the Gateway for several years to come.

'Do you miss working in your studio?' Clea asked him then interrupting his reverie.

'No not really' Geth told her sounding surprised by his own answer 'I was getting a bit bored to be honest' he continued 'the tattoos people wanted done were getting very samey and boring, plus my back was playing me up.'

'I didn't know you had back trouble.'

'Yeah, just wear and tear you know from years bent over people tattooing, especially the early years before I got the decent chairs and stuff.'

'How is it now?'

'Better.'

'That's good lovey, so you're happy just doing the odd tattoo for Eddie and maybe for us others then?'

'Yes, it's ideal really, I still get to keep my hand in, but I also get to work on my paintings, and now my flash art for this possible book.'

'Oh yes, the book, it sounds like a great idea.'

'Thanks, but why all the questions, are you worried I'm not happy here?'

'No, it's not that, I was just curious. I know it's not the same but I don't miss my old work either. I used to enjoy making people happy with my dressmaking and embroidery, but I can still make you lot and myself stuff. Besides, Sofia says if I wanted to go back to embroidering cushions and stuff like that the foundation could help me sell it online. I could even make clothes to order as long as it didn't involve fittings so I'm sorted, but like Eddie suggested you should talk to Sofia about your long-term excuse for being away from your business.'

Just then Sofia walked into the room.

'Ahh, just the lady we needed' exclaimed Clea.

'Oh yes' said Sofia 'What for?'

And so Geth told her.

'Looks like I have some work to do' stated Sofia when he had finished 'so I'd better get on with it' she said before heading off to the office opposite.

Ten minutes later Sofia returned.

'Okay, it's all in hand' she told them 'The big brains up at head office are going to think of the best excuse for you Geth and get back to us. They're used to this sort of thing remember so it's no problem. It'll be sorted I promise, they just need time to work out the best options. They'll only be suggestions; you won't be made to do something you don't want to do. The final decision will have to be mutual.'

'Great, thanks' said Geth.

It was still almost an hour before the shelter was due to open but Con decided to head back there and wait outside. He was not sure how busy it got and if they had to turn people away when it was full.

When he got there, he found a small queue had already formed outside so he joined the end of it to wait.

The queue began to build behind him. Some people chatted, some muttered to themselves, but most, including Con, waited quietly.

When the shelter opened Con filed in with the others. He was asked a few basic questions by a friendly, middle aged Asian woman with a clipboard who also told him the procedures and explained the rules. He was then allocated a bed for the night and instructed to join the queue for some food.

The food was basic, but descent and Con kept to himself whilst he ate although there were plenty of people around him. Con had never been good with strangers; he was not even that comfortable around people he knew. He noticed that the tables seemed to be split between those occupied by the chatty ones and those where the quiet ones sat.

One of the things he had been told when he entered was that if he wanted any information or help with something specific, he need only ask one of the staff. But although he did have a lot of questions, he did not feel up to talking to anyone about them tonight, maybe tomorrow he thought. He would also have liked to ask one of the other homeless people what they did with their time during the day, but he could not quite pluck up the courage to do that either.

Later, when he settled down for the night on the camp bed provided, despite the noise and unfamiliar surroundings, he actually fell asleep quite quickly. Maybe it was tiredness after a long, stressful day, or maybe it was because he was eager to dream.

When Con entered the Dream Realm Morpheus was there waiting for him.

The supercharged Dreambringer noticed the change in Con's emotions immediately. He could sense that the boy was sleeping somewhere unfamiliar and the feelings this was evoking in him. Those feelings being a mixture of fear, excitement and indecision. Was this to do with the secret that the soul held Morpheus wondered and did this effect how he should approach the dreaming soul this time?

Morpheus figured that this Dark Soul was beyond being scared off now, it was just a case of trying to glean as much information as he could in order to help him. Therefore, it was time to try a few questions.

He started with a simple greeting however finding connecting with the Soul easy now.
'Hello, how are you?'

There was a long pause before he received an answer, but he knew it was not due to a reluctance to communicate but more that the Soul was confused about how he was.

'I'm fine' was the eventual, uninformative, reply.

'What's changed?' probed Morpheus, then sensing uncertainty he communed 'You can trust me.' But there was no reply. He was sensing a conflict within the Soul as he tried to decide how, or even if he should answer.

'I'll wait until you are ready.' Morpheus communed deciding to give the Soul some time and not put too much pressure on him. For the time being he decided to set about his usual task of bringing the Soul a dream. He would start with the usual comfort dream of his mother and maybe the Soul would loosen up and communicate more later.

On his next attempt Morpheus tried a slightly different tack.
He sent the question 'Are you in danger?'
And received the worrying reply 'Maybe.'
'In what way?'

There was no reply and Morpheus sensed the barriers going up again. He would try again later, for now he brought the Soul dreams of safety and strength. As before he was not sure how the thoughts of safety and strength he conveyed would be portrayed in the Soul's dreams, but he was hopeful that they would work.

He concentrated his healing light on the Soul as it dreamt and then as the night drew to a close, he tried one last time to communicate with him. He probed with easy, gentle questions but learnt nothing new. Then just as he was about to give up, he received a faint answer, like it had escaped from the Soul without him wanting it to

'I am lost.'

What exactly did the Soul mean Morpheus wondered. Was he physically or mentally lost, or both? Either way it was something to work on. How could he know what sort of dreams to bring this Soul when it was so vague and guarded? He tried further probing but got no more details and when he probed the Soul's feelings, he could only detect a minor undertone of fear which was good. What he mainly detected was uncertainty.

His next communication to the Soul was not a question, it was a reassurance.

'I am here for you; you can trust me.'

Morpheus then set about bringing him a dream to convey how the Soul had a friend who would help him with whatever he was struggling with. He hoped it would mean that the Soul would learn to trust him in time and know he was there for him always through his dreams.

Morpheus hoped that upon waking from the dream Con would spend the day feeling like he had a friend he could confide in even if he did not know who or where that friend was. It might not make sense to Con when he was awake but if he lived with the memory of that dream for that day Morpheus hoped he would be more receptive when entering the Dream Realm the next night and that he would let his barriers down more.

When Con woke up that morning, he did not really remember his dreams at first, but unbeknownst to him and to Morpheus he had been given much more than they both realised.

Sofia was looking for Geth and came across Clea in the kitchen making bread. She was obviously happy in her work humming to herself as she kneaded some dough. And Sofia knew from experience that the bread would be delicious, Clea was a very talented lady.

'Do you know where Geth is, he wasn't in the art room when I looked in just now?' Sofia asked Clea.

'He's out on the patio with Eddie having a break, why?'

'I have some news for him about this thing with his business.'

'Ooh the big brains have come up with an idea then, what is it?'

'I think I should tell Geth first don't you.'

'Sorry, yes of course, but just let me put this dough in the proving drawer, then I can come with you and be there when you tell him?'

'Why?'

'Because I'm nosey and knowing him he'll tease me by keeping it to himself. I'm just really curious to know what they've come up with because with Geth being the way his is it's hard to think of something plausible to anyone who knows him.'

'How do you mean?'

'Well, he's not the sort to fall head over heels in love and make dramatic changes to his life because of it is he?'

'I don't know, anyone can fall in love at any time and with the most unexpected people.'

Clea noticed a strange nuance in the way Sofia said that last comment, but she was too wrapped up in talking about Geth to go into it.

'No, a new woman in his life is not a good excuse for Geth, and the story used by most of us that we were offered a place at a charity funded Art Commune and couldn't refuse it wouldn't sit well either even if it is the partly the truth.'

'I see what you mean, he was a hard sell to start with.'

'Exactly, because when people think of Art Communes they think of hippies and new agers right, and Geth is neither of those.'

'No, he definitely isn't.'

'Thats why I'm so curious about what they've come up with because I've been wracking my brains and haven't come up with anything.'

'Me either, but luckily the Foundation have people who are good at this sort of thing so as long as Geth's happy they have a solution.'

Sofia had to smile at Clea's cheek, but she did as she was told and waited until Clea had put the bread away to prove, then they went out to the patio together where the two men were having a beer and a chat.

'Hello ladies, what can we do for you?' asked Eddie when he saw them emerge through the open French doors.

'It's what we can do for you actually, or rather for Geth' Sofia told him.

'The Foundation has come up with a story for you' Clea interjected then with her hand over her mouth 'Oops sorry Sofia, this is your thing.'

Sofia was not offended by the older woman's behaviour, in fact she found it amusing, so in a mock stern voice she said 'Yes, thank you Clea I will take it from here.'

Clea smiled at her in appreciation of her understanding.

'Okay, so what have the brains at the Foundation come up with?' asked Geth.

'They suggest that you tell Chris that you have been offered a job abroad. At first you can say that it's a six month 'guest' slot at a tattoo studio and you felt like a change so couldn't say no. Then after those six months are up you can tell him that you like it so much there you are going to buy a share in that studio and stay on.'

'Whereabouts abroad am I supposed to be going?' Geth interjected.

'Well, for the most part that's up to you. The Foundation are going to email over a list of places where they have Foundation members who own a tattoo studio, and you can choose the place that sounds most like you. It being a real studio will make it all the more plausible.'

'Are there many to choose from?'

'A fair amount, yes.'

'What happens when I've chosen? How does it work exactly?'

'You give the name, number and email address for your chosen studio to Chris. The Foundation member who owns the studio covers for you if Chris calls. He then passes a message on for you to phone Chris back. You do this via The Foundation so they can make it look like you are calling from that country.'

'Sounds a bit complicated.'

'It is a bit, but the Foundation are very good at managing this sort of thing. Having said that they prefer if you encourage Chris to use email rather than the phone as that's less complicated.'

'Will I be the one receiving and answering the email or will the Foundation deal with it?' Geth's tone suggested he didn't like the idea of the Foundation dealing with it.'

'It's up to you. They can re-route them direct to you to deal with or they can deal with them for you, or some sort of compromise in between. It's something that will get sorted as you go along.'

'Okay, good.'

'Now, they have pointed out that once we're past the six months and you tell him you're staying away indefinitely you need to make a big decision, and depending on what you decide all this business with phone calls and email may not be relevant. What you will need to decide is what to do about Studio Ink. At the moment you have a good system going with Chris, but once you tell him you're staying abroad he's going to want to know where he stands.'

'Yeah, I see what you mean.'

'In the next six months you are going to have to weigh up your options.'

'Which are?'

'At the moment you still take a percentage of the profits with the proviso that Chris gets to stay in your flat rent free, so he gains too as he's the one doing the work.'

'Right, yeah, or rather the Foundation take my cut you mean.'

'Yes, but you know the money goes toward your upkeep here and securing your future when you leave here right?'

'Yes, I know, I didn't mean it as a complaint I was just getting the facts straight.'

'Okay, good, so when Chris is made aware that your absence is going to be long term or even permanent you need to decide between one of two options, but I must point out here that either option would make it difficult for you to go back to your business when you finish your work here. How do you feel about that?'

'I'm not a sentimental guy so I have no problem giving up the Studio as such, but what do I do when I leave here if the studio is no longer an option?'

'Whatever you want to do, within reason, and the Foundation will help you with it. Why don't I explain the options and that will make things a bit clearer for you?'

'Okay.'

'Option one, rather than taking a share of the profits you become the owner/landlord and hand the running of the business over to Chris completely but charge him rent for the studio and the flat. Then any profit goes to him and the other tattoo artists working there, and the rent money goes to the Foundation fund that will ultimately help you when you retire.'

'And option two?'

'You put the Studio and flat up for sale giving Chris first option to buy. Then the money from the sale goes into the Foundation fund. With option one there would be the possibility of going back to the Studio when you retire but it would be awkward as Chris would have been living there and running the place for years. With option two you are obviously giving up the Studio for good.'

'To be honest I think I'd rather just be rid of it, but I don't think Chris will be able to get the money together to buy it and I'd hate for him to get chucked out when someone else buys it.'

'No need to worry, if you want Chris to buy it the Foundation can arrange that.'

'What? How?'

'They'll use one of their property companies to go in and value the business etc, then they can recommend a mortgage lender to Chris who will obviously be part of the Foundation too and so they will give him guaranteed good terms etc. He won't know they are linked though.'

'And if he doesn't go for it?'

'We would deal with that problem if it arises, but don't you think he'll want the business?'

'I think he'll jump at the chance if he thinks its viable for him.'

'We'll make sure its viable for him then, so the problem won't arise.'

'What if he fucks up and the business goes bust?'

'The Foundation, like other big businesses, can take the hit, the money is small in the scheme of things to them, it wouldn't be a problem I can assure you. Anyway, if Chris does start to get into trouble, they'll help him out before it gets bad if he lets them so it's unlikely he'll go out of business.'

'They really have got it all sorted haven't they?'

'They've been doing this for a long time so yes.'

'So whatever option I go for I'm still covered when I retire, even if the business goes bust?'

'Definitely, yes. As you were told when you were first initiated the Foundation does take all your assets, but then whilst a Dreambringer you live at their expense and want for nothing. Then when you retire, they make sure you are set up for life.'

'And we can choose what set up for life involves?'

'Yes. If you want a job within the Foundation its yours or if you want to go out on your own with a new tattoo studio for instance, you will be given the resources to do so.'

'What if you ask to be set up as a millionaire, living the jet set life with boats and cars etc?'

'That may be a bit too much, and I did say 'within reason'. But as far as I know no one has ever demanded that, I don't think the kind of people who become Dreambringers as the sort to want that sort of lifestyle, do you?'

'No, you're right, that was a stupid question.'

'Don't worry about it.'

'What about those like Aaron who come into this without any assets? I know he'll be looked after too but will his 'fund' be less than others? We all came in with different levels of assets so how does it work exactly?'

'The Foundation run many profitable businesses some of the profits from which go into the retirement fund for those that have no assets when they join. Plus, if they make any money from their artwork whilst here that goes towards in too as it does for all of you. Believe me it is all fair and above board; you all get however much you need for your life after Dreambringing. If you really want more details, I'm sure someone at the Foundation can explain it further.'

'There's no need for that, I trust the Foundation and to be honest my heads spinning with too much information already.'

'That's understandable, therefore, regarding making your decision there's no rush. The Foundation are sending over the list of tattoo studios abroad that can be used as your cover tomorrow, but you can take all the time you need to make your decisions after that.'

'Okay, I'll give it some thought.'

'And if you have any more questions don't be afraid to ask me and if I don't know the answer, I'll ask someone who does.'

'Thanks.'

Eddie and Clea had stayed quiet throughout this exchange but now Eddie said, 'Makes me glad I came into this with nothing.'

'I must admit I kinda envy Aaron now' said Geth 'he hasn't got to worry about all this shit.'

'Mary too' stated Clea 'her flat was rented so all she had to sort was her car. Max has a house like me but no business, so his situation is less complicated too.'

'Are you going to continue to rent your house the whole time you're here, then go to live there again when you retire?' Eddie asked Clea.

'I haven't quite decided yet lovey. I feel the need to have it there to fall back on now, but I may change my mind over time.'

'It's a hard decision, but at least it's not as complicated as the business stuff.'

'Yes, thank goodness' and then to Geth 'If you need someone to sound off against regarding your business you can talk it through with me any time.'

'Same goes for me' added Sofia.

'Thanks.'

Clea had a feeling Geth would not take either of them up on their offer, he was not the chatty sort, but the offer was there.

'How about we change the subject to something less mind bending' suggested Eddie 'give your brains a rest and you can think on it in the morning when you're fresher.'

'What shall we talk about instead?' asked Sofia.

'Well, me and Geth were having a great conversation before all this started.'

'Oh yes lovey, what about?' enquired Clea.

'What was the best beer we've ever tasted' Eddie answered with a cheeky grin.

Sofia groaned and Clea laughed and though they did not carry on that particular conversation the mood was lightened and they found other lest mind bending things to chat about.

When Con left the Shelter that morning it was too early for the library to be open, so he headed for the train station. Although he had slept well, especially considering he had been in a strange, noisy place, Con felt fuzzy headed and not quite awake. He also felt a nagging at the back of his mind like there was something he was supposed to remember but could not.

Con walked slowly not really taking in his surroundings and when he got to the very busy train station, he plonked himself down on one of the outside benches hoping the fresh air would eventually clear his head.

He sat there going over his evening and night at the shelter hoping to jog his memory regarding this nagging thought. He searched his memory for what had happened but nothing he remembered seemed relevant. Nothing really remarkable had happened except for the general fact that he had spent the night in a very unfamiliar place.

He had not really spoken to anyone or done anything but eat and sleep. He was, however, aware that he'd coped with the strange situation a lot better than he had expected. He had thought he would lay awake partly in fear and partly just because of the strangeness of it all, but he had slept fine and had not felt the vulnerability he had expected too. He had even had some good dreams though this was more a feeling than a memory because he could not recall any specifics.

Dreaming was still a novelty to him, and he began to question now why he had suddenly started dreaming again. Or was it just that he had started to remember his dreams recently? What had he dreamt last night? He thought now that he had dreamt of his Mum again, of the two of them singing in the woods, or was he just remembering dreams from other nights? He was sure he had dreamt last night and tried to recall them now, but all he could get were vague feelings of being in a place where he felt safe.

He always felt safe in the dreams he had of his Mum in the woods (a feeling he was unused to in waking life) but there had been more to the dreams he'd had last night, he was sure.

Think, think, what was it? he thought mentally banging his head.

Then suddenly something occurred to him, there had been someone else in the dream, but when he tried to recall who that someone had been he came up against a mental brick wall again. He tried harder and it came to him that sometimes the person in the woods with him was his Mum and sometimes it was someone else, but who? Maybe it was not a real person and that was why it was hard to recall. So, he tried to remember what the other person looked like rather than their name. Instead of either he got a word; 'friend.' He had a friend. The thought made him smile and he decided not to strain his mind any further. He would just be content to think that he had a friend, even if they were only an imaginary dream friend, it was a comfort somehow.

A short while later Con realised that he had been sitting there in a daze for so long that it was now well passed opening time for the library. Getting a little shakily to his feet he headed there. His mind still felt a little foggy, but he managed to find his way back to the library and start the same pantomime as the day before. He still had some of the scrap paper he had been given last time, and he had kept the pen too. He hoped he would not be pulled up on stealing the pen but was ready to play innocent if need be.

"I'm a student studying, there's nothing odd in that" he kept telling himself.

After about an hour Con found he was feeling restless. Last time he had spent hours there quite content, but this time he was having trouble concentrating on his fake research. His mind kept wandering back to the friend from his dreams and now he realised that there was a place name involved somewhere too. It was there, at the back of this mind somewhere, the name of a place he would be safe and where he had a friend.

He tried to tell himself that it was just a silly dream, it was not important, and he should forget about it, he had more important things to work out, like how long should he stay around here using the shelter. But it was no good, his mind continued to worry over remembering names.

'Are you okay?'

Con jumped at the sound of the voice and his heart was hammering in his chest as he looked up to see who had spoken. It was the blonde library assistant with the fake Doc Martens. She stood over him with an armful of books and he cowered a little thinking that she was annoyed and wanted her pen back, but then he remembered she had asked if he was okay but as he'd taken so long to answer her, she now added 'It's just you were muttering to yourself and looking perturbed.'

'I was looking what?' Con answered feeling dazed.

'Perturbed, you know like nervous, agitated, that sort of thing.'

What Con wanted to say was 'get you with your fancy words' but what he actually said was 'I'm fine thanks, just studying hard.'

'Okay, well if you need anything just ask' she told him looking unconvinced.

Then to Con's relief she went off to shelve the books she was carrying leaving him feeling even more restless.

He made himself stay and keep up the student pretence for another half an hour so it would not look off, then he put away the book he had been pretending to study and left making sure he returned the pen this time.

The noisiness of the train station may mean it would be harder to think, but he thought he would look less odd there if he was sat staring into space. He was also less likely to be approached and disturbed by anyone.

After their animated conversation out on the patio Clea Sofia, Eddie and Geth had moved to the art room to get on with their artwork. After a while Clea left the room to go and put her now perfectly risen bread dough into the oven. As she was doing so, she remembered something she had been thinking about earlier whilst she kneaded the bread just before Sofia came in and she lost her train of thought.

It had suddenly dawned on her that no one outside of the Foundation had made a scheduled or surprise visit to the Gateway since her group had been there. Although regular visitors were not encouraged, occasional visits were allowed so no visitors in over nine months seemed strange.

Whilst all the trouble with Talionis was going on there were definitely no visitors allowed, and for the first few weeks after, as the new Dreambringers settled in, this rule had remained. For a few months now however, visitors had been permitted but none of the new Dreambringers had wanted any.

Most artists who became Dreambringers tended not to have much in the way of close family or friends, it was one of the elements that made them a candidate for the job. After all, if you had a close family, you would be less inclined to want to spend years away from them with only infrequent visits. It would also be harder to make excuses that people close to them would accept.

In the case of this new group of Dreambringers Aaron, Clea, Geth and Max had no family to speak of. Aaron also had no real friends due to his nomadic lifestyle. Clea had some friends, but they were from back in her arts and crafts days and she had seen little of them since she met her late husband Andrew and settled down. Andrew had been all she needed and since his death she had not made any new friends.

Although Geth got along with his employee Chris the two men did not socialise outside of work so were not what you would call friends exactly. Geth had other acquaintances within the tattoo world but did not count any of them as friends either.

In Max's case he had always been a bit of a loner and after losing both his parents nearly six years ago he had been even more of one. He was liked by the staff and kids at the youth centre where he had until recently volunteered but he had no real friends.

Mary was also a bit of a loner. She had been friendly with a girl at work called Stella, but they had not really seen each other outside of work and she had no other friends. Mary was, however, the only member of the group who had family. She had a mother and a stepfather, but although strictly speaking they were close relatives in reality they were not that close.

Mary's Mum Annabel had always resented the restrictions that having Mary had put on her life. A single mother at aged eighteen she had acted more like an older sister than a mother, often telling people, especially potential boyfriends, that was the relationship between them. She had often left Mary alone at home whilst she went out partying right from when Mary was far too young to be left alone.

Annabel had met Phillip, a businessman ten years her senior, when she was thirty-six and Mary was eighteen, and after a whirlwind romance Phillip had become her stepfather. The couple had been so wrapped up in each other that rather than becoming a real family Mary had been for the most part ignored. Phillip had a good job and for once Mary and her mother did not lack for the material things in life, but Mary was still made to feel like a burden.

Mary was working in the book shop by then and her so called parents, eager to be rid of her offered to subsidise the rent on a small flat and buy her a car. It was a situation a lot of teenagers would love, and Mary did appreciate the freedom of it, but rather than showing love as it would in a usual parent/child relationship it only highlighted the fact that they did not want Mary around.

They still retained a monthly family dinner, but it was the only time outside of Birthdays and Christmas that Mary saw them, and it was a bit of a torturous affair for all of them.

When Mary had phoned her Mum to tell her that she had taken a place in an art commune and so was giving up her job and the flat at first Annabel had scornfully said 'What talent do you have to offer an art commune.' She had gone on to tell Mary it was a risk giving up her job for a silly art commune, and that she was an ungrateful little cow for giving up the flat they paid for. But then as Mary explained more her Mum had changed her tune as she realised that this move meant her daughter would no longer be her problem financially or otherwise and she suddenly became all for the idea.

Mary had spoken to her mum on the telephone twice during her months at the Gateway. Both calls had been at Mary's instigation and lasted all of five minutes. Her Mum had shown no interest in what she was doing and definitely had not mentioned the possibility of a visit. But then Mary had no desire to see her or her stepfather either, therefore with no visits for the Foundation to worry about everyone was happy. Mary intended to continue to call her Mum occasionally but that was all she wanted, and she expected nothing more from her Mum.

Bearing all that in mind it was no surprise that none of them had received any visitors.

As for Eddie and Mason they too had no one outside of the Dreambringer world to visit them and were likewise happy with that. The family they had found at The Gateway had been more than enough.

If any of them did at any time want an occasional visitor there was a protocol to follow. A strict date and time had to be arranged and no overnight stays were allowed. If the visitor lived far enough away to warrant an overnight stay a hotel would be arranged.

The reasons of these limited visits were not so much due to a fear that the visitor would find out their friend/family members real reason for living at the art commune (that would be impossible for them to discover) but more that a visitor would disrupt the Dreambringer's routine and too many disruptions would be detrimental to their 'work'. For this reason, when a visit was arranged a Marshal would be present during the visit to help the Dreambringers deal with any awkward questions or situations.

Of course, there were other types of visitors, for instance the art communes were routinely visited by the Marshal that covered their house as well as the boost giving visits of the Dreamwishers. But as these were Foundation members these visits were no problem.

Other Foundation staff like accountants, lawyers and of course doctors occasionally visited but where possible their work was done over the phone or by email.

There was no post delivered to the houses, the few items of mail that were sent went to post office boxes and were collected by the Wardens. In this day and age goods are easily ordered online and delivered but this sort of service is rarely used by the art communes. One reason for this is that the houses tend to be in remote, hard to find areas making delivery difficult even in these days of satnav. The other reason being that there was no real need for it. Anything needed that the Warden could not purchase at nearby shops was ordered through the Foundation who had employees whose job it was to purchase things and deliver them when required.

As for Dreambringers leaving their art commune to visit family and friends this was only allowed in special circumstances. These being the illness or death of a relative, or on occasion a wedding or christening. However, with few family ties within the Dreambringer community these visits were rarely needed.

On the rare occasions when this was necessary a Dreamwisher team would be sent to the house to make up for the deficit created by a Dreambringers absence as even for a day it could have a detrimental effect on their Eternals.

Over the years it had been found that Dreambringers suffered almost as much as their Eternals if apart from each other for long and this in turn had an effect on the dreamers they helped.

This was something that Mason was all too aware of after the harrowing experience he and his Dreambringer group had suffered because of Talionis.

Dreambringers were not completely confined to their home and that of their Eternals, they were allowed to leave their houses for brief trips out to the shops or if they fancied an occasional meal out or a visit to the pub or cinema.

To some people this may sound extremely restrictive but those called to become Dreambringers were rarely unhappy with their lifestyle. Whilst a member of the group often accompanied the house Warden on essential shopping trips or went on the occasional luxury item shopping trip themselves, the Dreambringers were usually happy to socialise with each other in their home rather than venturing out to other social establishments.

Each Dreambringer house was large and set in ample grounds so the occupants could get plenty of exercise and fresh air. Some houses even had gyms if that was what the occupants wanted.

All in all, the life of a Dreambringer was strange but good.

As Clea pondered the groups lack of visitors she remembered something from a dream she'd had that morning. It was one of those buried memories that popped up when you were not really thinking about it and in Clea's case this sort of thing had a special meaning due to her particular Dreambringer talent.

Now the question was should she share the information she was now interpreting from her dream with her fellow housemates? And the answer was of course she should.

Not wanting to have to repeat herself Clea decided to save telling anyone about her dream until they were all together at dinner. For now, she returned to the art room and continued to work with the others.

Con spent some time sitting on an outside bench first. His mind was still foggy, and he was feeling mentally tired after all the brain strain from trying to remember his illusive dream. He had therefore decided to give it a rest for a while and just sit and watch the world go by. His thinking was that if he stopped thinking about it too hard it might just come to him.

After a while he decided on a change of scene and went inside the station. He was also a little hungry and thirsty so decided to get himself a cheap lunch. Con took a stroll around the shops inside the station to weigh up his options and in the end decided on a basic, cheap burger from the takeaway shop and the lowest-priced, litre bottle of water from the newsagents. Sitting on one of the seats in sight of the timetable boards he slowly ate his burger and sipped from the bottle of water. He did not have a big appetite so the burger would be sufficient for a while, but he wanted the drink to last.

When he had finished eating, he sat staring up at the boards without actually reading them. He let his vision blur and his mind wander. What he really should be doing was thinking about what his plans were, but today his mind felt too sluggish and foggy to think about that sort of thing. All he managed to decide was to go back to the shelter later and this time he would ask the staff for some advice. That was good enough for now, let someone else do the thinking for him.

For now, he went back to people watching.

A little while later he thought he should maybe get up and go for a walk but found that he just did not have the inclination, it was like he had taken root in that seat and that it was where he should stay for now. Why that was he did not know, it was probably just laziness but right then he did not really care.

Another hour went by, and he still had not moved but he had devised a new game. He would pick out a person headed for the ticket barrier, then look up at the timetable boards and try to guess which train they were going to catch and which of the stops they would get off at. It was pointless and silly, but it passed the time and did not take much thinking. It was just look at a person, look at the board and pick a random destination.

Con's next stranger pick was a young man dressed all in black with spiked up, dyed blonde hair and lots of piercings. Con thought that he might be wearing eyeliner too and wondered if he thought himself a goth, emo or punk, but either way Con thought he looked kind of cool. But where was he going? Looking up at the boards he began to scan through the destinations of the trains due to depart in the next ten minutes. In the second destinations list a name suddenly jumped out at him, but not like before. With the others he had just scanned until he saw a place name and thought that will do, they are going there. This time however it was like he recognised the place name even though he knew for a fact he had never heard of it before.

"What the hell?" he thought *"How can that be?"*

But then it just got weirder, because his next thought was *"I need to go there."*

What the hell was going on in his mind? Why would he want to go to a place he had never heard of? He could not let the feeling go though, and on impulse he was suddenly on his feet heading for the ticket booth.

A bored looking, middle-aged man with a bushy moustache sat behind the glass and Con purchased a single ticket to the unheard of destination from him like he was just a normal passenger. But this was far from normal. He was wasting his limited funds on a train ticket for no good reason. The thing was part of him knew this was the right thing to do and it was that part that was urging him on.

He only had five minutes until the train departed now and he needed to get to the platform so once through the ticket barrier he started running. This meant that he had no more time to think about what he was doing, he just did it, and before he knew it, he was sat on that train headed to somewhere that he somehow felt he needed to be. The thing was that now he was on the train he felt even more certain that he was doing the right thing.

Part of him still thought he was silly; how likely was it that there would be a homeless shelter in the place he was headed? He would probably end up spending the night on the streets, and he had no idea what sort of streets these would be. Well, he would soon find out that was for sure and the part of him that was certain he was headed in the right direction told him not to worry about it.

Just then he noticed another passenger on the train, the boy with the spiky blonde hair, and he had to laugh. At least he had got one thing right.

Clea waited until everyone had finished their meal before starting her waited for conversation.

'I need to tell you about a dream I had last night' she began 'or rather the feeling that the dream left me with.'

The group often discussed their dreams, but they sensed immediately that this dream of Clea's could be important.

'Okay, go ahead' prompted Max.

'First, I just want to say this; do you all realise that we have had no visitors since we've been here, us seven Dreambringers I mean. I'm not counting the brief ins and outs of Foundation drivers and of course Sofia and Morpheus, I don't really count them as visitors, they're more family. But it's a fact that we have had no visitors.'

'Well, yes' said Geth 'why would we?

'Does anyone here even have someone they would want to come for a visit?' added Aaron. The others indicated a no with a word or a shake of their head.

'So why point it out Clea?' asked Mason.

'Because I believe that we will be having a visitor soon.'

'What? Who?' enquired Mary.

'Did you invite someone?' queried Eddie.

'There are no visits scheduled' stated Sofia.

'I'm pretty sure this isn't a scheduled visit' Clea told them 'Well not exactly anyway.'

'Stop beating around the bush and tell us what you're on about' said Geth.

'I don't remember any details of my dream, which is unusual these days in itself, but my dream has left me with a strong feeling that we will be receiving a visitor soon.'

'And you believe this is a premonition dream?' enquired Sofia.

'I do, yes.'

'That could be very ordinary or very ominous' said Aaron 'I mean with it being you, the Seer of Dreams, it its more than likely going to happen, but the question is who is the visitor, and what do they want?'

'Who it is I definitely can't tell you I'm afraid. As to whether this visit is ordinary or ominous all I can say is I feel that whilst this visitor poses no real threat themselves the fact that they are coming here may be troubling, no that's the wrong word, I just mean that their appearance here will cause disruption.'

'How do you mean?' enquired a nervous sounding Max.

'I can't really explain it except to say that I feel this visit will herald another first in the Dreambringer world.'

'When will this visitor arrive?' asked Eddie.

'I don't know exactly, but it will be soon.'

'Are they just going to rock up at the gates and ask to be let in, or are they going to take us unawares like Talionis did?' Mason wanted to know.

'I'm sorry I really don't know.'

'But they won't take us unawares now will they' stated Eddie 'because we know they're coming. The security here is tighter now, an alarm will sound if they get through the perimeter, and we can spot them on the security cameras.'

'That's all well and good, but what do we do when we spot them, or if they blatantly buzz in at the gate do we let them in?' asked Geth.

'We bring them to the house and find out what they want?' stated Eddie.

'What if they're dangerous?' asked Mary.

'Clea doesn't think they are,' said Eddie.

'No offence Clea, but that's not a guarantee' Aaron pointed out.

'No offence taken lovey, but I think I'd sense it if the visitor was dangerous.'

'Should we let the Foundation know about this?' asked Sofia.

She got a no from Geth, Eddie and Clea, a yes from Max, Aaron and Mary, and a maybe from Mason. As to Sofia herself being a Marshal her training meant she should immediately think yes, but she was wavering for some reason. But then the only person who had not spoken so far made his feelings known.

'No' said Morpheus 'I say we wait and see. I trust Clea's judgement on this and if the visitor is no danger we can handle them ourselves and then let the Foundation know once we have found out what they want.'

'I'm not sure that's wise,' said Max 'surely it wouldn't hurt to get their input and possibly their help if needed?'

'We may need their help yes' Morpheus conceded, 'but not at this point. It's all a bit vague and despite my confidence in Clea there's always the chance that it won't happen, that she's misinterpreted her dream in some way, so I say we leave it for now, keep vigilant, and see what happens.'

'I don't believe that I've misinterpreted my dream, but Morpheus has a point, I think we should wait and see what happens.'

There was a little more back and forth, but in the end the group decided on the keep vigilant and see what happens strategy.

Con was disappointed when the guy with the spikey blonde hair got off the train two stops before his. He had thought that the guy was an omen and had somehow been the reason he had felt the need to get on the train. He had even thought that maybe he was the friend he felt he had without knowing who it was. Even so he had not felt the urge to follow him off the train so that obviously was not the case.

Con thought miserably that maybe if he had approached the guy and started a conversation things might have been different. But different how? He really did not know what to think. He had looked like he would be a cool friend though.

Finally, the train arrived at his stop. Judging by the size of the station he figured he was in a reasonably sized town but still did not know what to expect. The station was busy but there was no seating area and only a lone kiosk selling papers, drinks and confectionary.

It was late afternoon now and Con walked out of the station onto a busy high street. There was a double row of bus stops to his right, a pub opposite, and shops to the left. Turning left he took a stroll past the shops.

After about a quarter of a mile the road bent around to the right, but the pavement carried straight on becoming a pedestrian only shopping centre. Con continued to wander around the shops wondering what the hell he was doing there, and what he should do next. His head was clearer now but he was still basically lost, physically and mentally.

He did make one decision though, when coming across one of those shops that sell everything for a pound he went inside and bought himself a multi pack of crisps. As he would be missing out on dinner at the Homeless Shelter, he figured he had better get something to ease the hunger later and he would have some for the next day too.

After making his purchase he came across a bench and sitting down he took the bottle of water from his backpack and took a few gulps. It was quite warm, so he took off his jacket and hoody, then he tied the hoody around his waist and put the jacket back on. It was still a bit too warm even for that, but he figured it was easier to wear his jacket than to carry it.

The shops would start closing soon and he had no idea where he would be spending the night. Although he felt that the streets of this town would be a little less dangerous than the streets where he had grown up the idea of sleeping there still made him feel vulnerable. He felt a little foolish now for giving up on the shelter, but what could he do, he was here now, though why exactly he had no idea.

Getting up from the bench Con carried on his circuit of the shopping centre and went into two more shops. The first one was a large department store where he used the public toilet. The second was a charity shop where the window display caught his attention. The shop was advertising a sale they were having on books. He thought they must have had so many donations they needed to sell them off. Con was not a big reader having not read a book in years, but he used to love to read when he was younger. He decided that now could be the ideal time to start reading again. He needed something to pass the time and sitting reading a book could make him look less conspicuous in certain situations. As it was a charity shop, and it was a sale he figured the books would be cheap, so he went in to see how cheap.

Ten minutes later he came out with two books, both of which had cost him fifty pence each. He figured they were worth spending a pound on.

It was now almost closing time for most of the shops and thinking he may look odd walking aimlessly around the precinct after closing he headed back towards the train station to see what was on the other side of it.

Once out of the pedestrian shopping area he crossed the road so he was walking on the other side of the road to the one he had walked there on. This meant that when he got back to the train station he was on the side where the pub was. Just as he walked past the door of the pub it opened and a group of people spilled out. This meant that he heard a short blast of people chatting and glass clinking within and felt a blast of warm, beer scented air.

Con had never been inside a pub. Since he had been old enough to legally enter one and have a drink he'd not had the opportunity. He did not have any friends to go with and had not fancied going to one alone. He knew the guys from work often went for a drink after work, but he had never been invited. Not that he would have gone anyway, it was bad enough putting up with the taunting and insults all day, who wanted to prolong that. He had tried alcohol and did occasionally have a beer at home, but he was not a big drinker. Seeing the drunken state of his father on a regular basis for years probably had something to do with that.

For a second, he was tempted to go into the pub, but he did not have the nerve. It was only a case of curiosity anyway; it was not like he fancied a beer or anything. Besides, it was not the sort of thing he should waste his limited funds on. He carried on walking. There were a few more shops, a small café and on the other side of the road a supermarket. After that the buildings changed to office blocks and then a little further on blocks of flats and houses.

There were a few roads leading off the one he was on now as well as opposite. Glancing down each one as he passed, he saw more flats and houses, then as he glanced down the next one, he noticed a break in the houses on one side and not being able to make out what it was he decided to investigate. What he discovered was the entrance to a park, and from what he could tell it was a big one.

There was a small car park at the entrance and to the side and beyond that an expanse of green bordered by trees. Not far into this area there was a well-equipped children's playground which was currently occupied by about six children with their parents either pushing them on swings or sitting on the grass around it watching them play.

Scattered over the grassy area were a few other people lounging and taking in the last of the day's sunshine. Beyond them the ground sloped upward a little so Con could not make out what was beyond it. He headed past the playground and the sunbathers and walked up the slope. Stopping briefly at the top he took in the view. What he saw was a rather impressive lake with an island in the middle that held various trees. One of them was a willow its lowest branched gently stroking the water. The lake was populated by ducks, geese and swans. There was a path around it and bordering that was a thick layer of bushes and small trees. It was a picturesque scene and Con took a minute to appreciate it.

There were quite a few people around the lake, dog walkers and families with young children. Some were feeding the birds, other just strolling around the lake and Con decided to join them. It made a nice change from shopping centres and streets of houses.

Choosing to start on the side to his left he joined the path and began to follow it around the lake. As he walked, he wondered if sleeping under a bush by the lake would be safer than sleeping on the streets. It would be more sheltered and possibly more comfortable, but it was hard to know.

When he got to the opposite side of the lake to where he had started, he saw there was another, even larger expanse of grass stretching into the distance with a few large trees dotted about and more bordering it. Over to his right there was another, smaller entrance/exit to the park and just past that were wide, shallow concrete steps leading down to a small river. There were more people scattered around laying or sitting on the grass and a small group of children and adults having a game of cricket. Off in the distance he could see a large building which he guessed was some sort of sports centre.

Choosing to finish his circuit of the lake Con turned away from the idyllic scene and headed around the other side of the lake. He liked the feel of this place, even with the other people around it felt peaceful. Yes, there was the occasional shriek from an excited kid and parents and dog owners shouting random names and commands, but it still managed to feel serene.

With his circuit of the lake done Con headed back over the slope to find himself a spot to sit and have a drink. Taking off his jacket he laid it on the grass and sat on it, his back propped up against his backpack, he noticed that quite a few people were headed out of the park. They were obviously heading home for their dinner, and with this thought Con realised that he was getting hungry himself, so he got the crisps out of his backpack and worked his way through two packs whilst continuing to people watch.

There were only two children on the playground now watched by a slim young woman who was obviously their mother. There was a man walking a border collie around the tree line and two teenage girls sitting chatting and sharing a can of drink. Nearer to Con there was a young couple lounging on the grass. They were sharing a pair of ear bud headphones through which they were obviously listening to music together which Con thought was kind of sweet.

His meagre meal now finished he washed it down with a few gulps of water and decided it was the ideal time to start reading one of the books he had just bought. Using his backpack as a pillow he lay down and began to read.

The book was a thriller set in America about a seasoned and disillusioned L.A. cop who was partnered with an enthusiastic and bright female rookie on the hunt for a demented serial killer. Con had never heard of the author Jim Brooks, but he was soon riveted. He had forgotten how great it was to get emersed in a different world like this. It was an escape and an adventure without risk, and he wished he had rediscovered this love of reading before now. It would have helped him deal with his shitty life by taking his mind off it even if just for an hour or two a day. TV was his usual escape but there was not always something on that was engaging enough to hold his attention and take his mind off things, especially as his father mainly chose what they watched. If he had had a book to read, he would have had an alternative.

Con had read thirty-nine pages before pausing to look up from the page to see that he was now the only person left lounging on the grass. The only other person in sight was an old man walking an ancient looking mongrel dog. He realised he looked odd now laying on the grass reading. It was unfortunately time to move on.

Reluctantly leaving the park, his jacket and backpack back on, Con headed back towards the train station. He knew there was no seating in the station, but he decided he would find a place to sit on the floor and read some more. If anyone asked him what he was doing, he would say he was waiting for a friend whose train had been delayed. Later he would have to decide where to sleep but for the time being he could forget his own problems and immerse himself in the problems of a pair of L.A. cops.

After spending a couple of hours in the station – thankfully undisturbed – Con decided to go for a walk and scope out the town now it was beginning to get dark. The station was still quite busy, as was the area immediately around it due to the adjacent pub and bus stops. He headed toward the shopping precinct to look for possible sleeping places.

There were a lot fewer people about in that area and Con found it a bit eerie. Turning around he decided to head back to the park and see how the vibes were there at this later hour.

When he got to the park, he was surprised to see a group of people on the playground. He saw they were a group of six teenagers, four boys and two girls. They were laughing and talking loudly and Con almost turned and went back but decided to stay.

Sticking to the tree line around the edge of the grassy area he made his way hoping the trees and the semi darkness would hide him from their sight. As he got to the slope, he had a heart stopping moment when he heard someone shout 'Oy!' but when it was shortly followed by 'stop hogging the booze you dick, give me a swig' he realised they were not talking to him, so he carried on and then he was safely over the hill and out of their sight.

Now he was further into the park the darkness felt deeper, but it did not worry him, in fact he liked it for some reason. Even in the dark this park seemed safe and peaceful.

He headed for the bushes around the left side of the lake to look for a little hidey hole to spend the night in. He was not sure how comfortable it would be, but he would be out of sight and so surely it would be safer and comfier than the concrete of a shop doorway.

After scrabbling about in the bushes for about ten minutes he found the perfect place in a strange gap between two bushes, one behind the other. The gap between them was clear of branches low down but they had grown together higher up making a canopy for the space below. The hidey hole was big enough for him to sit, or lay curled up in. The ground was dirt strewn with leaves and twigs and although not as soft as grass he would have to make do.

Before crawling into the hidey hole, he took his backpack and jacket off, put his hoody back on properly and replaced his jacket. He thought that the three layers he had on would be enough to keep him warm enough during the night, he just hoped it did not rain.

After getting down on his hands and knees he crawled into the space pushing his backpack in front of him, then he flipped over so he was sitting with his backpack on his lap. He got the bottle of water out and took a few sips, then after putting it back he put the backpack behind him so he could lean back against it.

He felt cosy and safe if not completely comfortable. It was too dark to read unfortunately, and he wished he had a torch or something.

It was a bit early to go to sleep, but he was tired, and he thought it would be best if he got up really early the next day so he could come out of his hiding place without being seen by park visitors. It was unlikely he would sleep well in this environment; he had never slept outside before, not even on a camping trip with a tent etc, but he had to give it a try. Using his backpack as a pillow he curled up on his right side and tried to get comfortable. After brushing away a few twigs from underneath him he settled as best he could.

As he lay there, he found that he was less scared than he had expected even though there were a few strange noises, and it was very dark in his hidey hole. Attributing the noises to the ducks etc on the lake, or maybe the island, other small, harmless animals and the wind he did not let them worry him too much. The odd far away shout of the teenagers on the playground did not bother him either. He felt safe.

Con lay there for an hour trying not to feel sorry for himself. He tried to avoid it by thinking of this as an adventure, he was finally out in the world seeing new places. Maybe the places he had seen were not exactly exotic or exciting, but they were new, and he was free. Free form work and his father, therefore free of mental and physical cruelty.

He wondered how his father had reacted when he discovered he was gone, if he had even noticed yet. Maybe he should have left a note so his father knew he had gone for good. It was likely his father would be angry when he realised Con was not coming back, but would he be bothered enough to do anything to find out where his son had gone? It was doubtful his father would miss him as such, but he would definitely miss his money and having someone to clean the flat and cook his meals so he would want him back for those reasons. How would he cope without Con in those respects? A small part of him felt sorry for his father but mostly he was glad to be away from him.

The problem was what sort of life would he have now? Maybe the life he had had was the best he could expect and now things would get even worse. No, he could not think like that, he was moving on to better things he was sure, this was just the difficult intermediate stage, it would all work out in the end.

Eventually, despite all the thoughts going around in his head and the uncomfortable sleeping arrangement Con fell asleep. It was a restless sleep though and he woke up several times and felt disorientated and a little frightened for a few seconds before he remembered where he was. It was undoubtedly strange noises and discomfort that woke him, but after a while he got more used to it and drifted off into a deeper sleep.

From Morpheus' perspective Con's dream realm presence that night was troubling. The Dark Soul appeared earlier than usual but then disappeared again before Morpheus could do more than welcome him into his healing light.

The next time the Dark Soul appeared it was again only for a brief time. Although this was not unusual in the case of those dreamers that did not sleep well and was common for other Dark Souls, for this soul it was unusual. A new, interrupted sleep pattern was therefore worrying as it rarely happened for a good reason.

Eventually the Dark soul did make a longer appearance but fearing he would leave at any moment Morpheus was hesitant about interacting with him too much. Instead, he did a quick read of the soul's emotions. He was relieved not to detect any fear or other strongly negative emotions but there was a touch of uneasiness and a lot of uncertainty.

In light of all this Morpheus simply set about bringing the soul a dream hoping he would remain long enough to receive it. Not being able to glean any specifics regarding what the soul needed he brought him similar dreams to those he had brought him the night before. It was the only thing he could do until he learnt more about what the soul wanted and needed and what was causing this interrupted sleep.

The Dreambringer did his best to bring dreams that he hoped would instil the soul with confidence and security when he awoke. Again, he conveyed to the soul that he had a friend who could help hoping this would lead to the soul opening up to him more the next night.

When the Dark Soul disappeared again earlier than usual Morpheus could only hope that he had brought the soul enough of a dream to help. He also hoped that the soul would have a better night's sleep in the future, that this was just a one off because if it became the norm then helping the Dark Soul heal would be a much harder job. He needed time to heal this soul not just fleeting visits. But for now, he had done all he could and would just have to wait and see what happened next. If this did become a new sleeping pattern for the soul, he would have to come up with a new strategy.

For the rest of his time in the Dream Realm that night Morpheus concentrating on helping some of the normal souls that had, as usual, gathered around him.

Whilst in the midst of this he happened to catch a fleeting glimpse of what could only have been another Dreambringer out of the corner of his eye. Assuming it was one of the Gateway Dreambringers who often watched him work for a few minutes during the night he thought nothing much of it.

Chapter 9
The Visitor

Con woke early as he had hoped. He woke to the sound of birdsong and to the less pleasant discoveries of a stiff neck, numb right leg, cold hands and slightly damp clothing. Despite all that he felt strangely upbeat.

After crawling out from his hidey hole dragging his backpack with him, he stood, brushed himself down and had a good stretch. His bruised ribs still hurt a bit too but there was not much he could do about it. He did have one tip for himself *though "next time pull your hands up inside your sleeves"* he thought as he blew on his hands to warm them up. Apart from that he felt in pretty good shape considering he had not had a good night's sleep. At least he did not have a foggy head this morning, but he did need a piss. Moving a good distance away from his hiding place he peed up against a tree. Probably not legal but needs must.

Now he had to decide how to spend his day. His first thought was that he needed to walk to get his blood flowing properly again, shrug off the aches caused by sleeping on the ground and get rid of the pins and needles he now had in his right leg. So, he took a slow walk around the lake. It was so peaceful and beautiful in the early morning light. The only sounds were those made by the birds in the trees and on the lake. As he walked, he wondered how deep the water was, but after taking a closer look he could not answer his own question, the water was too murky. It would have to remain a mystery.

The early morning sunshine was weak, but it made everything look fresh and beautiful. Con decided that he liked being out and about at that time in the morning. The slight chill was invigorating, and he preferred the early morning sunshine to that of the warmer afternoon. The fact that he was in a beautiful park probably helped.

Once he had completed a circuit of the lake, he did another part circuit so that he ended up at the back end of the park. He wanted to check out where the other entrance/exit led to.

The disappointing answer turned out to be more streets of houses. He dare not got for a wander that way in case he got lost, so he went back into the park. There were a few people about now walking their dogs. One of the dogs had been let off its lead and it came running over to Con. It was a Golden Labrador Retriever with a sweet, kind face and a friendly manner. He wanted to pet it but was worried about its owner catching up and wanting to chat or something. Luckily the woman in question, rather than coming over, shouted at her dog to 'come here Peggy, leave that boy alone' and after giving Con a lolling tongued smile the dog obediently ran back to its owner.

Con now headed back through the park toward the larger entrance/exit. When he came in sight of the playground, he saw it was deserted it being too early for the kids to be playing. Strolling over to the swings he sat on one, after a night spent on the hard ground any sort of seat was more comfortable. He began to push gently against the ground with his feet making the swing move gently back and forth as he contemplated his next move.

Then his stomach rumbled, well why wouldn't it after only having crisps for dinner the day before. Should he get a good breakfast like he had done of his first day out? Was it worth spending money on something more substantial? After a minute's thought and more rumbling from his stomach he decided it was.

Remembering that he had passed a small café near the train station he set out towards it. He walked slowly hoping that the café was open this early. But he was out of luck, it was closed. The opening times taped to the door and a quick glance at his watch told him he only had twenty-five minutes to wait though. He spent those twenty-five minutes walking slowly up to the shopping precinct and back.

Being the first customer in the café he had his pick of tables and chose the two seater in the back corner. There were only five tables in the whole place and there was not much room between them. The menus on the tables were four sides of A4 laminated and were propped between a red sauce bottle and a salt, pepper and vinegar set. He gave the menu the once over and had made his choice when the waitress approached.

'Wot can I get ya darlin' she asked her pen poised over a small waitress pad.

She was about forty by Con's reckoning, with curly blonde hair, a curvy figure and badly applied lipstick. Her manner was cheerful and friendly.

'I'll have egg, beans and toast with a mug of tea please' he told her.

'Okay darlin' coming right up' she said noting it down then giving him a big smile before bustling off to the counter to hand the order to the cook, a tall, skinny man who took the piece of paper from her with seeming reluctance. Con wondered idly if they were a married couple.

Reluctant or not the cook was fast, and the waitress was soon placing his food in front of him.

'There you go darlin' enjoy' she said cheerfully.

'Thanks' said Con resisting the urge to add darlin' to the end of his sentence.

Only one other customer arrived as Con slowly ate his breakfast so without much to do the waitress and cook stood either side of the counter talking quietly. He wondered if they were talking about him, especially as they glanced over a couple of times, but he ignored them in case they tried to start up a conversation.

He'd nearly finished his food when the waitress approached.

'More tea darlin'?' she asked.

'Errmm, no thanks' he told her. He would have actually liked some more tea but did not want to stretch his budget too far.

'Or something more to eat darlin'?' the waitress continued.

'No ta' he replied.

'Okay darlin'' she said and walked away.

He was just taking his last mouthful of food when she came over with a mug of tea and two more slices of toast.'

'Here ya go darlin'' she said placing it on his table then picking up the empty mug and plate.

'I didn't order that' he told her alarmed.

'I know darlin', but I think you need it, look at ya, you're all skin and bones. And don't worry it's on the 'ouse, a treat from me.'

'That's so nice of you, thanks' he said returning her smile.

What was it with him and waitresses' he wondered; she'd been the second one to help him out lately? It was strange but he was very grateful to both of them.

When the waitress was not looking Con wrapped one slice of toast in his napkin and stashed it in his backpack for later. A cold piece of toast was not an ideal lunch, but it would be better than nothing he thought. He then slowly ate the other free slice and drank his tea.

He could not draw it out indefinitely though so all too soon it was time to leave. He had been looking at the bus stops across the road and had noticed that the shelters were the type that had the red, plastic half seats attached so he decided he would go sit over there for a while. He could read his book and pretend to be waiting for a bus. The other passengers would be too intent on catching their own ride to notice he did not get on one.

He paid for his food and said goodbye and thank you to the friendly waitress'

'Bye darlin'' she said as he left the café.

He felt bad not leaving her a tip in light of what she had done for him but then if he had left a tip it would have negated the freebee wouldn't it? Anyway, he thought she would understand.

Crossing the road, he chose a bus stop, sat on the strange half seat and taking his book from his backpack he was soon emersed in its pages whilst people got on and off buses around him.

After about half an hour he took a break from reading to take a look around him feeling that maybe he should be thinking about his next move rather than burying his nose in a book. The thought occurred to him that maybe he should head back to the Homeless Shelter, but that would mean shelling out for another train fare and that was not wise surely. He did not really want to think about what would happen when his money ran out, in fact he did not really want to think about any of it. It was much easier to just read his book.

Despite the nagging worry about money and his lack of plans he realised he was feeling surprisingly calm. Yes, stuff was constantly going around in his head when he was not reading, but he did not feel stressed about it. It was like on some level he knew what he was doing and that everything would be okay. Then a stray thought popped into his head.

"I have a friend I can go to."

Why the hell did he think that he had a friend? Then he remembered a dream he'd had that morning. Like many of his previous dreams he had been in the woods and the person with him had sometimes been his mum and other times someone else. When that person was Mum the two of them would sing, and when it was the other person, they would talk, and Con would mainly listen. But who were they and what had they said to him? Did he know them, or where they a made-up dream person? He could not recall what song he and his Mum had sung either, all he could remember were the feelings these things had evoked in him.

The singing made him feel safe, happy and free and the words spoken to him made him feel like he had a friend and somewhere safe to go.

"It was just a dream" he told himself, and it was good that it made him feel safe and positive, but it meant nothing, it was just a pleasant dream and that was all. Wasn't it?

Whilst Con pondered his dream the residents of The Gateway were gathering for breakfast. This included Morpheus and the group soon sensed that the big man was worried about something.

'Did it not go well last night?' Sofia enquired.

'No, not really.'

'Why, what happened?' enquired Clea as she placed a bacon sandwich in front of him.

'Not much, that's the problem' he told them, then went on to elaborate.

Once they had all the details there was a short silence as they processed the information before the usual chat ensued.

'We all have bad nights, well maybe not us Dreambringers, but normal dreamers do, so I'm sure it'll be fine next time' said Mary, always the optimist.

'Or he could be in real trouble' retorted Geth playing the devil's advocate as usual.

Clea tutted him before giving her own opinion 'I'm not surprised the poor lad has bad nights with the life he appears to be leading, but it's the first time he's been like this so let's hope it's a one off, or at least a rare occurrence.'

'We can only wait and see' added Max.

There was another short silence as there was not really much else to say. Then Aaron changed the subject.

'What about you Clea, did you dream anymore about a visitor.'

'Actually, I did' Clea told them.

'What are you waiting for? Tell us' urged Mary.

'It was only a brief dream. I was out in the woods near Morpheus' cabin I think, and I could hear voices.'

'How many, and what did they say?' Mary enquired.

'There were two. One said, *'I am here for you'* and the other one asked *'where are you?'* and the first voice just said, *'I am here, come'* like that, with a pause in between.'

'Weird, then what?' asked Aaron.

'Nothing, that was it. I told you it was brief.'

'And how does that relate to you believing we're going to receive a visitor?' asked Sofia.

'I don't really know; I just feel its linked.'

'Well, one voice did say come, like they were inviting the other, and you said you were in the woods here so that's obviously where it comes from' stated Geth sounding smug.

'Yeah, alright big head,' said Aaron.

'Did you recognise the voices?' asked Eddie detecting the slightly argumentative route that the conversation was taking.

'The second voice definitely not, but maybe the first now you mention it. It's hard to recall though because I know I said it was voices, but it was more like the telepathy thing we do with the Eternals you know, not verbal, more in the mind.'

'But you recognised it though. Who was it?' urged Mary.

'Wait, give me a minute' instructed Clea closing her eyes to concentrate, and they all stayed respectfully quiet as she ruminated.

'Oooh, I've got it' Clea suddenly exclaimed making them all jump 'It was you' she said pointing at Morpheus.

'Now that's interesting,' said Mason.

'It is' agreed Morpheus 'you know I think you might have been piggybacking the dream I gave to the Dark Soul.'

'You invited the Dark Soul here?' Max's tone was incredulous.

'Well, no, that wasn't my intention, it's just how Clea interpreted the dream. I just conveyed to the soul that he could trust me, that I was a friend, and I was here for him.'

'Where?' asked Geth.

'Nowhere specific, just generally here for him, you know, it's the sort of supportive thing you'd say to a friend who's struggling.'

'But if Clea interpreted it as an invite maybe the Dark Soul did too' suggested Geth.

'Morpheus just said that's not what he intimated' countered Max.

'Yes, but it's the message Clea got so why not the Dark Soul?' said Geth persevering with his argument.

'And that's why Clea believes we're getting a visitor because she feels the soul was invited here' added Mary.

'Maybe, but that doesn't mean he's actually coming,' said Max.

'This is doing my head in' Aaron told them.

'Let's not get worked up' said Eddie in a placating tone 'even if Morpheus did invite the Dark Soul here how on earth would he find his way? Did you give him directions Morpheus'?

'Of course not.'

'Well then he can't be coming can he.'

'But we didn't exactly get directions when we were called together' pointed out Geth 'Mason simply sent us dreams of the Artfest and we all found our way there'.

'That was totally different,' said Mary.

'How was it?' countered Geth 'Clea was in the woods near Morpheus' cabin in the dream so maybe that's what the Dark Soul saw too, and then Morpheus told him to come there.'

'It wasn't really that specific' said Clea 'and we don't know that the Dark Soul dreamt what I did exactly, besides we were all Dreambringer candidates and he's a Dark Soul who's only just started to dream again.'

'Exactly' agreed Eddie 'so we have nothing to worry about.'

'I'm not so sure that's the case' said Geth 'Morpheus is some sort of super powered Dreambringer, and we don't really know a lot about these Dark Souls do we, so maybe it is possible for Morpheus to bring the boy here in the real world.'

'I bloody hope not' said Max vehemently.

'Why ever not?' asked Clea.

'He's a Dark Soul, he could be dangerous.'

'That sort of Dark Soul isn't dangerous' Morpheus told him.

'Who says.'

'The Foundation, Xiu Bo and myself. I explained that those Dark Souls who shun help are the dangerous ones, this soul is just damaged and in need of our help.'

'That doesn't mean it's safe for him to come here' said Sofia 'I don't think the Foundation would like that.'

'Why are we worrying about something that isn't likely to happen?' asked Eddie.

'But the thing is it might happen' said Geth.

'For fucks sake, we're just going around in circles' stated a stressed looking Max.

In fact, everyone was getting a bit stressed now so Morpheus decided to put a lid on it all.

'Right' he began 'as far as I am aware I did not invite the Dark Soul here, but I'm still learning the extent of my new Dreambringer powers and breaking new ground so I'm not going to dismiss anyone's opinion, but I will reiterate that I truly believe the Dark Soul is no danger to us and if he is coming here then we will deal with that if it happens. I don't believe it's anything to be afraid of, it is just part of a learning curve that the Origination has set us on, and we should be excited rather than anxious. Some of you have been through a lot but if I could deal with Talionis I'm sure I can deal with one damaged but harmless Dark Soul, and so can you. Okay?'

After getting a nod or a yes from everyone he continued.

'Let's simply wait and see and deal with whatever comes our way together.'

Con had been at the bus stop for just over an hour now, most of the time he had been reading, but he occasionally took a break to look around and have a think. He still had not got anywhere in terms of plan making though. He had now put the book away thinking it was time he moved on. A little walk around the shops then back to the park for more reading he thought. And maybe a little thinking while he was at it, though he was not really in the mood. He felt quite apathetic really like there was no real need to make any plans, he just needed to go with the flow. Whatever that meant.

Just as he was about to set off a bus was approaching the stop and glancing at the destination displayed on the front of it, he stopped in his tracks. *"Oh hell"* he thought, it was happening again. The place name was unfamiliar to him, but he felt the sudden need to go there. He needed to get on that bus and before he even knew what he was doing he was rummaging in his pocket for some change and joining the queue of people waiting to get on the bus that had now pulled in.

He did not have a travelcard for this ride like he had been advised to get last time by the young waitress so he would have to pay in cash this time and he was not sure what the fare was in this area so he would have to ask.

'How much is the fare please?' he asked the driver, who was a grumpy looking bald man with a thick neck and very hairy forearms, and acted like the question was a big imposition.

'It's one pound sixty-five mate' he said with a heavy sigh.

Con put two pound coins in the little tray next to the ticket reader.

'I don't have any change mate' the bus driver informed him, 'most people use travelcards and contactless payment these days you know.' So Con rummaged around in his pocket to see what other coins he had. He was getting a bit panicked due to the unimpressed expression on the drivers face and the fact he could hear someone tutting behind him. In the end he managed to find a fifty pence and a twenty pence which he swapped for one of the pound coins.

'Don't worry about the five pence' he said.

'I won't,' said the driver.

It was a single decker bus and almost empty so Con picked a seat near the front, we wanted to see where he was going. He did not know where exactly he needed to get off, but maybe he would know when he was there.

"You're a crazy idiot" he thought to himself as the bus pulled away from the stop. What was he thinking of jumping on random buses just because he liked the name of the place it was going to? It was more than that though wasn't it, it felt more like a desperate need than an impulsive whim. It felt important but when you did not know why it was important that made it weird right? *"Maybe I'm going crazy"* he thought. Despite the craziness though it did feel like the right thing to do, so all he could do was go with it. *"This is an adventure remember, just enjoy it."*

The next couple of bus stops were within the confides of the town, but after that things began to get more rural. There were now fewer houses, and those houses were bigger and set well apart from each other. Then they were in the countryside. It was turning into quite a pleasant ride.

The bus made stops at a couple of small villages and then there was more open countryside. Con got the feeling they were nearly at their destination, and this was confirmed when he saw a sign with the destination on saying it was five miles away. He assumed the place was another little village and he wondered exactly what he would find there. How could he blend in in such as small place? What would he do there?

'Hey Geth, I have something for you' said Sofia as she entered the kitchen waving several sheets of A4 paper.

Geth was clearing up after the groups breakfast with Max and had his hands in a soapy bowl of washing up.

'What is it?' he asked.

'It's the list of Tattoo Studios from The Foundation like we discussed.'

'Okay, great, leave it on the table and I'll take it with me to the Factory and have a look. I've got as much time as I like to pick one, right?'

'Yes, take your time' Sofia told him placing the sheets of paper on the kitchen table.

'Okay, thanks.'

'Who's going out to the Factory with you?' Sofia asked.

'Aaron and Mary are coming with me when I'm finished here and Morpheus is already on his way there, eager as ever.'

'Oh right.'

Sofia was a little upset that Morpheus had left for the day without saying goodbye, but then he was not very good at basic etiquette, he always had too much on his mind. He did not really think about others, not in a bad way, he did care about people, he was just very single minded and committed to his work. If work was the right word, maybe vocation was better. Whatever the case she had to face the fact that what she was feeling for this man was not reciprocated.

'I'll be in the office if anyone needs me' she told the two men now and headed off to try to lose herself in her own work.

When the bus reached a crossroads Con had the feeling it should go right but then he saw a sign indicating that the place he was going to was off to the left. He was confused and felt a strong need to turn right but sat helpless when the bus turned left.

The bus travelled about half a mile down a tree lined road and then came out into another village. There were a few bungalows on their right and on the left a village green on the other side of which was a short row of detached houses. After passing the green and a few more bungalows the bus pulled into a road on the left and stopped outside a village shop and post office.

Up ahead the road terminated in a strange sort of dead end with a small roundabout. The pavement continued on however and it looked like it led to the main part of the village as he could see more shops ahead with people milling about. On the other side of the road there was a layby with another bus stop.

Although Con knew this was the destination of the bus and thought the place looked very welcoming and pleasant to him it was not exactly where he needed to be. But whatever he was feeling it was time to get off the bus.

By this time there was only Con and an old couple on the bus. They thanked the driver as they got off and Con found himself automatically doing the same even though the driver had been grumpy with him.

Once off the bus Con stood there like an idiot dithering as he watched the bus pull away, go around the dead-end roundabout and pull into the layby opposite. There the driver turned off the engine and Con watched as he got out of his seat and off the bus where he lit up a cigarette. He was obviously on his break until he was due to make the return journey.

The old couple from the bus were walking slowly towards the shops but Con realised he did not want to go that way. Instead, he started to walk back the way the bus had come. He tried to look purposeful as he walked, like he knew where he was going when in fact all he knew at this point was this was the direction he needed to go in.

Con walked for a little under a mile backtracking on the route the bus had taken. There was no actual pavement on the road beyond the first lot of bungalows just a narrow grass verge, so he walked on that. A few cars passed him, but he did not see anyone else walking.

When he got to the crossroads, he stopped for a minute to look at the sign. It was one of the old, white wooden ones with the arrows of wood sticking out in different directions with the place names and miles printed on rather than the modern metal board type.

There were four roads leading off the crossroads and therefore four arrows on the sign. One pointed back to where he had just got off the bus, one pointed back to where the bus had come from, and one pointed in the opposite direction with another destination name on.

The one pointing in the opposite direction to the village was however blank. Or rather on closer inspection Con saw that something had been there at some point but had been worn away making it unreadable. He wondered why only that one was worn away; the others were fine. Whatever the reason he realised that he needed to go in that direction, the direction with no name. Well, why not *"accept the weird"* he thought as he set off.

Like the road to the village there was only a narrow grass verge to walk on and it was bordered on both sides by trees and beyond the trees Con could see open fields. After about a mile he passed a narrow road leading off to his left. On the near side of this narrow road the trees and fields were open but on the far side a ten foot high barbed chain link fence had been erected. This fence carried on as far as he would see both down the narrow road heading left and ahead of him on the road he was walking. Behind the chain link the open fields had been replaced by dense woodland with all kinds of trees and bushes vying for room.

On the other side of the road the woodland was sparser and there was a low wooden post and rail fence midway between a grass verge and the treeline. Con chose to carry on walking along the chain link fence side.

However, after another half a mile the grass verge disappeared, and Con had to cross over to the post and rail fence side. He had not seen any cars since he left the crossroads, but then he figured not many people would follow a sign with no name on.

The road seemed never ending and Con wondered what he was getting himself into. He was walking into the middle of nowhere it seemed surrounded by woodland, dense on one side and more open on the other. Also, his backpack was hurting his shoulders and he was getting hot.

He considered turned back but knew somehow that was not what he should do. Instead, he stopped, took his backpack off and put it on the ground next to him. He then took off his jacket and hoody and hung them over the fence, then rummaged in his backpack for his bottle of water. It was only a quarter full now and the water was warm, but it was all he had. He drank a few mouthfuls and then put the bottle back in his backpack. He needed to cool down, so he sat cross legged on the grass verge and stared at the chain link fence opposite.

"I need to be on the other side of that fence" he thought and then mentally cringed. Why was he thinking these strange, random thoughts? Why on earth would he want to be on the other side of that fence, he did not even know what was over there, it did not even look like you could easily walk through the dense woodland. Then another of those strange thoughts popped into his head *"My friend is over there."*

Clutching his head Con groaned 'For fucks sake what is happening to me?!' he shouted, and why not, there was no one around to hear him. 'I'm a crazy man' he said still out loud but quieter this time 'I had a stupid dream about having a friend and thought that somehow meant I needed to be here, but where the fuck is here, and who is this dream friend? It's just ridiculous.'

He felt like crying then but managed to hold back the tears, just. He was stronger than this, he should stop acting like a baby and keep going. It was all he could do.

Getting to his feet he tied his hoody around his waist, put his jacket back on and then his backpack and continued to trudge on.

After about a mile the chain link fence suddenly branched off at an angle into the woodland and along the roadside it merged with a high field stone wall. The wall was an impressive twelve foot high and made up of varying colours and sizes of stones and was kind of beautiful in a way. Despite the wall's height Con could still see the tops of many trees reaching up above it. It looked old but sturdy and Con was impressed as it must have taken a long time to build because he could see that it continued on off into the distance. In fact, all that Con could see ahead was the almost straight road stretching on and on with the wall flanking it on one side and the fenced off fields on the other.

It was a warm day with very few clouds in a blue sky and so it seemed strange when looking at the road ahead now Con saw something that did not fit with the weather. Following the line of the wall at about waist height and stretching ahead he could see a thin ribbon of mist. Con did not think that mist was usual on clear, sunny days, plus mist was not normally in a single ribbon like that. But then he was not used to being out it the countryside so maybe it was usual there.

He noticed something else too, to add to his misery, the road ahead began to go uphill. It was a small incline to start with but got gradually steeper with the post and rail fence and wall continuing to flank the road. All he could hope was that when he got to the top of the hill, he could get a better idea where he was headed.

After walking another mile and a half, uphill, he finally reached the top where the road took a sharp turn to the left. On the fence side there was no right turn just more fencing built around the sharp corner and continuing on the right side of the new road to the left. The wall had been built in an impressive curve around the corner and continued along the left of the new road. He noticed that the ribbon of mist continued to follow the wall around the corner and now stretched ahead along the new road. It was definitely a strange phenomenon but he kind of liked it. It struck him then that maybe it was this ribbon of mist that he was following, that it was leading him somewhere and this thought brought strangely conflicting feelings of comfort and unease.

He only had two choices now, turn back or carry on and there was no way he was turning back now, he needed to follow this through to the end wherever it led, literality, because that was what he was doing, following the ribbon of mist.

This new road that the mist continued down was narrower than the one it led off, and tall trees close behind both the fence and the wall formed a canopy of branches high above it.

Con was really worn out and hot after the uphill walk and was glad that this new road was on a level and shaded. Deciding it was time for another break he walked far enough to be in the shade of the canopy of trees, and after divesting himself of his backpack, jacket and hoody he sat on the grass verge with his back against the bottom rail of the fence.

After a few more sips of water, he remained sitting needing a longer break this time.

He sat staring at the wall and the ribbon of mist which looked more substantial now in the dappled light under the tree canopy. Looking at it now he thought he could see little sparks of light within it which made it even stranger but somehow beautiful.

He sat like that for about twenty minutes before deciding he had better get up because if he did not move soon, he feared he would stay sat there for hours. He tied his hoodie around his waist again, then not wanting to put his jacket back on he tucked it around the straps of his backpack before heaving the backpack onto his back. It would be safe enough like that in this environment, he was sure he would notice if it came untucked and fell off. He was beginning to hate the feeling of the backpack on his shoulders and back, it felt heavier every time he put it on.

Con began to trudge slowly along the shaded road glad he was at least out of the full sunlight. He walked down the middle of the road to start with thinking he would hear any cars approaching, then he had the sudden urge to move over and walk into the ribbon of mist. He didn't understand why he had not thought to do it before.

Walking over he stood close to the mist and reaching out a tentative hand he slowly put it into the strip of strange diaphanous material. He felt a strong tingling sensation that was not unpleasant, and this gave him the courage to step forward so that his body was within the mist. There was more intense tingling as he walked a few steps and looking down it was like the misty ribbon was passing through his body rather than flowing around his body like normal mist would. It was a strange but pleasant feeling, but he felt that it would be wrong to remain in it like that, it was for following not merging with. It was a strange thing to think but he felt its truth.

Maybe he was being stupid, and it was just a strange sort of weather phenomenon after all, though he had never heard of fog making people tingle before. This thought caused him to do a strange hiccup of a laugh. 'Tingly mist' he said aloud with a big grin on his face. Then he gave himself a mental shake. What the hell was going on? Was he going crazy or something?

Stepping out and back into the middle of the road he continued to walk. The dappled sunlight reminded him of his dreams of his Mum, and he began to sing one of her favourite songs quietly to himself. It made him feel better about this crazy walk he was on.

The road stretched on in front of him for about half a mile and he thought he could see it bend round to the left up ahead, but what if it was a dead end? In the reduced light of the tree canopy, it was hard to tell at this distance. If it was a dead end, he would have walked all this way for nothing and would have to walk all the way back and he could not bear the idea of that.

He decided that if that happened, he would crawl under the post and rail fence and find a place to lay down and die. No, that was a bit melodramatic. He would just have a nice long rest and maybe a nap. The other worrying thing was his low supply of water. He could cope with only having a slice of cold toast and four bags of crisps to eat, he was not that hungry, but the small amount of water he had left would not last long, especially if he had to walk all that way back.

He did not know where it was he was going but he hoped that wherever it was he was nearly there, that it was worth the walk and that there was water there. It was ridiculous really to have walked all this way without knowing his destination. He just had to believe that something good would become of the craziness. He just had to carry on.

After walking for ten minutes, he could finally tell that the road did turn to the left ahead. It was good that it was not a dead end, but what if it just carried on like this for more miles?

As he neared the bend, he could see that it was like a reverse of the bend at the other end of the tree lined road. On the inside of the bend the wall continued around the corner built in another impressive curve, and on the other side the post and rail fence continued. He could also see that the ribbon of mist also disappeared around the corner.

He again had to admire whoever had put up the fences and built the wall, they had gone on for miles and engineered two sharp turns with great skill. But he wondered if this turn meant he would be going back on himself.

Rounding the bend, he found himself crossing his fingers and briefly squeezing his eyes shut. When he opened his eye's his heart plummeted for a few seconds when he saw that about a hundred yards ahead the road came to a dead end. The stone wall curved inward and continued off to the right across the bottom of the road where it then cut across the fence terminating it there. The wall then stretched off into the trees to the right.

Con had stopped in his tracks when he thought it was a dead end, but after a moments panic, he noticed something. About halfway down the road there looked to be a gap of some sort in the stone wall, or maybe a recess. He then saw that the ribbon on mist either terminated there or continued into the gap or whatever it was. This obviously needed investigation.

He walked quickly now; his tiredness forgotten in his eagerness for possible good news. As he got nearer, he saw that the wall had again been built cleverly around a corner and he could see it curved back out again a few feet further on, but what was in that gap? Another long road or maybe a building of some sort?

Then he was around the bend and what he saw evoked mixed emotions within him. It was a dead end of sorts, but it was also an opening, but to what.

The way in front of him was barred by a pair of huge, black iron gates. They were set in two rounded pillars built in the same stone as the wall. The pillars must have been about fifteen feet high because the gates they held were about twelve feet tall. Con was still moving forward but very slowly as he took in the ornate design in the iron work of the gates. It was like intertwined vines of metal ending in strange, flower like shapes yet more complicated and beautiful than that. Con had never seen anything like it. Its beauty and unusualness was made stranger by the fact that the ribbon of mist had followed the wall around the corner and then terminated at the gate where it twined around the metal vines. It was an awe-inspiring sight.

Stopping about ten feet away from the gates Con noticed something else. A couple of feet before the left-hand gate there was a metal post sticking up from where it was imbedded in the ground and on top of it was a metal box which was about twenty inches square. In the middle of the box there was a metal grill, above it a metal button, and below it a numbered keypad. Attached to the post under the metal box was a printed sign. The whole thing was about three feet high in total and Con realised it was an intercom. Moving a bit closer he read the sign, it said "Visitors Please Press Button and Wait"

His first instinct was to do as the sign said and me moved closer but stopped himself before pressing the button. *"What are you doing?"* he asked himself. If he pressed that button someone would speak through the intercom and ask him who he was and what he wanted and he only had an answer to one of those questions. He had no idea who would be on the other end and what he would say to them. Looking past the gate he could only see about a hundred yards of tree lined driveway before it twisted around to the right and that did not tell him much. He could also see another metal box topped post similar to the one in front of him.

Where did that driveway lead to? Maybe it was a scary old lunatic asylum Con thought, making himself laugh nervously. If it was he was probably in the right place. He should press the button and say, "Constantine Howard here, you have me booked in for an indefinite stay in a padded cell with complimentary straight jacket.' That was probably a bit outdated nowadays, but he was beginning to think that he might actually qualify for a stay in a mental health institute. At least he would have water and a place to sleep.

Or maybe the gates led to the spooky mansion of a reclusive millionaire who would lure him in and keep him as a slave. Now that was being really ridiculous, maybe he had heat stroke or severe dehydration or something. The truth was it was most likely one of those stately homes where some posh aristocratic family lived, cash poor but asset rich. If he pressed the button, he would probably be told by someone with a plummy voice to go away.

But whatever it was behind those gates Con had been drawn to this place. It was not like he'd just gone for a stroll in the country and come across it. He had felt a strong urge to get on that bus and then keep following this long, long road. Why do all that for no reason? He was supposed to be here and instinctively knew it somehow, even if he didn't know where 'here' actually was. If that was the case, why not press the button and see what happened? Even if it was all a strange fantasy in his head whoever answered might at least give him some water or even help him back to civilisation without that interminable walk.

There was a chance he would be putting himself in danger, but he did not feel that was likely. Even through his tiredness and confusion, and despite his silly imaginings this place gave him a good vibe.

Reaching out he pressed the button and waited as instructed. The intercom was at about waist height obviously as visitors were expected to arrive by car and he wondered if he would hear them answer okay or if it would be better to crouch down so he was level with the intercom grill. But then if he was in a car, he would be about the same distance away than he was now just at a different angle.

After a few minutes waiting Con was beginning to wonder if he was even going to get an answer at all when there was a sudden click and a crackling noise followed by a male voice asking

'Can I help you?'

'I errmm, yes, I mean I'm….I need some water' stuttered Con and cringing inside at his incoherence.

'You want water?' queried the intercom voice.

'Yes, I'm so sorry to bother you but I have been walking for a very long time, I'm very tired and thirsty and have very little water left' Con answered only just managing to keep himself together.

'You walked here?' the male voice enquired.

'Yes.'

'Why?'

'I errmm, I'm not sure.'

'You must know why you walked here.'

'No, not really, I just sort of came here on a whim, like I needed to be here. I know it sounds strange but it's the truth.'

'What's your name mate?'

This question surprised Con but he answered, 'It's Constantine, Con for short.'

Con thought he heard another voice in the background then, a female voice, but couldn't quite make out what she was saying. Then the man's voice was back.

'Con, could you wait a minute please.'

It was strange hearing someone call him Con rather than Missy or some other derogatory name. Con waited hoping that telling the truth had been wise. He'd sounded a bit crazy, but he hoped sincere. They were taking ages to come back though, which was a bit worrying.

Finally Con heard the click and crackle again and the male voice was back.

'Please wait there, someone will come for you, it may take a little while, okay?'

'Okay'

The conversation was abruptly terminated then with a click leaving Con's weak 'Thank you" went unheard.

Being told someone was coming for you could sound ominous but the tone of the man's voice had been reassuring rather than menacing so Con waited as he had been instructed to.

Con heard the vehicle before he saw it, and then around the bend in the driveway came a blue van. He could see two people inside, both men.

The van came to a stop about ten feet from the gate next to the other post and metal box and the driver reached a tattooed arm out of the van window and looked to Con to be punching in a code into a keypad. A few seconds later there was a strange clanging noise, and the gates began to slowly open inwards from Con and towards the van. Whilst this was happening the two men got out of the van and began to walk towards Con. As they walked Con got a good look at them. The driver was wearing jeans and a faded AC/DC t-shirt, he was tall and well-built with long,

119

strawberry blonde hair and a beard. The passenger was a tall, handsome, black man with short dreads and a neat beard, he was wearing green cargo trousers and a bright, white t-shirt. Both men could have looked menacing but their manner and the fact they were smiling soon diffused that impression.

Stopping a couple of feet away the driver was the first to speak.

'Hi, I'm Eddie' he said, and then indicating the other man 'and this is Mason.'

Con realised that this was the voice he'd heard and spoken to over the intercom.

'Hi, I'm Con' he told them even though he'd already told them his name.

'We came to get you in the van cos the house is still a distance away and you said you were tired which isn't surprising after you walked so far.'

'That's really good of you, thanks.'

'Come on then, get in.'

Con was surprised how comfortable he felt climbing into a van with two men that he didn't know. In fact, he felt that the two men to be more wary of him than he was of them for some reason. They were being polite and smiling but he could also sense a little tension, yet he was still happy to be sandwiched between them in the van.

Once they were all in the van the gates closed with a clang. Then Eddie manoeuvred the van in a tight three-point turn and began to drive the van slowly back the way they'd come.

For Con it was so good to be able to finally sit down on a comfy seat and he felt lulled by the gentle vibrations of the van as it travelled slowly on the driveway. No one spoke. The driveway was winding and bordered on each side by trees the whole way. Con found the sight of the woodland stretching away quite comforting, yet it also seemed strangely familiar.

He felt a sudden, strange tingling sensation all through his body then, but before he could think about the cause of it, they had reached the end of the driveway, and he had another amazing sight to take in.

The house was big and beautiful, made of red brick with large, white, many paned windows. It was the sort of house Con had only ever seen on TV.

'Wow, what's this place?' he asked, as the van came to a stop in front of the house.

'It's our home' Mason told him.

'What, just you two?'

'No, there are others, you'll meet them soon.'

'Are you a family?' It seemed unlikely on appearances, but you never knew.

'Sort of.'

'You're being very vague' accused Con and then feeling bad he added 'sorry, I didn't mean that to sound so rude.'

'It's fine' Mason told him 'You're obviously curious, but let's take this slow, okay?'

'Okay' Con agreed not really knowing what he was actually agreeing to take slowly.

Just then there was the sound of a mobile phone alert and retrieving a phone from one of the many pockets of his cargo trousers Mason glanced at the screen then nodded at Eddie.

'Good,' he told Con, 'we'll go inside now and get you some water, and something to eat if you like, then we'll introduce you to the others.'

'That sounds good, thanks' replied a grateful Con.

'They're here!' Clea had exclaimed excitedly just as a breathless Aaron and Mary entered the lounge/art room. But its wasn't the young couple she was talking about. She'd been stood by one of the windows in the lounge/art room looking out onto the driveway, but now she joined the others at the seating area as Sofia tapped a message into her mobile phone. Aaron closed the door to the room and he and Mary joined the group who now kept quiet as they listened to Mason, Eddie and their visitor enter the house, pass the closed door and head into kitchen as planned.

This plan had been hurriedly made after the drama of the gate intercom buzzer sounding and the ensuing conversation with the visitor.

The rarely heard sound had echoed through the house startling everyone within its walls. Sofia and Eddie had been in the office having a conversation about putting in a purchase request for a new microwave oven, and Mason, Clea and Max had been working in the art room. Morpheus, Geth, Mary and Aaron had been spared the initial drama as they were out at the Factory.

As they were in the office Eddie and Sofia had immediately gone to the security computer screen with the control box for the gate intercom in front of it to see who was at the door. There were hidden camaras in the gate posts giving them a view of anyone requesting to enter. The cameras showed them a young man with a slight build and shoulder length reddish brown hair. He was wearing jeans and a t-shirt and carrying a backpack.

Mason, Clea and Max soon joined them once they realised what the sound meant, and stood for a minute all staring at the image of the young man at the gate.

'Is this the visitor you dreamt was coming?' Sofia had asked Clea.

'It must be' replied Clea.

'So Isthat the Dark Soul?' queried Mason.

'There's only one way to find out' stated Eddie. Then he pressed the intercom button on the security system computer and began a conversation with the visitor.

When the young man told them his name Clea gasped and said 'It is him' sounding pleased about it. After telling Con to wait Eddie had clicked off the intercom so they could all have a conversation.

'Let the poor boy in' Clea had said. But the others had been more reluctant.

'He could be dangerous' suggested Max.

'Oh, look at the poor lovey, he's no danger to anyone,' Clea had pleaded.

'Appearances can be deceiving, Talionis was physically weak remember' Mason had reminded them.

'Yes, but It was half human Dreambringer and half Eternal Dreamer, this boy is just a Dark Soul and I thought It had already been established that he was no danger' Clea had pointed out.

'I wouldn't say established, just believed, we don't really know enough about these Dark Souls do we' Mason had countered.

'I don't believe he's a danger' Eddie had said 'but what the hell do we do with him once we let him in here?'

'Ask him how and why he's here obviously' had been Clea's answer.

'He may not be a danger as such but letting him in here could still be a security risk,' Sofia had then pointed out.

'I think it's worth the risk' had been Eddies view 'we need to know how and why he came here don't we?'

And the others agreed, Clea eagerly, the others reluctantly.

Their quick plan was then made and put into action. Eddie had told the boy to wait for someone to come and get him, and Sofia had called the group at the Factory and told them briefly what had happened and that they should get back to the house as soon as possible. Morpheus had been in the Eternals chamber communing with them and as it was unwise to interrupt them it had been decided that Geth would wait for Morpheus to finish, and Aaron and Mary would return to the house immediately. Then Eddie and Mason had set out to get the van and go pick the visitor up taking their time to give the couple a chance to get back before they did.

When Aaron and Mary arrived, they were to all gather in the lounge/art room with the door shut and to text Mason to let him know they were all there. Eddie and Mason would wait until they received that signal before bringing Con into the house. Their plan to take him straight through to the kitchen and to give him something to eat and drink first was so that he would not get too overwhelmed by the house and its occupants. They realised that they were not the only ones who would be feeling wary and on edge. If Con was just what he seemed, a tired, confused young man who had no idea where he was and why he had been drawn there they needed to make him feel as safe and comfortable as they could.

Con had been amazed by the size of the hallway with its wide staircase, but his attention had been grabbed by a statue displayed there. The striking figure dressed in long robes with long, flowing hair looked like something out of a fantasy story, yet seemed somehow familiar. His arms were outstretched, and in his hand, he held a strange sphere. It was a remarkable, captivating piece of sculpture and Con wanted to ask his hosts who it was but felt too nervous. His interest in the statue did not go unnoticed though.

The kitchen was the biggest one Con had ever been in but felt very cosy despite its size.

He took a seat around the big table putting his backpack and jacket under the table on the floor just in front of his feet.

'I'll get you a nice big glass of water to start with' Eddie told him 'Then I'll make you a sandwich, how does that sound?'

'Like heaven' said Con making the two men smile.

Con downed the glass of water in seconds and Mason filled it again for him whilst Eddie got out some of Clea's homemade bread.

'Would you like ham or cheese in your sandwich?'

'Cheese would be good' Con requested between gulps of water.

He felt comfortable in the company of the two men even though they were strangers, and the house gave him a good vibe too. When the sandwich was put in front of him he took a couple of bites and told them it was the best bread he had ever tasted, and he meant it.

'I've never tasted anything like it' he told them.

'Clea does bake good bread' Eddie said.

'So is Clea one of the other people who live here?' Con asked.

'Yes, we'll introduce you to her and some of the others when you've finished eating.'

'Some of the others? How many of you live here?'

'There are nine of us at the moment' Mason told him 'You'll meet another five of them shortly and then the other two later. We understand it might be daunting for you meeting so many new people at once so it's why we'll stagger the meetings a bit.'

'Thanks, I'm not very good with new people' Con admitted, then added 'well actually I'm not good with people in general, but strangely I am looking forward to meeting the others.'

'That's good, we don't want you to feel uncomfortable' Eddie told him.

'They're all very nice people I promise and they're looking forward to meeting you too' added Mason.

'Really? Why would they be looking forward to meeting me?'

'Well, the fact that you have just turned up here like this means that you must be very special and they're curious to find out more about you' Mason explained.

'I'm not anything special'

'We believe that you are but let's leave that conversation for later. You just enjoy the rest of your sandwich and then we'll go make those introductions.'

Con was torn between savouring the fantastic sandwich and gulping it down so he could meet these mysterious others a bit sooner. He was surprised at himself for looking forward to meeting new people, which was not at all like him, but he knew somehow that these people were good people and that he was on the brink of the new life he had set out in search of, and he was more confident now that it would be a good life.

As for Eddie and Mason they were beginning to relax. Con was coming across as innocent and honest and they felt sure he was no threat, but neither of them intended to let their guard down completely, you just never knew.

When Con had finished his sandwich (at a sensible speed in the end) it was finally time for the big meeting.

Whilst Eddie put the kettle on and prepared to make them all some tea Mason went to fetch the others.

Clea was the first to enter the kitchen and Con instinctively knew that she was the bread maker.

'Hello lovey I'm Clea and I'm very happy to meet you' she said with a big welcoming smile and resisting the temptation to give him a big hug she took the seat to his right.

'Hi' Con replied returning her smile.

Sofia was the next to greet him and Con thought she was the most sophisticated woman he had ever seen. Even in jeans and a casual blouse she looked elegant and refined.

Mary and Aaron's hellos were friendly and easy going, and Max's quiet, shy hello was still welcoming.

Once everyone was sat around the table with a mug of tea in front of them Mason started things off.

'I'm sure you have lots of questions Con and so do we, but I think rather than us bombarding you with questions why don't you start by telling us a little about yourself and how you come to be here today.'

'I'm not used to telling people about myself' Con told them 'But I'll do my best. My full name is Constantine Howard and I'm eighteen years old. Until a few days ago I lived with my father and worked in the building trade' he was not sure this was the sort of thing they really wanted to know and at first he was going to keep it simple, but once he started it all came flooding out. He told them how much he hated his life and why. When he told them about his Mum's death Clea reached out and took his hand in hers, a gesture he found comforting.

Con was not used to being touched like that, he was used to manhandling and blows from heavy fists. The warmth from her gentle hands gave him the strength to talk about the abuses he had suffered, and he did not stop to think why he was being so open and honest, it just felt right. These people were total strangers, but he felt comfortable with them as well as experiencing an innate sense of trust.

Once he had told them about the life he was escaping he went on to the escape itself. He noticed that they did not bat an eyelid at some of the stranger aspects of his story. In fact, when he talked about his dreams some of them even nodded like they knew exactly what he was talking about.

When he got to the bits about his urges to get on the train, then the bus and then to follow the road with the ribbon of mist here they were literally on the edge of their seats taking it all in. And when he had finally finished there were a few seconds silence before the comments and questions started.

'You really have had a time of it haven't you' said Clea 'and you've been so brave.'

'You think I'm brave?' queried a surprised Con.

'Yes, even just walking out your front door was brave, but spending all that time on the streets and not panicking is something to be proud of don't you think?'

'I guess, but I don't feel brave because apart from taking that first step in leaving I haven't really felt scared much.'

'But the whole things brave' added Max 'don't you see, you have made such a big change in your life, and it always takes bravery to do that.'

'I don't know what sort of life I've left my old one for though, I don't know where I'm going or what I'm going to do when I get there.'

'Maybe we can help you with that' Clea told him.

'I would like that I think, and I do feel I need help though in what way I don't know.'

'We'll help you work it out lovey.'

'But who exactly are you, and what is this place?' Con finally asked the question they had been expecting.

Now it was the turn of The Gateway residents to give Con some information. What they would tell him had also been hastily decided before letting him in. The group would treat him like they would a family/friend visitor and as a Marshal was usually there on these rare outsider visits it was down to Sofia to take the lead now.

'You have been very open and honest' she began 'and now it's our turn to tell you about us. This house is called The Gateway and it is an Art Commune. Everyone here but me lives here, I'm just a regular visitor. The people around this table are all very talented artists who have earnt a place here on their artistic merits, a place given to them by the organisation that runs it and whom I work for. They are called The Somnium Foundation and they are a Global Organization that funds art communes like this one around the world as part of their charitable works.'

'Wow, you're all so lucky?' exclaimed Con 'you get to live in this amazing house and just do art stuff, that's gotta be so great, but what about you Sofia, why are you here?'

'I'm the area manager and I look after this and four other art communes. I visit them on a regular basis to make sure everything is okay.'

'Sounds like a nice job.'

'It is.'

'But not as nice as being an artist and living here.'

'No, you're right.'

'Sofia does have artistic talent too' interjected Eddie.

'Cool, well I guess it helps with the job if you're an artist just like the people you look after.'

'Yes, it does' agreed Sofia.

'So, what sort of art are you all good at then?'

The Gateway residents took turns to tell him what sort of artist they were, and Con was impressed. He was particularly interested in Eddie's field of art having been a big fan of comics when he was younger.

'I'd love to see some of your work' he told Eddie, then not wanting to offend the others added 'and all yours too.'

Just then there was the sound of a mobile phone alert and Sofia retrieved her phone from her jeans pocket and read the text that had just arrived before announcing to the group that the other two resident were on their way back to the house.

Morpheus had intended a much longer session with the Eternals, but it had been cut short when the Eternals made him aware that there was an unexpected visitor at the house. Well, not entirely unexpected, but still it was an unusual situation. The Eternal Dreamers had been alerted via their connections to their Dreambringers and Morpheus had agreed it was worth cutting their commune short to go and see what he made of this visitor as it was somehow down to him that he was here.

Morpheus had emerged from the Eternal's chamber to find Geth waiting for him.

'Looks like the little bugger's turned up' Geth told him though he could sense that Morpheus already knew.

'We'd better get to the house quickly' stated Morpheus

'I'll text Sofia and let her know we're on our way' said Geth.

Geth explained the basic plan the group had made as the two men walked quickly through the woods and Morpheus nodded his approval.

'Just so you know the Eternals agree with me that this young man is no threat to us' he then told Geth.

'I get that he's no physical threat, and not even a mental one like Talionis was, but he's still a threat to the secrecy of this place surely?'

'No, not if we deal with him correctly.'

'And how's that exactly?'

'Like the plan, we treat him like a family/friend visiting. The Foundation have never had any problems on that front, so we just follow the usual protocols.'

'But this kid found his way here somehow so it's not the same, he's not some normal clueless visitor, there's something more to him, there has to be for him to come here and you know it.'

'I'm not denying that I just think we can handle it. Yes, we'll have to play it by ear as we go but I don't think we have anything to worry about. I think this is exciting rather than frightening.'

'You would.'

'What does that mean?'

'I don't know, it's just you're thing I guess, taking risks and leading us all into strange new territory.'

'It all works out in the end though doesn't it right?'

'Until now yes.'

'Why should this be any different?'

'Oh hell this is doing my head in a bit now, so let's shut up and just wait and see.'

'Sure.'

Back at the house the rest of the group were keeping conversation light as they waited. Clea was fussing over Con asking him if he wanted anything more to eat or drink. Con told her he was fine and thanked her for the lovely bread he had eaten earlier which pleased her.

Clea had been studying the boy intently since she entered the room and thought that Con was a strange mix of young and old. Physically and mentally, he appeared younger than his eighteen years, but when you looked into his big, brown eyes he seemed like an old soul, there was so much depth there, and pain, you could definitely see the pain he had suffered in those deep, beautiful eyes.

She tore herself away from those eyes then as she got up saying she was going to put the kettle on in case the two new arrivals wanted a cuppa.

'Looks like I need to go get another chair' said Eddie before leaving the kitchen on that errand.

Luckily Con did not ask them any awkward questions about where the two men they were waiting for were coming from. The truth was Con was far so preoccupied with chatting to the amazing new artists he'd just met that it had not even occurred to him to ask.

Taking Clea's vacated seat Mason asked Con 'Do you have any artistic talent?' partly as a distraction but also Mason thought it might be relevant. If this young man had a talent for art in some way, it may be part of the reason he had managed to find them.

'Me, no, I can't draw or paint or anything like that.'

'But what about something like photography or playing a musical instrument?'

'Nope, none of those things…. unless'

'Unless what?'

'Well, I can sing a bit. My mum used to tell me I had the voice of an angel, but she might have been exaggerating, you know how mothers can be.'

The look on Con's face then had been heart-breaking and Mason had almost regretted asking the question, but he persisted with it 'Maybe you could sing for us, and we'll tell you if your mum was exaggerating or not.'

'I.. errmm don't know if I could, I've never sung in front of anyone but Mum.'

Again, this made Mason feel a bit bad, but he was determined to find out the answer to his question, he felt it was important.

'You could just sing for me then maybe.'

'Ermm, okay' agreed Con reluctantly.

'Not now though, later' Mason said giving Con a little reprieve.

They got the conversation back on a safer track and Eddie returned with another chair.

'It's starting to get a bit crowded around this table now' Aaron pointed out with a laugh as they all shuffled around to make room for the new chair.

Any more conversation was stopped then as Geth and Morpheus arrived.

Con was sitting with his back to the door so did not see the two men come in. Geth walked around the table until he was in Con's sight and introduced himself whilst Morpheus hung back waiting for his turn.

After making his own introduction Geth said 'And this is Morpheus' and Con just had time to think what a strange name before the man himself came into his field of vision.

Recognition sent an electric shock through Con's body.

'It's you' he said without really understanding what he was saying. And then the strange ribbon of mist was back, this time it snaked across the short distance between himself and the man he had just learnt was called Morpheus.

The group watching could see it too as could Morpheus who was feeling both shock and excitement. Con was still feeling shock waves through his body and now he was seeing flashes of his dreams in his mind's eye. He saw the trees and he saw his mum, but he did not see this man who stood before him. Yet he recognised this man, but how?

He remembered the statue he had passed in the hallway then and although he was in no doubt that it was sculpted in the image of this man, he also knew that it was not the reason for this recognition.

The rest of the group stood watching, stunned. Whatever they had been expecting of this visitor it was not this.

Now, several minutes after appearing the ribbon of mist dissipated, the electric tingling Con had been experiencing throughout his body abated and Morpheus regained enough composure to speak.

'Hello Con, it's good to meet you' he said as if everything was normal.

'It's…ermm…good to meet you too' stammered Con wondering if he had imagined what had just happened. But then he looked around at the others in the room and the looks on their faces told him it had really happened.

'What's going on here?' he asked no one in particular, but no one had an answer for him.

Con came over a bit faint then and almost fell off his chair, but Mason managed to catch him and place him back on the seat.

'Are you okay lovey?' asked a concerned Clea after witnessing it all.

'I'm not sure' Con replied, 'I don't know what just happened, but it was very strange.'

'We know lovey, but don't worry, it was a good strange okay. I'll get you some water.'

'None of us are quite sure what just happened' Morpheus told him. He had recovered from the strange encounter a lot quicker than Con being used to that sort of thing, but he had not yet had time to process what had happened let alone analyse it.

'If you're not sure, how do you know it's a good strange as she put it?' Con enquired.

'We just know' Morpheus told him in what he hoped was a reassuring voice.

It was then that Con noticed something else strange about Morpheus. His eyes. Looking into them now he could see a strange, white light in their depths.

'Your eyes…' he said and noted that the man immediately broke his gaze.

His comment was ignored so he didn't say anything further thinking he must have imagined that light.

Con had a thought then that maybe he was still laying by the roadside. Maybe he'd fallen asleep there and this was all a dream. It was pretty detailed and vivid for a dream though. What if he was not simply asleep though but delirious from the heat, dehydration and exhaustion and maybe this was a delirium dream? What were they like? Was this one? But then had he really been that badly off to become so delirious?

'Am I dreaming this?' he wondered aloud.

He heard the man called Aaron give a snort of laughter and Morpheus said 'Not this, no.'

"What the hell did that mean?" Thought Con, and now he was getting a headache.

'I don't feel too good' he told them all.

'Maybe he needs a lay down' suggested Mary.

'Yes, he should drink some more water and then lay down for a rest' agreed Clea, then to Con 'Would you like that lovey?'

Con could only nod, he felt suddenly very drained. He drank the glass of water Clea handed him as a whispered conversation went on around him about an attic room, then he was told that Eddie would take him somewhere he could have a lay down.

'Come with me mate' Eddie said, and Con grabbed his backpack and jacket and stood up slowly before walking to where Eddie waited by the door. Eddie took the backpack and jacket from him and putting a steadying hand under his elbow led him from the room.

There were rooms nearby that did not involve stairs for their tired visit to traverse, but there would be distractions on the way if he took him through the art filled lounge/art room to Sofia's room, or into his or Mason's rooms that were full of their stuff. It was better to take Con to one of the newly converted, neutral attic guest rooms

Eddie walked beside Con up the main staircase and then across the landing at the top keeping a hold on his arm to steady him the whole time. The staircase up to the attic rooms was much narrower though so Eddie walked behind Con so he could catch him if he fell.

Despite the lack of visitors to The Gateway the two attic guest rooms were always equipped and ready for visitors. Each room contained a small wardrobe, a chest of draws and bedside tables, with one room containing two single beds and the other a double bed. Both rooms were painted in a pale grey with a darker grey carpet, and both had a small en suite bathroom with shower.

Eddie steered Con into the first room, which was the one with the two single beds, and put his backpack and jacket down on the top of the chest of draws saying, 'You can have a shower once you've rested if you want to, there is soap and towels etc, and when you're ready just come back downstairs, okay?'

'Yes, thanks' said Con before sitting down on the nearest bed to take his trainers off. Eddie left him to it with a cheery 'See you later mate.' Once he had gone Con took off his jeans and after settling under the duvet, he fell asleep within seconds.

Eddie went back downstairs a lot quicker than they had gone up and joined the others who had now assembled in the lounge to chat. They had waited for him before staring so now he had arrived they could begin.

To start with everyone began to talk at once so Morpheus decided to take charge.

'Everyone quiet for a minute!' he shouted, then once he had quiet, he continued 'You'll all get your say but for now let me start by asking if you all agree that his young man is no danger to us.'

They all agreed with a nod or a brief comment, but Sofia elaborated with 'It's not a matter of him being a danger so much as how do we deal with him in the long run? How much do we tell him, and where do we go from there?'

'Exactly, that's what we need to discuss, but first you need to catch me and Geth up by telling us what he told you so far.'

Sofia was elected to repeat Con's story and the rest of them sat quietly whilst she did so. Then when she had finished the discussion started.

'It looks like you did invite him here somehow then doesn't it Morpheus' said Max

'I concede that it must have been something I did that brought Con here, but believe me when I say I didn't do it on purpose…'

'We believe you' said Sofia and no one contradicted here.

'Good, so now I have to work out how I did it and what happens from here.'

'Is it time we let the Foundation know what's going on?' asked Max.

'Not quite yet' replied Morpheus, 'let's just talk it through a bit more and then I need to think on it for a bit. The Foundation are going to want answers and I need to have something to tell them first.'

'Won't they be angry when they find out we delayed telling them?' queried Mary.

'Probably, but I'd rather deal with that than have to answer 'I don't know' to all their questions.'

'But it could take ages to work out the answers' countered Max.

'I'm not going to put it off for ages, I will call them today, but later, I just need a little time to put all the facts together and have a think, so let's start with the facts; Con is a Dark Soul within the Dream Realm, I healed him enough to be able to bring him simple dreams. I then tried to break down his barriers to learn more about the type of dreams I needed to bring him in order to heal him completely. Unable to fully break through his barriers I brought him dreams I felt he needed based on the emotions I was reading from him. I sent him dreams of comfort and support in an effort to give him confidence and win his trust. I continually tried to convey that he could trust me and that I was a friend who was there for him. Due to the barriers he put up I was unable to see how he interpreted all this in his dreams. Today he told us what he dreamt. Now the question we need to answer is how did these seemingly simple dreams lead him to us?'

'You're right' said Clea 'even after he'd told us what he dreamt it's still not clear how those dreams brought him here. He dreamt of his mother which is no connection, and although they were in woodland in the dreams they could've been anywhere. Con never saw this house, or the nearby village in his dreams and he didn't mention hearing place names or anything in his dreams, yet he was drawn to them when he saw them.'

'And I didn't tell him to come here which is clear from his recounting of the dreams' added Morpheus.

'It is similar to how we were called to the Artfest though, yet not quite,' said Aaron.

'It's like a warped version of it I guess' commented Mason 'when I called you all I just gave you an image of the Artfest advertisement that I'd seen and had to prey it got through to you. But I was one weakened Dreambringer calling five of you and Morpheus is much stronger and was focusing all his energy on one soul.'

'But that one soul was a Dark Soul' stated Geth 'so it must be something to do with that. The difference between these Dark Souls and the Dreambringer candidates' souls.'

'That's obviously the key' added Mason 'to the nature of the Dark Souls.'

'The problem with that being we know so little about them,' said Max.

'We now know why he became a Dark Soul' commented Clea 'because of the trauma of his mother's death and the subsequent abuse from his father and others, but that still doesn't answer the question.'

'Is Con a special case or would this have happened with any Dark Soul?' said Eddie.

'Bloody hell what we need is answers not more questions' blustered Geth.

'I asked Con if he had any artistic talent?' Mason told them then.

'What made you ask that?' enquired Eddie.

'I'm not sure, I just thought the answer might be relevant in some way.'

'And does he have artistic talent' prompted Clea.

'He said no to start with, but then told me he could sing but wasn't sure how good he was.'

'He told us that he sang with his mum in his dreams' interjected Aaron.

'That's right' agreed Mason 'so maybe that is why he was able to find his way here, he has artistic talent so maybe if he hadn't been traumatised, he would have been a Dreambringer candidate.'

'But he hadn't dreamt for years and us Dreambringers have a great dreaming talent' stated Geth 'and what about the fact that Morpheus didn't purposely call him here?'

'Yes, but we've not been traumatised have we, and that's my point.'

'Let me get this all straight' said Sofia 'what you're saying Mason is that if not for childhood trauma Con could have been a Dreambringer candidate and that fact, plus the fact that Morpheus' new powers are still not quantified means that the combination of the two has created yet another - for want of a better word – mutation within the Dreambringer world.'

'Yes, that's what I'm saying' agreed Mason 'it would explain the thing with the ribbon of mist that led him here and when he met Morpheus, and the eyes thing, he saw the light in Morpheus' eyes, you all noted that right, and they're the sort of thing that happen to Dreambringers not some random kid.'

Mary gave little gasp of realisation then and said, 'What if all the Dark Souls are Dreambringer candidates that have suffered trauma.'

'That's a bit of a stretch' scoffed Geth.

'No, wait, she may have a point' said Morpheus 'maybe our definition of the Dark Souls is a little off. It could be that some of those Dark Souls that won't be helped are normal dreamers who have been traumatised and the rest were born warped somehow. But those that are more accepting of help are souls like Con who had a Dreambringer talent until it was taken away by trauma.'

'Right, like there are three levels of Dark Souls, the ones like Con, the traumatised normal dreamers and then there's the evil bastards' suggested Aaron.

'Something along those lines yes,' said Morpheus.

'Whatever the case it all boils down to the fact that we don't know enough about these Dark Souls' stated Geth.

'But we're learning now so that's a good thing' said Morpheus 'and now Con is here we might learn some more.'

'It's a bit risky though, isn't it?' argued Geth.

'There's always an element of risk involved with this sort of thing. Back in the old days the Foundation had to take lots of risks as they learnt more about the Eternal Dreamers and Dreambringers. They've had it easy for a long time, but I took a risk with Talionis and that paid off, so why shouldn't this?'

'The Talionis thing is still a risk if you ask me, what we don't know about your new talent is part of all this remember.'

Noting the mounting tension between Geth and Morpheus Sofia decided to cut in.

'Let's not argue okay. In light of all that's just been said we can only speculate at this point. What we need to do now is make a plan as to what to do about Con.'

'I know what I'd like to do first' said Morpheus 'I'd like to go and commune with the Eternals and see what they think. Con is asleep so the Eternals can monitor him within the Dream Realm and tell me what they think.'

'Good idea' agreed Sofia.

'I'll just go for an hour of so then when I come back, we can see where we are. Hopefully Con will sleep for at least that long.'

'The poor boy was very tired' said Clea 'but what if he wakes before you get back?'

'Just keep him occupied, treat him like you would an invited guest.'

'And what if he asks awkward questions?' asked Max.

'Do your best to answer him without giving anything away that you shouldn't.'

'You make it sound easy' said Geth sarcastically.

'I'm sure between you, you can think of something.'

'We'll be fine' Sofia told him 'You go off to the Factory now and I'll talk through a few strategies with the others for dealing with awkward questions, it's part of my job after all, I was trained for it.'

'Thanks Sofia.'

Sofia tried not to show how much his thanks meant to her so just nodded. And then he was gone, and Sofia turned her attention to the task she had given herself.

Sofia gave them a few tips on question evasion and misdirection then went through the Foundation guidelines she had been trained in regarding dealing with outsider visitors. There followed a brief discussion on Foundation policies before Geth began a very odd discussion.

'Have the Somnium Foundation ever killed anyone in order to protect their secrets?' he asked.

'Fucking hell mate, that's dark even for you' exclaimed Eddie with a laugh, then to Sofia 'but it is a valid question, so, have they?'

'I dare say that back in the beginning that sort of thing went on, but I'm not aware of it happening in modern day times.'

'Ah, but would you know about it if it did happen' said Geth 'maybe the Foundation have a top secret 'wet work' section like the CIA do.'

'I really don't think that's likely, even a big organisation like the Foundation would have trouble getting away with stuff like that.'

'I think they would get away with it' stated Aaron 'they could use a patsy.'

'I think you and Geth watch too many movies' said Max.

'What's 'wet work' and what on earth is a patsy?' asked Clea.

'Wet work is a euphemism for murder and assassination' explained Geth.

'And a patsy is someone who takes the blame and if necessary, the punishment for something someone else did, usually an organisation of some sort' added Aaron 'and I reckon the Foundation could find someone loyal and brave enough to be a willing patsy and take the fall for the good of the cause.'

'You think someone would kill and or die to keep our secrets?' asked Eddie.

'Yes, I do, and I think back in the past they probably did it too.'

'Would you?' asked Geth.

'I'd do it if it meant keeping Mary safe.'

'Really? That's so brave of you' said Mary before leaning over to give Aaron a big kiss.

'Ah, breaks my heart' said Clea whilst Geth makes a face and fake retching noises.

'Okay, that's enough of that now' said Mason 'I think we need to keep ourselves occupied with some artwork until Morpheus gets back. We can all still mull things over as we work and if we have any good ideas we can share with the group, but in the meantime let's give the Eternals an extra boost to help them help us.'

'Great, let's get on with it' agreed Eddie.

Upstairs Con was having a restful, dreamless sleep. Without Morpheus in the Dream Realm the Eternals could not help him, they could only watch over his dark presence as it roamed on the edges of their realm. But right now, Con needed rest more than he needed dreams, with Morpheus' help he was already where he needed to be, now they just needed to work out how to restore him fully to a healthy dreaming soul.

With the help of the energy being produced by the artists back at the house the Eternals communed with Morpheus relaying their thoughts and observations to him.

Morpheus returned to the house after nearly two hours. Con was still asleep, but the group had been getting a bit antsy so were pleased to see him. He did not waste time with pleasantries, he just got on with it.

'I have a lot to tell you. There's been a bit of a breakthrough that I have to admit has given me a bit of a mental slap. I have let the human side of me have too much of the reigns, or rather I've not been paying enough attention to the Eternal Within. Yes, when in the waking world, like now, the Eternal Within is pretty dormant and my human side comes to the fore. But since I stepped into that spiral circle and the Eternal Within was made stronger when in the Dream Realm, I have been focusing too much on what it brought to my human Dreambringer talent and not the talents the Eternal Within brings itself. The Dream Realm is their domain after all, and I've been a fool to forget this.'

The group were a little startled, and in some cases glad, to hear this from Morpheus. His confidence whilst usually a good thing had obviously in this case veered towards arrogance and though most forgave him that, some, namely Geth and Mason and to a lesser extent Eddie, were pleased he had been given this wake-up call. But no one said anything, they were too eager to hear what else he had to say.

'As you know when in the Dream Realm, I give out a strong light that brings comfort. I am aware that this light comes from the Eternal Within, but my mistake has been to think that this is the extent of its powers. I believed that despite the recent boost to its strength being enclosed in human flesh still made it weaker than the other Eternals and it appears that is not quite the case. Rather than being weaker it just works in a different way.

This is a good thing, but the problem has been that my human and Eternal sides have not yet learnt how to communicate properly so have been working to some extent independently. Therefore, I was sending basic dreams to the Dark Soul whilst the Eternal Within was healing it with its light but also adding little, unconscious notes to the dreams like they do when they help to call new Dreambringers and so this is how Con came to find his way here.'

There were a few noises of realisation from his audience and a muttered 'Now that makes sense' from Mason. They sensed Morpheus was not finished though, so no one else spoke.

'I feel like a fool for not realising all this' he continued 'but I have learnt my lesson and I have some more learning to do. You're probably wondering why the Eternal Within hasn't communicated this to me before, but again as I've said this is all new to It too and It didn't quite understand what was going on either. This was all basically down to a lack of communication which is something I'd always thought I was good as which makes my failing worse. I can only apologise for this and assure you that I will do better from now on.'

'So why did the Eternal Within lead Con here?' asked Sofia partly to carry the conversation on without someone having a go at Morpheus.

'That's not completely clear' said Morpheus 'the Eternal Within didn't actually do it on purpose, like I've said Its not sure of Its new powers either and It just tried to do what It used to do without realising the consequences. The good news is that the Eternals are sure that Con is no threat, in fact they think he's rather special and basically one of us.'

'Oh, that's such good news' gushed Clea.

But a much less enthusiastic Geth asked 'So what do we do with the boy?'

'The Eternals and I believe that Con should be treated in a similar way to a new Dreambringer recruit, or at least he should once he has been healed fully.'

'And he stays here until then does he?' queried Geth not sounding happy about it.

'Yes, that seems best.'

'But that means we have to keep up a pretence for however long it takes, and I don't think that's good for us.'

'I don't believe it will be long before we can start to initiate Con into the Dreambringer world so this pretence as you call it will only be for a short time.'

'It won't feel short when we have to spend our days avoiding awkward questions.'

'I don't think it'll be a problem' Clea interjected 'I get the feeling Con likes it here already and he's just glad to be safe and away from his life of abuse. He's going to be too busy enjoying being here to ask too many questions.'

'I agree' said Morpheus but Geth gives out a harrumph of displeasure.

'What about telling the Foundation?' asked Sofia.

'I'll update them later today now that I actually have something to tell them.'

'Okay, good. Do you want me to be there when you make the call? I can help smooth things over if Cedric gets angry about us not telling them sooner.'

'Yes, that would be good, thanks.'

Sofia gave him a beaming smile and he rewarded her with a beautiful, rare smile in return.

'So, what happens next regarding you're ongoing work healing Con?' asked Mason.

'Now that I'm working in sync with the Eternal Within, we can work better together tonight on the healing and bring Con dreams to reassure him that he is safe here. I think that after spilling the beans with us in person about his trauma he will be much more open and receptive to our help. And we keep doing this until he is fully healed.'

'And in the meantime, we continue to tell Con that we're just a happy group of artists living the good life' said Geth sarcastically.

'Yes, that's right' confirmed Morpheus ignoring the sarcasm 'he'll be fine. So let me now lay out the plan for the next few days. I suggest that myself and a couple of you go out to the Factory for a couple of hours as the Eternals will need all the energy they can get later. The rest of you should feed the Eternals with your art from here. When Con wakes up, you keep him occupied and if he asks about the missing members of the group tell him we're out on some errand. Then we'll all be back here for dinner and after, whilst you enjoy your leisure time me and Sofia will update the Foundation then join you.

Tonight, working in tandem with the Eternal Within this time, I will work on Con and see how being here has impacted him and hopefully find out more about what he needs to heal. Tomorrow, hopefully, I will have some news to tell you and the Foundation about Con. We will work from there in whatever way seems best with what we learn as we go.'

It was in some respects a vague plan, but it was a plan they could follow easily, the problem being the variables. Still, everyone was feeling quite positive despite this including Geth and Mason, if reluctantly so.

'Who's coming out to the Factory with me then?' asked Morpheus.

'I'll come' volunteered Geth 'I don't fancy being here when the boy wakes up just in case, despite what you think Morpheus, he does ask me some awkward questions.'

'Fine, anyone else want to come?'

'Me, I'll come' said Max for the same reason as Geth though he did not say so.

Minutes later the three men had got their stuff together and set off for the Factory whist the others got started on their artwork.

Con woke slowly from a restful, dreamless sleep. He felt a moments disorientation and a touch of panic at the unfamiliar surroundings, but then memory returned, and he relaxed. He lay on his back looking up at the ceiling wondering how on earth he had ended up in the big house with these people. It was like something in a movie.

This adventure he was on certainly seemed to have taken a turn for the better, if in a bit of a weird way. It would have all seemed reasonably normal if not for that ribbon of mist, and then the strange reaction when he saw the man called Morpheus. And then that phrase was in his head again '*accept the weird.*' It seemed this would need to be his new philosophy in life.

These people had treated him well and he did not want to do anything to make them regret that, or to make them chuck him out. He did not want to rock the boat, he needed to go along with things and just enjoy the ride. There was no danger here, just a little strangeness, but it was worth putting up with the oddness of some things in order to enjoy the rest.

He lay there a while longer enjoying the comfy mattress beneath him and the peaceful feeling that being there was giving him. Soon though he felt the need to get up and seek out the artists. Then he remembered Eddie telling him he was welcome to take a shower and realised he was probably unfit for company without one.

The shower was great, it seemed brand new and much better than the one he was used to. After drying himself on a wonderfully fluffy towel and combing his damp hair he fished out clean jeans, underwear and a t shirt from his backpack and got dressed.

Now he was fit for company he headed out of the room and down the narrow staircase. There were five doors off the wide landing below and he was tempted to peek in each room but resisting the temptation he carried on down the main staircase.

As he descended the stairs he heard voices, and when he got to the bottom, he worked out they was coming from the room accessed by the door ahead on his right. He was momentarily distracted by the sculpture of the man with the strange name. It stood on its pedestal table commanding the attention of anyone passing. Con experienced the same strange feeling he had when he saw it the first time. There was something special about this man, not least that Con felt like he'd met him before today.

A burst of laughter distracted him from the sculpture and turning Con entered the room. Six pairs of eyes were immediately upon him as he took in the scene before him.

132

Con had never seen such a big room; it was larger than the whole of the flat he had grown up in. On the walls there were many works of art and within it's walls were the artists.

Behind a workbench near the windows stood the man called Mason who was doing some sort of woodwork. Con could not remember the name Mason had given to his art/profession, but he knew that the man made guitars so that must be what he was working on.

A little way back from Mason the young man called Aaron stood in front of an easel obviously working on a painting but from where he stood Con could not see what it was of.

The rest of the artists were over to the right sat on various armchairs and sofas. The young woman called Mary who Con remembered was a writer sat on one end of a sofa with her legs tucked up, a laptop balanced on them.

The kindly bread maker lady called Clea was sat in an armchair doing some sort of sewing, embroidery if Con had remembered her name right.

The sophisticated and sexy Sofia sat at the other end of the sofa to Mary with a large sketch pad on her lap and a pencil in her hand.

In another armchair sat biker Eddie also with a large sketch pad but he was working with a sharpie pen.

All the artists stopped what they were doing when Con walking in and there were a few seconds silence before Clea spoke.

'Hello lovey, did you have a good nap?'

'Yes, it was good thanks.'

'Come and sit down' she said indicating the space on the sofa between Mary and Sofia, and as Con walked over and took a seat she continued

'We're all working on our art, it's a shame you haven't got anything to work on, but we can talk whilst we work.'

'Okay, but I do have a book in my backpack that I could read so you'd be free to get on with your work.'

'You're free to go and get it if you like lovey, but I can sew and talk, it's not a problem.'

'I wouldn't want to disturb the others though.'

'Okay, you go get your book then.'

But before Con could get up Mason had another idea.

'Maybe you could sing for us.'

It was a risky comment likely to put Con on edge judging by his earlier reaction, but Mason could not help himself, he was too curious to hear the boy's voice. He received a cross look from Clea who was of course all for coddling the boy, and some of the others looked like they did not approve, but it was too late now.

'Do you have some LPs I could sing along to, cos that's the only way I'm used to singing' said Con surprising them all, including himself. The idea of singing for an audience had frightened him earlier, but now, after his nap and in the calming presence of these nice people he felt he could give it a try. It wasn't that he was no longer nervous, he just felt a little braver now and for some reason in the mood to sing.

'We have some CD's' said Eddie pointing to a small stereo within the shelving unit of the TV system set up. Underneath it were two short rows of CD's 'it's a small but pretty varied collection as we all have different tastes so you should be able to find something you know.'

'Most of the songs I know are from the 1960's and 70's because that's what my mum used to listen to. We used to sing along to her albums. I don't know any modern stuff' Con told them as he walked over to the CDs on slightly shaky legs.

'There isn't much modern stuff there' Eddie told him.

Flicking through the CDs Con was pleased to see a few by bands and singers he knew, but what should he choose. Then he saw it.

'I can't believe you have this one he said holding up the selected CD.'

'Oh, that's mine' piped up Clea 'good choice.'

'Mama's Big Ones, are you having a laugh' exclaimed Eddie.

'Shush, Mama Cass was an amazing woman' Clea told him.

'Sorry, I can pick something else out if you like,' suggested a worried Con.

'No, sorry mate, you pick what you like I was just joking' Eddie told him feeling bad for his silly outburst, how likely would it have been for the kid to pick one of his heavy metal albums anyway.

'Let me put in on for you' Eddie offered getting up.

Con gave a nervous nod and handed the CD to Eddie who turned the stereo on and put the CD into it.

'What track do you want on?'

'Track three, thanks, but can you hold on a minute.'

'Okay.'

Con nervously cleared his throat in preparation for possible embarrassment. He did not think these people would be cruel enough to ridicule him, but it could still be awkward if he sang badly. Yes, he had sung by himself recently, but he had not really taken note of how good or bad his voice was, he had just revelled in the act of singing. He decided that should be his approach now, he should lose himself in the singing and just enjoy it no matter how good or bad it was. He had never done karaoke before but decided to approach it like that, he was out having fun with friends on a karaoke night.

He gave Eddie the nod, and the rocker guy moved the CD onto track three which was 'Make Your Own Kind of Music' then quickly sat back down as the music started.

Con stood facing his audience but set his gaze above their heads afraid to see disappointment on their faces.

The first few notes came out a bit croaky but Con continued, and after a few lines his voice grew stronger. By the time he got to the first chorus his voice was at full volume and he began to enjoy it.

His audience were enjoying it too. Con's voice was a joy, it had a sweet, high but full tone. It was beautiful, he did indeed have the voice of an angel.

Mason had a big smile on his face the whole way through the song, his theory having been proven. In fact, all those listening had big smiles on their faces.

When the song finished, they all clapped and cheered and called for more. Con looked at their faces then seeing they truly had enjoyed his singing. He felt flushed with joy and pride, his Mum must have been right, they loved it. He could not help the little voice of doubt in the back of his mind though 'they're just being nice' it said, but he pushed it away preferring to believe in his Mum's judgement and that the applause was warranted.

His audience urged him to sing another song so Con went back through the CD collection as Eddie got back up and ejected the Mama Cass CD from the stereo.

Con's next choice was a best of Eagles CD, and he chose the song 'Take It Easy' which was a better choice in Eddies mind, but the CD actually belonged to Max.

Again, at the end of the song there was rapturous applause.

After that Con sang another Eagles song, then found a Beatles CD and sung a couple of songs off of that too.

When he had finished the second song, he asked if he could have a break.

'Oh lovey, of course you can, you must be thirsty after all that lovely singing. Would you like some water, or maybe tea, or I think we have some lemonade if you prefer.'

Con admitted he was a little thirsty and told her that tea would be nice. Both Clea and Eddie volunteered to make everyone tea at the same time. Eddie persuaded Clea to stay and talk to Con – it did not take much – and off he went to the kitchen.

During the singing they had all been so enthralled that they had stopped working and Mason and Aaron had even moved to sit on the other sofa. Now Con retook his seat between Sofia and Mary. They chatted about Con's singing and song choices until Eddie came in with the teas on a large tray. After he had handed them out, he sat back in the armchair and the chat turned to music and what their individual tastes were.

They talked, laughed and drank tea and Con felt comfortable amongst them. In the end he had to ask for some water after he had drunk all his tea because he had not talked this much in years and on top of the singing, he was feeling a little hoarse.

'Why don't you come with me to the kitchen for your water, it was time I started making the dinner and you can keep me company whilst I do it' suggested Clea.

She figured that way the others could get on with their artwork for a bit longer and chat about Con without him there.

Con seemed okay with the idea, so they went off to the kitchen taking the tray of empty tea mugs with them. Con then offered to wash up the mugs and although he was basically a guest Clea let him do it thinking it would make him feel even more at home because for some reason that's how she wanted him to feel.

So, Con washed and dried the mugs whilst Clea started preparing dinner for everyone. It was pork chops, roast potatoes and veg and she felt it would stretch easily to an extra person.

After Con finished with the mugs Clea asked him to help prepare the veg and they set to it chatting away the whole time. Clea was careful about which subjects she chose as she did not want to answer any awkward questions on her own. Con joined in the conversation here and there but mostly listened, he was not much of a talker, and he liked the sound of Clea's voice, it was jolly and warm and made him feel safe.

Clea need not have worried about Con asking questions because he was enjoying himself too much to even think of questioning why he was there. He was here in this lovely house with these amazing people and for now the whys and how's did not matter to him.

In the lounge the others were discussing Con's singing and how the quality of his talent gave the idea of him being a Dreambringer candidate if not for his childhood trauma more weight.

'There's definitely something special about Con,' said Sofia. The others nodded and murmured their agreement.

'It's a bit strange that he hasn't asked any question though,' said Mary.

'I think he's been too preoccupied with the singing to even think about it' suggested Mason.

'Yeah, that was a good call on your part Mason' Eddie told him 'it worked on two levels, getting us more info on his talent and keeping him occupied.'

'And he enjoyed it too' added Aaron.

'He did' agreed Mary 'he's been through so much this must seem like paradise to him even if it is all a little strange.'

'It'll be interesting to see what happens in the Dream Realm tonight' commented Mason.

They talked a little more about their visitor then got back to their artwork.

When Clea and Con had finished preparing the meal as far as they could for the time being Clea suggested they went back to the lounge with the others until it was time to put the veg on. As they walked back, she talked overloudly to Con, she had a feeling the group would be talking about Con and wanted to make sure they would hear them coming and therefore stop talking about him before they walked in. She need not have worried though as they were all intent on their work at that point.

'Dinners on, and will be about forty minutes' Clea announced, then sitting down in the armchair with her embroidery she added 'the boys should be back by then' with a meaningful glance at Eddie.

Understanding her meaning Eddie left it a minute before excusing himself saying 'I just need to go make a call.'

Con had sat down next to Sofia who was now showing him the charcoal sketches she was working on, so he did not really take much notice of what was said. They had an excuse ready for Geth, Max and Morpheus' absence, but it turned out not to be needed.

Eddie went to the kitchen where he used his mobile phone to call Geth and tell him it was time for them to come back to the house for dinner. Geth of course asked how it was going and Eddie filled him in regarding the singing and lack of questions asked.

'I hope he's not saving them up until I get there' was Geth's half joking reply.

His errand done Eddie returned to the lounge where there was a relaxed atmosphere as people chatted and, in some cases, got on with their artwork.

A while later Clea went to the kitchen to put the veg on and set the table. Con was having a conversation with Aaron about his art and was happy enough.

Whilst Clea was in the kitchen Max Geth and Morpheus returned.

They had a quick conversation with her then went through to the lounge. Once the hellos had been said Eddie suggested he take Con on a quick tour of the house before dinner. This was again a diversionary tactic to stop him asking about where the three men had been.

Eddie took Con upstairs first explaining as they walked up the large staircase, 'There's not really a lot to see but I just wanted to let you know what rooms are where.' He then had the sudden realisation that he had no room to point out as Morpheus' bedroom suite and had a moments panic over what to tell Con before he came up with a plan.

'You've obviously seen the guest room above where you had your nap, so we won't go up to look, but there's another guest room next to it which is where Sofia is staying.' He would get to Morpheus later.

They were now on the large, upstairs landing and Eddie pointed to each of four of the doors explaining whose bedroom suite each one led to.

'I won't show you inside, it's not my place, it's up to the others to show you their rooms' he explained, and Con nodded his understanding.

'But I can show you that room' Eddie said pointing to a door between the two rooms to their right.

Opening this fifth door he showed Con the laundry room saying 'If you need any towels or bed linen this is where you come. Oh, and that reminds me, you might want to sleep in the other single bed tonight, I'm not being funny, but you were a bit grubby when you had your nap and clean sheets are always nice, right. We can put the other sheets in the wash tomorrow.'

'Thanks' said Con feeling happy that he was obviously welcome to stay the night. '

Eddie then led him back downstairs and across the hall to the door on their left.

'This is the office' he said opening the door to let Con through adding 'The door across the room there is to Mason's room.'

Con's gaze skimmed over the items which you would expect to find in a room named the office, but what really captured his attention was all the artwork on the walls.

'Who did all this artwork, and all the stuff in the other room?' he asked.

'This house has been an art commune for a long time' Eddie explained 'and the work was done by various artists who have lived here over the years.'

'Is there anything by the artists here now?'

'Not in this room, not so far, but there are a few things that were recently put up in the other room. Plus, the sculpture in the hall which Max did.'

'It's a great sculpture, Max is very talented. It's of Morpheus, right?'

'Yes, that's right.'

Con was obviously impressed and luckily his questions were easy and safe to answer.

As they walked out of the office Eddie gestured into the lounge/art room saying casually 'The door across the room is to Morpheus' bedroom suite.'

He would have to explain things to Morpheus and Sofia later, but he felt it was better to say Sofia was in the other guest room and Morpheus had a bedroom suite as it made more sense regarding what Con knew about the Gateway set up. Plus, Con would be more likely to notice Morpheus' night-time absence than if he had explained the rooms the other way around. It might cause Sofia a little inconvenience having to move but it was the best he could come up with at short notice.

Then he took Con out to the kitchen to show him the utility room and toilet. He then showed him to his own room which was across the hall from the kitchen, and this time he actually showed him inside.

Again, Con was impressed by the size of the room which contained a double bed with bedside table, large wardrobe and tall chest of draws plus a seating area with sofa, coffee table and TV. There was also an old fashioned piece of furniture that had a record turntable set in the top and two cupboards containing Eddie's vinyl LP collection.

'All the other bedroom suites are similar' he told Con as he led him back out of the room.

Lastly, he showed Con the terrace through the French doors at the back of the house where they stood looking out over the sloping lawn and woodland beyond.

'You're welcome to sit out here if you want some fresh air, but I wouldn't advise going into the woods in case you get lost, okay?'

Con nodded and said 'Okay' then, gazing off into the distance he asked, 'Do the people who own the house own all this land too?'

'Yes, the Foundation own it all.'

'How much land is there?'

'I don't know exactly' Eddie lied. He did know exactly how much land there was and where everything was on it, but it wasn't information he thought Con needed to know, 'we tend to keep close to the house, a lot of the woodland is too dense to walk in anyway' he added as an extra deterrent to questions and possible wandering. Con seemed happy enough with his answer thankfully.

As they went back into the house Clea called to them from the kitchen 'I'm ready to dish up dinner' she called 'Con can you go tell the others that dinner is ready, and Eddie can you give me a hand dishing up.'

Dinner was a raucous affair with lots of talking and laughing. Con told Clea it was the best meal he had ever had making her blush, and he was not lying. The dinners he cooked for himself and his father were a lot less impressive, he was not a natural cook and had had to teach himself over the years. His food was edible but basic and far below the skills Clea obviously possessed.

Eddie managed to get word around the noisy table regarding the bedroom situation he had explained to Con without Con hearing. In return Sofia let him know she was okay with the change and others congratulated him on his quick thinking.

When they had finished eating it was Mary and Aaron's turn to do the clearing up, but Sofia and Morpheus made a show of it being a four-person job with so much to clear up. It was obvious to everyone but Con that this was an excuse for Sofia and Morpheus to slip away to the office for their call to the Foundation.

Usually, the others stayed in the room whilst the clearing up was done but today those not involved headed for the lounge straight away. They had decided over dinner to find a movie to watch on Netflix, a task that was no mean feat with ten people involved, which was the excuse Mason had given for deciding that Con, being the guest, should choose which movie. The others all realised that the real reason was to keep him occupied enough not to notice Sofia and Morpheus' extended absence and went along with it.

So, whilst Mary and Aaron cleared up and the others watched Con skip through Netflix in search of a film Sofia and Morpheus slipped off to the office to make their difficult call.

As expected, the delay in informing the Foundation did not go down well. Cedric Neale's listened silently as Morpheus explained the basics of what had been going on, but when he had finished Cedric's usually moderated, cultured tone became unusually loud and harsh when he exclaimed 'Why have you not informed me of this situation before now? I have expressly told you several times that I need to be updated on a regular basis. This delay is a breach of Foundation policy, and I am not happy about it!'

'I apologise for the delay' said Morpheus 'but I really didn't want to call you until I had some answers to give you to the questions that this whole situation has brought up.'

'That is no excuse' Cedric told him 'And you should have known better Sofia, you should have insisted Morpheus call me, or done it yourself, I'm disappointed in you, I hope you were not coerced into this secrecy.'

'I understand your disappointment' Sofia said embarrassed by the telling off but keeping her cool 'but I was not coerced into anything, and it wasn't about secrecy. Holding off on the call was a joint decision and I still believe the right one. We could have spoken to you earlier but would have had nothing of real significance to report, it would have just been our vague wonderings and theories, there were so many questions we did not know the answer to, and we wanted to know more before we contacted you.'

'You should have still reported it, however insignificant you thought it' Cedric insisted though his tone was now less harsh.

Morpheus was glad that Sofia was with him, she was doing a better job than he would have done in placating their boss. Much as he respected the man, he found him a little bit stuffy and old fashioned at times.

Morpheus had spent a lot of time with Cedric Neale and the other Foundation leaders in the months after the origination. A lot of boring, frustrating time. He could picture Cedric now, seated at his huge, oak desk wearing one of his old, but exquisitely made three-piece tweed suits, his bald head shining as if polished and his white moustache neatly groomed as always. Although facially dissimilar, with his bald head, cultured voice and manner he had always reminded Morpheus of the actor Patrick Stewart.

The man was a good leader, but was far too cautious for Morpheus' liking, though he was more receptive than some of the other high up members, those months after the Origination had shown him that.

Morpheus understood the element of fear they must have felt when first dealing with the new being he had become, but he had done nothing to warrant the continuation of that fear. And despite his view on their old-fashioned ways, he had never shown and inclination for, or even felt within himself the need to take over as leader. He may have flouted their rules a little at times both before the Origination and after, but it was never done to harm anyone or anything, or to assert control over anything but his own actions, it was just the way he worked, and everything he was working for was for the good of the Foundation.

He had always felt that they had spent too much time testing him. He, and even they, should have realised that keeping him in a safe house in the middle of nowhere for months was wrong. It was now obvious that he should have been here, with these people and the Eternals all along, because being with the Eternals had turned out to be the key to it all. Their lack of trust had been understandable but frustrating and had cost him time. It was easy to realise all this in hindsight, he understood that, but it did not help with his feelings of frustration at the time he had lost because of it.

What he realised then was this fear of theirs, that his power meant that they would lose control of him, and possibly their rule over the Foundation, was the root of Cedric's anger now. What he didn't know was that Cedric wasn't the one he had to worry about.

Sofia had begun the job of placating their boss but now it was his job to gain the man's trust going forward.

'I understand that my holding out on you can be perceived as worrying behaviour but rest assured that I still have respect for you and the whole of the Foundation. I didn't keep things from you for deceitful purposes, I just wanted to have something tangible to report before I came to you. I can assure you that I only want what's best for everyone within the Dreambringer world. All I ask is that I be given enough trust and freedom in order to do things in my own way.'

There was a slight pause as Cedric mulled over his words before he said, 'I understand where you are coming from, and I agree that you have done nothing to warrant any mistrust, but we are used to things being done a certain way and it will take time to adjust to your way of doing things. You will have to be patient with us, but I must also make it clear to you that the hierarchy within the Foundation is still in place and must be respected, you are still required to come to us before making any important decision, I cannot stress that enough.'

Morpheus conveyed his understanding of the points Cedric had made and the conversation moved on to the situation at hand. Cedric asked for more details on certain points and talked through the conclusions that Morpheus and the other Dreambringers had come to. He went on to ask Morpheus what his immediate plans were and after hearing them gave him permission to proceed but as usual stressed the need for Morpheus to keep him updated at regular intervals.

With that the call was ended and Morpheus and Sofia let out sighs of relief in unison.

'I'm so glad that's over with' said Sofia 'it was a bit tricky to start with, but it went okay in the end didn't it.'

'Yeah, it could have been worse I guess' agreed Morpheus 'but now I can get back to making my plan for tonight.'

In his own office Cedric Neale was steeling himself to pass on the latest news to the others in his group of command. Most felt the same way he did and trusted his judgement, but one particular member, Patrick Chapman had been giving him a hard time. Strangely, the man had been a bit quieter lately but for some reason rather than reassuring Cedric this fact made him more nervous.

He would impart the day's news by the usual medium of a Zoom meeting as it was always hard to get them all in a room at the same time. He sent them all a request to join the meeting in an hours' time and then worked on updating his own report for the records whilst he waited.

When the time came, he welcomed them all to the meeting one by one, the last to appear being Patrick, his clean shaven, pudgy face almost filling the small screen.

Cedric managed to get the update out without interruption, but as soon as he was finished the questions began. He fielded them as best he could and had time to note that Patrick was quieter than normal. Although he did make it clear he wasn't happy with how things were going at the Gateway, and with Cedric's handling of it, he was less vitriolic than usual.

After the meeting Cedric found himself pondering what was going on with Mr Chapman, because there was definitely something going on with him and whatever it was, he did not like it.

Morpheus and Sofia joined the others just after Con had made his movie choice. Luckily it was universally acceptable, if not everyone's ideal choice, and they all settled down to watch it. Morpheus was not concentrating on the screen; however, he had things to work out and decide.

After hearing Eddie's whispered message about the bedrooms, he had realised that he could not go out to the Factory until Con went to be bed, so a plan was needed to make sure he retired as early as possible. Therefore, when the time was right, on the pretext of getting drinks and snacks for everyone, he asked Clea to come out to the kitchen with him.

'I need you to make sure Con gets an early night' he told Clea as they got the drinks and snacks together 'can you feign tiredness and suggest he must be tired too or something?'

'No problem lovey' she assured him.

'Good, I'll signal you when the time is right.'

'Okay,' and with that agreed they returned to the others with the goodies.

After watching the movie, the group spent the rest of the evening chatting and listening to music with Con consenting to a second rendition of 'Make Your Own Kind of Music' so that those that had been absent could hear his voice.

The three men were impressed, and the evening continued in a relaxed manner with a lot of laughter.

Con was having the time of his life and even Geth and Max were beginning to relax in his company. The time between dinner and bedtime was the Dreambringers leisure time and it was nice to have another person there to chat to. It wasn't that they had run out of things to say to each other or were bored with the company, it was just nice to have a little variety.

Morpheus was the quietest in the group as he had a lot to think about, but even he enjoyed the evening. Then when he felt the time was right, he gave Clea a nod to say it was time for Con to retire. During the evening Clea had managed to recruit Mary in her task thinking two hints would work better than one.

At a fitting moment Clea gave an exaggerated yawn and stretch and said 'Well I don't know about the rest of you, but I think I'm ready for bed. Lovely as this evening has been I'm pretty tired' and she added another yawn, just by thinking about it, to illustrate her point.

Taking her cue Mary yawned too, yawns were strangely contagious after all, and said 'Yeah, me too, it's been a great day, but tiring.'

Aaron gave her a quizzical look knowing she was never usually tired this early, but luckily Con did not see it.

'How about you Con?' asked Clea 'I know you had an afternoon nap, but things must be catching up with you after your long journey here.'

'I guess I am a little tired' Con admitted reluctantly realising it was true and joining in the infectious yawning. He was a little torn between a need for more sleep and wanting to spend more time talking to his new friends though. But by now Aaron and the others had realised what Clea and Mary were up to and so Aaron and Max both expressed their intention to go to bed soon and that made Con's mind up.

'Yeah, I do think it is time I went to bed' he told them all not realising just how happy that made them, especially Morpheus.

As the five who had professed their intention to retire got up Sofia said 'The rest of us won't be far behind you' adding to the pretence.

The thing was it was not much of a pretence as the Gateway residents tended to go to bed reasonably early in order for their Dreambringer talents to be used to their full extent anyway. This was a bit earlier than was normal, but they realised that Morpheus needed to get out to the Factory as soon as he could in order to be within the Dream Realm for as long as possible. It was not ideal walking through the woods in the dark, but Morpheus had no fear of it, he was just eager to get there.

Sofia needed to wait until Con had gone up to his room before she did as she needed to grab her things from her usual room first and without him seeing. It would be strange spending the night in a different room, but it was necessary for now.

As for Geth, Mason and Eddie they intended to stay up until their usual time.

As soon as Con was upstairs Morpheus was off taking only a minute to get a torch from the kitchen to light his way. Sofia chatted with the other three men for a short while before getting her things and following the others upstairs.

Con was in bed but not quite asleep when he heard Sofia pass his room, but he obviously could not see that she carried a small suitcase full of her belongings with her. Once in the room Sofia unpacked a few things quietly before preparing for bed.

One storey down, in their room Mary and Aaron were cuddling on their small sofa and quietly talking through the events of the day. In her own room Clea was softly humming to herself as she got ready for bed and reflected on the eventful day.

Nearly an hour later Geth, Mason and Eddie retired for the night. By then Con was fast asleep as were Sofia and Clea, and Mary and Aaron had just drifted off after an excitement fuelled love making session.

Morpheus had almost run to the Factory, or as near as he could over rough ground in torch light. Upon arrival at the Eternal's chamber he wasted no time in making his connection with them and for a short while he communed with them, the shimmering ribbons of mist linking them together. Then, as soon as he felt it right to do so Morpheus slowly got up from the crib he had lain on, moved towards the spiral circle and stepped inside. He embraced the sudden, shuddering jolt and the strange sensation of lightness that followed and was soon floating in his newly established state of conjoined sleep.

Morpheus found Con's Dark Soul within the Dream Realm very quickly, only he was no longer such a Dark Soul. The dark, vaguely human shape that represented Con was now shades lighter and, most notably, although its outside edge was still dark, just beneath that was a band of bright light following its edge, kind of like an aura. To Morpheus this was a sign that the Dark Soul was more than partially healed. The work he had done so far had started that healing, and now, being in closer physical proximity to the Eternals had enhanced that work. Being at the Gateway was a definite positive for Con, and his beautiful singing had obviously benefited everyone.

But now Morpheus had more work to do.

As the (not so) Dark Soul moved willingly into his healing light Morpheus began his usual work, but this time with an added element. This time he made a concerted effort to commune with the Eternal Within, an effort that was reciprocated. This time they worked together rather than as two separate beings to bring Con healing dreams.

They started simple with the dreams of his mother but this time, with their combined effort the dreams would be more lucid and detailed giving Con happy thoughts for the day to come.

Next it was time to probe the Dark Soul to gauge what other dreams he needed in order to heal. The soul's lighter appearance gave Morpheus more confidence in his hopes of Con having let down his barriers to some extent at least.

Morpheus initiated the mind probe with a simple question *'Hello Con, how are you?'*

'I'm good' was the gratifyingly immediate reply.

'I'm glad to hear that. I'd like to help you so that you feel even better, will you let me do that?'

'Help me how?'

'Open up to me and I will help you in whatever way you need'

The reply Morpheus got then was not words it was just like a series of question marks. Con's soul was obviously more open now but being unused to this sort of commune he did not quite understand what was happening.

'What is it you need?' was the question Morpheus then conveyed to nudge the soul into the right sort of commune. There were a few moments pause before Morpheus was struck with words conveying the soul's feelings.

'Safety, friends, love, security, peace.'

They were basic, human needs and Morpheus needed something with more depth, but this was a start, the next stage would give him more to go on.

Making sure that the human Dreambringer and Eternal Within were working as one Morpheus communed the command *'let me in'* and moments later he was engulfed in the muddled, wounded thoughts and feelings of the Dark Soul. It was more intense than was usual and expected so it took Morpheus a minute to get a grip on things. But once he did, he was in his element. The amount of work he realised needed doing was exhilarating rather than daunting and he set to it with relish.

Morpheus was so intent on his work that he was totally unaware he was being watched. A Dreambringer who really should not have been there was shadowing him, stealthily spying on all that he did.

Morpheus awoke lying awkwardly on the floor of the Eternals Chamber. The ribbons of mist still linked him to the other Eternals and the Eternal Within was back within its human shell. Feeling physically drained but mentally buzzing he got up slowly and walking on shaky legs made it to the nearest crib where he collapsed. The Eternals were rejoicing as he drifted off into a revitalising sleep.

Con drifted slowing into wakefulness a gently smile on his face. He opened his eyes and when he remembered where he was his smile widened. He turned onto his back and stretched, then relaxed again. *"Wow, what a dream that was"* he thought. He was tempted to drift back off to sleep but then remembered that he now had something to get up for. Would his new friends be up yet? He reached over to his watch on the bedside table and checked to time. Eight thirty-eight. That wasn't too early, surely someone else was up by now. He decided to take a leisurely shower first though to make sure he was not the first up.

Con need not have worried, Clea had been up and downstairs since just after eight fifteen and Sofia entered the kitchen not long after her. By eight forty they had been joined by Eddie, Mason and Geth. Then just before Con arrived Max sauntered into the kitchen to join the others.
Historically Aaron and Mary had always been the last ones downstairs of a morning, but now, mainly due to having to walk back through the woods, Morpheus had taken on that role. This morning Con beat all three of them to the kitchen.
When he walked in Con was glad to see most of them were there. There was no awkwardness either, they all greeted him warmly and he felt at home.
'Geth's been making us all scrambled eggs' Clea told him 'It's the only thing he can cook well' she added with a cheeky grin provoking a semi-serious 'Oi!' from Geth.
'Do you want some?' Geth asked Con.
'Yes please' Con said taking a seat at the table. He noticed that Clea and Sofia had finished their eggs, Mason and Eddie were in the middle of eating theirs and Max had just started his.
'I don't want to put you out though' he said to Geth 'it looks like you've already done loads and haven't even had some yourself.'
'It's no problem' Geth assured him 'it's easier to do in smaller batches and I'm gonna have mine now with you.'
'What about the other three who aren't here?' he asked.
'I'll do theirs when they get here, don't worry about it kid, it's how we work.'
Con had to stop himself from blurting out that he loved it here. It would sound too gushy.
The eggs were soon cooked, and he tucked in joyfully as he listened to the light conversation going on around him.
Just as he finished his last mouthful Aaron and Mary arrived.
'Great timing' Geth told them having not long finished his own breakfast. He got up now to make more for them. Con marvelled at how well everyone got on, a lot of people would be annoyed about making breakfast over and over again, and Geth was even the grumpiest of them all he had discovered.
Now the only person missing was the Marvellous Morpheus. Con wondered if the others would find his nickname for their friend funny or a bit weird. He decided to keep it to himself.
'How did you sleep Con?' Sofia asked him then.
'Great thanks, I had some fantastic dreams' as soon as he said it, he regretted the last bit knowing what would come next.
'Oh yeah, what did you dream about?'

Con cringed a little inside, what should he say, if he told the truth they might think him weird. But he wasn't very good at lying. He realised then that they were all waiting expectantly for his answer which made him panic.

'You were all in it' he blurted and then blushed. Oh hell, how would he explain this without sounding like some weird fanboy.

'What were we doing?' enquired Mary.

'Oh, I don't know, it's a bit vague' Con lied 'we were out somewhere having a good time, it was just a nice, vague little dream that's all.

It was not a complete lie and he thought he had got away with it okay.

'I thought you said it was a fantastic dream' said Geth questioningly.

'Oh, I ermm, I was just exaggerating, sorry' stammered Con.

'Leave the boy alone' Clea told Geth 'he doesn't have to tell us the details of his dream if he doesn't want to.'

'I dreamt I'd grown an extra nose on my elbow' said Aaron making them all laugh and dispersing the slight tension in the room.

'Good grief was there any real need to share that disturbing image' said Max making them laugh harder.

Con laughed with the rest of them glad the spotlight had been taken off him and feeling happier than he could ever remember.

Although he was eager to get back to the house Morpheus decided to take a detour to his cabin for a shower and a change of clothes. After spending a whole day and night in the same clothes he felt it necessary.

He showered and changed as fast as he could though and headed for the house where he found everyone in good spirits. Geth thrust a plate of scrambled eggs in front of him and he ate it whilst watching Con's behaviour without seeming to and also avoiding direct eye contact. He was gratified to see that the boy was smiling and joining in.

Morpheus really wanted to update the group on last night's goings on, though he figured they had worked out things had gone well by the way Con was acting. It dawned on him then that the day ahead needed careful planning under difficult circumstances, so he began to work on them himself.

Ten minutes later he had the start of the day sorted at least, now he just needed to convey his plans to the others.

Firstly, he engineered a quick, quiet chat with Eddie then waited for Eddie to put the plan into action which he did faultlessly.

'Hey Con' Eddie said, 'I need to go out for some supplies and could do with a little help, but all these buggers will whine that they'll miss out on artwork time if I ask them, so do you fancy joining me?'

'Okay' agreed Con though he was in two minds. He liked Eddie as much as any of the others, but he would have preferred to stay at the house with more of the group. Then again, he did not want to seem unhelpful, they were putting him up and feeding him for nothing without even knowing him so maybe he should do something to pay his way.

'I'm in' he added to sound keener than he felt.

'Great, we'll leave in about ten minutes okay, I've just got to get everyone's list together.'

The rest of the group had cottoned on to the plan and so they all gave Eddie one or two items they needed, even if they didn't, to go along with the ruse.

Ten minutes later Eddie and Con got into the van and set off for the art supply shop the group used.

'Right, they'll be gone for nearly two hours' stated Morpheus 'so I need to catch you all up and we need to make plans and think of excuses. Someone can update Eddie later. So let me catch you up first.'

He proceeded to tell them about Con's new, lighter Dream Realm appearance and his new-found receptiveness. They all expressed their pleasure at the news and waited for Morpheus to elaborate on what he thought this meant.

'I believe that Con is well on the way to becoming a normal dreaming soul, he just needs a few more days in this house and a few more nights of supercharged Dreambringing.'

'And then what? You realise he loves it here already and the longer he stays the less likely he will want to leave' said Geth.

'I know and I understand it's not ideal, but we have time to work out what to do once he is fully healed, besides until that has happened, we can't really know what needs to happen next. In the meantime, we need to devise plans on how best to keep working as near to usual as possible with Con here. There are two main elements, the first is how to explain the absences of those who go out to the Factory. The second is to think of ways to keep Con occupied with as little disruption to the artwork we do here as possible.'

'We need to keep it simple' Sofia said 'when we have normal visitors they don't really worry about what the other artists are up to, only the person they're visiting. I know this is different, but I think we just need to tell Con that those who have gone to the Factory have gone out on some errands.'

'It works in the movies' interjected Aaron 'someone wants to go out to do something in secret and they just casually say "I'm just going out to run some errands" and no one ever questions what those errands are.'

'This isn't a movie Aaron' said Geth.

'I know, I was kinda joking.'

'You have a point though I think' Sofia told Aaron 'Con just wants to fit in here, he'd not the type to rock the boat, he's hardly asked any questions, so I think we're safe to just give him very basic information and anything more only if he asks.'

'You seem to have got a good grasp on the boy's character in such a short time' said Geth.

'Well, I monitored Con through the Eternals last night, it's part of my job remember, to vet people for jobs within the Foundation and that's where I got my grasp of his character from.'

'I apologise' said Geth looking abashed 'I forgot you had that talent.'

'Don't worry about it' was Sofia laid back reply.

'Let me get this clear' said Mason then steering the conversation back to its original course 'we don't offer an explanation for those who aren't here but if he asks, we tell him they're out on an errand?'

'Yes, simple as that.'

'And if he asks what errand?'

'We just fob him off with vague things like they had a few things to do in town or something. It'll be fine, I'm sure.'

'But what if he sees them walk in or out of the woods, what sort of errands do you go on in the woods' said Geth a little scathingly.

'We can get around that' Sofia told him 'I know it'll be a little bit bothersome, but I suggest those going to the Factory go out the front door, get in the van, or even Max's VW maybe, and drive off. They then pull over somewhere along the driveways and walk to the Factory from there. Then on the way back they walk back to the vehicle and drive it back to the house.'

'It's a bit of a palaver isn't it?' said Mason.

'Maybe, but it won't be for long, and it's the best option we have, unless anyone else has any ideas?'

'I think it'll work fine' Morpheus told them 'but I would like to make a little change regarding my reason for being away.'

'Of course you do' said Geth at the same time as Sofia said 'Okay, go ahead.'

Morpheus chose to ignore Geth's comment and continued 'I want to tell Con about the cabin, and before anyone says anything I'll tell you why. It will help with any awkward questions if he sees me coming to or from the woods as I'll be doing different hours to the others at the Factory. We'll explain that it's my special refuge and that no one else goes there unless invited. We can use my musical talent as an excuse, say it's so I can play what I like, when I like without disturbing anyone. I might even show him the cabin one day just so he knows what I'm talking about.'

'Okay, that works' said Sofia.

'I'm not too sure about showing him the cabin, but apart from that I'm okay with it I guess' was Geth's comment and no one else had any objections.

'Good, that's the plan then, and I'll update Eddie when he gets back.'

And Morpheus added 'I'll review the idea of taking Con to the cabin in a day or two, see how things are going.'

'One more thing' added Sofia, 'we need to find ways to keep Con occupied all day. We should each think about how to spend some time with him, showing him our art or something, okay.'

She received nods of agreement all around, and so with that discussion over they moved on to the last decision of who would go to the Factory that day.

Con was having a great time looking around the art supplies shop whilst Eddie made his purchases. There were so many lovely art materials it made him wish he could draw or paint.

When Eddie was ready Con helped him carry his purchases out to the van and they set off on the forty minute drive back to The Gateway.

'How often do you do this?' Con asked Eddie as he drove them out of the small town centre.

'I usually do a run once a month for the big stuff like clay for Max and Canvas' for Aaron, then we do one or two trips in between for the smaller stuff.'

'Do you always do it?'

Eddie was about to simply say yes, then thinking better of it in light of their need for excuses for leaving the house he lied a little saying 'I usually do the big run with Mason, but it varies who does the other ones.'

'What about other suppliers like food and stuff?'

'Same sort of thing really, a big monthly shop, plus smaller shops in between when needed.'

'It's a bit of a long drive to the shop though isn't it, what with the house being in the middle of nowhere. You can't just pop to the local shop for milk or something can you?'

'No, true, but we plan well, and we think the peace and quiet we get at the house is worth the effort.'

'Yeah, I guess that's true, I'm just not used to it, it's so crowded and busy where I'm from.'

'Where I'm from it was too, but I prefer it here.'

'I like it too.'

Eddie glanced over at his passenger then and seeing the gentle, quizzical smile on the boy's face realised he was beginning to like the kid. At eighteen he wasn't really a kid, but he looked young for his age so that's how Eddie thought of him, and his fears about him being a danger were definitely abating.

When they got back to the house Con helped Eddie carry everything into the lounge/art room where the other artists took their supplies off them and put them away. Con noticed that they were all there apart from Morpheus.

Clea then suggested Con came out to the kitchen for a drink in order to give Mason time to update Eddie.

Once Mason had finished updating him Eddie told him and the others in the room about the conversation he'd just had with Con in the van.

'That was great thinking of you about us sharing the shopping trips, it fits right in with what we'd decided.'

'Yeah, I must be psychic or something' said Eddie with a laugh.

'I'm going out to the Factory shortly with Clea and Max' Mason told him 'and Morpheus has already gone, eager as ever. And everyone now knows what to tell Con if he asks.'

'Great, and I think he'll be fine, I'm warming to the kid, he seems genuine and descent which is a miracle after what he's been through.'

'Maybe this place is working on him already, on top of Morpheus' work of course.'

'Yep, the magic of the Eternals and Dreambringers restorative talents strike again.'

When Clea and Con came back into the room Mason took the leap of trying their lie.

'Right Max and Clea, its time we were off' then to Con 'us three have got some things to do in town, we'll see you later.'

Con looked a little perplexed, but nodded and said 'Okay, see you later' but he didn't question what they had to do in town. He wondered for a second why they had not come with him and Eddie, then realised there was only room for three in the van. The only other thought he had about the trio leaving was he wished they would all stay here all day so he could get to know them better, but he didn't want to voice that wish.

For their part Eddie, Mary and Aaron were poised ready to distract the boy, Sofia was ready with vague answers to any questions and Geth was just hoping the boy would not ask anything but intended to keep out of it if he did.

When Con did ask a question it wasn't about the three who had just left.

'Where's Morpheus?'

So, then it was time for Sofia to put Morpheus' other part to the plan into action.

'Morpheus has gone to his cabin out in the woods. He likes to be alone sometimes so he can play what he wants, when he wants, as loudly as he wants without disturbing the rest of us.'

'Oh, I see' said a disappointed Con 'but if he plays well why don't you want him to play here?'

'He does play here sometimes, and although a bit of live, background music can be quite nice whilst we work at times, when he's practicing a new piece of music for instance, it can be distracting. Plus, Morpheus is quite a private person who prefers to work without an audience a lot of the time' Sofia explained basically making it up as she went.

'I see, okay.'

At first Sofia thought that Con's tone meant that he didn't believe her, but then looking at his face she realised he did, he was just disappointed at the news, she recognised that feeling, she knew it well.

'Now we just need to find something for you to do whilst we work on our art' she continued in order to redirect his attention.

'I can go get my book to read' Con suggested.

'That would be good, but we won't leave you reading all day. Go and get the book for later, but when you've done that how about I give you a drawing lesson.'

'I'd like that' said Con brightening up.

'Good, go and get your book and I'll get some supplies ready.'

Sofia smiled as she listened to Con run up the stairs, he seemed like a sweet boy. Aaron, Mary, Eddie and Geth were busy getting themselves set up for the day and Sofia went to a storage cupboard and dug out a couple of rough sketch pads, some pencils and some charcoal sticks ready for her lesson.

The lesson went well. Con wasn't exactly a natural, but he enjoyed it and his efforts were pretty good for a beginner.

After the lesson Con did a bit of drawing by himself, then after a while decided to read his book.

When Geth saw that the lesson was over he took the opportunity to ask Sofia for a quick word in private, so they went over to the office and sat in the chairs by the window.

'I've made some decisions about how to proceed regarding my studio' he told her.

'That's great, what have you decided?'

'Regarding the fake new job, I'd like it to be the studio in New York. If I was ever to go abroad that's one of the few places I'd like to visit so it's believable.'

'Okay, good choice.'

'As to my studio I've decided it would be best to sell it, preferably to Chris.'

'I know it's been a hard decision, but I think you've made the right one. I'll get straight on to the Foundation now and get the ball rolling.'

'Thanks. Then when you get all the information on the New York Studio I can ring Chris myself and tell him about it right?'

'Yes, give him the story and then relay their phone number and email address, but remember to stress that it would be better for him to contact you via email what with the time difference and the price of overseas calls.'

'Yep, okay, got it. Then in a few months I call him and give him the spiel about staying there indefinitely and selling the studio giving him first option to buy.'

'Yes, exactly. We will just need to sort a date with the Foundation so they can put the sale into motion.'

'Okay.'

'I'll get the ball rolling then' said Sofia getting up and walking to the phone on the desk whilst Geth headed back to the lounge/art room.

For the rest of the day Con spent some time with each of the other artists with bouts of reading in between.

Geth took his turn next letting Con look through his new flash art and gave him a little tutorial on how his tattoo guns worked which Con found fascinating.

Sensing that Geth would not be as chatty as the others Con kept his questions to a minimum and ended by saying 'I think I'd like a tattoo, but I know they're expensive and I can't afford it' and Geth, surprising himself as well as Con, replied 'When you're sure you want one and know exactly what you want, I'll tattoo you for free.'

'That's amazing, thanks' Con gushed

'I'm going to stress here that I'll only do it if you're sure and you really love what you want tattooed. I don't want no nonsense about picking some random, common design just for the sake of it, you need to really want it because it's going to be on you for life, okay?'

'Okay.'

'You can look through more of my flash art, or you can think about it and tell me what you want, and I'll design it for you, just don't rush it.'

'I won't, I promise.'

Con had no idea what he wanted at this point, but he was serious about having a tattoo and so added 'I'm not worried about the pain by the way. I'm used to pain so I won't be a wimp about it I promise. At least I'll get something good out of the pain won't I'

Knowing the boy's history this was a little heart-breaking even for a hard bastard like Geth, but he didn't let that show, he just said 'I'm sure you'll sit great mate.'

Geth was just glad Clea had not been there to hear that, it would have really set her off. As it was by the looks on the faces of both Mary and Sofia, they have overheard it and Mary particularly looked close to tears.

Luckily Eddie announced it was lunchtime then giving them something else to think about when he asked them what they would like.

After lunch they switched things around on Con and asked him to sing a few songs for them. The singer gladly went over to the CD collection and found another five songs he knew to sing for them. He enjoyed it immensely as did his audience.

With Aaron Con opted to just watch Aaron paint whilst asking him questions about how he worked which Aaron was only too pleased to answer. Aaron had taken his self-portrait to the

Factory to work on there as it was too awkward and risky to keep carrying the canvas back and forwards through the woods. The one he was working on now was of Clea's deceased husband Andrew.

The idea to do the portrait had only come about recently. Clea had been showing Mary an old photo album and he had overheard Mary comment that Andrew looked like a lovely man and gone to have a nose himself. The photo they were looking at had been a great, natural head and shoulders shot with the man smiling into the camera.

'That's an ideal photo to do a portrait from' he had casually commented and so when Clea had cried out 'Oh Aaron, would you paint Andrew for me, that would be so lovely' how could he refuse. It meant taking time out from his Dream Realm portraits of his fellow Dreambringers, but it wouldn't take long. It had in fact turned out to be good for him to work on a new subject, and a challenge to depict Andrew's spirit from a photo alone having never met him.

Con was very impressed with Aaron's portrait which the artist himself felt was coming along well so they had a good time together.

When it came to Mary's turn she apologised as there wasn't really anything for him to watch and as she wasn't letting anyone read her novel until it was finished there was nothing for him to read either except her poems.

Con told her he would love to read her poems even though he wouldn't really know if they were good or not as he didn't know very much about poetry. She gave him some to read anyway (though not the Dreambringer ones).

After reading the first one he had a frown on his face.

'What's wrong?' Mary asked him.

'It doesn't rhyme' he told her.

Mary laughed good naturedly and explained that not all poetry rhymed.

'Really?' said Con and so Mary went on to tell him about the different types of poetry there were, like hers which were written in what was called Free Verse. She was afraid he would find the subject boring, but he seemed interested and now armed with his new knowledge he went on to read some more of her poems. He still wasn't sure if they were good, he told her, but he said he liked them which made her smile even if he was possibly just being nice.

Con then told her of his newfound love of reading and asked her some questions about being a writer, some of which were hard to answer, but she did her best.

Their session ended with him telling her he would love to read her novel when it was finished.

Lastly Con spent some time with Eddie who started off by showing him some of the new drawings he had done for his Graphic Novel. Con loved them and asked Eddie if he could give him a lesson in drawing comic style characters as it was a genre he loved.

Eddie did his best, and they had a good laugh at Con's rather wonky first attempts, but with a little help he did improve.

Whilst working they chatted about their favourite comic heroes which then moved on to talk of movies based on comic's and graphic novels. Con had not seen as many as he would have liked so Eddie promised to help him look for some to watch on the different TV apps they had at the house. Eddie thought it might make a good distraction for the boy on other days as long as it wasn't disruptive for the others to have the TV on whilst they worked.

The only two questions that Con asked about those that had gone out during the day were "Will they be back for lunch?' the answer to which was no, and 'Will they be back for dinner?' the answer to which was yes.

By the time they did return Con had spent quality time with all the artists at the house and had nearly finished reading his book. For the artists part they had all enjoyed having him around.

He had caused minimal disruption to their day and although he had asked many questions none of them had been awkward.

As for Con, there was only one question he wanted to ask but hadn't dared, and that was 'Can I stay here forever?' He dare not ask it because the answer was likely to be no, and even if it was a possibility him coming on all over enthusiastic and nerdy at this early stage might put them off the idea of him staying and he would be asked to leave immediately.

As to the questions about where Clea, Mason and Max had gone, and why, he was of course curious, but again didn't want to make himself a nuisance by asking too many questions.

At just after five thirty Eddie got a call on his mobile, and once he'd hung up, he announced to the group that the others were on their way home, so he was going to make a start on dinner. Con offered to help and being taken up on it he followed Eddie out to the kitchen asking, "What are we cooking?'

'Spaghetti Bolognaise.'

'I've never had that; my Dad won't touch pasta.'

'Well, you're in for a treat then' Eddie told him supressing the urge to ask what the hell the boy and his father had eaten in case the subject upset him.

Con was a little subdued after bringing up his father, but he soon brightened up as Eddie began a lesson on how to cook the perfect Spag Bol.

Eddie wondered as he worked about Con's father. The man was obviously a wrongun' but what had he thought when he found his son missing? And more to the point what had he done about it?

If he had called the police Eddie could have been strolling around the art supply shop with a missing person. It could bring trouble which was something no one had considered so far so he made a mental note to speak to the others, and in particular Sofia, about it when he got the chance. He thought it likely to be something that the Foundation could find out about and deal with, so he needed to get their views on it and ask Sofia about talking to the Foundation.

Con and Eddie were still in the kitchen cooking the best Spag Bol ever when Clea, Max and Mason returned from the Factory via their new circuitous route. It felt weird to them all coming in through the front door let alone the short, weird van ride.

They went straight into the lounge/art room, but when they heard where Con and Eddie were Clea went to let them know they were home.

Morpheus returned the usual way a short while later his cover story being different. Con didn't care where they had all been or take note of the way they had returned; he was just glad they were back. He did not know how long they would let him stay, or what he would do if they asked him to leave, he just intended to stay of their good side and hope for the best. He did not want to dwell on the weirdness of his arrival, he just wanted to enjoy the company of his new friends for as long as possible.

The group enjoyed their meal and gave Con much appreciated praise for his part in it. They then spent another pleasant evening together.

The next three days were spent in much the same way and apart from the rigmarole of the fake comings and goings and having to watch what they said around Con everyone was happy enough with the situation.

As for the nights Morpheus continued to work on Con's Dark Soul which was becoming progressively lighter as he worked his magic. Con's soul was so much more receptive which made Morpheus' work much easier.

Working in tandem with the Eternal Within was beginning to come as second nature now which was good. And although his reports to the Foundation – and the other Dreambringers in small groups – sounded samey and uneventful he was happy with the progress he was making.

He believed the time Con was spending with the artists, and singing for them, was doing his soul good too.

Chapter 10
What Should He Know?

On the fourth day Morpheus decided to take Con to his cabin. He had let the others know his intention first and as they all felt comfortable around Con now, they agreed it would do no harm.

Con was excited by the news as not only would he get to see this mysterious cabin, but he would also get to spend time with Morpheus. The man was the only one he had not spent any real time with so far.

Con had spent some time sat out on the terrace with some of the other artists and had even taken a walk around the very edge of the woods the day before with Clea and Max, but now he would get to walk through the woods properly which was another plus.

As they set off down the sloped lawn towards the trees Morpheus explained 'You can stay for an hour or so, then I'll bring you back and go back alone, okay?'

'Okay' agreed Con, happy for any time with Morpheus the magnificent.

He felt very small walking beside the tall man, and he had to do little, quick hoppy steps now and then to keep up with his longer stride, but he didn't mind.

When they got in amongst the trees it was beautiful and peaceful but also strangely familiar. One piece of woodland was much like another Con figured, and he had never walked in any himself so it could not be familiar he told himself.

Then he remembered his dreams of walking through the woods with his mum and the unknown other. Where these woods the ones in his dream? No, they couldn't be surely, that was too weird. Or would it just be kind of cool. Maybe he had some sort of special power where he could dream about places he had never been? He had been having more, different types of dreams lately, really good ones, and in those he had been in other strange places but had assumed they were just made up by his dreaming mind.

None of the places in his dreams had been places he actually knew though, but that was a good thing. If he dreamt of his old flat or workplace that would have been more like a nightmare. He did not miss his old life, but he did sometimes wonder what his father and work colleagues had made of his disappearance. What did they think had happened to him, and did they even care?

Con decided to push all that to the back of his mind where it belonged and concentrate on now.

Morpheus didn't say much as they walked and that was fine by Con, he just wanted to enjoy the surroundings.

And then Con saw the cabin.

Like everyone before him the word cabin had conjured up visions of a little wooden shack, but this was something else.

'Wow' was all he could manage to say on first sight, and then when they went inside, he had exclaimed 'This place is awesome!' and then he had laughed and said 'I don't think I've ever used the word awesome before' which caused Morpheus to let out a short bellow of laughter.

Morpheus let Con do a slow circuit of the cabin before offering him a drink.

After drinks were sorted Morpheus began to show Con his musical instruments and of course the first one Con wanted to hear was the hurdy gurdy.

The musician happily played the strange instrument for him and watched Con's face light up with a mixture of delight and awe.

'I've never heard anything like that' Con said when Morpheus stopped playing 'can I hear some more?' and so Morpheus played on.

Whilst Con was out of the house, and before some of them headed for the Factory the rest of the group were discussing some news Sofia had been given by the Foundation early that morning.

After Eddie had shared his worry about Con's father calling the Police Sofia had spoken to Cedric Neale about it. The other Dreambringers and Morpheus had been made aware too.

Since her call the Foundation had been checking up on this via their contacts within the Police Force and other areas and had found out some startling news. Con's father Donald had reported Con's disappearance, which wasn't totally unexpected, but what was unexpected was rather than reporting him as a missing person he had reported him as a thief who had absconded with all his money.

It was disgraceful and everyone was appalled at the man's behaviour, not least for the fact that the money Con had taken had been his own, he had earnt it, not his father. That was obviously not what the despicable man had told the Police though, as far as he was concerned it was his money.

Luckily the police had understood it for what it was, a young man escaping from an unhappy home and taking as much money with him as he could. They could not know the extent of abuse Con had received from his father, but they got an idea simply from the man's drunken, belligerent demeanour and the fact that he was reporting his own missing son as a thief. They had fobbed him off with promises to do their best to 'apprehend' Con, but in truth, at eighteen he was an adult so the police had simply written him up as a missing, at-risk adult, as there wasn't much else they could do.

As part of their small investigation the police had spoken to Con's boss and work colleagues, but none of them had any useful information about where the boy might go, and they did not seem to care that he was gone either.

Now, armed with this information the decision the Gateway residents needed to make was whether or not to tell Con what they had found out, and if they did tell him how to explain how they knew it.

'I doubt Con will be surprised by the news' said Sofia, 'but whatever he thinks of his father this will still hurt him.'

'The poor boy' said Clea 'it would hurt him yes, but he's probably wondering how his father has reacted to him going missing and it might help him in a strange way to know. Plus, we can help heal his hurt.'

'But would it set Morpheus' work back?' asked Mason.

'I don't know, we'd have to ask him that,' said Sofia.

'Wouldn't Con be a worried if he thought the police were looking for him?' enquired Mary.

'Maybe, but we could reassure him that it wasn't like that, he's in no real danger of arrest especially with the Foundation in his corner.'

'And are they in his corner?' queried Geth.

'Yes, of course they are.'

'How would we explain how we found all this out to Con?' was the next question, this time from Max.

'That's pretty easy' Sofia told him 'we'd explain that a big organisation like the Foundation will always have connections in places like law enforcement, it wouldn't seem odd to him I don't think and telling him that information about the Foundation doesn't put our 'secret' at risk.'

'No, I guess that's true' agreed Max.

'I think we should tell him' said Mason 'Clea's right I think he needs to know so he can move on. We just need to run it past Morpheus first regarding the possibility of it setting his work back.'

'Okay, so does everyone agree on that?' asked Sofia.

Everyone did, but the conversation was not finished.

'Have the Foundation let the police know where Con is?' enquired Eddie.

'Not exactly, their contacts are obviously aware that the Foundation know where Con is but that's all. They are foundation members themselves remember so they don't question the work the Foundation asks them to do. Their investigation on behalf of us was done covertly and the fact that the boy's whereabouts is known has not be officially recorded. The Foundation do have a plan on that score though, they are going to report that Con turned up at a homeless shelter that they fund and that he is safe but will not be returning home.

If Con's father continues to kick up a fuss about the money Con took the Foundation will return the amount Con took to him and the police can then close the case. The Foundation will make it clear to the police that Con's father should not be informed of his son's whereabouts. If he starts demanding to know they will threaten to arrest him over allegations of abuse that Con has made, hopefully that will scare him off and he will leave well alone.'

'They should arrest him anyway if you ask me' said Clea.

'It's a thought' agreed Sofia 'and the Foundation have the lawyers to see he goes away, but I think that might be something that's up to Con to decide, don't you?'

'You're right, yes' agreed Clea.

'Any more questions?' asked Sofia.

There were none so now it was back to the usual business of the day.

After the hurdy gurdy Morpheus had played a couple of classical pieces on his violin. This was another novelty for Con in that he had not really heard much classical music, but again he thoroughly enjoyed it.

Next Morpheus moved on to the acoustic guitar and played a few more modern songs. When it was discovered that Con knew one of the songs Morpheus asked him to sing along with him. Con was a bit nervous, the talent that the big man possessed making him feel a little intimidated, plus he had only ever sung along to records rather than a live musical accompaniment. But he gave it a go, and although he messed up a bit to start with, he soon got into it and the pair started to sound good.

They discussed what other songs they might both know and found a couple more to play and sing. On Morpheus' part he was enjoying it almost as much as Con was. It wasn't such a novelty to him, but the boy had such a great voice it was a pleasure to play, and at times sing along with him.

All too soon for Con it was time for him to go back to the house.

Morpheus walked him back through the woods and this time they talked more.

As they were nearing the edge of the woods Con suddenly said, 'You sound like the voice in my dream.'

'Do I?' Morpheus enquired unphased.

'I ermm… I don't know why I said that' replied a flustered Con. The thought had escaped his lips before it was even properly formed and he did not really understand why he had thought it, let alone said it aloud. Did he really think that it had been Morpheus' voice in his dreams? If so, how could that be as the dreams had started before he had even met the man. He remembered then the strangeness of their first meeting and it made him feel a bit weird.

Morpheus did not appear to be bothered about his comment, but then Con wasn't very good at reading people and Morpheus was particularly hard to read, he was always so composed.

Con decided that it was just a bit of fanciful nonsense, and as for the weirdness of their meeting that had just been him being tired, dehydrated and in a strange place.

'Forget I said that' he told Morpheus now 'I was just being silly.'

153

'There's nothing silly about dreams' was Morpheus's slightly cryptic reply.

In truth he had been a little shocked when Con came out with his revelation, but he wasn't bothered by it. He was, in fact, quite pleased that the boy had made the connection. He wasn't afraid of awkward questions like the others were, he would have liked to explain a few things to Con before now but was making himself stick to Foundation protocols. He decided to probe the boy a bit now he had been given an 'in' though.

'I believe that dreams are very important' he told Con 'don't you?'

'I've never really thought about it 'cos I didn't dream for a long time.'

'But you dream now?'

'Oh yes, I have great dreams now.'

'And do you not think that having dreams is a good thing, that it helps you in waking life somehow?'

Con took a moment to think before answering 'When I've had a good dream it makes me feel happy when I wake up if that's what you mean.'

'Yes, there's that, but do you think what you dream helps you through your day and maybe even helps you make decisions.'

'Now you mention it I did have some dreams that I think maybe helped me decide to leave home.'

He wanted to mention his thoughts about the woods being familiar but was afraid to, his blurted statement had been bad enough, though Morpheus had taken it well.

They were out of the trees now and heading up the sloping lawn to the house so having sewn a little seed of the information Con would soon find out more about Morpheus ended it by stating 'So you see dreams can be important' and Con had given a nod of agreement.

Con did not have much time to contemplate their conversation though because as soon as he saw the others he was busy telling them about his time at Morpheus' cabin.

Whilst Con chatted to the others Sofia made a point of following Morpheus as he headed back out. He was halfway down the sloped lawn eager to get to the Factory when she caught up with him.

'I won't keep you long' she said a little breathlessly as she kept pace with him 'but I just need to run something by you.'

She then proceeded to tell him the news about Con's father and the police before asking him what his thoughts were on telling Con.

'I suggest you tell him. Like you say it might hurt him, but it will also give him some closure knowing what happened after he left. I think the closure will offset any hurt in terms of my work, but if not, it shouldn't put him back much. If you tell him sometime today, then I will make sure I bring him the right sort of dreams to deal with it tonight.'

'Okay, I'll wait until later when he's come down from his excitement over the cabin visit then I'll tell him what we've found out.'

'Good. Do what you can to help him deal with his emotions afterwards and I'll continue the work tonight. I think it could be a good thing though. Its better he knows his father for the bastard he is and then he can move on and forget about him, rather than worrying about how the man's coping without him.'

'Yes, I see your point.'

'I'll be back at dinnertime for a bit so you can update me then.'

'Okay, will do.'

And with that he continued to walk on, and Sofia turned around and went back to the house. She wasn't looking forward to telling Con about his father, but she agreed with Morpheus that it was best he know rather than continuing to speculate.

Sofia chose to speak to Con after lunch and so whilst the artists that were at the house went to the lounge/art room to carry on working she asked Con to join her in the office.

She could see that Con was nervous as they sat in the armchairs by the window, so she told him 'Don't worry, you're not in trouble or anything I just have something to tell you, and although it's not exactly good news, I want you to know that we're all here for you.'

Con nodded his understanding, but he didn't look any less nervous. In fact, Con was thinking it was something to do with his stay at the house and he was worried, despite her words, that he was going to be told he had to leave. Therefore, her next words surprised him.

'I need to tell you something about your father.'

What could she have to tell him about his father? Had he found out where Con was somehow? Had they told him where Con was? Was he coming to get him and take him back home? Con was starting to really panic now, and it showed in his face.

'Please calm down Con' Sofia soothed 'I can tell you have all sorts of things spinning around in your head, but just listen, okay?'

Con took a deep, calming breath and told her 'Okay.'

'First of all, let me assure you that your father does not know you're here and we have no intention of telling him in the future.'

Con visibly relaxed a little at her words but still looked nervous as Sofia continued.

'But you have to understand that we cannot let you continue to stay where without checking a few things out. As we have told you, this house is part of The Somnium Foundation which is a large organisation and so as such it has many contacts throughout many other organisations and industries, and one of those organisations is the Police Force.'

Seeing the panic rise in Con again she added 'Don't worry, you aren't in trouble with the police. Let me explain. Using their contacts, the Foundation has discovered that your father did report your disappearance to the police, but I'm afraid to say that rather than report you as a missing person he reported you for theft.'

'What!' exclaimed Con.

'He told the police that you'd run off with his money.'

'It's my money, I earnt it.'

'We know, and so do the police.'

'They do?'

'Yes, despite what your father told them their small investigation soon revealed that the money you took was your own.'

'So, what are the police going to do.'

'Nothing much. They will tell your father that as far as they're concerned there has been no crime committed and so that's the end of it. They have however put you on the missing at-risk adult list which means although they won't put many hours into looking for you, they will give your info out to homeless shelters and places like that so if you turn up they can check you are okay. In light of that its looking likely that the Foundation will let the police know that you are safe. They will tell them you turned up at a soup kitchen they fund and that you are well and will be given help to get you off the streets.'

'So, you won't tell them or my father that I'm here?'

'No, it's easier this way, less complicated, okay?'

'Yes, that's fine by me.'

Con realised that staying in a strange house where no one knew you were could be sinister, but that's not how he felt about it. He felt safe here.

'And I can carry on staying here?'

'For the time being yes, we won't just throw you out I promise. There are things to sort out and I can't say how long you will be staying here, but you won't be leaving until you have somewhere else to go.'

The 'for the time being' bit worried Con a little, but he felt mostly reassured by her words. Now that his initial fears about the police and having to leave this house had been allayed the rest of what Sofia had told him was starting to sink in.

His father had dobbed him in to the cops! The bastard didn't care that his son has left home, he'd only cared about the money his son had taken with him. Although Con understood how important that money must be to his father the fact that he was less important hurt even though he realised that he wasn't surprised by this fact.

He had no illusions about how his father felt about him, his mental and physical abuse had shown him that the man had little love for his son, or at least lacked the sort of love parents should have for their children. He was about to ask Sofia if his father had shown any sort of concern about his wellbeing, but he realised he didn't really care. He would always have a little bit of love for his father deep down, but this news had now wiped away any pity he may have felt for leaving the man to cope on his own without the money he earnt to keep them. He was sure the bastard would find a way to keep himself in fags and booze. So as his father had pretty much wiped his hands of Con, why should he in turn worry about him? No, he didn't care if he ever saw that man again, they had gone their separate ways and that's how it would stay. His life was his own now, he was free.

Sofia sat quietly and watched the emotions wash over the boy's expressive face. First came the hurt, then a little anger, and finally a strange look of what appeared to be relief.

'Thank you for telling me' Con told Sofia with a weak smile.

'I have a question for you Con. Do you want to press charges against your father for abuse and or defamation regarding the theft allegations? The Foundation have plenty of lawyers who could help you if you do.'

'What? No, I ermm… no, I don't think I want that' said Con sounding panicked.

'Okay, I understand, but if you want to talk about it, any of it, I'm quite happy to talk things through with you.'

'No, it's okay, I just want to say that I'm glad I ran away and that my father is out of my life. I don't want anything more to do with him even to pay him back for the things he's done to me, I just want to forget him and move on. What he did, the reporting me for theft thing, that hurt me, but I'm free of him now which can only be a good thing, and that's how I want it to stay.'

'I must say Con, I think you are dealing with this very well, but if you ever do need to talk, I'm here for you and so are the others.'

'They all know?'

'Yes, I hope that's okay.'

'Its fine, at least I won't have to explain to anyone what a bastard my father is.'

'No, but feel free to vent about him to any of us' Sofia offered with a smile.

'I might take you up on that' said Con returning her smile.

'Why don't you go back and join the others' Sofia suggested 'And I'll get on to the Foundation and tell them to inform the police you're safe. There's a small chance that the police will want to speak to you to verify that, but I doubt it.'

'Okay, thanks.'

Con joined the others, and after a brief conversation about how he was feeling he opted to do some reading. He had already finished the two books he had bought in the charity shop and had just started on one that Mary had lent him from her own collection.

He found he could not concentrate very well though. He had told them he was feeling okay about what his father had done, and basically that was true, but the full truth was he had so much going on in his head he didn't really know how he felt. There was definitely hurt there, plus a bit of anger but also relief. He really did feel he was free now. The problem was that this newfound freedom was actually a little scary. He felt safe here in this house, but he wasn't sure how long he would be allowed to stay, and it was the not knowing what he would do then that was scaring him.

There was also the weirdness of his journey to the house and some of the things that had happened when here. His adopted mantra of *'Accept the weird'* was wearing a bit thin and he was starting to lean more towards *'Question the weird.'* He had been reluctant to question things before now for fear of being rejected and told to leave. But now the questions were becoming increasingly harder to keep in. What was that ribbon of mist that had led him here and why had he felt compelled to follow it? And why had something similar appeared again when he first met Morpheus? Had he really seen a strange light in Morpheus' eyes? Why did the woodland surrounding the house seem familiar? And Morpheus too, why did he feel like he knew him before he came here? Then there was his strange comment about Morpheus' voice being the one from his dreams?

He thought back then to his conversation with Morpheus earlier about dreams being important. This in turn made him think about how the artists here often discussed their dreams, and he had even begun to join in. So, dreams were important to them all he thought, but why? Was it an artist thing? His head was becoming full of questions, and he did not like it. What he needed was a distraction.

'Would anyone mind if I put on a CD and had a sing-along?' he announced to the room.

No one objected so he went and put on a CD. He found that singing tended to clear his mind and that was just what he needed right now.

After a few songs he felt calmer. The questions were still there but he had pushed them to the back of his mind so he could enjoy his day.

When Morpheus returned for dinner along with those who had been working at the Factory, he pulled Sofia aside to get an update on how it had gone with Con.

She told him he had taken the news pretty well, but that he had seemed very restless all day.

'It's like he keeps wanting to say something but then changes his mind' Sofia said.

'I guess he's got a lot on his mind and is likely to be a bit confused. I'll get more of an idea what's going on with him tonight. I can scan his emotions and ask a few questions. It's safer to do it in the Dream Realm than in the waking world right now.'

'Yes, I get that. Hopefully you can bring him some dreams to help him process and deal with the turmoil that must be going on in his mind.'

'I'm sure I can help.'

That night Morpheus set about giving Con that help. First however he noted another change in the Dark Soul's Dream Realm appearance. The lighter 'aura' that had developed around the dark shape had now spread into the whole figure so that it was more similar in appearance to the normal dreaming souls, a vague, light, human shape. But there still remained a thin, dark band around it's edge, and within the new lightness there were swirling eddies of darkness and at its core a roiling ball of darkness.

The dark ball represented what was left of the darkness that had taken the boys dreams, the remnants of his Dark Soul. It was this last piece of darkness that Morpheus needed to work on eradicating. But before he did that Morpheus felt that the dark eddies within the light figure were the manifestations of the turmoil of questions and doubts that Con was currently dealing with, and these were what he needed to deal with first.

To start with Morpheus probed Con's soul to gauge his emotions. The soul was now completely open to him, so it was easy to 'read'. The emotions he perceived were as expected, hurt, anger and confusion, but in all that the soul felt closer to joy than sorrow.

When Morpheus sent him the question *'How are you?'* he received a similar reaction to one he'd had on one of his earlier tries. It was like a barrage of questions without actual words. The problem was that although Con's soul was now fully receptive and could communicate simply questions and answers, he still hadn't fully mastered the art of communing without speaking as was the way in the Dream Realm. Any complex thoughts became unreadable jargon to Morpheus. It was a problem Morpheus had hoped would be rectified soon, but tonight his progress in this matter had actually been set back.

Morpheus could not know exactly what questions were clouding the soul's communication skills, but he could give it a good guess. And that's what he would have to do, guess what questions needed to be answered in the soul's dreams.

He knew he had to work on healing the hurt and anger the news of his father had caused, that was the easy part. These questions, however, were a product of Con spending so much time at the Gateway yet having been given very little information about what went on there. This was obviously not something Dreambringers were used to helping with in the Dream Realm. Con was very much a new case study, a phenomenon within the Dreambringer world. Morpheus realised that the confusion the soul was feeling would ultimately need to be dealt with in the waking world. He would do his best this night, but some serious decisions needed to be made, and soon.

Con awoke from a restful sleep full of dreams feeling clearer headed. He still had questions, but they weren't buzzing around his head constantly. He felt calm and the hurt and anger caused by his father's behaviour were dampened down by this calmness and he was looking forward to another day at the Gateway. Every day was a good day here, and he was only just getting used to that. He was beginning to put his old life behind him and was ready to be who he should be. He was free to make his own way in life now and although he didn't quite know what he wanted to do with that freedom it gave him hope for the future.

There was one particular dream that had stayed in his memory that morning. He had dreamt that he was in his old flat, his father was there sat on the sofa, and he was demanding that Con made him a cup of tea. Instead of doing that Con stood in front of him and started to sing. His father had looked angry and had stood up. Con had remained where her was and continued to sing despite the fact he knew his father was about to hit him. Then suddenly, they were both outside on a busy high street. His father was standing still as Con walked away from him. Then the street and his father disappeared, he was in the woods, and he heard voices in his head saying *'Sing for us'* and as he began to sing, he woke up.

It was one of those strange, nonlinear dreams but it had meant he woke up feeling good. Like Morpheus had told him the day before, he was now believing in the philosophy of dreams helping you in waking life. The dream hadn't given him any answers as to where his life was going, but it would continue to make him feel good for the rest of the day.

Morpheus and Sofia were in the office ready to make their morning update call to Cedric Neale. They had got into a routine over the last few days where they would head to the office after breakfast and Morpheus would update Sofia on his nights progress before they made the call.

Afterwards Morpheus would update those who came out to the Factory and Sofia would find time to speak to the others away from Con and update them. These updates were usually very brief, so it wasn't too much of a chore. Today was different though, because after his conversation with Con the day before, and his interaction with him in the Dream Realm Morpheus had come to the decision that Con needed to be told about Dreambringers.

Morpheus put his case to Sofia and then they phoned their boss. After a brief preamble Morpheus repeated his decision and the reasons for it.

'We need to tell Con about the real work we do here' he told Cedric Neale. 'We've been lucky so far in that Con hasn't asked too many awkward questions, but that won't be the case for much longer. The boy is bursting with unasked questions, this is clear from my observations of him in the waking world as well as the Dream Realm. On top of the news about his father yesterday this put Con's mind in turmoil. I managed to soothe him through dreams, but it can't go on. I feel that in order to heal properly the boy needs some knowledge as to why he felt compelled to come here.

The Eternals can remain a secret as can the whole Talionis thing and the Origination. As far as Con will know I'm just a sort of head Dreambringer stationed at the Gateway. The knowledge we give him will be on a par with that we would give those who become Wardens.'

'But he is not like those we choose as Wardens is he' Cedric interrupted 'he is a Dark Soul and therefore an unknown entity.'

'I agree he's different, but I believe that his differences are a reason for this move rather than against it.'

'How so?'

'We here at the Gateway have all vetted him in our different ways and find him no threat. Having spent time here he is already a part of this Dreambringer family. He can't go back to a normal life after being here, he will remain within the Foundation whatever happens right?'

'Agreed.'

'So, as we have stated before, we think that, due to his singing talent, Con would have been a Dreambringer Candidate if not for his childhood trauma and subsequent abuse. Although he is still having trouble communing complex feelings in thought words in the Dream Realm, he can read my thought words and even emotions easily. I therefore believe that if we put him through a version of the initial Dreambringer induction it will help us discover his true talent.'

'Firstly, why is discovering his true talent, if in fact he has one, important?'

'Because it could be useful with in the Dreambringer world.'

'I'm not sure I see that at this point, but secondly, how exactly will telling him about the existence of Dreambringers help you help him. He will not be able to properly interact with you within the Dream Realm, will he? That only happens with Dreambringers once they have been bonded to their Eternal Dreamer.'

'Yes, in the case of normal Dreambringers, but I think that Con is already bonded with me in some way, how else did he find his way here? He can be told that I'm the strongest Dreambringer here without the knowledge that I have an Eternal Dreamer within me. I strongly feel that being aware of his own potential Dreambringer talent in the waking world will mean I can really connect with him in the Dream Realm. This will mean not only will I be able to heal him, but we will find out more about his potential and in turn possibly more about Dark Souls in general. It could lead us to find out if Con is a one off, or if more Dark Souls have the same potential and who knows what else.'

'There is a lot of conjecture on your part here, and the "who knows what else" bit worries me.'

'I know, but I'm confident in my assessments and we can't move forward without taking some chances.'

'There are some here who believe there is no need for us to move forward, not in this way, and that Dark Souls should continue to be left alone. They feel there is no need to know more about them and that it is safer to leave them be.'

'Are you one of those?'

There was a slight pause before Cedric answered.

'No, I believe we should move forwards, but with caution.'

'We have been cautious, and what do those who believe we should leave the Dark Souls alone think we should do with Con? Should we just chuck him out of the street? That's hardly in line with the Foundations charitable reputation, is it?'

'Of course he would not be thrown out on the street, he would be found a suitable place within the Foundation.'

'I believe that this house is the suitable place for him, for now at least anyway.'

'Before this escalates any further, I just want to say that I agree with you, I have not disagreed with you on anything so far, have I? I was simply making you aware that what you are attempting is not popular with some members, and that I am continuing to urge caution.'

'So, are you giving me permission to go ahead and tell Con about the Dreambringers?'

'I am, but if there is even the slightest hint of a problem you must inform me immediately. I do have faith in your judgement, but I do not like it when you do things without informing me first.'

'Thank you. I know that my confidence can come across as arrogance sometimes, but you must know that everything I do I do to help people and benefit the Dreambringer world.'

'I do know that which is why I let you have such scope, but I have to retain some semblance of control at least, I am the head of this division after all.'

'I understand, and it's never my intention to undermine you, I just like to do things my own way, I like to check things out for myself before passing them on to you.'

'I am not keen on that side of the way you work, but I cannot force you to change. I do have a question though. How will Con be able to have a proper Dreambringer presence within the Dream Realm and therefore, be assessed as a Dreambringer if he is not tested as new Dreambringers are before meeting and communing with the Eternals?'

'As you know it was the Eternal Within that brought Con here, albeit unintentionally, and that there was a strange happening when Con and I first met.'

'Yes, the business with the ribbon of mist.'

'Right, well I think that means that as the Eternal is part of me, I can connect and commune with Con in the waking world much as he would with his allotted Eternal Dreamers if a normal Dreambringer recruit. I also think that in finding his way here Con has actually passed the first big test that the Dreambringers are usually tasked with, that of finding their way to their Eternals home. Therefore, I propose to perform a variation of the final test, the Bonding Ceremony. In this case I would refer to it as a Communing Ceremony though. This is an unusual route I know, but in view of the unusualness of Con's 'calling' it seems right.'

'And what exactly would this Communing Ceremony consist of?'

'As you know the Bonding Ceremony usually consists of the retiring Dreambringer relinquishing their strong connection to their Eternal and their replacement taking up that connection, and if done successfully the new Dreambringer has passed the final test.'

'Yes, go on.'

'In Con's case the Eternal he has a link with is within me and I cannot relinquish it, I can only share it to some extent. Therefore, my soul and the Eternal Within will consciously form a strong link whilst in the waking world and then we will extend an invitation to Con's soul to link with us. If he is able to do that then he has passed the test just as the new Dreambringers usually do with their Eternals.'

'And where do you intend this commune to take place?'

'I thought I would take Con to my cabin and do it there.'

'Alone?'

'Yes.'

'No, I do not like that part of this somewhat audacious plan. I would like you to take at least one person with you, and I suggest Mason. He may have had a recent, unusual downgrade to Dreamwisher, but Mason is still the strongest Dreambringer after you at the Gateway. I just feel you need extra support in case something goes wrong.'

'Okay, I agree that Mason can come too.'

'Good. So, when do you propose to reveal the secret to Con, and how soon after do you intend to attempt the Communing Ceremony?'

'We'll speak to Con later today, then tonight I will assess how he has taken the information whilst he's in the Dream Realm, then if I am happy the ceremony will happen tomorrow.'

'Right, well, there is no further discussion needed then. I agree to your daring plan.'

'If Con passes this communing test, do I have permission to tell him all?''

There was a pause as Cedric thought this over, it wasn't a decision you came to lightly.

'I'll have to think it over and get back to you on that' he said.

And with that they ended the call.

Having had the call on loudspeaker Sofia had heard it all. So now she asked, 'When exactly do you intend to speak to Con?'

'I'm going to come back from the Factory earlier today and I will suggest that the others do too. We will tell him when I get back, although I think it should be just you and me with him when we tell him so he doesn't feel too overwhelmed. The others should be here to help deal with the outcome whether good or bad, though as I told Cedric, I'm sure it will be good.'

'Okay, I'll let those who stay here today know what's going on when I can.'

'Good, and I'll obviously tell those who come out to the Factory. When I commune with the Eternals I will obviously get their opinion on the decision too, and although I'm sure they'll agree with my plan it's always good to get their input.

'Okay, good.'

With that all settled Morpheus, Geth, Aaron and Mary headed off to the Factory by their circuitous route for the last time leaving the others to hold their tongues in front of Con for one final day.

Whether told about it by Morpheus or Sofia all the Dreambringers were glad the lying would be over and were happy that Con would finally know enough of the truth to give them breathing space to go about their lives as usual. He would be told about the Factory, but that only the artists could go there just as the Wardens and other trusted Foundation employees were.

If it went as well as Morpheus expected it to then this final little secret would not be a problem. If what Morpheus believed of Con to be true Con would accept it as Eddie and many others had before him

Con, as usual, did not question the errands that those leaving the house were going on. He continued to dampen down the need to ask questions. But he did pick up on a strange atmosphere in the room. An atmosphere that intensified as the day went on. It wasn't a bad atmosphere, but he could not quite put his finger on the cause of it. Everyone was acting as normal, but it was like they were all waiting for something. Something that Con was very much unaware of. It would have made him nervous if they had started to treat him differently, but they didn't. They were still as friendly and chatty as usual so Con decided to just go with the flow. He was sure something was about to happen so would just have to wait to see what it was.

As he had expected Morpheus' commune with the Eternals went well with them being all for letting Con in on the Dreambringer secret. The Eternal Within was particularly happy with the idea and the Passenger Soul, a usual, was happy that It's host and the attached Eternal were happy.

When Morpheus emerged from the Eternals chamber to tell the artists it was time to go back to the house, they were more than happy with the plan. Even Geth was keen to see how it would all pan out. He had warmed to Con the way he had warmed to his fellow Dreambringers so even he felt now that the boy deserved to know what he was involved in.

Con was pleased when the other artists returned but when he was asked to come into the office for a chat with Morpheus and Sofia he began to feel a bit nervous.

Indicating that he should sit in one of the armchairs Sofia sat in the other whilst Morpheus wheeled over the desk chair. It had been decided that Sofia would give Con the initial induction spiel whilst Morpheus noted his reactions. Then Morpheus would continue to explain the commune session he intended Con to take part in. That was if he was happy to, it was not something you could force someone to do.

It was part of Sofia job to vet Warden candidates, and although it was the trained Dreamtellers who usually conducted the induction she knew what was usually disclosed and what wasn't even if she had never actually done it before. As had been agreed in this special case the Talionis story would be left out as would the Origination. She felt a little nervous though not wanting to botch it up, especially in front of Morpheus. On the other hand, it was quite a thrill to impart such life changing information.

She started by saying 'We have decided to trust you with some very secret information Con, and we hope that you prove worthy of our trust.'

'You can trust me, honest' Con told her sincerely his eyes widening with anticipation.

'Here goes then. There's more to the people at this art commune than their artistic talents. They have another, very important and special talent.'

She went on to explain what that talent was.

Morpheus watched the emotions plays across Con's expressive face. At first, he had looked apprehensive, then at Sofia's first words he had looked excitedly expectant. At first he noticed a touch of understandable disbelief until Con heard more and made connections with things he had witnessed and experienced himself. By the end of Sofia's induction speech Con was smiling and fidgeting in his seat.

'Do you have any questions so far?' Sofia asked.

'No, I think you've answered all the questions I had, plus some I didn't even think of. I knew there was something special about this place and the people in it, but I never imagined it was something this amazing. I love the whole 'Souls Domain' thing. I may have some questions later, but for now I just need to take in all this information, Wow!'

'You take a few minutes' she told him 'then Morpheus has more to tell you.'

'More? I think my head might explode' said Con with a nervous laugh.

'All the more reason for us to give you a few minutes to take it all in.'

The three of them sat in comfortable silence for nearly ten minutes whilst Con stared out of the window thinking about what he had been told so far. So, there were special people who helped you dream, how bizarre and incredible. And he was living with some of them, how cool was that.

It was Morpheus who broke the silence.

'Are you ready to hear some more?'

'I guess so.'

'First, I want to ask you something. Before your mother died did you dream a lot?'

After a moment's thought Con answered 'Yes, I did, and so did my mum, we used to talk about our dreams a lot. I'd forgotten that 'til now.'

'I thought as much. As Sofia explained, being a Dreambringer is a calling. There are people all around the world that are at some time in their lives possible Dreambringer candidates. Only a few are actually chosen, the others miss out due to timing or a change in their circumstances. I believe that you Con possessed the potential to become a Dreambringer candidate, that was until your Dreambringer talent was taken away by the trauma of your mother's death and the subsequent abuse you suffered.'

'Me? But I was only eleven when Mum died.'

'I didn't mean you would have been a viable option at eleven, but you had the potential to be one in later life. If your mum had lived you would probably not have been called either, not with that strong a family tie, it's just the potential we're talking about here.'

'How do you know this?'

'I don't for sure, it's just a feeling I have because of your singing talent and the fact that you were drawn here in much the same way that the artists here were, and many before them.'

'Is that to do with my compulsion to get on the train and then the bus, and that ribbon of mist thing I followed?'

'That's a big part of it yes.'

'But I've not been called here to become a Dreambringer have I?'

'No, not exactly.'

'Why then?'

'I brought you here in my efforts to heal your dreaming soul.'

'And it's thanks to you that I can dream again, isn't it?'

'Yes. Originally that's all I intended to do, heal you so you could dream again, but in the process, I inadvertently called you here.'

'So, I wasn't supposed to come here?'

'That wasn't the original plan, no, but I'm glad you did come.'

'I'm glad I did too. And I was right about you being the unseen person in my dreams, wasn't I?'

'Yes, you were.'

'So, am I healed?'

'Not fully, no, I still have some work to do, and I was hoping that letting you in on the Dreambringer secret would help.'

'How?'

'Well, firstly, it will help clear your mind and soul of all those questions you had, and with the confusion gone I can concentrate on healing the deeper hurts.'

'And how will you do that?'

'The same way I've been doing it so far, by bringing you the dreams you need to heal.'

'What happens now?'

'Tonight, I will continue my usual work, and with your soul cleansed of big questions I can get more done. But in order to really heal you, and also to explore your Dreambringer talent, I will need to make you able to become aware of your own presence, and mine, within the Dream Realm.'

'What does that involve?'

'Tomorrow we will need to perform a Communing Ceremony. Don't worry, it's not difficult, and it won't hurt, it will just seem a little strange.'

'What will it do?' Con asked.

'To be honest I'm not sure exactly, but it won't do you any harm, I can promise you that.'

'Is it some sort of test then?'

'Yes, it's similar to the tests that Dreambringer candidates have to take. So, are you up for it?'

'Of course. I'm a little bit nervous I must admit, but I want to do it.'

Sofia smiled 'Okay, good.'

'Do I have to do anything tonight to prepare?'

'No, just get a good night's sleep, I'm the one with the work to do tonight.'

'Will I remember what happened in the morning, you know, seeing you in the Dream Realm or whatever.'

'No, not tonight, that will come after the Communing Ceremony.'

'And that's gonna be tomorrow?'

'Yes.'

'But what if I fail the test?'

'I'm confident you won't.'

'I wish I was as confident' Con said letting out a heavy breath and slumping in the chair.

'Are you okay about everything?' Sofia asked him.

'Yeah, I'm fine, I'm just kinda exhausted after all that.'

'That's understandable. Do you want to sit here quietly for a bit whilst I go and get you a mug of tea?'

'That would be good, thanks.'

With that Morpheus and Sofia left him alone in the office. Morpheus went to tell the others that it had gone well whilst Sofia went to make the promised tea.

After putting his tea down on the table in front of the armchair Sofia told Con that he could take as much time as he liked to get his head straight before joining the others but pointed out that dinner would be ready in about an hour.

'We can keep yours warm until you're ready' she added.

'No, its fine, I'm sure I'll be with you all long before then, I just need ten minutes or so.'

'Okay, good, we'll see you soon.'

It was actually almost half an hour before Con joined them in the lounge/art room, but he was obviously in good spirits.

'Hello, Dreambringers', he exclaimed as he walked into the room with a big grin on his face. 'I was a little overwhelmed earlier, but it's all good now. I knew this place was special, and now I know why it's just awesome.'

'We get it, we've all been there' Clea told him.

'We're glad you're in the know now cos we were dreading you asking probing questions. I don't know how you didn't,' said Eddie.

'It was hard not to at times' Con admitted 'but I didn't want to be a nuisance, I didn't want you to ask me to leave. I kinda adopted a philosophy about it.'

'What do you mean?'

'Well, when strange things happened like me feeling the need to get on that bus, and the weird ribbon of mist thing, I would just tell myself to 'accept the weird' as a way to cope it guess.'

There was a gasp from Clea then and Max exclaimed 'What the hell?!'

'What?' questioned Con 'what did I say?'

'Your 'accept the weird' philosophy isn't exactly original' Clea explained 'I used it to help Max cope with the strangeness of our meeting, and then the group adopted it. I don't know if its coincidence, or if you picked up on it from us somehow, but either way I reckon that really does mean you're one of us.'

'Cool' said Con.

For the next half hour or so they all chatted answering Con's questions about how they had all met and what it was like being a Dreambringer.

Now that he knew about the Factory (if not the Eternals) they told him the truth about the room set ups which would make thing simpler and meant that Sofia would be able to move back to her usual room.

They couldn't tell them the full truth about Morpheus, but they did explain that the fact he was the 'head' Dreambringer was why he spent more time at the Factory and that the cabin was his own place.

The conversation continued through dinner and eventually moved on to more mundane subjects. Con was really beginning to feel like part of the group now. He didn't know what the future held, and how long he would be able to live with these special people, but he knew he was part of something now and would always have a place to stay. The group had made sure he knew this, and he was very grateful to them for it.

Con went to bed that night happier than he could remember being. He was still a little nervous about the coming 'test', but it was a good nervous, an excited nervous. He had potential apparently and he had never been told that before. As for the thing he had potential for, well that was just remarkable.

After giving Cedric Neale the promised update Morpheus headed out to the Factory. He was on a high too, it had gone well so far, and he had hopes of more good things to come. He now thought of Con as his protege and that was exciting.

As Morpheus expected Con's appearance in the Dream Realm had changed again in that the eddies of darkness no longer swirled within his lightened form. The dark edge was still there, as was the knot of darkness at its core however and that was what Morpheus needed to work on dispersing. Without the turmoil of unanswered questions clouding his mind Con would hopefully be even easier to work on.

Morpheus' initial scan gave him even more hope. Con was manifesting feelings of real happiness for the first time. Yes, there were still notes of other negative emotions like hurt and uncertainty, but happiness was a big deal. And so, Morpheus continued with his usual first question without words.

'Hello Con, how are you?'

'I'm good' was the instant answer.

'Can you tell me why?'

'I am safe now.'

'Anything else?'

'I am part of something, and it's something amazing.'

'It is indeed. And you are amazing too.'

'Am I?'

'Of course, only amazing people know what you know.'

Morpheus could almost physically feel the waves of joy his last words produced.

'Is it time for me to dream now?' Con enquired hopefully.

'Yes'

And so, the healing dreams began. There was no question of what Con needed and Morpheus was more than aware of the dreams he brought. The soul's mind was completely open, his communication skills improved, now he just needed to heal the soul's deep wounds. His work would not be finished this night, there were more steps to follow, but things were moving on now. He would heal, and he would learn until Con was whole again, and his potential, whatever that was, could be reached.

Patrick Chapman was not a happy man. He had gone to bed unhappy after receiving the latest update from Cedric Neale and the conversation that he'd just had with another colleague had not improved his mood.

The other colleague was his cousin Matilda Chapman, an ex Dreambringer who now worked as a legal secretary within the Foundation. She had been helping him with some work that he felt necessary but could not do himself, and he was not exactly pleased with her efforts.

Matilda had been a Dreamcatcher for eleven wonderful years and had now been retired for nearly seven years. Although the Chapman family had held important roles within the Foundation over the years, usually within the law department, Matilda had been the family's one and only Dreambringer. Being from a Foundation legacy family meant she was that rare kind of Dreambringer that had family ties, but as that family were mostly 'in the know' to some extent at least, it had not been a problem.

Her Dreambringer talent was something she was very proud of, but she had noted a touch of jealousy from some family members over the years. It had never been a dangerous sort of jealousy, but it had been there.

She missed Dreambringing of course, but she was settled and happy in her new role within the Foundation. At fifty-six she was still single, but she had the other members of her ex Dreambringer group who were both friends and a second family to her. They were all still very close as was usually the case and she saw them often. In fact, she felt closer to them than she did to her actual family.

When her cousin Patrick had called, she had been very surprised, and when he had told her he needed help with something she had assumed he meant help with law secretary work, so had agreed to meet with him in his office later that day. She did not usually work directly with him and had wondered why his own legal secretaries could not help so had been very curious to find out what it was she could help him with.

As soon as she entered Patrick's office, she sensed that he was very wound up about something, there was a strong aura of discontent about the man that made her a little nervous.

Matilda was one of the few people who knew about his impending divorce and wondered now if it was anything to do with him wanting to see her, not that she could work out exactly why that would be. She had heard it from Irene rather than Patrick, so she didn't think he knew she knew. She hadn't spoken to him before that day knowing that he wasn't the type of man to take sympathy well. What on earth did he need her help with?

Sitting on the chair across the desk from him she smoothed her grey skirt over her chubby knees and patted her blond curls with both hands, which was something she unconsciously did when nervous.

He had not minced his words and she had soon discovered why only she could help, and it was nowhere near what she was expecting.

'I need your Dreambringer skills' he had told her.

'What on earth does that mean?' she had enquired, and he had told her.

She was of course aware of the Origination, she had felt it herself, and so had some idea of what had happened, but detailed information did not filter down to Foundation employees at her level. The more detailed information she did receive both before and after the Origination had come via a member of her ex Dreambringer group who had gone on to be a Dreamteller. Her name was Pam Weaver and she had been the one to induct the new Dreambringers for The Gateway art commune. Of course, Pam did not know everything herself, only the top leaders within the British division knew it all. But what she did know she had passed on to her friend Matilda. There was no harm in that.

When her cousin Patrick began to tell her about Morpheus, she had been more shocked by the fact he was telling her about it than what he was actually telling her. The information itself had been very interesting and thrilling but the mere fact that Morpheus existed was phenomenal.

'Why are you telling me all this?' she had asked during a pause in his narrative.

'Let me tell you what this thing called Morpheus is up to now and then I will tell you why I have asked you here.'

Matilda could not understand the distain in Patrick's voice when he mentioned Morpheus, but she listened intently wanting to hear everything. She wasn't sure that she liked where things were going, her cousin sounded so angry, but she was willing to hear him out. She did not know him well, but he was family. Besides she was a very curious person, some would say nosey, but she preferred to say she had an inquiring mind.

'I appreciate you telling me all this' she had told Patrick when he finished 'but what has it got to do with me.'

'I need your help Matilda. I do not trust this thing that calls itself Morpheus and I need your particular skills to check up on the creature.'

'Check up on It how?' she had enquired. Referring to Morpheus as It had felt wrong to her, but she had felt the need to placate her cousin at this point.

'I need you to spy on It in the Dream Realm, I need to know exactly what It is up to.'

'Wwwhat? How?' she had stuttered.

'I would have thought that was obvious' Patrick had said sounding a little impatient 'you have a presence in the Dream Realm, you can find Morpheus there, watch him and report back to me on what exactly he is doing there with this Dark Soul' he had said spitting out the words Dark Soul like they were swear words.

He had started to make her nervous then, but she had felt it best to go along with him.

'I see your point, but it's not as simple as that' she had told him.

'What do you mean?' he had almost shouted.

'Please don't shout, if you calm down, I will explain.'

She had not realised what a temper her cousin had, and it worried her, but she had kept calm and explained herself.

'Although my Dreambringer talent does mean that I do have a presence in the Dream Realm, the fact that I am no longer connected to an Eternal means that presence is not as strong as it was. I can help dreamers if I choose to but on a much weaker level, and it's not really my place to do that anymore. The Dream Realm is more than adequately covered by the current Dreambringers and it's bad manners to, for want of a better phrase, 'work someone else's patch'.

'I'm not asking you to bring dreams am I' Patrick had interjected again showing impatience 'I want you to spy on that arrogant son of a bitch Morpheus.'

'I understand, but you see when I was a Dreambringer I stuck to my own area of the Dream Realm as is usual, I never travelled it then, and now in my weaker Dreambringer state it may be hard for me to find Morpheus within it.'

'But not impossible?'

'Well, no, it's definitely possible, I'm just pointing out that it won't be easy, plus there is another problem.'

'What problem!' he had barked.

'How do I watch him without him knowing I'm doing it?'

'I don't know, that's for you to work out Matilda. I just need to know if you are willing to help me.'

'I am, yes, but can I ask why you are coming to me with this, if the Foundation mistrust Morpheus there must be more talented and experienced people they could use?'

'I am asking you because Cedric Neale and the other heads are idiots and they trust this thing, I do not, this is off my own back and I must stress at this point that we are to keep this between us, do you understand?'

'I do, and I will help you' she had told him having seen the whole picture.

The truth was she did not understand his problem with Morpheus. Cedric Neale and all the others had obviously decided he was no threat, but for some reason Patrick did not agree with them. She was not sure how she felt about what she had learnt of Morpheus and this Dark Soul he was apparently helping, but she had decided to go along with her cousin for two reasons. The first was because she had felt a little afraid of his reaction if she had said no. The second was pure curiosity. Whether he was a force for good or not, now that the idea had been put into her head, she could not resist the chance to spy on the mysterious Morpheus. It would take some doing though.

It had taken Matilda several nights to find Morpheus within the Dream Realm. When she finally did locate him, she had been too stunned by his impressive appearance to do much but stare in wonder from a distance for the short time she had left before being pulled back into sleep.

She had awoken with his image imprinted on her brain. She had never met Samuel Raven in the waking world and although she had heard he was a handsome man she had not been prepared for just how beautiful this newly formed creature Morpheus' Dream Realm appearance had been. And that light he gave off, she had felt its healing power even at a distance. She had felt a little of that power when the Origination happened, but this was next level.

What she could not understand was why Patrick thought that Morpheus was anything but good. Her cousin had become increasingly frustrated during the time it had taken her to find Morpheus and although initially happy to hear she had found him he had been less than pleased by her first report. When she recounted that although she had not had enough time to check out what he was actually doing, her first impression was that he was a force for good Patrick had become very angry. She had been shocked by the vitriol that had poured out of him and was glad that the exchange had been by telephone and not in person. Once he calmed down a little, he had made it clear to her that she needed to do better and to change her attitude.

'Do not be fooled by this creature's charm' he had told her 'you need to be wary of him and do what I have asked you to. I need more information on exactly what he is up to with that evil entity they call a Dark Soul.'

Matilda had agreed to do better not wanting to anger him further. The truth was she had become very confused and a little afraid. There was no way she could do what Patrick wanted her to do without being noticed, and she had no way of knowing what the consequences would be if anyone found out what she was doing. So, she decided she would simply seek Morpheus out each night and watch him whilst fobbing Patrick off with vague observations for a few days whilst she worked out what to do for the best. Her cousin's attitude and anger were troubling, but he was family, and she did not want to get him in trouble.

As she had expected it had been quite difficult to spy on Morpheus without being noticed. In the Dream Realm she had a distinct human form, an ethereal recreation of her human form that was smaller, and less impressive than that of a practicing Dreambringer, but it still meant she stood out amongst the normal dreaming souls.

She did not have to lie to Patrick regarding her lack of information because beyond telling him that Morpheus was making progress in his efforts to heal the Dark Soul there was not much else to report. He wasn't happy, but what could he do about it except shout at her to do better. She was growing accustomed to his anger, but that did not mean she liked it. The inborn affection she had felt for her cousin was diminishing with every conversation they had.

Patrick kept asking her to get nearer so she could read the Dark Soul herself and gauge just how evil It was. She did not even try to persuade him that as far as she could tell the Dark Soul was not evil at all, she just explained that she did not have the skill to do what he wanted, not unless he was happy for her to get caught in the act.

Their last conversation had not ended well. She had reported that it looked to her like the Dark Soul was almost healed and he had yelled at her saying that maybe she should risk getting caught because she was 'bloody' useless anyway and he should maybe find someone better.

She had managed to placate him not wanting him to get another person involved. That could only go one of two ways, they could end up under pressure and afraid like she was, or they could be more sympathetic to his views and do some harm. There wasn't much they could do in the Dream Realm, but they could stir up trouble if they were less discreet than she was. She felt it more likely to be the first scenario as all those who were chosen to be Dreambringers were inherently good people, but then she had thought the same of all Foundation employees, especially those high up in the hierarchy, but her cousin was proving her wrong every chance he got.

This latest conversation had made her mind up though. She had thought long and hard about what to do and had finally decided on a plan of action. Now was the time to make a start on that plan. Almost as soon as the call to Patrick had ended, she was making a call to someone else.

Unbeknownst to Matilda however, Patrick had an alternative plan of his own. He had been awake most of the night after hearing that Cedric had given the go ahead for the Dark Soul boy to be told 'the secret'. He was so angry at the decision and in the end had decided to take things into his own hands. Therefore, he too had made another call directly after his call with Matilda had ended.

Con didn't eat much at breakfast, he was too full of nervous excitement. He was a little disappointed that he had only had the usual sort of dreams the night before, he'd been hoping for more even though Morpheus had told him nothing like that would happen until after the Communing Ceremony thing.

He was enjoying taking part in the usual breakfast chatter when Geth suddenly moved the conversation into strange territory.

'I think I saw something weird last night' he said gaining everyone's attention.

'What sort of weird?' asked Eddie.

'I thought I saw another Dreambringer, well sort of.'

'It's possible' stated Mason 'we don't usually stray into another Dreambringer groups territory, but it can happen.'

'What do you mean by sort of?' queried Clea

'What did they look like?' Mary inquired at the same time.

'It was a woman' Geth told them 'and she didn't quite look like we do, she was distinctly a Dreambringer but not as impressive, more like Mason and Eddie look in the Dream Realm.'

'She's probably a Dreamwisher then' suggested Eddie.

'Maybe, but she didn't look as impressive as you two either, she seemed weaker somehow.'

'What was she doing?' asked Aaron.

'Watching Morpheus, I think.'

'Can you blame her,' blurted Sofia.

'No, not really' agreed Clea giving Sofia a knowing smile.

'We've all spent some time watching Morpheus, she was probably just a curious Dreamwisher' suggested Max.

'But why was she in this area?' asked Sofia 'I'm not aware of any Dreamwishers visiting anywhere near here.'

'That's a good point' said Mason 'but I don't think by the description that she was a Dreamwisher, I think she may have been an ex Dreambringer. I've been there briefly remember. Ex Dreambringers can still access the Dream Realm, they just have less influence, they're weaker, therefore that's how they look.'

'That still doesn't explain why she was in this area,' said Sofia.

'No, but if she lives near here, it could explain it' Mason suggested 'and if you were roaming the Dream Realm and you came across Morpheus wouldn't you stop and watch him.'

'I think we already established that was a yes' said Clea.

'What do you think Morpheus?' asked Mason.

'I was just remembering that I caught sight of something one night, I thought it was one of you, but maybe it was this mystery woman.'

'Should we be worried?' asked a nervous Max.

'I don't think so' Morpheus told him 'I believe I would have sensed danger if there was any.'

'How do you know that?' questioned Geth.

'Well for a start what danger could any Dreambringer be to me in the Dream Realm, or to anyone for that matter?'

'After Talionis you never know do you?' proffered Geth.

'Even Talionis was no danger in the Dream Realm' Morpheus reminded him.

'Okay, maybe not, but that doesn't mean another rogue couldn't be.'

'I think you're just finding problems where there aren't any.'

'I'm just playing devil's advocate'

'I'd rather you didn't,' said Max.

'Okay, let's all calm down' soothed Morpheus 'and I suggest that tonight Mason and Eddie stick by me and take turns looking out for this mystery Dreambringer and we can get their take on her, if she turns up.'

Everyone was happy with the plan. Con had stayed silent throughout the whole thing not really knowing what to make of it. He didn't really want to think about some stranger watching them, he had enough to worry about.

Sensing Con's uneasiness Clea steered the conversation onto a more casual topic making sure the boy was part of the discussion. Morpheus was thankful for her thoughtfulness, he needed Con to be as relaxed as possible for the upcoming Communing Ceremony. He wasn't too worried about this Dream Realm onlooker; he had just wanted to make sure the group were reassured. Now he could concentrate on what he had to achieve today because it wasn't some small thing. He was moving into unknown territory again and although he felt confident in his own abilities, he could never be sure how Con would cope.

The phone rang in the office then and Sofia went to answer it.

She came back a few minutes later with a frown on her face.

'We're going to be having another visitor' she told them all 'that was a man called Patrick Chapman on the phone, he's the head of law at the Foundation and he's coming here to talk to Con about the legal side of his situation. He says the police want to speak to Con about his father. He's convinced them to do it by phone and he wants to be with Con when he talks to them.'

'I thought that was all sorted.' said Morpheus.

'Obviously not.'

169

'When is he coming?' asked Clea.

'He's on his way now,' said Sofia.

'What the hell' exclaimed Morpheus 'we have the Communing Ceremony to perform today, he must know that, so why the hell is he coming now?'

'I really don't know; he was pretty short with me on the phone.'

'Is he coming to see me?' queried a worried sounding Con.

'Yes, but don't worry you're not in trouble' Sofia assured him 'it's just routine, I think the Foundation just want to cover themselves.'

'It does seem a little odd though' said Mason 'the lawyers very rarely come out to the art communes; he could have been in on the call remotely.'

'I know, it is unusual' Sofia said without much conviction.

'I take it Cedric Neale knows about this' Morpheus stated.

'I did ask, and he said Cedric had authorised his visit.'

'Did you believe him?'

'Well yes, why would he lie.'

'You're right, he's the top guy in legal so he must know what he's doing. I'm just annoyed that I'm going to have to put Con's Communing Ceremony on hold.'

'Do we all have to stay at the house to see him?' enquired Aaron.

'No, he said the only person he really needs to see is Con. I'll be around too, but the rest of you can carry on as you would have done.'

'I'll go out to the Factory then' said Morpheus 'I can commune with the Eternals and get my energy up for when we can finally do the Communing Ceremony rather than just waste time waiting.' He was annoyed and thought that this could be some sort of payback from Cedric Neale and the other heads for doing things without their say so, a way of showing him they were still in charge. Maybe they were wavering over the Communing Ceremony, and this was a delaying tactic. Whatever the reason he intended to make sure the ceremony went ahead. He would play their game for now, but it would happen whether they liked it or not. Right now though a session with the Eternal was what he needed to calm him and help get his mind straight.

Whilst Morpheus quietly seethed over this seeming stalling tactic the others were making their plans for the day.

'Me and Mary want to go to the Factory today,' said Aaron.

'Me too,' said Max.

'I'll go too' added Geth.

'I'm going to stay here' said Clea 'I want to see this man.'

'Why?' asked Max

'Oh, you know me, I'm just nosey' she told him, but that wasn't the whole truth. She had a bad feeling about this visit, but she didn't want to admit it out loud because she didn't have anything to back it up, just an odd feeling. She couldn't quite put her finger on what was worrying her either and just hoped it was simply a manifestation of nervousness on Con's behalf, because the boy looked really anxious. He'd had a lot to deal with recently and he did not need some stuffy suit confusing him with legal jargon.

'It looks like me and Mason are staying here then' stated Eddie and for some reason Clea felt relieved it was those two men who would be staying.

About forty minutes after Morpheus and the others had set off for the Factory the gate buzzer echoed through the house.

'Wow, he really is in a rush,' said Mason.

Eddie went to buzz the man in whilst Clea tried to calm Con.

'It's just routine, nothing to worry about, and we're all here for you' she said as much to calm herself as him.

Clea then elected herself as lookout and went to stand a one of the lounge/art room windows.

'He's here' she called when she saw a white BMW pulling up on the driveway. Sofia went to open the door whilst Clea continued to watch as the man got out of the car. She noted the ill-fitting suit and the man's nervous energy. *"Why would he be nervous?"* she thought.

Sofia brought Patrick into the lounge/art room and introduced him to everyone. His manner was polite and friendly but there was something fake about him in Clea's view. She made a point of shaking his hands and noticed it was hot and clammy. Con did not like the look of him either.

'It's nice to meet you Constantine' Patrick said when introduced to the boy.

A weak 'Hello' was all Con could manage, his throat constricted and his mouth dry with anxiety.

'There's nothing to worry about, just boring legal stuff' the man told him, but to Con his friendly manner seemed forced. There was a look in the man's eyes that he did not like, it reminded him of his father for some reason.

'Is there somewhere I can speak to the boy in private?' Patrick asked no one in particular.

'You can use the office, but I would like to sit in, Con's a little nervous with strangers and I think he'd feel more comfortable if I was there,' said Sofia.

She noticed a flash of annoyance wash over the man's face before he broke into a forced looking smile.

'I'm not sure that's necessary, but if you insist, please join us. If you could lead the way to the office, we can get this sorted as quickly as possible.'

Sofia led the way with Patrick behind her and Con reluctantly following.

Mason, Eddie and Clea watched them go. They were all fighting uneasy feelings about the man. He was giving off worrying vibes, but he was a lawyer with a top job within the Foundation therefore he could be trusted surely.

Patrick Chapman was not happy with how things were going. He had wanted to get Con alone and these idiots were making that difficult, he needed to think on his feet. He now realised how flimsy this plan of his was, but he was pretty confident he could still make it work.

Once they were in the office Sofia asked, 'Would you rather sit at the desk where the phones are, or shall we start off in the more comfortable chairs?'

'The desk would be best. Con and I can sit there whilst you sit more comfortably' he said with another false looking smile.

Sofia had never felt uneasy about a Foundation member before so the feelings she was getting about this man were worrying her. She had met him briefly a while ago and he had seemed okay then, but now something was off.

Con followed the man over to the desk and sat in the chair at the side of the desk whilst Patrick sat himself behind it. He did not like this man at all, and again he thought how the look in the man's eyes reminded him of his father. Con wondered then if the man had come to take him away after all, maybe the Foundation had changed their mind, or the police had decided he should be arrested after all. Con felt frightened and cornered and it was only Sofia's presence that was keeping him from freaking out.

Just as Sofia was about to sit down on one of the armchairs across the room from them Patrick said 'Sofia, why don't you go and make us some tea, I'm parched and I'm sure Con would like one too.'

'No, I'm fine' Con said his heart lurching in panic at the thought of being left alone with the man, but what Sofia said next reassured him a little

'Sure. I'll go and ask Clea to make it' Sofia suggested.

'I wouldn't want to put the lady to any trouble, shouldn't she be working on her art.'

'Yes, but she won't mind' Sofia told him having noted another flash of annoyance on the man's face.

As Sofia was leaving the room Con saw the man's expression change and what he saw scared him. He had been free of this sort of fear for days now and he did not welcome its return. This could not happen to him again.

Sofia was halfway across the hall on her way to speak to Clea when the office door suddenly slammed shut behind her making her jump. Twirling around she headed back towards the closed door whilst shouting 'Mason, Eddie, come quick.'

She was trying to open the door when the two men joined her.

'It slammed shut behind me and now its locked' she told them shock and fear distorting her fine features.

Clea was now hovering behind them her hand over her mouth, her eyes wide with fear.

Sofia stepped aside to let Mason try the door, it wasn't that he disbelieved her, he just needed to make sure it wasn't just stuck.

Discovering it was definitely locked he pounded the door with a fist shouting 'What's going on in there? Open up!'

'Was it the lawyer guy who locked it?' Eddie asked Sofia.

'I don't know for sure, but why would Con do it, I never should have left him alone with that man.'

'You weren't to know. And it could just be innocent, he might just want privacy.'

'He wasn't keen on me being in there, but this seems a bit extreme.'

Mason shushed them then 'Sorry, I just want to try and hear what's going on inside' he explained as he placed his ear against the door.

For a few seconds he heard nothing, then he heard a voice say 'What are you doing? Put that away' it was the man's voice. There was then a strange scuffling noise followed by a cry of surprise, again from the man who then yelled, 'you little devil, look what you've done' then after a brief pause, he said 'no, don't' then yelped in pain. There were more scuffling noises then, but Mason had heard enough and telling the others 'There's something bad going on in there, I'm gonna try to break the door in' he stood back and gave the door a hard, high kick. The door was old but well made so did not budge.

'Let me try' said Eddie thinking he would try shoulder barging the door with his full weight. But before he could try the door suddenly flew open.

Patrick stood in the doorway. There was blood on his right cheek, and he was holding the top of his left arm with his right hand through which more blood was seeping.

'The boy attacked me' he told them.

Pushing past him Mason rushed into the room to find Con slumped on the floor in front of the desk. He was unconscious and there was blood on his forehead.

'What did you do to him?' Mason shouted.

'What did I do to him? I just told you; he attacked me. He locked the fucking door after Sofia left and then attacked me, I was just defending myself.'

Eddie, Sofia and Clea had now come into the room.

'He's just a little slip of a thing, how could he be a threat to you?' asked Clea as she rushed to where Mason was still crouched over Con.

'The little shit had a knife' Patrick explained 'look it's there' he added pointing.

The small penknife lay not far from the outstretched arm of the unconscious boy. There was blood on the knife and on Con's hand.

None of the Gateway residents could believe Con would have done such a thing but the evidence was in front of them.

'What did you do to him, why is he unconscious?' Sofia asked Patrick.

'After he slashed me with that knife a second time I decided to fight back, he went for my stomach, but I managed to grab his wrist and stop him, then I shoved him away and he fell hitting his head on the desk on the way down.'

It was plausible, but at the same time unbelievable. There were so many questions the big ones being why did Con have a knife on him, and why would he attack Patrick?

Whatever he had done though Con needed medical attention. Clea and Mason were both kneeling beside him and having established that he had a pulse and was still breathing Mason said 'Eddie, I think you need to call that special number and get an ambulance here.'

Both Mason and Eddie were now having unpleasant flashbacks to the terrible incident involving their friends Mahesh, Claude, Gina and Blake at the beginning of the trouble caused by Talionis. But they managed to keep it together.

'I'll make that call' Patrick suddenly announced 'I can get through faster and get someone here, I need medical treatment too you know' he added sounding a little indignant.

'How bad are you hurt?' enquired Sofia.

'We'll let the paramedics decide that' he told her going around the desk and picking up the phone and dialling.

'This is Patrick Chapman, there's been an incident at the Gateway art commune, we need paramedics here straight away. We have one unconscious male and I have sustained knife wounds' he told the person on the other end, then after a pause to listen 'the unconscious patient is the one who inflicted my wounds, he may need restraining if he regains consciousness' then after another short pause 'good, thank you.'

'An ambulance will be here within twenty minutes' he informed them all after hanging up the phone.

Clea was now holding Con's unbloody hand and whispering assurances in his ear. She was feeling guilty about not voicing her worries about the lawyers visit. She did not trust his version of events, there was no way that Con would have attacked this man.

Mason, Eddie and Sofia were reserving their judgment. Whilst none of them really believed Con would do something like this past experience told them that it was possible. The gentle giant Claude Grey had murdered his friend Mahesh whilst under the influence of Talionis so maybe something similar had gone on here. Or maybe they just did not know Con as well as they had thought. The boy had been abused for years and maybe all the recent stress had pushed him over the edge. Whatever the case the Foundation would get to the bottom of it.

'I'm going to wait outside for the ambulance' Patrick told them now 'and whilst I wait, I'm going to make a few more calls on my mobile to update Cedric and the others.'

Clea remained by Con whilst Mason and Eddie paced the office not knowing what to do and Sofia stood at the window watching Patrick making his calls out on the driveway. What he was doing would usually be her job and she was feeling at a bit of a loss as to what she should be doing.

'We have to let the others know' she suddenly blurted.

'Of course.' agreed Eddie 'I'll call Geth's mobile and tell them to get back here straight away.'

'What about Morpheus, he'll be with the Eternals' said Sofia.

'Well. I know it's not usually done, but someone will have to interrupt him. I'm sure he won't mind under the circumstances.'

In fact, no one needed to interrupt Morpheus, he already knew something was wrong. The Eternals had alerted him that something bad was happening at the house. They could not give him details, they just sensed there was something wrong.

He made his way upstairs to the others, his legs a little shaky after having to end his communing session so suddenly.

'We need to get back to the house, now' he shouted as he emerged from the sunken staircase.

'Why?' queried Geth.

'Something bad has happened' was all he could tell them.

Dropping everything instantly they all headed back to the house and were halfway there when Geth received the call from Eddie.

'We know mate, we're on our way' he said before Eddie could speak 'Morpheus got some sort of tip off from the Eternals, we'll be there soon.'

'Okay, good' said a stunned Eddie before Geth hung up. 'They're already on the way' Eddie told the others 'somehow the Eternals knew and told Morpheus.'

'This is some craze shit' said Mason his hands buried in his short dreadlocks.

'It sure is mate' agreed Eddie 'I'm gonna go out to meet them and fill them in, I don't want them all rushing in here.'

'Good idea' Sofia told him whilst still watching Patrick who appeared to have finished his calls and was now standing staring out at the driveway entrance.

Eddie intercepted the returning artists halfway down the slope.

'What the hell happened?' Morpheus asked him.

'Con attacked the lawyer guy with a knife and was then knocked unconscious.'

'Why would he do that?'

'I don't know, but that's what the guy told us.'

'What do you mean what he told you, did none of you see it happen?'

'No, we got locked out of the office, there was only Con and the lawyer guy in there.'

'How the fuck did that happen? Why were they left alone?'

'Sofia was with them, but she came out for some reason and the door was slammed shut behind her.'

'How badly hurt is Con?'

'We're not sure, he's still unconscious, the ambulance should be here soon though.'

'And where's this lawyer guy now?'

'Out on the driveway making calls to Cedric Neale etc and waiting for the ambulance.'

'So, he's not badly hurt then?'

'No, I guess not.'

Morpheus was feeling bad now for leaving Con, what on earth had happened. He could not believe that the boy would harm anyone, it must have been in self defence or something, but why would the Foundation lawyer want to harm Con?

'I know you're all concerned about Con' Eddie said now as they reached the terrace 'but please don't all rush into the office. The ambulance should be here soon, and Clea is with him. I suggest you all go into the lounge, there isn't anything you can do anyway.'

They all nodded their agreement except Morpheus who said, 'I need to see the boy' and no one argued with him.

Eddie decided to go to the lounge with the others and answer their questions as best he could whilst Morpheus headed for the office.

Upon entering he quickly surveyed the scene then hurried over to Con.

'He's breathing okay but still unconscious' Clea told him tearfully.

Crouching down Morpheus told the unconscious boy 'Hold on kid help will be here soon.'

He then stood up and went to join Mason and Sofia who were both stood at the window.

'Where's this lawyer guy then?' he asked them.

Mason pointed out the window and just as Morpheus spotted the man the private Foundation ambulance appeared. It pulled up on the driveway and two paramedics got out and after speaking briefly to Patrick they retrieved a stretcher from the back of the ambulance and headed for the house.

Mason went to the office door and motioned the paramedics into the room.

Clea was asked to move out of the way and reluctantly did so as the paramedics began their examination.

'How long has he been unconscious?' one of them asked and it was Mason who answered them.

Within minutes they had checked his vitals, dressed his head wound and loaded him carefully onto the stretcher and as they were taking him out one of them said 'His vitals are stable, but we need to get him to hospital for a head scan as soon as possible.'

'Can I go with him?' asked Morpheus.

'I'm afraid there isn't room in the ambulance sir, not with our other patient,' the paramedic told him meaning the lawyer and with that they took Con out to the ambulance.

'They'll be taking him to the nearest Foundation hospital, I know the way' Mason told Morpheus 'we can take the van and follow on in a bit.'

The stunned Gateway residents watched as Con was taken outside and loaded into the ambulance. Patrick went in the back too with one of the paramedics whilst the other one climbed into the driving seat. Then they were gone off down the driveway.

Eddie ran over to the gate intercom and made sure the gate was open so they could get out quickly.

The Gateway residents now all congregated in the lounge. Clea and Mary hugged each other, both close to tears and everyone took a seat except for Mason, Eddie and Morpheus.

'Me and Mason are going to the hospital' Morpheus told them all 'and we'll update you when we can.'

'I'll see you out the gate then make this lot some tea, I think they need it' said Eddie looking around at all the shocked faces.

Morpheus and Mason went out to get the van and Eddie went back to the gate intercom in the office. Then once he had seen them out the gate he went to the kitchen.

The atmosphere in the van was tense, both men lost in their own thoughts of how they had failed Con in some way. Morpheus was convinced that whatever Con had done was in self defence whether justified or not. The stupid man had probably scared the boy, but why on earth had Con had a knife. In Mason's case he was berating himself for not getting into the office sooner. He should have broken that door down as soon as he got there.

They saw no sign of the ambulance on their journey to the hospital, but it had a good head start on them plus the luxury of being able to speed through traffic.

Upon arrival at the Foundation run hospital they hurried to the reception desk.

'One of your ambulances just brought two patients in' Mason said to the receptionist 'we would like an update on the patients please.'

'Let me just check for you' the receptionist told them.

She picked up a phone and relayed their request to someone on the other end. She listened, then asked 'are you sure?' listened again, frowned, said 'okay, thanks' and putting the phone down she told Mason 'I'm sorry sir but we haven't sent any ambulances out today, let alone had any come back in.'

'What? That can't be right' he told her 'a Foundation ambulance picked two men up from our art commune and said they were taking them to the hospital.'

'Are you sure it was this facility they were coming to sir?'

'Where else would it be?' queried Mason 'this is the nearest facility to the house.'

'I don't know what to say sir, except we know nothing about it here, sorry. You can use our phone to call someone at head office to check where they might have gone if you like.'

'That's fine, I have a mobile' Mason told her, and not knowing the level of the receptionist's knowledge the two men returned to the van before carrying on their conversation.

'Who should we phone?' Mason asked Morpheus.

Morpheus, who was looking as sick as Mason felt answered 'We need to speak to the big man himself, Cedric Neale, this could be down to him.'

'How do you mean?'

'I mean the man may have used this incident to get Con away from me. They probably want to lock him up and test him for months like they did me' he explained the bitterness clear in his voice.

'I thought Cedric trusted you, he gave you the go ahead on letting Con in on the Dreambringer secret, didn't he?'

'Yes, but maybe this incident gave him second thoughts. Whatever actually happened he would have only heard that lawyer's version and it would have sounded bad, so maybe he's had Con whisked off somewhere he deems safe.'

'This is all sounding a little far fetched and crazy. Let's just phone the man and see what he has to say.'

Mason dialled the Foundation emergency number then when prompted keyed in a code that would get him through to Cedric Neale immediately. As it began to ring, he put it on speaker then handed the phone to Morpheus sensing the man wanted to do the talking.

'Hello Mason, this is Cedric Neale' the Foundation division leader said after reading the emergency call readout.

'This isn't Mason, its Morpheus.'

'Ah, I see, what can I do for you Morpheus, I take it there is some kind of emergency.'

'You know there's an emergency.'

'Do I?'

'Don't play the innocent with me old man.'

'Please refrain from talking to me that way and explain to me what on earth you are talking about,' said a now indignant Cedric Neale.

'I'm talking about the incident at the Gateway and the fact that the ambulance that took Con and your lawyer friend away has not arrived at the hospital. Where have you sent it?'

'I can honestly say I have no idea what you are talking about.'

'What?'

'I know nothing of any incident at the Gateway let alone where some ambulance has been sent, what the hell is going on?'

The man's tone of voice was beginning to penetrate through Morpheus' anger, and he realised that the Foundation boss really did not know what was going on.

'Shit!' exclaimed Morpheus 'I am sorry for the way I spoke to you just now, but something is seriously wrong here.'

Between them Morpheus and Mason then quickly explained what had happened.

'Good grief' Cedric exclaimed when he had finished 'the nerve of that man.'

'What man?'

'Patrick Chapman, the lawyer.'

'Oh him.'

'I have a feeling this is all down to him. I don't have time to explain, I need to set some wheels in motion at this end to find out exactly what's going on here. I suggest that you and Mason head back to the Gateway and I will update you when I can.'

'Is there nothing we can do?'

'Not at this point no, it's up to me to sort this mess. I want to assure you that I do not sanction whatever it is Chapman is up to.'

'Good, and I'm sorry again for thinking this was down to you.'

'Well, we'll let that go for now. Sorting this problem out is more important than your opinion of me. I will update you shortly.'

And with that Cedric ended the call.

'Why is the drama always focused on the Gateway?' mused Mason.

'Because its where all the changes are taking place' was Morpheus' enigmatic reply.

Matilda was very nervous as she approached Cassandra's desk.

Cassandra had been Cedric Neale's PA for nearly nine years. Matilda guessed her age to be about fifty and she had always found the woman a little intimidating. Her dark, chestnut hair was cut in an immaculately kept, chin length bob and she wore well cut, fashionable pants suits matched with silk blouses and sensible shoes. She gave off an air of neatness, confidence and efficiency which Matilda was a little jealous of. Matilda was as good at her own job as Cassandra was at hers, but Matilda always looked a little dishevelled and had a far less confident air about her.

That morning Matilda had spoken to her fellow ex Dreambringer Pam Weaver and had confided in her all that had been going on with her and her cousin Patrick. Pam had listened intently then said, 'I don't like the sound of all this. Patrick's attitude is a little alarming if you ask me.'

'I know, that's why I'm asking your advice. I'm really worried about what he might do next and am not sure what I should do about it.'

'I think you should report everything to Cedric Neale, and soon.'

'But I will get in trouble over this, what I did was definitely outside of acceptable Dreambringer behaviour.'

'That may be, but you will get into even more trouble if you're found out after Patrick does something worse.'

'You're right, I should own up now, it's gone too far already. I can't say I relish the idea of standing in from of Mr Neale and telling him what I've done.'

'It will be hard, but I think he will be more concerned with Patrick's behaviour than yours.'

'I guess so, and you're right, I should go and see him now.'

'Good girl. And good luck. Call me later and let me know how it went.'

'I will, thanks.'

Now, arriving at Cassandra's desk Matilda patted her blond curls and cleared her throat 'Hello Cassandra' she began 'I was hoping I could speak to Mr Neale.'

Looking up from her computer screen Cassandra explained 'I'm afraid Mr Neale is very busy right now Matilda, can it wait?'

'Errmm, it's kind of important actually.'

'Well, he's dealing with an emergency at one of the art communes right now so it would have to be very important to come before that.'

'Which art commune?' Matilda asked a feeling of dread creeping over her.

'I'm not sure I can divulge that I'm afraid, I should not have told you that even.'

'Is it The Gateway art commune?'

'What makes you think that?' Cassandra asked looking a little taken aback.

'Because what I need to talk to Mr Neale about concerns the Gateway and a possible problem there, so I thought maybe something had already happened. If I'm right, then I think I really do need to speak to him.'

'In that case I will see if he can speak to you.'

'Thank you.'

Picking up the intercom handset Cassandra buzzed through to her boss' office.

'I'm sorry to bother you sir' she said after a short wait 'but I have Matilda Chapman here and she would like to speak to you urgently concerning the Gateway, I think it may be something to do with the problem there.'

There was a pause as she listened to her boss, then she said, 'Yes sir' and replaced the handset.

'He will see you now' she told Matilda indicating the door to her left with a well-manicured hand.

She thanked the PA and let herself into the office. The room she entered looked more like a study in a stately home than an office. The walls were painted dark green, the carpet a thick pile burgundy, there were shelves of leather-bound books, two upright, leather armchairs, and dominating it all a large, oak desk behind which sat the man himself.

'Hello Matilda, please take a seat' said Cedric indicating one of the armchairs which was placed in front of the desk 'I understand you have something to tell me regarding the Gateway.'

'Yes sir' she said taking a seat and smoothing her skirt over her knees, 'though what I have to tell you is more precisely about Patrick.'

'Patrick Chapman?'

'Yes. As I'm sure you know he is my cousin and, well, he recently asked me to do something for him that I am ashamed to admit I agreed to.'

'Go on' he encouraged.

And Matilda told him everything about what Patrick asked her to do and what she actually did and then she tried to explain why she had done it.

'I will admit it was mainly curiosity on my part I'm afraid, I mean who wouldn't want to witness Morpheus in the Dream Realm. Anyway, I promise you, whatever motives Patrick had, mine were in no way malicious. I was just there to watch and monitor and that's all I did. But when Patrick started to get frustrated with me because I wouldn't go nearer to learn more I really started to worry. After talking it through with a friend I came to you.'

'Which friend?' Cedric asked causing a ripple of panic in Matilda at her stupidity for putting Pam in the frame too.

'It was Pam Weaver' she admitted 'but you can trust her, she wouldn't tell what I told her to anyone I promise.'

'I believe you; she will not be in trouble; I just need to know who knows what.'

Matilda nodded her understanding.

'Am I in trouble sir?'

'I'm not going to rule out any future disciplinary action where you are concerned, but you are not in any serious trouble, especially now you have owned up to what you have done. We won't worry about that now though; I have other things to deal with. I will not go into what your cousin has gone on to do, that's need-to-know information as far as I'm concerned, but I want to thank you for coming and telling me this, though I would rather you had done it earlier.'

'Yes, I'm sorry, I should have come to you when this all started, but he's family, you know.'

'I understand that and am just glad you came to your senses in the end.'

'What should I do now?'

'You should keep quiet about what you know, carry on as normal and contact me immediately if Patrick contacts you. I have a lot to do here but I will ask Cassandra to give you an emergency code so you can get through to me quickly if you hear from your cousin.'

'I doubt he will contact me now but if he does, I will definitely let you know.'

'Good, now if you could leave me to it and go get on with your day, I'm sure you have things to do.'

'I do yes, thank you sir.'

'Goodbye Matilda.'

'Goodbye sir.'

Matilda left the office not knowing how she would be able to get on with her day as if she knew nothing of the problems her cousin had made. She dreaded to think what he had done now. She stopped at Cassandra's desk to get her emergency code and then headed off to her own office to try and concentrate on her own work.

Meanwhile Cedric had things to do, he had Matilda's information now and was beginning to build a picture of what had gone on. His next job was looking into the ambulance business.

'So why has this lawyer taken Con?' asked Clea her face ashen with worry.

'We don't know, and if Cedric Neale does, he hasn't told us yet' Mason told her.

'Whatever reason he had it can't be good' said Geth.

The whole group had obviously been shocked at the news Morpheus and Mason had returned with and they were all very confused.

'So did Con attack the lawyer guy cos he knew he was here to take him away?' asked Aaron.

'Maybe' said Mason.

'Or maybe Con didn't attack the man at all' added Morpheus.

'But he had knife wounds' said Mary in a shaky voice.

'We don't know what exactly happened in that office and we don't know where Con has been taken or why' stated Morpheus 'I'm hoping Cedric Neale will call us soon and hopefully he knows more.'

'What do we do until then?' asked Geth.

'We wait'

'Well, that sucks.'

Con woke up with a start finding himself laying on a strange bed in a strange place. His head was bandaged and hurting, and he felt dizzy and nauseous. Holding down a strong feeling of panic he sat up and, when the room had stopped spinning, he looked around him.

He was in a strange, small room. It was about ten by twelve feet with a slate paved floor and whitewashed stone walls. He was sat on the bare mattress of a small, single bed and the only other pieces of furniture in the room were a small wooden table and a shabby looking armchair. On the table there was a small bottle of water and at the bottom of the bed Con saw a large bucket. There was also a wood burner, which was currently cold and empty, and in a niche in one wall an oil lamp, which again was unlit. The meagre light in the room was coming from a small, narrow window set high up over the bed.

The room reminded Con of a jail cell and the thought sent a shiver of fear through his body. Carefully standing up from the bed he walked over to the sturdy looking wooden door across the room.

Con banged on the door a few times with the side of his fist then shouted 'Hello, is anyone there?!'

There was no answer.

The banging hurt his hand, and the shouting hurt his head, but he tried it again, and then again, but still received no answer. Feeling weak, dizzy and scared he went back to sit on the bed. He tried to remember how he had got to this room but the last thing he could recall was having breakfast with the Gateway artists and a conversation about someone watching Morpheus in the Dream Realm. Now he was here, wherever here was.

He had been sat there for what must have been about ten minutes trying not to scream in panic and remember how he had got there when he heard a noise. It sounded like someone unlocking a door, but it was not the door in front of him. The next thing he heard was a voice.

'So you're finally awake then boy?' the male voice asked.

Con managed a weak 'Yes' in answer, not sure if he'd have been wiser staying quiet.

'I've left you water and a bucket to piss in and that's all you're getting for now. I still need to decide what to do with you, so you'll be in there for a while. Don't try anything stupid.'

'Why have you brought me here? What have I done to deserve being locked away?' asked a very confused Con.

'You're an abomination and a danger to others' was the answer he received though it wasn't said with much conviction.

'I've not hurt anyone, I'm just looking for a new life, one without pain. I thought I'd found it, but now you've taken it away, why?'

'I just told you why boy, now shut up.'

After that Con heard a door being locked again and then nothing.

The sound of the man's voice had triggered some memories, and now it was coming back to him in little flashes. The man was the lawyer who had come to see him and something frightening had happened in the office at the Gateway house. It was a bit of a blur, but he knew that the man had somehow knocked him unconscious and had then obviously brought him here.

How had he got him away from the Gateway without his new friends stopping him? They would have stopped him, wouldn't they?

Con felt sick then but managed to hold the vomit down, he didn't fancy adding the aroma of vomit to this already dismal place. He did not manage to stop the tears though; he just lay down on the bed and let them flow down his cheeks thinking it was inevitable that something like this would happen, that his so-called new life had been too good to be true.

Patrick Chapman left the garage cell that had once held Talionis and returning to the Custodians cottage a few feet away he sat at the kitchen table. He felt a bit sick too, he had acted impulsively, and did not know what to do next.

What should he do? Who could he trust?

Matilda had let him down badly and he could not trust her anymore. Richard had helped him with the ambulances, but would he help further?

Richard Norman was the Foundations head of transport and the other dissenter in the group regarding Morpheus and the work he was doing with the Dark Soul. He was a small man, and the only other word Patrick could find to describe him was grey. Grey haired, grey suit wearer, just grey. Although he didn't have such strong views on the danger posed by Morpheus and the Dark Soul as Patrick did, he had been the only other one to voice concerns and question Cedric Neale's handling of it all.

Because of this Richard had agreed to arrange the ambulance for Patrick even though it was not really in his job description. However, he was a cautious man who had not wanted to know Patrick's plans. He knew it was to do with the Dark Soul but had wanted to be kept out of it and would definitely not have done something so bold and impulsive himself. Nor would he have agreed with Patricks plan if he had known the extent of it which meant Patrick could not rely on him for further help.

There was no one else he could turn to; he had made a big mistake.

Whilst in the throes of rage that morning his plan had been to get the kid away from the Gateway and to kill him, making up an excuse of self-defence. But now he realised two things; firstly, the plan had been too weak to get away with; and secondly, he did not now think he could actually go through with it. He wasn't a bad man, just a very angry, scared one and one who had started to doubt his own convictions.

The boy had sounded so sincere and pathetic just now, and at no time in the presence of the boy before knocking him unconscious had Patrick felt any threat from him. His worry that like Talionis the boy may have mental powers that could put him, and others in danger seemed unfounded now.

Had the stress of his wife's betrayal and his health diagnosis caused the extreme paranoia he'd been feeling over this Dark Soul and the way the Foundation had been dealing with it? Thinking about it now he'd had no real basis for his strong, negative feelings about the boy. If the boy was in anyway dangerous surely someone would have picked up on that, someone with much more Dreambringer talent than himself. The Gateway Dreambringers definitely hadn't, they had championed the boy, had affection for him even going by their actions after he'd locked the office door on them.

'What have I done?!' Patrick cried despairingly out loud feeling regretful and alone.

He had sent the Foundation paramedics away after they'd helped put Con in the cell. They weren't too happy about leaving an unconscious patient in such a strange place, but to allay their inbuilt professional fears for the boy's welfare he had told them a Foundation doctor was on his way to look at the boy. They had no reason to doubt him and being Foundation employees they did what they were told without question. He had sworn them to secrecy citing his authority and telling them it was top secret Foundation business that should not be talked about with anyone.

It was likely someone would question where they had gone with the ambulance and why sometime soon though and he had no guarantee that they wouldn't eventually tell all. He really hadn't planned this well. The Foundation were bound to find out what he'd done soon.

His plan had been so very weak, and he was in deep trouble now with the Foundation, he had effectively ruined his own career. Could he use mental health issues as an excuse to get out of this trouble, just return the boy and apologise? Would he be forgiven? Would he keep his job? He doubted it.

His life was ruined.

He could only see two ways out for himself. One was to run, cut his ties with the Foundation and try to start a new life. It was a risky venture, and would probably fail, the Foundation would seek him out and likely find him. As for the second option, well that was really drastic. And regarding the boy, either way he would leave his future up to fate. If he truly was good, then surely, he would be saved. If not, he would die in that cell.

When the phone finally rang Morpheus answered after the first ring.

'What have you found out?' he enquired before any greetings were given.

Cedric Neale wasn't happy about the lack of politeness, but he understood Morpheus' need for information and knew he'd been disappointed with the small amount of information that Cedric had been able to glean.

'Not much I'm afraid, but I'm hopeful of some news soon.'

'What sort of news?'

'I currently have people working on trying to locate the drivers of the ambulance and will let you know as soon as I have news. My other bit of news does not help us find Constantine, but it may be of interest to you. Patrick Chapman has long been critical about your work with the Dark Soul and my letting you have such a free reign with it. He fears that Con is a threat to the Dreambringer world. He has recently become quite vitriolic on the matter.'

'And you didn't think I needed to know this? I mean I knew some members of the Foundation were very wary of me, but if this Chapman guy was that against me should you not have warned me?'

'No, whyever would I? It was down to me to deal with the man and you knowing about it helped no one. Now if I may continue, I have discovered, quite by chance, that Patrick had someone spying on you and in the Dream Realm.'

'What the hell did he think that would achieve?'

'I believe he wanted some sort of proof that the Dark Soul was a threat.'

'He never would have got that proof because it's just not true.'

'Quite. The person he persuaded to do the spying tried to convey that, but he was having none of it.'

'Who did the spying?'

'That is none of your concern, and no harm was done, I am just letting you know all the facts.'

'Fair enough, and thank you,' Morpheus told him finally finding his manners to Cedric's relief 'is there anything I can help with?' he continued.

'Not in terms of the sort of thing I am already dealing with, no, but I suggest you do what you do best and commune with the Eternals as they may have some insight into how Constantine is, if not where he is.'

'You're right, that's a great idea, they may be able to sense something of his situation.'

'Exactly. Call me once you have finished your commune.'

'I will, thank you. And you will call as soon as you have news.'

'Of course. Goodbye for now then.'

'Bye.'

After letting the others know what Cedric Neale had said Morpheus set off for the Factory. He didn't know why he hadn't thought of this before. The Eternals wouldn't be able to locate Con exactly, but they may be able to get a read on his welfare. Morpheus wasn't sure if they could glean anything if Con was still unconscious, but it was worth a try.

When he returned to the house Morpheus had little to tell them.

'It would seem that Con is most likely conscious as the Eternals have been able to sense some vague feelings from him' he told them 'what they sensed was that he was confused, afraid and trapped.'

This news was obviously upsetting but not unexpected and it could have been worse. The boy was at least still alive, him being dead having been an unvoiced fear they'd all had at some point.

'So, they couldn't tell you where he is?' queried Clea.

'No, in order for them to do that Con would have to know where he is and from the confusion, I'd say that he doesn't know so they can't 'read' that from him. They will continue to monitor him and see if they can get something from him as to his whereabouts. I'm going to go back out there to help them.'

'Can you not find him through your dreams, you know, the way you found Talionis' hiding place in the woods before?' asked Sofia.

'I've thought of that, but no, I don't think so, not yet at least. Con would need to be present within the Dream Realm for me to do that and the Eternals inform me that's not the case right now. If and when they do sense that he is asleep and therefore in the Dream Realm I will enter and see what I can do, but until then all they can do is monitor his general wellbeing.'

'Oh, I see.'

'Now I need at least one of you to come back to the Factory with me so that if Cedric phones with any news it can be relayed to you, and then you can come to the Eternal's chamber and let me know.'

'I'll come with you' volunteered Geth.

'Me and Mary might as well go back out there too' said Aaron 'what about you Max? We might as well stick to the same group and get on with the work that was interrupted. If we can concentrate on it that is.'

'Yeah, I'll come' agreed Max.

'Right let's get going then,' said Morpheus, then to Sofia 'call Geth as soon as you hear anything.'

'Of course.'

And with that the group set off for the Factory.

All the gateway residents did their best to concentrate on their artwork, damping down their worry and frustration at not being able to do anything else.

Back at head office Cedric Neale and others were doing their best to locate the paramedics who had taken Con. He was also actioning other avenues of investigation like tracking Patricks mobile phone.

Morpheus and the Eternal Dreamers did their best to get a location on Con through the vague connection they had with him but all they could glean was that he was trapped in a small area. As to his emotions there was obviously a strong sense of fear, but they also sensed despair and sadness.

Morpheus could not figure out what Chapman's game was. Why had he orchestrated this kidnap? What was his ultimate aim? Surely if he thought Con was some sort of danger then the boy's life was in danger, but so far, he was still alive and simply being held hostage. How long would that remain the case though?

As to his physical state the extent of Con's head injury was unknown. The Eternals link was with his soul rather than his mind, but they believed that he was conscious which was a good sign physically speaking. It was not clear if the Eternals would be able to 'read' anything from him if he returned to unconsciousness though.

If Con were to fall asleep however, as Sofia had suggested, Morpheus would have a better chance of locating him, but it was unlikely that the boy would sleep normally, not in the predicament he was in, not anytime soon anyway.

It was, frustratingly, a waiting game.

Con was unaware of all the effort that was going into finding him, he was too immersed in his own fears and self pity. He really didn't know what he had done to deserve this imprisonment. The tears had dried up, but he lay on the bed staring up at the ceiling his mind in turmoil.

As for Patrick, he had now realised that he had effectively trapped himself as well as Con making the 'escape to a new life' option more difficult. His own car was back at the Gateway and the paramedics had obviously driven off in the ambulance, so he was stranded in the middle of nowhere. In order to get away from this place he would need help from a Foundation member and that just wouldn't work.

He could call an outside cab firm but that would bring its own problems. This place was well off the beaten track and not easily found even with satnav, the Foundation had made sure of it. Not to mention the trouble bringing outsiders here could cause. He was in enough trouble as it was.

There was only one course of action he could take: option two. It was drastic, as drastic as things got, but he could see no other choice. He had hunted around the thankfully still equipped kitchen and found what he needed.

Now he just had one other thing to do before the final act. Taking his mobile phone from his pocket he turned it back on, typed an email and set it to be sent at a specific time, then he turned the phone off hoping it hadn't been traced in the time it took to do it. But then, even if it was traced it was unlikely that anyone would get there in time to prevent him following his plan through, the time delay was just a failsafe.

The email had been easy, now came the hard part. He needed to psyche himself up for it so he thought *'my wife humiliated me, I have a serious medical condition that will affect my job and shorten my life, I have effectively ruined my career anyway, I will be punished severely by the Foundation, my life is over'* and that was it, he was ready.

It was late afternoon when the paramedics were finally tracked down and questioned by Cedric Neale himself.

At first, they were very confused as after having been sworn to secrecy by a high up member of the Foundation, they were now being questioned directly by that man's boss who they had thought had given the order in the first place.

Once it was made clear that Patrick Chapman had acted without permission however, they gave all the information they had though when it came to telling the exact location where they had left Con and Patrick it was hard for them to explain. They did not know the name or address of the place; they had simply followed Patrick's directions and even the one who had driven was not sure he could find his way back there. They did mention Patrick giving them a code to key in to open a gate and that gave Cedric an inkling of an idea.

To check his idea he asked them to describe the place and, being very distinctive their description plus the key code thing confirmed to Cedric that it was the old Custodians place.

The Foundation boss then had to quickly decide who best to send to the rescue. He decided on a two phase 'rescue' mission.

First, he briefed and despatched a security team telling them to get to the location ASAP but to wait at the gate at the beginning of the road leading to the cottage. Knowing the security teams ETA, he then made a timed call to the Gateway house.

Sofia took the call and relayed a message to Geth to get Morpheus to call Cedric back immediately.

Geth relayed the message to Morpheus in the Eternals chamber, and they returned to the workroom upstairs in order for Morpheus to make the call from Geth's mobile phone.

Cedric got straight to the point.

'Patrick has Con at the old Custodians place and is keeping him in Talionis' old cell. You need to get there ASAP and liaise with the security team I've already despatched. I've timed it so that they should be there just before you because I don't want you going in without back up as we don't know if Patrick is armed, and I don't want them going in without you as they may need your guidance to resolve this hostage situation. I suggest you take Mason and Eddie with you too. I wish I could be there myself, but it would take me far too long to get there.'

'I understand' Morpheus told him, his heart racing.

'Good, and good luck. Please contact me as soon as you have news.'

'I will.'

The group raced back to the house and Morpheus, Mason and Eddie immediately set off in the van. The atmosphere inside the vehicle was tense and nothing much was said during the short journey.

As they had been told the security team were waiting for them. The team consisted of three men and one woman all armed and serious looking.

The leader of the team was a tall, muscled bald man who introduced himself simply as John. The other two men were equally as tall, the dark haired one muscled and bearded, the other one slim and wiry, his blond hair cropped short. The woman was smaller but looked equally able to look after herself her brown hair pulled back into a neat bun at the nape of her neck. None of the three offered their names.

Their complete party totalled seven, giving them a strong numbers advantage. That was assuming the paramedics information that it was only Patrick and Con at the location was still correct.

There was a brief exchange between the two groups, then after John entered the code to open the gate (as previously supplied by Cedric) both vehicles were driven nearer to the cottage before they traversed the last part cautiously on foot.

The woman and the dark haired guy went to the front door and John and the blond guy headed around the back with the three men from the Gateway a short way behind them. The three men then stopped at the garage that housed Talionis' cell, holding back, whilst the two security men carried on to the back door of the cottage.

Using two way radio's the two security teams coordinated trying the doors. The front door was locked, but the back was open. The man and woman at the front door stood poised, ready. The two men at the back door entered the cottage slowly and carefully, guns drawn.

Seconds later Morpheus, Mason and Eddie heard an expletive of 'Fucking hell!' from inside the cottage then the blond security man came back outside and promptly threw up in the shrubbery next to the door. John followed shortly after looking pale and shocked.

'You stay there' he told the three watching men, then into his radio he spoke to the two at the front door saying, 'kitchen secured, we are about the check the rest of the house, please stay where you are for now.' The two men then when back into the house, the one who'd been sick a little reluctantly.

A few minutes later the two men re-emerged, John again on his radio telling the other two that the cottage was secured and that they should come around to the back. He was holding some keys and headed towards the three men outside the garage.

'What's going on?' Morpheus asked him.

He held up his hand and said 'hold on a minute' then waited until the other two had joined them before addressing them all.

'We have located Mr Chapman in the kitchen. He's dead.'

'What the fuck?' exclaimed Eddie.

'There is no one else in the house' John continued 'and he appears to have died by his own hand.'

'It's damn nasty in there' added the man who'd puked 'the crazy bastard slit his own throat with a kitchen knife.'

This was a shocking bit of news that made them all feel a bit queasy.

'Who fucking does that?' said Eddie.

'Now we need to check the garage for the boy' said John holding up the keys 'you all stay back, I'll go in, I don't know what I'm gonna find.'

Morpheus' heart was racing. Was this a case of murder suicide? He felt pretty sure he'd know if Con was dead, but he couldn't be certain especially if his death was recent.

Mason and Eddie were equally alarmed as the security guy started to unlock the first door. He went inside and they heard as he unlocked the second door.

Whilst all this was going on, back at the Foundation head office an email notification pinged up on Cedric Neale's computer. Seeing who the sender was he opened the email immediately.

As he scanned its contents Cedric's face paled, and he covered his mouth with a shaking hand.

'Good grief' he muttered.

What he had just read was basically a suicide note with a heavy note of confession.

Patrick Chapman cited the stress caused by his wife's betrayal (which Cedric knew of) and his Multiple Sclerosis diagnosis (which he did not) as the reasons for his recent paranoia and erratic behaviour. He apologised for his conduct but stated that he still felt he may have had grounds to be worried about the Dark Soul's potential to do harm, but he did not elaborate, obviously being unwilling to admit totally that he had been in the wrong.

The email ended with Patrick stating clearly his intention to end his own life on the basis that it was 'ruined' but there was no mention of what had happened to Con.

Cedric was shocked and appalled by the whole situation. That someone holding such a high position within the Foundation could have become so mentally unstable was very rare, and very troubling. The question was had the man actually gone through with it? Cedric wouldn't know until he heard back from the two groups that had gone to the cottage.

He found himself uncertain as to what to do next. Should he try to contact the security team, or wait to hear from them?

He decided to wait, he was sure they would be in touch very soon, and in the meantime, he would think how best to deal with a kidnap, possible suicide and potential murder within the Foundation.

They'd dealt with the murder of Mahesh Choudhary at the Gateway easily by passing it off as an unfortunate accident, but this was much more complicated. He had a lot to think about and plan.

Back at the cottage Morpheus and the others were waiting anxiously to find out if Con was still alive. They heard John opening the heavy door to Talionis' old cell, then they heard him say something though they could not tell what it was he had said. Was it another expletive of shock, or was he talking to someone?

Then they faintly caught the brief sound of another voice. Con's voice? It had to be.

There was a short silence, then they heard John's voice again, at first indistinct, then he clearly shouted, 'All clear, we're coming out.'

There was more indistinct talking and it sounded positive, but Morpheus didn't relax until he saw the security man immerge with his arm around a quivering, but alive Con.

When Con had heard the doors being unlocked, his initial thought had been that the horrible lawyer man was coming in and he was afraid. The man meant him harm, he knew it.

The man who entered the room, however, was a total stranger though initially just as frightening as he was holding a gun. Con stifled a gasp and scuttled into the corner at the head of the bed.

After doing a quick visual check of the small room the man had lowered his gun a little and asked, 'Are you okay son?'

'Yes, I think so' Con had answered not really feeling okay at all.

The man was really looking Con over now whilst staying at a distance.

'Show me your hands' he said then raising the gun again.

Con did as he was told and the man holstered his gun and shouted, 'All clear, we're coming out' before saying to Con 'Come on son, out you come, you're safe now.'

When Con saw Morpheus he ran the short distance to him flinging his arms around the big man's waist and laying his head against his chest.

'Whoa there boy' said Morpheus taken aback, but then he laid a big hand carefully on the boy's injured head 'It's okay, I gotcha, you're safe now' and Con was finally reassured. Morpheus had come to rescue him like he should have known he would. He was happy to see Mason and Eddie there too, and although he didn't know the other four people, he was grateful to them as well.

'Thank you, thank you all' he said stepping away from Morpheus a little.

'How's your head?' asked Morpheus.

'It hurts, but I'm okay' Con told him in an effort to be brave. He actually felt a little dizzy and groggy but was too glad to be saved to want to worry his rescuers about it.

'I'll update Mr Neale now and ask for further instructions' John told them all. He then pulled a mobile phone from his pocket and made the call.

They all listened in as he gave his report and Con visibly jerked in shock when he heard details of the lawyer man's suicide. It was then the security guy's turn to listen as he received his boss' instructions nodding occasionally and saying things like 'yes', 'okay' and 'got it'.

Ending the call with 'Will do sir, thank you' he then passed his boss' instructions on.

Him and his team were to wait at the cottage for what he called a 'clean up team' to arrive. The three men from the Gateway were to take Con back to the house where a Foundation Doctor would be sent to check him over.

The three men thanked the security team and headed to the van with Con. As there were only three seats in the van Eddie volunteered for the uncomfortable ride in the back and as Mason was driving it was Morpheus who put in a call to Sofia to put the rest of them out of their misery with the news that Con was safe.

After the call was ended Con had a question.

'Do any of you know why that man thought I was some sort of threat and put me in that cell?'

'He didn't understand the work I was doing to help you. For some reason he thought you might have powers that could do him and others harm' Morpheus told him.

'Powers? Me? He called me an abomination but I'm just a normal person.'

'That's not strictly true Con, we've explained to you how special you are, but I get your point.'

'If he thought I was so bad, why did he kill himself and not me?'

'We're not really sure, he obviously wasn't in his right mind.'

'Could he be right? Might I be a danger to people somehow? He must have been sure to do what he did.'

'No, there is no chance you're dangerous Con, please believe me. The lawyer guy was just paranoid because of something that happened at the Gateway, and more specifically, to me a while back. It was actually me I think he was more scared of, but you were the weaker target. He knew there was no way he could do me harm like he did to you.'

'What happened to you at the Gateway?'

'Now's not the time, but I will explain soon, I promise.'

'Okay.'

Morpheus realised that the plan not to tell Con about Talionis and the Origination would now have to be revised.

When the van pulled up outside the house Sofia and Clea were standing in the doorway waiting. Clea ran to Con as soon as he emerged from the van and engulfed him in one of her big, motherly hugs whilst Sofia remained in the doorway.

The six of them then entered the house and went to the lounge/art room where the others were waiting.

A big fuss was made over a rather overwhelmed Con until Morpheus stepped in.

'I think Con had better go for a lay down' he suggested 'the Foundation are sending a Doctor to check him over and they should be here soon.'

'He should use my room' suggested Sofia indicating the door at the back of the room 'it's a better option than the attic room whilst he recuperates.'

And so Con went to lay down and Clea went to sit with him (at her insistence) until the Doctor arrived.

The sight of the doctor when he arrived gave Mason and Eddie a jolt of recognition as bad memories were evoked. Dr Gordon was the same doctor the Foundation had sent to examine their friend Claude and pronounce Mahesh dead at the beginning of the Talionis problem.

The doctor was a small, bespectacled, balding man carrying a large, black, old fashioned doctors' bag. Sofia escorted him to his patient and then she and Clea left him to it.

When he returned to the lounge area a short time later, the doctor was greeted by the whole group, all wearing similar worried, expectant expressions. It was a little daunting for the man and his magnified brown eyes flicked from one to another not really knowing who to address.

'The young man has a concussion. I have redressed his head wound and given him some painkillers, and I have left some more painkillers and clean dressings for him. He will need lots of rest and peace and quiet with no stress. An ice pack for the swelling may be helpful on occasion over the next couple of days too. Apart from that physically the boy's fine' he told them 'as to his mental state I'm not really qualified to say but although he has obviously suffered some sort of trauma he appears to be coping well' he added experiencing his own flash backs to his previous visit.

'Thank you doctor' said both Sofia and Morpheus at the same time.

'If there are any problems, please do not hesitate to arrange for me to visit again' the doctor offered and again he was thanked. He then said his goodbyes and left.

'I wonder what he makes of all this' Aaron mused once the doctor had gone.

It wasn't something the others could answer.

The truth was that Dr Jeremy Gordon really didn't give it much thought. He was a kind but unimaginative man, a man of science who didn't really want to know other people's business. Only treating their aliments interested him, it was what made him an ideal Foundation employee.

That's not to say he didn't have a touch of curiosity on occasion, but as he got into his car and drove off now the details of what had gone on with that poor boy did not really trouble him. He'd performed his duty and he would spend very little time thinking about it now it was done.

With the doctor gone Sofia and Clea went to check on a very dozy Con. Clea elected to stay with him at least until he had fully fallen asleep, and Sofia returned to the others.

It was now time for Morpheus to update them all on the news. They were all obviously shocked and appalled by it and there was a rush of exclamations followed by questions, most of which the three men who had been to the cottage could not answer.

'I intend to phone Cedric Neale but not quite yet' Morpheus told them 'I expect he is very busy dealing with the situation at the cottage and I want to give him some time. He may have some answers for us but even he probably won't know everything.'

When Morpheus did call Cedric it turned out he did know pretty much everything thanks to the e mail Patrick Chapman had sent him.

'It seems he was a very disturbed man' Cedric told Morpheus.

'I'm not sure that having a few stresses in your life excuses assault and kidnap though, lots of people have similar problems and don't do stuff like that.'

'I know, and to be honest its very worrying that it was a trusted Foundation leader that was so weak of mind. It's a precedent that I hope remains a one off.'

'I take it the incident is being dealt with within the Foundation only?'

'Of course. I feel I'm becoming quite adept at dealing with major incidents to do with The Gateway.'

Morpheus didn't know what to say to that slightly barbed comment. The Foundation leader was obviously a bit stressed himself, so Morpheus chose to ignore the comment as Cedric continued 'I don't understand how this could have happened with all the screening and monitoring we do on Foundation employees. How did I not pick up on the fact that Patrick was troubled, I just thought he was averse to change and a little afraid of the unknown. It seems we need to beef up our system, keep a closer eye on those higher up to make sure something like this never happens again.'

'It wouldn't hurt to make some changes' Morpheus agreed 'but putting things in perspective, one mental breakdown like this within a huge, worldwide organisation over many, many years is a very small percentage, and no system is perfect.,'

'It's still one too many though.'

Morpheus couldn't argue with that, so he decided to change the subject slightly.

'Con is going to need a couple of days rest so the Communing Ceremony will unfortunately have to wait. I take it that Chapman's actions have not caused you to change your mind about going ahead with this?'

'No, no, I haven't changed my mind' Cedric confirmed so Morpheus continued with another question.

'In view of what's happened, if he passes the final test of the ceremony, do I have your permission to tell Con about the Eternals and the Origination? He's asking questions about why Patrick did what he did to him and with everything that he's been through I think he deserves to know everything.'

'I'll have to give it some thought' Cedric said after a short pause and Morpheus thought he sounded tired.

'I understand' he told him though he was frustrated by the lack of a definite answer.

Morpheus couldn't help but feel bad for the man though, he'd had a lot on his shoulders as leader over the past months. He'd had to deal with a lot of changes within the Dreambringer world, and although he wasn't the only one directly affected, he was the one who had to make the important decisions on behalf of the whole Dreambringer community. It was a heavy burden.

'I promise you that some good will eventually come from all of this' Morpheus told him hoping his boss believed it.

'Let's hope so' was Cedric less than enthusiastic reply.

'I'll talk to Con tomorrow, and I'll call you after to let you know how he's doing.'

'Good, thank you.'

They ended the call and after putting the phone down Morpheus felt that Cedric's tiredness had rubbed off on him. He felt emotionally drained. To him this meant there was only one thing to do, he needed to be with the Eternals, they would 'recharge' him. He would need to be at full strength that night in order to heal Con after his traumatic experience. It was frustrating that Con's progress had been put back, but he was safe again now and Morpheus had faith in his own ability to help the boy put the recent events behind him.

That night Morpheus got to work on Con's dreaming soul as soon as he appeared. He was pleased to see that Con's Dream Realm appearance hadn't changed significantly which meant the damage done wasn't too severe.

On a first reading he deduced that Con's prevailing emotion was confusion mixed with understandable fear and self pity.

'You are special' he told Con without words *'you are good, you belong. Be brave and all will come right.'*

Con did not answer but Morpheus sensed self doubt in him.

'Trust me and believe in yourself' Morpheus encouraged.

'I'll try' was the tentative reply he received.

After that Morpheus set about bringing Con dreams to boost his confidence and self belief.

The next morning Clea was the first to check on Con and found him still fast asleep. She left his room briefly to fetch herself a cup of tea and some water for Con so he could take his tablets when he woke.

She then told Eddie, who was the only other person up, that she would be sitting with Con until he woke and took the drinks to what they all thought of as Sofia's room.

It was nearly an hour before Con stirred from sleep.

'How do you feel lovey?' asked Clea once he was able to focus on her.

'My head hurts a bit, but I'm okay' he replied blearily.

'Here, take these, they'll help' she told him proffering the pain killers and glass of water.

Con did as he was told. He was a little groggy but seemed in pretty good spirits which Clea assumed was down the Morpheus' nights work.

'I had some good dreams' he told her as he settled back on the pillow confirming her assumption. His eyes closed and he drifted back off to sleep. Clea left him too it for the time being and headed for the kitchen.

By this time everyone else was in the kitchen except for Morpheus.

'How is he?' Sofia asked Clea.

'He's a bit groggy but seems okay. I gave him some more painkillers and he's gone back to sleep. I'm going to grab a quick breakfast and then go and sit with him. I don't want him to wake up alone.'

'Good idea' agreed Sofia.

Morpheus entered the kitchen then and Sofia had a similar question for him.

'How was Con last night?'

'He wasn't too bad considering. A bit confused and sorry for himself but I don't think any lasting damage was done.'

'That's good news.'

'Has anyone been in to see him yet?' Morpheus enquired.

'Yes, me' Clea told him.

'How was he?'

And so, she repeated her assessment adding 'and he said he'd had some good dreams.'

'Good, I just wish I could've stayed in the Dream Realm longer to help him. I guess I can always go back in if he's still asleep later, but it might drain me somewhat.'

'Don't worry, the Eternals will look after him' Clea reassured him.

'True.'

Clea then told him of her intention to take some work and sit with Con until he woke, and he nodded his approval.

'The Eternals can monitor him in the Dream Realm and let me know when he wakes up, but if you could get word to me to confirm he's fully awake that would be good. I want to see how he is for myself, have a little chat, explain what we know about Chapman's state of mind, assess how he's coping and let him know that his Communing Ceremony will have to wait until I've healed any damage caused.'

'How long do you think it will take?' asked Eddie.

'I'm hoping just a couple of days, but it's not something I can put an exact timeline on. I couldn't detect any severe damage caused by the kidnap last night, he's just a little shaken by it as we all are, so I'm hoping it won't take too much time.'

'That's good,' said Sofia.

'I'm going to go back to the Eternals chamber' Morpheus told them, and no one was surprised.

'So Clea will be staying here, and I think I'd like to go to the Factory, what about everyone else?' asked Mason.

'I think I'd better stay here' said Eddie 'I know the danger is over, but I'd feel better being near Con for safety.'

Aaron and Mary decided to stay at the house too and Geth and Max opted for the Factory so with that decided they started their day.

A little over two hours later Con woke up.

'I'm hungry' he said which Clea took as a good sign.

She would have been happy to bring him breakfast in bed, but he insisted on getting up and having it in the kitchen.

Whilst he ate Clea made the promised call to let Morpheus know he was up via Geth, and he turned up a short while later.

They were still in the kitchen when he arrived. Morpheus noted that Con seemed happy enough considering and appeared pleased to see him.

'How're you doing?' Morpheus asked Con.

'I'm okay' said the boy with a shy smile 'thanks for the good dreams' he added.

'You're welcome. I'm just gonna make myself some coffee and we can chat. Do you want a drink?'

'No, I'm fine' said Con indicating the half full mug of tea before him.

'I'll leave you to it then' said Clea before leaving the kitchen.

Having made his mug of coffee Morpheus sat down next to Con.

'Right then' he said, 'I need to tell you some things we've learnt about Patrick Chapman.'

Morpheus then began to tell him about Patrick Chapmans state of mind as gleaned from his suicide note.

The boy was a good listener, he didn't interrupt once, and Morpheus felt a little guilty that he wasn't able to tell the boy the whole truth yet, but he was abiding by his boss' wishes.

When he'd finished Morpheus asked Con if he understood what the whole kidnap thing had been about now.

'Yes, he did what he did to me because he was having a hard time in his personal life, and it made him go a little crazy.'

'That's pretty much it though I'm not sure crazy is the right word, disturbed would be more accurate. I'm glad you understand it more now though.'

'Me too, so what happens now?'

'Our Communing Ceremony will go ahead but not for a couple of days.'

'Why not? I feel fine.'

'Maybe so, but you're recovering from a traumatic experience and concussion, so I think it's best to wait a bit.'

'Okay, if you think its best, I guess I am still a little shaky.'

'This is the plan then. You relax for a couple of days, let Clea and the others fuss over you during the day, and I will continue to heal you as you sleep then we can review things, okay?'

'Okay.'

'Good, let's go and join the others.'

So, for that day and the following two Con relaxed and got spoilt. Clea had to relinquish her mother hen duties to Sofia on the second day as she'd missed going to the Factory for two days, but she was back at her post the day after. And Morpheus worked on Con in the Dream Realm returning him to the condition he'd been in before the kidnap and maybe even improving on that.

On the third day Morpheus phoned Cedric Neale to inform him of his intention to conduct Con's Communing Ceremony the next day. Morpheus then asked if Cedric had made up his mind on the question of Con being told about the Eternals, Talionis and the Origination if he passed the Communing Ceremony.

Cedric was feeling very tired, but luckily, he had already made that decision. He had stuck with Morpheus so far, so why change that now.

'Yes, you can tell him everything' he had agreed much to Morpheus' delight.

The reason for Cedric's tiredness was that he had spent the past few days dealing with the fallout from Patrick Chapmans suicide whilst keeping it within the Foundation family.

It wasn't that it was difficult to arrange as such, it had just been quite an emotional and trying few days for the division leader.

Plus, news had gotten around to other divisional leaders and Cedric had dealt with a lot of questions from them all.

Although the original problems caused by Talionis had only really affected the Gateway and therefore the British division of the Foundation, the Origination had affected all and so any developments concerning Morpheus were of interest to everyone in the know.

After three days of it Cedric Neale was seriously considering resigning as division leader. It wasn't something he could give up easily, but he couldn't deny that this last incident had taken its toll on him. He wasn't a young man anymore and so maybe it was time to step down, though not quite yet. He had to see this thing with young Con through. Then he could consider his position and what he would like to do next. He may be nearly done in his current position, but he wasn't ready to retire from the Foundation completely.

Chapter 11
A New Chapter

After breakfast on the fourth day Morpheus and Con sat on the comfy chairs in the office and had a long discussion about how Con was feeling.

Physically Con was doing well but Morpheus was more concerned about his mental health. Within the Dream Realm he felt that he had successfully restored Con to the same level as before, but he just needed to check that Con was ready for the next step, the Communing Ceremony.

After their long, general chat Morpheus asked the question 'Do you think you're ready for the Communing Ceremony Con?'

'Yes, I am,' said Con without hesitation and that was good enough for Morpheus.

Morpheus had spoken to Mason the day before requesting that he be present for the ceremony if it went ahead as suggested by Cedric Neale. Mason had happily agreed. So now Morpheus went to seek out Mason and tell him it was on for later that morning.

For Mason's part he was glad to be the one to go with Morpheus and Con. This ceremony would be another ground-breaking moment in Dreambringer history and he was more than happy to be a part of it. Like everyone else, there was part of him that was a little bit worried about how it would go, but he was mainly excited. Also, at the risk of seeming arrogant, he thought that he was the best man for the job and Cedric Neale had obviously agreed having volunteered him for the role.

Now that the ceremony was a go it was arranged that most of the other Dreambringers would go to the Factory in order to boost the Eternals power as much as possible. Sofia and Eddie would be the only ones to remain at the house, and Morpheus, Con and Mason would head to the cabin for the ceremony.

With the plans made it was all put into practice as they all headed to their designated places.

Sofia and Eddie set about a couple of quick Marshall/Warden duties after which they would settle in the lounge to work on their art.

Those going to the Factory set off in a chatty group.

And Morpheus, Con and Mason set off for the cabin.

Once at the cabin they sat themselves in the comfy chairs to the right of the door in order to first talk through what was going to happen. This was mainly for Con's benefit. He looked a bit nervous but that was understandable and its was still obvious that he was up for it. Morpheus also wanted to wait until all the others were hard at work so the energy feeding the Eternal Within would be at its best.

Soon enough it was time to begin.

As instructed Con went over to the bed in the opposite corner to where the other two men remained seated. Con felt a little self conscious as he made himself comfortable lying on his back on the large bed. He had been told that he should close his eyes and relax but keep his mind alert and 'open'.

Meanwhile, under the watchful eye of Mason, Morpheus relaxed in his chair and began to consciously commune with the Eternal Within. Then once the human soul and Eternal were fully linked, they set out to connect with Con. This manifested in the usual twisting rope of mist extending from Morpheus' chest and heading towards Con.

The first thing that Con noticed was that his nervousness disappeared, and he felt calm. Next, he felt a strange sensation against his chest like someone was pressing on it with gentle hands. He then felt a pleasant tingling penetrate through his chest and shoot through the whole of his body. His body tensed, unused to the strange feeling, but then he relaxed again as the feeling took on a soothing note.

Sensing the time was right Morpheus sent the first thought words.

'Hello Con'

Con's body jerked on the bed as he was shocked by the strange sensation of words without a voice, but he wasn't afraid, and he knew immediately who the 'words' were from.

'Hello Morpheus', he replied without really thinking about it and felt a little thrill of surprise at the ease at which he had managed to speak without his voice.

'Well done' Morpheus congratulated him.

'This feels good' he told Morpheus.

'I know' he replied, *'and this just proves how special you are.'*

'You've told me I'm special like this before, in my dreams.'

Now it was Morpheus' turn to be surprised.

'You remember that?' he queried.

'Yes', replied Con as images of Morpheus in the Dream Realm flashed through his mind meaning that Morpheus also experienced them. It was very strange seeing yourself from someone else's perspective, but also exhilarating especially under these circumstances. Con was exceeding all of Morpheus' expectations.

Although he did not know exactly what was happening Mason felt the exhilaration with them and understood it was all going well.

'If I'm special you are exceptional and unlike anyone else. Someone, or something else is here with us, I can feel it.'

Again, Morpheus was pleasantly surprised by Con's ability, he was sensing the Eternal Within.

'We can speak about that later, for now I am pleased to say that you have passed the test.'

Both parties were reluctant to end the communing session, but both felt it was time and so released their link. Con felt the pull as it was released. Then after a few seconds he opened his eyes and sat up.

Morpheus sat smiling at him from his chair and Con returned the smile.

'I take it that went really well' stated Mason.

'It sure did' said Morpheus and Con in unison making them all laugh.

Those at the Factory and back at the house sensed that things had gone well but waited expectantly for confirmation that Con had passed the test.

Morpheus and Con told Mason the details of the communing session and he was suitably impressed. He then left to go pass the news on whilst they stayed at the cabin to talk.

'You've passed the test, you're one of us now so I'm going to tell you everything, all the bits we've left out until now' Morpheus began. He then proceeded to tell Con about the Eternals and the story of Talionis and the Origination.

Again, Con listened without interruption, but his reactions were clear on his very expressive face. These expressions mainly told of wonderment and awe.

When Morpheus had finished there was a short silence before Con spoke.

'Wow, that's all so amazing, I knew there was something special about you, but I never could have imagined that you had two souls and an immortal dream being inside you.'

'And how do you fell about being part of the secret world of Eternal Dreamers and a strange, new being like me?'

'I feel honoured. I'm in awe of it all.'

'Don't forget you are special too; you have some sort of Dream talent'

'But what exactly?'

'To be honest I'm not entirely sure, we still have things to learn about your talents as we do about mine, but now we can discover them together. Now we have been linked by the Communing Ceremony I think the answers will come soon.'

'It's all so exciting.'

'I agree.'

'So, what happens now?'

'Now we wait and see what happens tonight. Although I've said that you passed the test, which you did, tonight will still be another test, or rather the morning will. The fact that whilst we were communing you saw flashes of me as I appear in the Dream Realm gives me hope that my theory behind the reason for the communing will work, but I can't know for sure.'

'What's going to happen tonight then?'

'Nothing new is going to happen tonight as such. We will work together to heal you even further in the same way we have been doing. The test will be if you remember what happened after you wake.'

'Oh right, I see, you Dreambringers always remember what goes on the Dream Realm, but all the rest of us remember are our dreams to varying degrees. But if I remember what happens in the Dream Realm tonight then I really do have Dreambringer talent.'

'You've got it. I have to tell you though that I don't believe your talent to be dream bringing as such.'

'But how can I be a Dreambringer if I can't bring dreams?' Con asked his face registering his confusion.

'I've discovered that my new dream talent is to help Dark Soul's like you to dream, and the fact you are the first alone makes you special, but I believe there is more to you than that. This bond we have, the fact that you have made a connection with the Eternal Within means that you are now integral to my work. We make some sort of team, a partnership. What we need to discover now is exactly how that partnership works. I am the Dreambringer in this collaboration, but what's your role, that's the big question.'

'I see what you mean. Will we find that out tonight, or rather in the morning?'

'I think it will take a little more time than that. Let's just concentrate on you remembering your time in the Dream Realm for now. As eager as we are to find everything out it's not something we can rush, okay?'

'Okay?'

'Good, now let's get back to the house and in a while, when everyone is back there, we can have a good old Gateway chat and see what the others think. It's always good to get feedback from others.'

After Morpheus and Sofia had updated Cedric Neale the Gateway chat took place, unfortunately no one had any more insight into Con's talent than Morpheus had already thought of. They were all very excited though and keen to find out if Con would remember his time in the Dream Realm.

There was some chat about a couple of promises that Morpheus had made though. Back when they had shown him their Origination inspired artwork, he had promised that when he discovered his new talent, he would wear the t-shirt Clea had made him and let Geth tattoo him with the design he had created.

'So, when can I tattoo you then, and will you be wearing Clea's t shirt when I do it?' asked Geth with a mischievous glint in his eyes.

'Well, as I see it my talent hasn't been finally discovered properly until we find out what Con's is as I'm sure they are linked.'

'I knew it, a cop out' exclaimed Geth. He'd never had much faith in Morpheus keeping his promise.

'Not at all, I'll keep my promise, but it's not quite time yet. I actually can't wait until I can wear Clea's great t shirt, and as to the tattoo I've actually grown quite keen on the idea.'

'I'll believe it when it happens' was Geth's typically pessimistic reply.

'What about me?' Con piped up then taking on Max's usual role of deflecting from conflict 'I'd like a tattoo, not to mention a custom t shirt.'

'Ooh lovey, what a great idea' said Clea 'I don't know why I haven't thought of it before, I'd love to make you a t shirt.'

'Great, thanks' said Con giving her a beaming smile.

Clea returned his smile. She was actually pretty busy with her ambitious embroidery product, but she was happy to take time out to make Con a t shirt, though for now it would just be the garment, she had no inspiration for the embroidery design yet.

'I'd love to tattoo you kid, but not until I come up with a design' said Geth echoing Clea's problem.

'Maybe we'll get inspiration after tonight' suggested Clea.

'Let's hope so,' said Con.

'I'd be happy to paint your portrait sometime' Aaron added then.

'And I'll sculpt you if you like, when I get time' Max told him.

'I'll write you a poem once we know what you're called,' said Mary.

'What I'm called?" queried Con.

'You know, like me and Aaron are Dream Mate's and Clea is the Seer of Dreams.'

'Will I get a name like that then?'

'Of course you will if you're a kind of Dreambringer' Clea confirmed.

'But Morpheus says I'm not exactly a dream bringer.'

'You're still one of us and part of the family so it counts' said Clea 'and even if the Foundation don't give you an official name we will, okay?'

'Okay, thanks.'

Con really was looking forward to becoming a proper part of this group, he just hoped it all worked out.

Soon enough it was time for bed, and they all went to sleep hopeful of good things go come.

That night in the Dream Realm Morpheus noted the slight difference in Con's Dream Realm appearance. His shape was more noticeably human and although it still had the dark rim the ball of darkness at its centre was noticeably reduced. This was a good sign as were the emotions he was reading from the soul. There was a strong note of positivity, something that had been lacking in the past. He also read happiness and even a touch of confidence. All good so far.

Morpheus had decided to make their Dream Realm thought communication particularly challenging and memorable for two reasons. Firstly, he wanted to make it challenging to see if their new stronger connection made it easier for Con to express himself within thought conversations. Secondly, he wanted to make it memorable so that he would have something to 'quiz' the boy on to test his Dream Realm memory if he had one. He started simple though with

Hello Con

Hello Morpheus

Con was using his name that was a good sign, it showed consciousness of what was going on.

How are you feeling?

Great thanks

Now some more challenging questions.

Do you know where you are?

Yes, the Dream Realm.

Within the Dream Realm what are you known as?

A Dark Soul.

Do you feel different now to how you did the first time you encountered me here?

Yes.

In what way?

Less dark.

This comment made Morpheus do something he'd never done in the Dream Realm before, he laughed, but a laugh of the mind. It was still conveyed to Con though, and he didn't need the laugh explained, he understood how his comment had been perceived as comical and joined in the 'thought laugh' too. Their thought conversation was definitely on another level now.

With Con's improved skill now confirmed Morpheus moved on to the memorable with some simple but random questions, the sort of questions Con would not be expecting and therefore couldn't guess at the next morning when quizzed.

'If you were an animal, what would it be?'

'What?'

'It's a simple question, don't think about it too long, just answer. If you were an animal, what would it be?'

'A deer.'

'What's your favourite colour to wear?'

'Blue.'

'What's your favourite type and flavour of crisp type snack?'

'Roast beef flavour Monster Munch.'

'Good, good.'

'What were those crazy questions for?'

'I'll tell you in the morning.'

Con realised then what was happening, they were test questions to make sure he didn't lie about remembering being in the Dream Realm. He could have been offended but he wasn't, it was fair enough. He never would have lied about it, but Morpheus couldn't know that for sure.

The connection was now so strong that Morpheus was aware of these thoughts going through Con's mind without him emoting them. Another positive sign.

Morpheus now had something else he wanted to try.

'It's time for me to bring you dreams now, what sort of dreams do you need?'

Up until then Morpheus had had to deduce what dreams Con needed, but now he wanted to see if his soul was closer to a normal dreamer's in that he could communicate what dreams he needed to Morpheus more clearly himself. It wasn't exactly how it usually worked between Dreambringer and dreaming soul, but felt it was an important experiment.

'I'd like to dream of Mum but in a way to give me confidence rather than just comfort.'

Another success, Con really was a special soul and Con was happy to give him what he wanted and needed.

Unbeknownst to them both Con and Morpheus woke up at exactly the same time that morning.

Morpheus awoke in the Eternals Chamber and was up and heading out within seconds.

Con woke up in Sofia's room feeling like a new person. His dreams had been magnificent and that was the least of it. He lay in bed savouring the dream memories deciding to stay there for the time being. Although he was eager to see everyone, he wanted to see Morpheus before he saw anyone else. He had a feeling that if he stayed where he was Morpheus would come to him.

When Morpheus entered the kitchen, he was greeted by Clea, Sofia Geth and Eddie.

'Has anyone seen Con this morning?' he asked before exchanging any kind of greeting.

'Rude' muttered Geth.

'No, not yet lovey' Clea answered.

'I'm gonna go see if he's up' Morpheus told them already heading out of the kitchen.

'Someone's eager' said Eddie to the room.

'Do you blame him' said Sofia 'he wants to check it worked.'

'I'm sure it did' Clea stated with confidence.

Morpheus knocked on the door and sitting up in bed Con told him to come in.

Entering the room Morpheus again cut to the chase without the usual pleasantries.

'What do you remember about last night Con?'

'Everything' Con answered with a big grin.

Morpheus' large frame noticeably relaxed a little, but he still had to check.

'What questions did I ask you?'

'You asked me what animal I'd be, what colour I liked to wear and what my favourite crisp type snack was. I told you deer, blue and roast beef Monster Munch. I believe that means I've passed your test.'

'You definitely have' and now it was Morpheus' turn to smile broadly.

'Am I healed now then?'

'I believe you're healed enough for us to move on yes. You still have a little of that dark core within your Dream Realm self but it's possible that will never fully go away.'

'I feel healed. I'll always miss my mum, but it doesn't hurt half as much to think about her now.'

'That's good to know.'

'And by the way you look beyond cool in the Dream Realm, I mean the Dreambringers artwork gave me some idea how you would appear, but the reality of it is far more astounding.'

'Your Dream Realm self may not be as impressive as mine or that of the Dreambringers, but it is still unique and special.'

'Is it?'

'Yes, it makes you stand out as something new, something important.'

'But what exactly am I?'

'I have a theory, but we need to do some work in order to find out if its correct.'

'What's your theory?'

'I'll explain soon, but for now get up and washed and dressed. I'm gonna go give the others the good news then head to the cabin to clean up. I'll meet you all back here in a bit.'

'Okay.'

'Today is a good day' Morpheus added before leaving the room.

Con received a hero's welcome from those in the kitchen. When the others appeared and were told the news they all congratulated him too.

'You're one of us now' they all told him in varied ways.

As promised Morpheus returned and then the celebrations really began. It was a strange sort of breakfast party full of high spirits and good food.

Sofia and Morpheus briefly left the party to give Cedric Neale the good news.

They were too hyped up from the celebrations to notice that their boss' mood was a little flat. Although he was happy that things had gone well Cedric was the one who would now have to let others know that there was yet another big deal going on at the Gateway. That another new type of being had been… what… discovered? Or created? Either way it was big news that may scare some people and he did not relish the job.

Patrick Chapman's behaviour may have been extreme due to his domestic circumstances, but Cedric had lately begun to sense notes of Patrick's misgivings from other quarters.

He really wasn't enjoying this job anymore.

Unaware of the rumblings they were causing within the Foundation the Gateway residents were winding up their party. There was still work to do. It was time for Morpheus to tell them what they needed to do next.

The congregated in the lounge to hear what he had to say.

'As you know I believe that my new, improved Dreambringer talent means that I am able to help Dark Soul's to dream again' he began 'but what we need to establish now is exactly how Con fits into all this. I feel he is healed enough for us to move on and explore his talent.

We have established that he has a strong artistic talent and have therefore deduced that this fact plus the fact that he made such a strong connection with the Eternal Within means that he would have been a Dreambringer candidate if his life had gone differently.

What we need to discover now is if other Dark Soul's like Con are the only ones I can help, those that could have been Dreambringer candidates. Or if I can also help the other normal dreamer type Dark Soul's.'

'So, does this mean you think that our summary about there being three types of Dark Soul's is true?' interrupted Mason.

'I'm pretty convinced of that, yes. I believe that the work that we have ahead of us will prove this, but obviously it may also disprove it. Either way I think we will know soon. As to Con's place in the Dreambringer world I also have a theory on that.'

There was a short silence as Morpheus waited for any comments, but when none were forthcoming, he continued.

'My theory is that in the same way that Dreambringers are the conduit between the Eternal Dreamers and normal dreamers, Con is the conduit between me and the Dark Souls.'

There's another brief silence as they all take this in. Then Mason is the first to speak.

'That makes total sense.'

'Is it really that simple though?' questioned Geth.

'And exactly how would it work?' added Max.

'That's what we need to work on' Morpheus told them 'Con and I need to try to approach Dark Soul's within the Dream Realm and experiment.'

'That sounds a bit risky to me,' said Mary.

'Not really, they can't harm us, not even those that are Dark Soul's because of their dark nature' Morpheus assured her.

'But that's not a proven fact' stated Aaron.

'Maybe not, but there is no recorded incident of a Dark Soul harming anyone in the Dream Realm is there.'

'No, but we've always left them alone until now,' stated Eddie.

'I think you're all just trying to find problems where there aren't any' Morpheus told them.

'We're just being cautious' countered Mason.

'You sound like Cedric Neale,' said Morpheus.

'And that's a bad thing?' questioned Mason.

'No, but it's all I seem to hear when I'm trying to move things on, to find things out.'

'We appreciate that you're a brave visionary Morpheus, but us mere mortals are instinctively more cautious' said Geth.

'Okay, this is getting a bit combative now' Sofia interjected 'so let's just cool down a bit and let Morpheus finish telling us what he proposes to do.'

Everyone nodded or vocalised their agreement, so Morpheus continued.

'My proposal is simple really; I think that to start with me and Con should find and approach various Dark Soul's to see how they react to us. Their reactions, and ours, particularly Con's will then dictate how we move forward.'

'That sounds okay' said Aaron, a glint in his eyes 'as long as you do it with caution' he added with a cheeky grin.

This caused a ripple of laughter breaking the tension that had built up.

'Right, that's decided then' stated Morpheus with a smile 'Con and I will start work tonight.'

That night the new Dreambringer partnership began its work.

Morpheus and Con met up in the Dream Realm and set out for its outskirts and the Dark Souls that lurked there.

Once they drew near Morpheus let Con take the lead. Con understood the logic to this, he was far less intimidating than his partner and he took to his allotted role with ease and confidence. He was discovering himself as well as gathering information on the Dark Souls.

The Dark Souls all avoided contact with Con, which was not unexpected, they avoided each other too, but he noted differences in the way they reacted to his presence. Some simply moved around him as if he was an inanimate object that held no interest to them. From them he felt little emotion, just apathy. A few took a few seconds to study Con before they too moved away but they also showed little in the way of emotion and interest. The others actively fled from his presence and from them he gleaned dark emotions of fear, distrust and general negativity aimed not just at him but everything and everyone.

This first time Con did not try to interact with any of them, he simply wandered amongst them. It was a strategy that he and Morpheus had worked out before going to bed.

Morpheus shadowed Con just outside the dark habitat of these wounded souls, watching and making notes of his own, this first foray mainly being for gathering information.

After a while both Con and Morpheus began to note that there were small differences in the appearances of the Dark Soul's, and they soon equated them with the way the souls reacted to them.

Those that showed no interest had a less distinct human form and the darkness within that form was like gently roiling mist. The ones that studied Con briefly had a very similar appearance, but the mist moved a little faster within them. As to the ones that actively avoided Con, he perceived that their dream selves were darker, the mist within them denser.

That first night Morpheus and Con left the Dream Realm having achieved what they had set out to do.

For the next couple of nights, they did the same thing in order to verify their data.

Each day they discussed their thoughts and feelings on their findings with the Gateway artists and on the third day they came to the following, simple conclusions.

Those Dark Souls that showed no interest in Con represented the souls of normal dreamers that had been severely damaged by trauma and could no longer dream.

The ones that showed a little interest were less damaged but still handicapped by their trauma.

As for those that actively avoided Con, the ones with the dark emotions, they were the 'evil dreamers' (a tag given them by Aaron). These were the twisted souls of those that did not want to dream.

The group concluded that the 'evil dreamers' were beyond help and should be left alone. As to the others, although put into two different groups, they were basically the same, they just represented different levels of traumatised souls. Therefore, it was decided that Con and Morpheus would now concentrate on the less damaged souls, those that took an interest, however brief.

It was noted that they had not yet come across a Dark Soul as receptive as Con had been. None of them ever ventured out of their dark fringe to investigate the healing light being given off by Morpheus as Con had. It was not yet known if this meant that Con was a one off, or if his 'kind' were rare. Only time and the continued search would tell.

Cedric Neale was of course updated on all the news and he in turn passed it on to other division leaders as was normal. He was still hearing rumours of discontent from some quarters and was still very much considering retiring, but had not informed anyone of his intent yet. It wasn't a decision to be made lightly, plus the last thing the Foundation needed at this time of change was a change in leadership.

He would have to see this thing with Constantine through whether he wanted to or not, the Foundation as a whole was more important than just one man.

On the fourth night Morpheus and Con began their attempts to interact with those amongst the Dark Souls they felt they could help, those that showed even a fleeting interest.

This is when they discovered a new, startling, but wonderful development.

The plan that Morpheus and Con put in place was that Morpheus would come nearer to the Dark Souls domain and do his best to shine his light through the gloom to infuse Con's soul with it. This would hopefully mean that the healing light would help to entice the most receptive Dark

Souls and at least hold their attention for longer giving Con time to try to make a mental connection with them.

The new discovery was that when Morpheus concentrated on sending his healing light through the gloom to surround Con what actually happened was that the light became concentrated into a beam that then hit Con's dream form with intensity lighting it up. Then several beams of the light shot from his form and out into the gloom.

Assuming that these beams of light needed to be aimed at the most receptive Dark Souls Con set about trying to do just that. But it did not work. He would spot a Dark Soul that had been momentarily halted by the light and try to focus a beam in their direction. However hard he tried though the beams just skittered off in other directions.

It was frustrating but he and Morpheus persisted with it thinking it was simply a case of perfecting the skill.

After several nights of fruitless effort however they realised they were taking the wrong approach.

Instead of trying to shine the beams of light at a specific target they should concentrate on one particular beam and follow the direction in which it shone. Maybe the beams were showing them the way to those Dark Souls that were responsive to it.

Again, it was easier said than done as the beams were hard to follow, and sometimes simply dissipated, but they persevered.

Then one night the beam finally led them to its target.

The shaft of healing light ended within a specific Dark Soul creating a small ball of light within its centre.

Con approached the soul and sent it thoughts to calm and soothe it.

'We are here to help you' he emoted hoping his message would penetrate.

There was no answer from the soul, but it did stay put.

Con tried to read the soul's emotions. What he received was curiosity with a touch of fear.

Before he would do more though the nights work was over, and he and Morpheus were pulled back to their own healing sleep.

It was frustrating for them, but they knew that if they had achieved it once they could do it again. Persistence would eventually pay off.

As word of this latest development spread through the Foundation fear within the dissenting members grew. This Morpheus 'thing' was going too far now as far as some were concerned. But what should be done about it?

Two nights later Con and Morpheus were successfully led to another Dark Soul, and on this occasion, they had more time to work with it.

Con once again sent out thoughts to calm and soothe, followed by his message of help.

There was no immediate response but again the soul stayed put.

Morpheus continued to concentrate his light on Con and Con continued to send calming messages of help.

Finally, they received a weak message in return.

'Help me.'

And once again the Dreambringer world was changed forever.

Printed in Great Britain
by Amazon

29888988R00116